W9-CCE-390

THE FAR REACHES

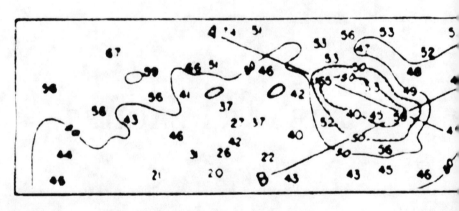

Also by Homer Hickam

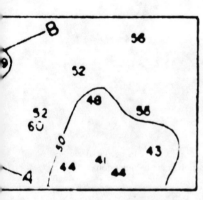

THE
FAR
REACHES

Homer Hickam

THOMAS DUNNE BOOKS
ST. MARTIN'S PRESS
NEW YORK

This is a work of fiction. All of the characters, organizations, and events portrayed
in this novel are either products of the author's imagination or are used fictitiously.

THOMAS DUNNE BOOKS.
An imprint of St. Martin's Press.

THE FAR REACHES. Copyright © 2007 by Homer Hickam. All rights reserved.
Printed in the United States of America.
No part of this book may be used or reproduced in any manner whatsoever without
written permission except in the case of brief quotations embodied in critical articles or reviews.
For information, address St. Martin's Press, 175 Fifth Avenue, New York, N.Y. 10010.

www.thomasdunnebooks.com
www.stmartins.com

Library of Congress Cataloging-in-Publication Data

Hickham, Homer H., 1943–
    The far reaches / Homer Hickam.—1st ed.
        p.   cm.
    ISBN-13: 978-0-312-33475-8
    ISBN-10: 0-312-33475-3
    1. United States. Marine Corps—Fiction. 2. World War, 1939–1945—
Campaigns—Pacific Area—Fiction.

PS3558.I224 F37 2007
813'.54—dc22   2007010369

First Edition: June 2007

10 9 8 7 6 5 4 3 2 1

To Linda, my island girl, and Carl, who has shared many an adventure, and his father, who waded across that awful lagoon

PART I

Tarawa

Watchman, tell us of the night,
What its signs of promise are.
Traveler, over yon mountain's height,
See that glory-beaming star!

Watchman, does its beauteous ray
Aught of joy or hope foretell?
Traveler, yes; it brings the day,
Promised day of Israel.

—JOHN BOWRING, A HYMN

1

"Sister, we die now?"

"If it is God's will, Nango."

The American bombardment had gone on for nearly an hour, and it seemed the big sand fortress might collapse beneath the weight of the mighty shells. Still, even as the thunderous assault sent down a rain of sand and coral dust on top of them, Sister Mary Kathleen smiled encouragingly at the muscular and intricately tattooed young man who had asked her the most pertinent question. She reflected, even at that awful moment, that they were quite the pair. Except for a wrap of bright red lava-lava cloth about his waist and a necklace of white cowrie shells and shark's teeth around his thick brown neck, Nango was essentially naked. She, on the other hand, was completely clothed from the top of her head to her slippered feet in the white shrouds of the habit of her sisterhood, the Order of the Sacred Blood. She allowed her smile to fall on the other fella boys, too. They had backed against the wall and were regarding her in anxious silence. "Prayers, me boys," she told them, pressing her hands together and letting her smile broaden to show them she wasn't afraid, even though she was. "Let them flow up to heaven. I'm praying to me little Saint Monessa, God bless her. She'll get us through this. I'm certain of it."

One of the fella boys replied in their native tongue, a dialect of the Marquesan language, which was itself a subgroup of ancient, premissionary Tahitian. "I think the Japanese will kill us soon, Sister."

"Japonee no killem me!" another of the fella boys replied hotly in pidgin. It was Tomoru, a giant of a man, covered like the rest with elaborate blue tattoos. He puffed out his hairless, muscular chest. "Me killem Japonee, Sister. You say, me do."

"No, Tomoru," she replied in his language. "Do not say such things, even in pidgin. They may understand."

"They" were the Japanese troops, the *rikusentai,* Imperial marines, who had crowded inside the sand-covered fortress to stoically wait out the ferocious American naval artillery pounding of Betio, the main island of the atolls called Tarawa. In contrast to the near-boredom of the Imperial troops, most of whom were quietly sitting on the earthen floor, Sister Mary Kathleen observed a nearby naval lieutenant whose legs were trembling. Each time a shell landed nearby, his startled eyes darted toward the dull roar of the explosion, and then he would visibly swallow. Sister Mary Kathleen's heart went out to the man. He was clearly terrified, yet so constrained by his nationality and rank that all he could allow himself was an inner scream that she could hear quite clearly.

When a lull in the bombardment went longer than a minute, Sister Mary Kathleen caught the Japanese lieutenant's eye, and he hurried over. "May I help you, Sister?" he asked, breathlessly.

She nodded and said in a near whisper, "I'm sorry, Lieutenant Soichi, but I really must go."

"Go?"

She nodded again, her summer blue eyes modestly downcast. "Go," she reiterated.

"Ahhhh," Lieutenant Soichi said, understanding now. "Go. Well, I understand why you would not care to squat over a pot like the others. I will be pleased to accompany you outside now that the shelling has stopped for the moment. But we will have to hurry."

"I am quite able to hurry, Lieutenant," she said, smiling at him.

He tried to smile back, but he was too nervous, and it came out a bit crooked. "Let me just explain the situation to Captain Sakuri." He cast an uneasy glance at the native men behind her and confided, "Those men, they always look like they want to murder me."

"Aye, Lieutenant. That is because they do."

"Ah, well," he shrugged. "I suppose they have good reason."

She nodded. "Yes. Very good reason. More than you might imagine."

After absorbing her comment, Soichi bobbed his head and then picked his way through the lounging troops and thence to a *rikusentai* officer who harangued him about something for several minutes, then dismissively waved him away. Soichi bowed to the man deeply, then put on his helmet and hurried back to the nun. "We may go now, Sister. If you'll follow me." He nodded toward an aperture in the fortress, one of two.

The aperture led to a zigzag corridor lined with sandbags stacked ten feet high. Since he had designed the sand fortress, the lieutenant proudly explained the purpose of the crooked opening. "If a bomb or artillery shell should explode outside, Sister, its force and shrapnel have no direct path to the interior of the fortress. My design also forces attackers to come through the corridor no more than one or two at a time. This makes it easier for defense."

"Faith, 'tis a grand design, indeed," Sister Mary Kathleen said with feigned enthusiasm, feigned because she wished to continue to curry the lieutenant's favor. He had been kind to her and her fella boys since their arrival on the atoll, and she feared what might happen without his influence. "Where did ye learn to build such a truly magnificent fort, Lieutenant?"

Soichi shrugged, though it was plain from his expression that he was pleased by her compliment. "I studied a few books on field fortification architecture," he said modestly, "and I used my imagination."

"It shows, Lieutenant. Aye, it does."

Soichi nodded in gratitude, then led her through the sandbagged corridor to the outside, where dawn was struggling to appear. The sand and powdered coral covering the flat atoll was made pink by the rising sun, which glowed like a distant ember through the dust raised by the barrage. The air stank of scorched gunpowder. It burned her nose and made her sneeze.

"God bless you, Sister," Soichi said without irony.

She sneezed again. "Oh, this awful sulfurous smell! It is a hellish stench!"

Soichi sucked loudly between his teeth. "Yes, Sister, the stink of hell, indeed." He chose a path behind a steep wall of sand. "Here we will be safe. I designed this embankment to stop naval artillery, which tends to come in flat. The shells hit and throw up dirt but otherwise have no effect. I had many such walls built all over the island." Soichi stopped and pointed toward a grove of palm trees and low bushes that were sheltered by the sand wall. "Now, Sister, if you'll go there, I will stay here to ensure your privacy."

She expressed her gratitude, then had her private moment in the bushes and returned to find Soichi consulting his wristwatch. "I think the Americans will be starting their bombardment again soon," he told her. "You must hurry back to the fortress. Just follow the path."

"Yer not going with me?"

"Yes. I mean no. I'm sorry. Answering such a question with a negative when it should require a positive is a peculiarity of English that is hard for most Japanese to grasp. But never mind. Yes, I'm not going back because I intend to find a hole to crawl into and somehow survive the coming battle. Captain Sakuri, as you may have noticed, is not pleased with me. He thinks I am weak because I do not share his enthusiasm for dying. If I go back with you, I think he intends to force me to lead some kind of insane *banzai* charge."

"I shall miss ye, Lieutenant," she said truthfully. "Ye've been like a knight to a lady in distress."

He bobbed his head. "It has been my pleasure, Sister. Now come with me. I wish to show you something."

He led her up the slant of the embankment and then bade her to lie down beside him so that they could just peek over it. Her flowing white habit rustled as she flattened herself against the warm sand. On the other side, she observed a cratered moonscape and a grove of shattered palm trees. Beyond was a glittering lagoon, and past it lay an astonishing number of big gray ships strung broadside to the beach.

"The American fleet," Lieutenant Soichi advised. "Aboard those ships are many rough, angry men. Admiral Shibasaki has laid down a challenge to them. He says a million Americans could not take Tarawa in ten thousand years. I think it will take considerably less. They will be landing very soon." He inclined his head in her direction. "Why don't you go with me, Sister? I think there's a chance we could even make it to the next island. The crossing is shallow."

She could not take her eyes off the ships, wondering about the men aboard them, imagining them looking back at the atoll, and what they might be thinking. Were they frightened? Or perhaps they were eager for a day of fighting. The only Americans she had ever been near were rich yachtsmen who had pulled into the harbor near the convent on Ruka. Of course, she had not been allowed to talk to them. Only the older nuns and the priests had enjoyed their fellowship. Her impression of them, based on brief observations, was that they were a bit loud, and their women a bit aloof.

"Sister? Did you hear me?" Soichi asked.

"Aye, Lieutenant, I heard ye, but surely ye know I cannot abandon me fella boys."

Soichi sucked between his teeth. "You don't understand, Sister. The *rikusentai,* haven't you noticed their preparations? They can hardly wait to die. This battle is going to be a bloody nightmare. I beg you to escape it. Come with me."

Her smile was grateful but her answer firm. "No, Lieutenant. I cannot. If I die here, then God's will be done. Me fella boys and I have come far together, and together we will stay."

He nodded. "I understand. You are loyal. It is a fine thing to be loyal."

"Dear lieutenant," Sister Mary Kathleen said, "how was it you came to this terrible place?"

His answer was bitter. "My father thought it best if I joined the militarists. It was a business decision, you see. We import and export a variety of goods and require many government permissions. So, despite my most excellent American education, I entered the navy and was sent here to this awful place. I do *so* hope this pleases my honorable father! And you, Sister? How did you come to be here? It has never been clear to me."

"I suppose ye might say it began when I took me vows in Ireland," was her wistful answer. "'Tis a long story."

"Then I regret I shan't stay to hear it," Lieutenant Soichi replied cordially. He led her down to the base of the embankment, then waited while she shook the sand from her habit.

Although there was little doubt he was ready to leave, and quickly, Soichi tarried long enough to give her some final advice. "Stay in the fortress, Sister. I designed it well. It will survive the bombardment, although your ears will surely ring from all the noise. When the invasion comes, find a dark corner, you and your Polynesians. Crouch down and keep yourselves quiet. From their talk, I fear some of the *rikusentai* may decide to vent their frustrations on you. Never look them in the eye, that's my counsel. To them, it is a sign of aggression to which they must respond. Be meek and humble and perhaps you will get by."

She put out her hand to him. "Meek and humble. 'Tis the nun's stock-in-trade, Lieutenant! Thank ye for looking after us so far."

"Sister, my countrymen are all going to die. Pray for them, if you will. They are brave men who think they are doing the right thing."

"Yes, all right, Lieutenant," she answered. "God go with ye now."

"We'll find out if He's with me soon enough, Sister," Soichi answered, then bowed to her, put his hand on top of his helmet, and ran like a rabbit. Sister Mary Kathleen watched him go, watched him pick his way through a scruffy bramble of wilted sea grapes and then pause before making a run across an open field. He was heading for another long barrier of sand, and he almost made it. Halfway across the field, there came from overhead a horrible screeching noise, and Lieutenant Soichi froze, then looked up as if God had called him to show his face to heaven. That was the last time Sister Mary Kathleen, or anyone, ever saw him. The hideous screech ended in a vast, terrible roar of orange fire, molten steel, and flying sand.

Lieutenant Soichi, Sister Mary Kathleen's only Japanese friend on the atolls of Tarawa, was gone forever, vaporized by a huge American naval artillery round that otherwise dug a shallow crater in not much of anything. She looked resentfully toward the sky, then angrily crossed herself. "Saint Monessa!" she called. "Fly to God, my dear sweet child. Beg for me. Ye are my only chance!"

As if in reply, angels in heaven shrieked back their hatred of her. Shaken, it took a moment before she realized it was not a snarling heavenly host but screaming death hurtling anew from the sea. Sister Mary Kathleen cast another pleading look at the sky, then put her head down and ran for her life.

2

Booms and shrieks shattered the morning tropical mist, and black smoke rings from gray naval guns floated prettily across the crystalline blue, lagoon. Distant thumps and pale yellow smoke boiling aloft announced the multiple hammer blows falling from the sky to batter the tiny atoll. Aboard the troopship *J. Wesley Clayton,* a big, wide-shouldered man wearing navy khakis and a Coast Guard officer's cap watched and marveled as more naval artillery pierced the moisture-laden air. The cascading thunder of the outgoing rounds was leavened by the clanking of gears and the high-pitched, energetic shriek of pneumatics turning the big guns. The United States Navy had been busy all morning, showing her marines how she could pummel a tiny island into submission. It was a fiery demonstration of the power of the great American fleet off the atolls known as Tarawa and one in particular, called Betio.

The Coast Guard officer marveling at the amazing bombardment was Captain Josh Thurlow. A legend of the Pacific war, though officially not part of it, he had the square-jawed look appropriate to seafarers, a face deeply tanned and properly weathered by the wind and waves, and a stout build and muscular legs adapted to a rolling deck. There was also a livid scar on his chin, a result, so the story went, of a confrontation with a polar bear when he was but a young officer on the old Bering Sea Patrol. At the present, however, as Josh stood on the troopship before the beaches of Tarawa, his rugged face reflected not past adventures but major unhappiness, and not a little worry for the day's endeavor.

Josh had observed the mighty barrage of the navy, smelled the wafting stink of the expended gunpowder, and reached the first of several unsettling conclusions, which he felt compelled to voice to the pug-faced little Marine

Corps colonel who stood beside him. "The navy's too close, Montague," he announced. "They need to back off, and you marines would be wise to shift your beaches away from that dodging tide, too, or wait another day."

The puggy little colonel was none other than Colonel Montague Singleton "Monkey" Burr, who was also something of a legend, though, as his troops gossiped, mostly in his own mind. "What a crybaby you are, Thurlow," he chided. "Today's *the* day, that island is *the* island, and we're going ashore, hell, high water, or dodging tides, whatever the hell that may be."

"We, Montague?" Josh asked mildly, even though he knew it would make steam blow out of Burr's ears.

"Damn you to hell, Thurlow!" the colonel snapped, confirming Josh's expectation. "I don't like being a staff officer, you know I don't, but," he sneered, "at least I ain't Frank Knox's tattletale."

Josh didn't reply, mainly because Burr had him dead to rights. He was in the Pacific courtesy of the secretary of the navy, and he had no portfolio save as an observer. Of course, that hadn't kept him from fighting on Guadalcanal, or going up the Slot with Jack Kennedy to chase after President Roosevelt's cousin who, some said, had deserted and gone over to the Japanese. But now, here he was, only an observer again.

It was November 1943, and the United States Navy was beginning her grand strategy of throwing her marines at island after bloody island across the Pacific. If all went well, so the admirals believed, the triumphant leathernecks would ultimately stand in the emperor's palace in Tokyo as they'd once stood in Montezuma's great hall with Old Glory fluttering on its highest rampart. The United States Army, meaning General Douglas MacArthur, believed the navy's strategy to be mad. It required light infantry to go up against determined, even fanatical defenders who loved concrete, big guns, carefully prepared fields of fire, land and sea mines, snipers, and human wave attacks compressed onto tiny battlefields from which there was no escape save death. The little atoll in front of Josh and Colonel Burr was the first island chosen for this great strategic sweep across the Pacific. On this rock, the Marine Corps was determined to build its New Church of Amphibious Assault. It would do it without the United States We-Grind-Slowly-but-We-Fucking-Grind Army, too.

During a lull in the bombardment, Burr began to lecture Josh and anyone else within the range of his voice, which meant most of the ship, even down in the boiler room, about his beloved marines. "War may be the Corps's vocation, Thurlow," he roared, "but glory is our real work. The navy knows that and is pleased to allow us marines to occasionally wade in

glorious blood, though it ain't pretty to them in their crisp whites and polished decks. We will be victorious this day, make no mistake, and the harder
the enemy fights, I say, all the better. Through hardship comes experience
and knowledge. Through adversity comes strength and greatness. Through
privation comes triumph and glory!"

"Glory, Montague?" Josh replied, maintaining his mild tone. "Do you
really think these young gents about to go ashore are as fond of glory as
you and the other professionals of the Corps?"

Burr stared at the wounded atoll, which seemed adrift in smoke and flame.
"Now listen to me carefully, Thurlow," he said in a low growl. "I followed
you out here to tell you to keep your yap shut. I won't have you infecting
these marines with your defeatist nonsense. You ain't part of this operation.
Don't forget that."

Before Josh could reply, the dawn was again shattered, this time by the
battleship USS *Maryland,* old, obsolete, bombed and sunk at Pearl Harbor,
but by God afloat again to fight another day. In a gigantic broadside, the
warship erupted with a bone-rattling display of her power. A mighty spew
of plumed orange and white smoke flew away from her, and the sky seemed
to fall apart like a window struck by a flying brick. Then Betio seemed to
be gripped by an earthquake as the shells struck, the atoll trembling beneath
a storm of dust and sand.

"Oh, God love you, old girl," Burr admired, beaming in rapture at the
resurrected vessel. "Pound 'em into dust, my darling!"

Standing around the bridge high above the deck, the *J. Wesley Clayton*'s
duty officers were cheering, goading the huge shells to fly straight and true.
But straight was the problem, in Josh's view. "You know your artillery theory,
Montague," he persisted. "Those shells are on a flat trajectory. They're throwing up sand, I'll warrant, but they're not digging Jap out of his hidey-holes. If
the navy would back off and raise their tubes, the shells would come down at
a steeper angle and penetrate the sand before exploding. I think Jap's just
hunkered down right now behind and beneath all that sand, waiting us out."

Contradicting Josh, there was a sudden explosion on the island, sending
a massive shock wave flying across the water, so thick that Josh and Burr
could feel the pressure on their faces. Burr laughed out loud. "As per usual,
you're wrong, Thurlow!"

Josh caught a whiff of the acid stink of exploded gunpowder, the odor
conjuring up the terrible battles he'd fought over the years against his
country's various enemies. "There's still that dodging tide," he remarked
stubbornly.

"What in God's fucking underpants is a dodging tide? You keep repeating that damnable phrase!"

Josh was always a patient teacher of the sea, especially with marines who thought the ocean but a nuisance across which they had to endure in order to get at the throats of the enemy. "There's spring tides, neap tides, and dodges," he explained. "It all has to do with the sun and the moon and where they are to one another. When both of them big fellows line up and start pulling in tandem, you've got a dodging tide, and, as bad luck would have it, Montague, that's what you've got on that atoll before us right now. That means this very minute the tide's going out, way out, and the reefs are rising. Soon they'll be as dry as your Aunt Sally's picket fence, and your boys will have to get over them."

Burr spat a brown stream of tobacco juice over the side. His temper was not helped when a good portion of it blew back in his face. He used the sleeve of his crisp new camouflage utilities to wipe his face, then spat again for good measure, this time with the wind. "Again, you're wrong. We'll get over the reef with our amtracs and then we'll dig out the few Japs left alive after this barrage and we'll kill them, see, and bury them. All in a morning's work."

Josh knew he was wasting his breath, had known it all along. A kind of desperation had made him voice his fears even though he knew Burr was too low on the totem pole to do anything about them. Josh had seen it happen before, a kind of momentum that took hold during the planning of an operation that buried errors in judgment beneath wishful thinking. Since Guadalcanal, it was the belief of every navy and Marine Corps staff officer that their marines could overcome any obstacle, including poor tactics. But Josh loved his history and knew Napoleon at Waterloo and Lee at Gettysburg had also come to believe their men could do anything, even charge up a hill into the teeth of cannon. Defeat served up on a cold plate was what those great generals had received, and now Josh feared these islands called Tarawa, and especially this atoll called Betio, were the next cold serving of error, this time for General Holland M. "Howling Mad" Smith and his cocky leathernecks. They were about to launch themselves onto a hot, sandy beach where a determined enemy waited, no matter how many flat, skipping rounds were thrown at him courtesy of the United States bluewater, pleated-pants, brown-shoe Navy.

"Jap's figured out he's not going to win this war, but he thinks if he bloodies us enough, we'll sue for peace," Josh said, thinking aloud.

"That will never happen," Burr swore.

"I agree, but them folks on that island, they don't know that. And they ain't just your normal Japanese soldiers. Those are Imperial marines. They call themselves *rikusentai* and are tough as they come."

Burr screwed up his ugly face. "Marines, did you say? There ain't a Jap boy born yet who deserves the title *marine*. We'll brush them aside and be across that spit of sand in an hour."

Josh looked away, then shook his head. "If you say so, Montague," he replied wearily.

Burr registered surprise at Josh's sudden surrender and eyed him for a long second. "How long's it been? Us knowing one another?"

Josh smiled, though it was a sad smile. "Since the Bering Sea. You headed up a marine detachment that came aboard the old *Comanche*, and I was at the time the lowest ensign on the duty roster. I was told to look after you." Josh recalled Burr as a young man, climbing eagerly up the gangway to board the cutter in Ketchikan. Burr had been filled with piss and vinegar, like a boy playing war in his brown khakis, leggings, and flat tin helmet. He'd had a big forty-five-caliber pistol strapped to his waist. It occurred to Josh that it was probably the same one Burr had in the holster on his belt, though the belt wrapped around a waist that was considerably thicker than during the old days in Alaska.

"I didn't like you the first time I laid eyes on you, Thurlow, and nothing has changed my mind since," Burr announced.

Josh put out his hand. "Maybe so, but isn't it about time you and me made a peace?"

"You can just go ahead and put your mitt away, because I'll never shake it. Don't look at me that way. You know why. You married the woman I loved and then you got her killed. Do you think I could ever forgive you for either of those things?"

Josh lowered his hand. "I loved Naanni, too."

Burr's reply was a sneer. "Sure you did."

If you only knew how much, Josh thought, remembering Naanni's face when she'd looked up at him from their marriage bed. Though he tried not to, he also saw her face when it was cold and bloody and as empty of life as the frozen tundra in midwinter.

"You loved her just as much as you love your present girlfriend, I'm sure," Burr sniped, then laughed harshly. "The coconut telegraph has been alive with the news that you impregnated the black wife of that cannibal coast-watcher on New Georgia! I wonder what Miss Theodosia Crossan, Killakeet Island, North Carolina, is going to think about that? Isn't that her name and address? Why, I suppose anybody could write her a letter, tell her all about what her boyfriend's been doing out here while she sits home pining away."

The naval artillery stopped, and Josh looked toward the battered atoll, the dust settling around it. It was shining bright yellow in the sun. "That 'anybody' won't be you, will it, Montague?"

"Don't worry, Thurlow. I won't do it, though God knows somebody should."

Now came a sudden heavy thumping and the muffled shouts of men behind plated steel. "You boys keep it quiet in there!" a thin voice shrilled, and Josh turned to see a tall, skinny ensign and two sailors pushing against a watertight door. The ensign looked frightened.

Josh could never stand to see a thing caged, neither a raccoon in a road-side zoo nor even a bunch of marines on a troopship. "Let them boys out," he demanded, advancing on the ensign, who looked at Josh with wide eyes.

"Those men are kept inside for a reason," Burr called over his shoulder from the rail.

"That might be," Josh muttered, "but it ain't a good one." He thrust himself between the sailors and pulled open the door. "You fellas get on out here, get some fresh air."

He didn't have to say it twice. A flood of marines, dressed in their smart new camouflage utilities and canvas field packs, fell outside, their sweaty faces raised to the blue sky and breathing deep the first fresh air they'd had in hours. They headed for the rail to bask in the cooling breeze and take in the thoroughly pummeled, smoke-shrouded atoll that lay before them. The naval guns boomed again with great claps of thunder, and the shrieks of their rounds flying over, followed by the hollow thumps of explosions on the is-land, caused the marines to cheer.

"Thanks, Captain Thurlow!" a gunny sarge named Pinkerton called out, then clapped his mouth shut when he saw the scarlet visage of Monkey Burr, who looked ready to chew nails. Burr said nothing, though, and waded through the marines and stomped up the ladder to the bridge.

A young marine slipped up beside Josh. "What's going to happen today, sir?" he asked. Josh looked at the boy, fuzzy cheeked and wide-eyed beneath his helmet. Two months ago, maybe less, this boy had been in a boot camp in San Diego or Parris Island. Before that, he'd been at his mother's knee.

"What's your name, son?"

"Randy Hewatt from Atlanta, Georgia, sir."

"Drink your water, Randy," Josh said.

"Sir?"

"Before you go over this rail, fill up with water. Don't wait until you get thirsty. It's going to be a hot day, and a long one."

The youth puzzled over Josh's advice for a short second, then said, "They say you killed a hundred Japs in one night on the Canal. Pretty damn good for Coast Guard, sir. I hope to get a hundred myself today."

It hadn't been a hundred—twenty, maybe—but, yes, Josh had cut throats that night on Wilton's Ridge. The next morning, he'd pulled off his boots and poured a sticky black liquid from them into the mud. It stank like rotten blood, which it was. "Oh, the glory of it all," he muttered.

"What was it like, sir? On Guadalcanal?"

"Easier than it'll be on this sandy spit," Josh said beneath his breath, too low for the boy to hear. "Drink your water, I said!" he snapped and lurched off to another position on the rail where he wouldn't have to look at the dead boy who wasn't dead yet but was headed in that direction, sure as the tide would fall and the reef before them would rise. He imagined the boy's mother standing at her door holding a yellow telegram from the Navy Department. The boy's father was rising from his easy chair, a newspaper in his hand, a quizzical look on his face . . . Josh shook the vision out of his head and tried to think of something else, anything else.

The clock ticked on. Two battalions of the Second Marines had been in their amtracs and the slab-sided, ramp-dropping Higgins boats for five hours, riding around in circles. Josh suspected the men inside were probably desperate to get off what had turned into a boxy inferno of vomit, urine, gun oil, diesel fumes, and sweat. He had seen that even off Guadalcanal, where the landings were mostly unopposed.

Now Josh was surprised to see a line of amtracs and Higgins boats making their way toward the *J. Wesley Clayton,* which had been named after one of President Roosevelt's financial advisors. The company of infantry aboard her had been designated as part of the reserve. Apparently, someone in the command structure had decided to go ahead and send it in on the first wave. To Josh, this represented the first sign of nervousness from General Smith and his staff. "You're starting to figure it out, aren't you?" he whispered, then shook his head. "Too late. Too late."

There was no planned second wave. The Sixth Marine Regiment was in the troopships, but no one thought it would be necessary to send them in. *No one.* Every time there was a briefing, the briefing officer always ended with that note. The Sixth Marines were there just in case, but *no one thought they were necessary.* From his voracious reading of history, Josh knew the capricious gods of battle especially loved to spoil the certainty of staff officers.

Then, abruptly, the thunderous naval bombardment once again stopped. On the atoll, the breeze tumbled away the yellow smoke, and beneath the tropical sun, the spit of sand began to glow like a sliver of gold lying atop a vast blue tabletop. It was pretty, Josh thought, postcard pretty. All that was needed was hula girls, their hands making erotic movements of welcome. *Come you, marines. Come you, and make love to us.*

Josh's mind flew aloft and looked down at what lay before the invasion fleet. Two miles long, Betio was flat, nothing higher than thirty feet on the entire island. It was shaped like an eel with its head facing west and its limp tail hanging east. The widest part was where the crucial airfield was located, seven hundred yards from beach to beach. Most of the island was barely the width of a football field. The American fleet was aimed at the northern coast of Betio, where there was a protected lagoon behind a long reef. It was easy to see why the planners of the assault figured it would take only a morning's work to seize it.

But Josh had seen General Smith's detailed topographic map of Betio. It showed what was known from numerous aerial photography missions. The Japanese clearly had been working tirelessly for months to prepare for an invasion. Dozens of big coastal artillery pieces, embedded in concrete bunkers, were in place, and the Japanese were famous for being competent artillerymen capable of accurate, rapid fire. There were also long sand embankments stretching across the island. There had been an argument about what those embankments were for. Most of the staff officers felt they were lines of defense. Only a few had divined their true purpose, the absorption or deflection of the preinvasion artillery rounds.

The map also showed a vast array of steel bar obstacles on and near the beach, designed to snag landing craft. And just back from the beach was an assortment of palm log bunkers, probably used as machine-gun nests. Josh had no doubt that snipers were also dispersed across the atoll behind every sand dune and in the tops of palm trees. Betio was, in effect, a hornet's nest. But the best defense for the Japanese this day, Josh believed, was not anything they had built. It had been provided by the gods of war.

The reef.

Josh's mind flew down Betio's reef. It completely surrounded the atoll, except for the eastern tip of the eel's tail, which led to the shallows between it and the next atoll up, named Bairiki. Josh knew reefs, even loved them. They were the protective home of vast numbers of fish, lobsters, crabs, and other sea life. They were alive themselves, the calcic outer shell of millions upon millions of tiny creatures that came out at night to feed on plankton. When the creatures died, their progeny kept building one on top of the other. The result was a dense wall of layered brain and lettuce corals, jutting pillar corals, sharp staghorn and elkhorn corals, all laid down in a rainbow of colors, all gloriously beautiful and, put together, a formidable barrier.

The plan to assault Betio was to grind over its reef in amtracs, which were small boats with tractor treads. But what of the larger Higgins boats following behind? They were nothing but tricked-up plywood barges. When they plowed into the reef . . . Josh pressed his mouth into a tight line of worry. Between the reef and the atoll was a wide, shallow lagoon. A killing ground.

Josh felt vibration in the soles of his brown shoes. The engines of the *J. Wesley Clayton* were rumbling awake. The old freighter was making headway. He saw the other transports were shifting, too. Sergeant Pinkerton appeared at his side. "Why are we moving?" the sergeant wondered.

"To get back into position. The current's been pushing us away from the beaches all morning," Josh answered.

"Situation normal, all fucked up," Pinkerton concluded wearily.

The transports slogged up-current, the amtracs and Higgins boats chasing them, and the clock kept ticking. Josh looked at his watch and was shocked to see how late it was. The morning was nearly gone and not a single marine had started toward the atoll. "Jap will be coming out of his hole to take a breath and maybe a smoke," he said, thinking aloud. "If our battlewagons let loose again, they might catch him in the open."

"Then they'll do it," Pinkerton said.

But they didn't. The battleships *Maryland*, *Tennessee*, and *Colorado*, the heavy and light cruisers, and all the other naval artillery platforms remained silent as gray ghosts. Then, *there*! A big splash in front of the old *Maryland* indicated the Japanese shore batteries were not only still alive but capable of challenging the American fleet. Soon, a dozen splashes around the big ships indicated more guns opening up from shore.

"Damn!" Pinkerton grunted. "How the hell did them Japs live through all that blasting?"

Josh said nothing, even though he recalled one of old Captain Falcon's axioms: *When you send a man into battle, tell him the truth, especially if the going will be hard. A man should be allowed a certain contemplation of his likely fate.*

"You know a lot about stuff," Pinkerton persisted. "Tell me what you think the situation is so I can get myself and my boys ready."

After a moment's reflection, Josh said, "There's a seawall that runs the length of the beaches. I've seen it in aerial photos. It looks to be about three or four feet high and built out of palm logs. My advice is to get yourself and your boys to it as quick as you can."

"Then what?" Pinkerton demanded.

"Stay alive," Josh replied. "And fight like hell."

On the wind now came a wild cheering from the island. It was the Japanese rising up out of their holes. Some of them were yelling, in perfectly understandable English: *Come you, marine. Today you die!*

When some of the marines began to look worried, Sergeant Pinkerton called out to them. "Let 'em yell. They'll all be dead soon."

Then there was an ominous fleck of yellow on the sea. Josh raised his binoculars. Just as he feared, a dodging tide was in fulsome retreat, and the reef was rising in front of the invasion fleet like a gigantic stone fence.

And still no marines went forward.

3

The mood inside the sand fortress had changed from stoic acceptance to jubilation. The *rikusentai* were running in and out, clutching each other by the shoulders, and yelling excitedly to one another as if a great victory had just been won. Sister Mary Kathleen supposed that survival after the terrible barrage was something of a victory, though what lay next, if Lieutenant Soichi had been correct, was a landing by the Americans. She caught Captain Sakuri's eye, and the officer stomped over to her. His uniform was impeccable, as if he were heading to a dress parade. He was grinning beneath his helmet. "You Americans die today!" he screamed triumphantly. "Babe Ruth go to hell!"

"I'm Irish," she replied quietly, then regretted saying anything. It seemed to set the captain off. He drew a long sword from its scabbard and waved it about, screaming threats at her she couldn't understand. She heard her fella boys stir behind her, and then Tomoru was by her side. She put a restraining hand on his arm. "No, Tomoru. Please sit down."

Nango rose and put his hand on Tomoru's shoulder to further restrain him. "You will sit," he ordered, and, with a grunt, the big man backed off.

Captain Sakuri's attention was mercifully diverted by the appearance of a Japanese naval officer who barked a command. Sakuri, after insolently waving the tip of his sword near the nun's face, sheathed it and pushed through the milling *rikusentai* for a word with the officer. He bowed deeply, and the nun supposed the naval officer had brought orders from someone higher in the chain of command. Translated to her world, a bishop had sent word to a priest through a monk. Sakuri yelled something; then he and all the troops inside the fortress streamed through the twin apertures and disappeared outside. An unnatural quiet and calm inside the dark bunker was the immediate result.

"They are going outside to meet the Americans," Nango said, in the dialect. "They seem confident."

"However they seem," Sister Mary Kathleen answered, " 'tis good to be rid of them for the moment."

"Maybe they won't come back," Nango said hopefully. "Maybe the Americans will kill them."

"Aye, there's that," she answered. "Perhaps we will fulfill our quest yet. But first the Americans must win. We must pray that they do."

"I have been praying to Juki," the fella boy named Agoru said mischievously. "She is a fickle god, like all of them, but she at least knows what we need."

"Juki has no power here," Nango snapped. "She is a god of the Far Reaches. But Sister's god, he is here and everywhere. Pray to him, instead."

Agoru shook his head, making his cowrie shell necklace rattle. "Sister's God is too big and is surely overwhelmed and confused by all the prayers coming at him. I am sorry, Sister. It is what I think. How can just one God control everything? He must have help."

"Aye, He does," she admitted. "He has His saints and His angels and of course His son, the Christ. You might also pray to the Virgin Mary, who is much like your Juki, except not fickle, of course."

"I wonder who the Japanese pray to?" Nango mused. "On Ruka, some of them had shrines, and there they burned incense. They said it was for their ancestors. I concluded they worshipped ghosts, who are the most unreliable spirits of all. It is little wonder the Japanese are such odd creatures."

"I will not be happy until they are all dead," Tomoru growled. "Every one of them, including their children." He took a breath, then shrugged. "Sister, I talk too much at times."

"Talk is our only solace at this moment, Tomoru," she answered quietly, "and prayer our only weapon. Let us all pray in whatever fashion suits us."

"You pray to your little saint, Sister?" Nango asked.

She smiled. "Aye. 'Twas a sweet child, she was, to die upon baptism. A perfect spirit. She is with me always."

"Perhaps all children who die become saints," Nango offered.

"Perhaps so, Nango. Perhaps so."

She turned, startled, when Captain Sakuri came running back inside. He looked at her and the fella boys, then put his hands on his hips and threw back his head in a great shout of laughter. "Marine no come!" he screamed in an apparent mixture of joy and relief.

But behind him suddenly came a flood of *rikusentai*. They pushed around him and then crouched down and assumed their stoic expressions. Captain Sakuri looked at them in astonishment, then walked to an aperture and peered outside. Then he looked up, grimaced, and angrily made a fist and pounded a sandbag. Sullenly, he gave Sister Mary Kathleen a murderous glance, then touched the hilt of his sword. She had no doubt he meant to kill her. For a moment she felt grateful and even lifted her eyebrows at him as an enticement. But then she remembered all she had to do, and why. *Saint Monessa,* she silently prayed. *Not yet, not yet.*

4

The sun baked the *J. Wesley Clayton,* the steel hatches and exterior bulkheads almost too hot to touch. The marines on the deck sought out what little shade there was, and some of them even went back inside, hoping to find a cooler place.

A deep drone indicated the arrival of aircraft, and Josh looked up to see a formation of Dauntless and Avenger dive-bombers majestically soaring above the armada. The aircraft carriers, though hidden beneath the horizon, were getting into the act. For seven minutes by Josh's watch, the bombers ranged up and down the island dropping their bombs, each sortie producing spouts of smoke and fire. Then, abruptly, they lifted into the sky, wheeled around, and raced back from whence they'd come. Unimpressed, the Japanese shore artillery opened up again.

For at least the tenth time in the last thirty minutes, Josh checked his watch and then peered at the location of the sun. If the invasion didn't get started soon, it would have to be called off. Josh was no longer certain that was a good idea. The marines in the landing craft were surely ready to go and would be put in a sour temper if they had to wait another night. Worse, the naval artillery was probably running low on shells. The next morning would find the Japanese refreshed, eager for battle. No, even though he dreaded what they might find, he now believed the marines had to go in today, come hell or, in this case, low water.

"They're here, girls," Pinkerton called, and Josh saw an amtrac bump alongside the freighter. As if they'd been invisible, marine lieutenants and captains suddenly appeared, though they stood aside and let the gunnies direct the men down the rope mats.

Josh became aware of an awful retching and was surprised to discover it was the young marine he'd told to drink water. The boy had found a clear place on the rail and was heaving his guts out. Blinking away tears, he looked over his shoulder at Josh. "I drank my water like you told me, sir, but it made me sick."

"What are you talking about?" Josh demanded and unbuckled the boy's canteen and took a swig, then spat it out. It was foul with oil. "Where'd you get this?" Josh yelled over the shouts of marines clambering over the side and the rumbling noise of more amtracs clustering alongside.

"Out of the scuttlebutt they gave us to fill our canteens, sir," the boy said, clutching his stomach.

Somebody said, "There they go. I sure feel sorry for them little yellow bastards."

Josh turned toward Betio and saw, sure enough, the Second Marines, God bless 'em, finally heading in stately fashion toward Red Beaches One, Two, and Three. Bosun Ready O'Neal, yawning from the nap he'd enjoyed throughout the bombardment, appeared at Josh's side. Ready was a Killakeet boy and a pleasant young man who rarely saw harm in anyone. He was also an ugly fellow, no two ways about it, with a nose too big, and eyes a little too close together, and a brow a bit too heavy for his face. No matter, he was a cheerful sort, and smart, in that he tended to be thoughtful. In other words, Bosun Ready O'Neal was a good man to have around. "Ain't them Higgins boats gonna get hung up on that reef?" Ready asked, after a moment of scrutiny.

Josh didn't have the heart to reply to the good-natured man who had seen instantly what nearly everyone else had missed, or denied. The Second Marines were creeping closer to the reef, and now huge explosions were hitting among them and—*there!*—one of the amtracs was struck by an enemy shell and upended, its human cargo spilling overboard. No heads bobbed up, just a white froth marking where they'd disappeared. Each man carried nearly one hundred pounds of gear strapped on tight with canvas webbing. At that moment, those men were drowning while trying to strip off their equipment. Not many would succeed.

Josh needed to get higher to see what was happening. He headed for the bridge and burst in on a surreal scene. The watch officers were laughing and slapping one another on their backs as if they were watching a football game. Josh shut the hatch, then ventured to a portal. The good news was that the amtracs were advancing across the reef, not even slowing down—Burr had been right about that—but the bad news was plentiful. The Higgins boats, one by one, were running aground on the reef. Stuck, unable to move, the Higgins coxswains had no choice but to let down their ramps within a storm of bullets and artillery.

A groan rose among the *J. Wesley Clayton*'s watch officers at the sight of an amtrac exploding inside the reef, bits of steel and men thrown high into the air, a greasy plume of smoke left to mark the sinking machine. Then another of the tracked troop-carriers was struck and sent wheeling aimlessly in the water. Josh swept the beach with his binoculars. Not a single landing craft had yet made it ashore. Then he looked over his shoulder at Burr, who stood with binoculars pressed against his eyes, his mouth a grim line. Behind him, other marine officers stood in shocked silence at what they were seeing, the savage skill and cold discipline of the *rikusentai* as they tore the heart out of the invaders of Tarawa. *Come you, marine. Today you die!*

5

"Keep going, keep going!" the gunnies brayed, pushing their boys toward the rail. Over they went, gasping as they took the weight on the unsteady netting, their packs and rifles and bandoliers of ammunition pulling them backward, their boots slipping on the wet hemp as they clambered down to the tossing Higgins boats. Josh left the bridge and descended to the deck, where he stood with his hands on his hips, then walked closer until he was at the rail. He watched the marines, most of them teenagers, going up and over. Josh had been in many battles, against the poachers and pirates of the Bering Sea with Captain Falcon, then captaining the little cutter *Maudie Jane* against marauding German subs off the Atlantic coast, then against the Japanese infantry in the Solomons, and more. Yet here he was, but an observer, while young, inexperienced men were being sent forward to fight and die. *This is all akilter,* he said to himself, and then something snapped inside his mind, like a cord stretched too taut.

He had to go.

Without another thought, he put his leg over the rail and went hand over hand down the netting until he dropped into the landing craft. There, he sought out a quiet corner until the last marine climbed down and the Coast Guard coxswain steered the boat away. Josh worked through the silent troops, a few already seasick, or perhaps sickened by the oily water in their canteens. He climbed into the cockpit. "What's your orders, son?" he asked the coxswain, a boy with big buck teeth that stuck out over his lower lip.

The boy looked at Josh with more than a little surprise. Clearly, he had not expected a captain in khakis, brown shoes, and a soft cap with the stiff eagle crest of the Coast Guard to show up among the heavily armed, helmeted marines. "I juth driff around until the lead boat goeth in, thir, then I follow it," he explained, still staring. "What the hell're you doin' aboard my boat, thir, if you don't mind me afking?"

"You ever hear the story of the fireman's horse put out to pasture?"

"No, thir."

"Every time he heard the bell at the firehouse, he jumped the fence and raced the wagon to the fire."

"Why'd he do that? Wath he thtupid?"

"Pretty much."

"You ain't got no weapon, thir."

"I'll find one," Josh predicted and unstrapped his binoculars and handed them to the driver. "Have a souvenir," he said.

The coxswain put the binoculars around his neck, then steered the Higgins into a clockwise turn, joining a line of landing craft going around and around. The sun beat down and the temperature rapidly rose. Oily exhaust fumes from the other circling boats turned the air a pale blue. Marines, their utilities soaked with sweat, began to choke. Josh saw three marines doubled over, puking. A foul odor, a mixture of oil and vomit, filled the floating box. Marines drank from their canteens, to rid themselves of the awful taste of the air, only to spit the water out and wipe their mouths in disbelief. From without, a terrible din of machine-gun fire and rifle shots rose and ebbed. The men cursed and spat and raised their faces to the sky in a futile attempt to gasp in a breath of fresh air. Howls of outrage rattled the boat. "Let's go!" the marines screamed. "What are we waiting for?"

Josh climbed up on the steel frame around the cockpit, balancing himself with one hand on the coxswain's shoulder. He could see dozens of Higgins boats snagged on the reef, and in the lagoon marines were slogging ashore through chest-high water, their rifles raised above their heads. The sea was leaping all around them, marking bullet strikes. The sudden disappearance of individual marines told Josh when they were hit. Remembering his duty as an observer, he said to the lad at the wheel, "I need to see this up close. Let's go in."

The coxswain shot Josh a wary glance. "I'm thuppothed to wait until the lead boat goeth first, thir."

"I said take us in, son," Josh growled. The young man opened his mouth to object, thought better of it, and pushed the throttle forward and cranked over the wheel.

"Marines!" Josh called down. "I need to get on that beach. So do you. It's our job, boys. So get ready."

"Anything to get off this crate!" someone yelled, followed by cheers.

Sergeant Pinkerton, the gunny Josh had talked to aboard the troopship, yelled out, "We're with you, Captain Thurlow!"

Beside Pinkerton stood the young marine who'd drunk the foul water when Josh had suggested it. His eyes stared beneath his helmet like white marbles, and it appeared he was on the edge of puking again. Josh looked away.

Something big opened up from the atoll, and two huge splashes, like sudden boils from an underwater volcano, erupted no more than a dozen yards away from the charging Higgins boat. The coxswain started to weave the boat back and forth, but Josh stopped him. "Full throttle dead ahead, son. No time for maneuvers."

As they neared the reef, Josh saw with a sudden shock hundreds of bodies floating in the lagoon. He also counted eight amtracs adrift; oily bubbles indicated where others had sunk. He could make out only two amtracs on the beach, and black smoke was pouring from both of them. Tatters of water and coral flew as bullets peppered their way back and forth across the reef, chewing up the Higgins boats stuck there with their ramps down. No one appeared to be alive aboard them.

"Steer for that boat there," Josh told the boy at the wheel, pointing at a random Higgins in the long line. When the sailor hesitated, Josh reached over and jammed the throttle to its stops. "Ram it! Knock it off the reef and follow it in!"

The coxswain gasped, then slumped down, blood pouring from a wound in his neck. Josh grabbed the wheel from him and kept the Higgins on course. Then something stung his arm, and something else whizzed past his ear. The Higgins plunged on, its engine howling. "Get ready!" he yelled at the marines, who screamed their readiness back. They turned as one toward the ramp.

The Higgins plowed into the stern of one of the stuck boats, though the impact knocked it only a few yards forward. Josh backed off, then threw the throttle full ahead again, the sound of shredded steel informing him he'd thoroughly abused the transmission. Then it felt like a mule had kicked him in the ribs. He clutched his side but kept his hand on the throttle. The Higgins plowed on until it struck the stuck landing craft again. This time, the impact was enough to knock it off the coral, and it slid ahead, leaving behind a channel of clear blue. Holding his side and gritting his teeth against the pain, Josh drove his boat through the gap just as the transmission tore itself to pieces and the engine seized. A pall of dense blue smoke poured from the exhaust.

"Far as I can get us, boys!" Josh yelled above the hammer of bullets splintering the Higgins's ramp. He saw a marine fall, and another was tossed back by the impact of a bullet ricocheting into his face.

"Get on the beach any way you can!" Josh yelled, then lowered the riddled ramp. He saw Sergeant Pinkerton lead the charge, only to disappear beneath the waves. Others went in behind him, most of them finding their footing, Pinkerton apparently having had the bad luck of stepping into a hole. Thrusting their rifles over their heads and wading toward the distant shore, not many of them survived more than a few seconds. The next marines across the ramp went into the water, then curved around to use the landing craft for cover. They began pushing the boat toward the beach, step by step.

Josh was aware that he was wounded, maybe mortally, but he'd have to worry about that later. He started to go down the ramp but then was startled to see several marines slogging back toward the reef. "Where are you men going?" he demanded.

"Back to the troopships, sir," one of them called. "We lost our rifles."

"Turn around," Josh ordered. "Take a weapon from the dead and start fighting."

Dutifully, they turned around, only to disappear moments later when a stitch of machine-gun fire laced through them. A flurry of bullets was tossed Josh's way, too. What sounded like a swarm of hornets buzzed past his ears, and Josh knew it was time to follow his own advice and get to the beach. He leapt off the ramp and fell, apparently into the same hole Pinkerton had found. He came up swimming, bumping into bodies every time he lifted his arms. When his feet finally found bottom, he discovered he was walking on dead marines. He couldn't take a step without stepping on one. Josh picked up a rifle in the shallows and ran to the seawall and threw himself down. He was heartened to see a dozen or so marines were also there. One of them, sitting with his back against the wall, looked over and nonchalantly asked, "Can I have that rifle, sir? I lost mine. Do you know you've been shot in the arm? Your side's all bloody, too."

"I'll trade you for your K-bar," Josh said, then made the switch, buckling the sheath on his belt and drawing out the knife. "Who's in charge?"

The boy scratched up under his helmet. "Nobody, I guess. Except for you, I ain't seen no officers or gunnies on this beach yet. They gonna send some boats to take us back to the troopships?"

"Nobody's going to send any boats to take you anywhere," Josh growled. "You're here to stay."

"I was afraid you'd say that," the marine answered. "I don't think them navy guns killed a one of them bastards. And didn't nobody know about that damned reef?"

A Japanese officer, screaming and waving a sword, suddenly appeared at the top of the seawall. A marine rose up and tackled him, and they both landed heavily on the sand. The marine's K-bar won the short argument that ensued. "Why'd he do that?" the marine wondered as he wiped his bloody knife on the officer's shirt. "He's got to know he's gonna get killed."

"He knew it. They all know it, every one," Josh explained. "That's why they're fighting so hard."

"What should we do, sir?"

Josh gave the question some thought and decided what he needed was a working radio to report his observations. "Keep fighting," he told the marines. "I'm going to see if I can find a radio."

A dozen yards down the beach he instead found a lieutenant, his helmet inexplicably on backward, squatting behind the seawall in front of another knot of survivors. "All right, men," Josh heard him say, "we're going up and over. These bastards can't stop us."

Before Josh could say a cautionary word, the lieutenant climbed up on the seawall and looked over his shoulder at his men. "Follow me!" he yelled just as a furious swath of bullets struck him. Spurts of blood leapt out of him and he fell backward onto the beach. His men dragged his lifeless body, his face shattered, his helmet still on backward, and placed him sitting up against the seawall. His head fell forward, as if he'd decided to take a siesta.

"What outfit?" Josh asked in near despair.

"We're none of us from the same one, sir," a corporal answered.

"Any gunnies around?"

"No, sir. Just us pissants."

A nearby Japanese machine gun opened up, and Josh had to raise his voice to be heard. "Anybody know where I can find a radio?" When no one responded, Josh said, "All right, listen up. The Japs are right over there. What you've got to do is start using your rifles. I know it's hard to put your head above this seawall, but you either start shooting at them or you're going to be overrun."

"Sir, we ain't never gonna take this island," the corporal said. "Ain't they gonna come and get us?"

"You boys keep asking me that," Josh replied. "The answer is no. You're either going to take this island or you're going to die on it. Those are your choices. Now, you boys get to shooting. Throw a few grenades. Mix it up.

That's an order. I'm going to go find a radio and see if I can't get us some help. Savvy?"

The marines savvied and turned toward the seawall. A few of them bobbed up and fired, and there were angry Japanese screams as their bullets struck home. They also began throwing grenades, and a machine gun no more than ten yards away was silenced. A young marine grinned at him. "Like that, sir?" he asked.

To Josh's surprise, it was the young marine who'd drunk the water and gotten sick on the *Clayton*. "Just like that," Josh said, patting the boy on the back. "Keep up the good work, Randy. I know your mother would be proud of you."

Josh headed down the beach at a low crouch, the hot sun beating on him. When he heard the crunch of boots in the sand, he thought the young marine had decided to follow him, but when he turned, he discovered it was actually a small Japanese soldier chasing after him with a long, bayonet-tipped rifle.

Josh was an expert at this kind of infighting and almost nonchalantly stepped aside, grabbed the rifle at its handgrip, pulled it forward until the young Japanese was off balance, and then buried his K-bar in the man's innards, feeling a flood of hot blood around his hand. Twisting it, he pulled out the knife and let go of the rifle. The Japanese marine gave Josh a pitiful look, then quietly fell. Josh, surprised at the regret he felt for killing the young man, considered telling him he was brave—but then something hot hit Josh in the back of his neck. He slapped at it, thinking he'd been stung by a bee. It was, however, something hard that had lodged beneath his skin. He plucked out the thing, which proved to be a black and bloody bullet. It had struck him after being spent, possessing only enough energy to wound him. He considered for a moment putting it in his pocket as a good luck charm but decided there was nothing but bad luck to be found on this beach today. He flicked it into the sand, then went on, dodging past burning amtracs with marines hanging lifelessly from them. Everywhere in the lagoon were numerous floating men, their faces immersed in the rancid sea. Only a marine here and there had made it to the seawall, where they crouched, confused and spent, silently raising their faces in helpless supplication as Josh sprinted past.

6

Bosun Ready O'Neal slogged out of the water and fell onto the beach. He was a bit shaken but unscratched—*a bit of luck for sartain*. When Ready had discovered Captain Thurlow was no longer on the troopship, he'd figured out what his skipper had probably done. To find him, Ready had come in with a bunch of engineers who'd been sent to defuse a line of underwater mines near the reef that fronted Red Beach Two. After motoring in as close as possible, the engineers had jumped into the water. Ready followed, ducking machine-gun bullets, and swam around until the lead engineer announced that, as far as he could tell, none of the mines were armed. "Guess the Japs got in too much of a hurry," he concluded before being struck in the head by a bullet.

The engineers swam back to their boat, pulling their dead sergeant with them. After a moment of indecision, Ready decided to strike out on his own for shore. His captain was surely there, and there he had to go. He swam steadily, an occasional bullet plinking nearby, until he arrived at a long pier jutting perpendicular from the beach. Ready had taken off his shoes before going into the water, so after crawling ashore beneath the pier, he took a dead marine's boots that looked like they would fit. Since he'd also taken off his shirt, he put on the dead man's utility shirt as well, then plopped aboard his helmet, too. Finally prepared, Ready clambered from the protection of the pier and set off down the beach, hoping to find Captain Thurlow. Before long, he came upon three live marines squatting beside a dozen dead ones. "Any of you seen a Coast Guard captain?" Ready asked politely.

The three marines stared at him. "No, sir!" one of them chirped. "Do you have orders for us, sir?"

Ready was surprised at the response. "I don't have any orders. I just want to find my captain."

"All the officers we've seen on this beach are dead, sir," the marine answered, "except for yourself, of course."

That was when Ready realized he had taken the clothes off a dead marine officer. He wondered what his rank was and surreptitiously glanced at his collar. He was astonished to discover that he was a major and that, based on his reading of his name tape, his name was Deer.

"Sir, if we stay here, we'll get killed, for sartain," one of the marines said urgently.

Ready lit up like a bonfire when he heard the marine's brogue. "Where are you from, boy, and what's your name?"

"North Carolina Outer Banks. Hatteras Island. I'm Frank Tucker."

"I knew a Bill Tucker," Ready said. "He came down to Killakeet to stomp clams from time to time."

"Bill's my brother."

Ready felt like hugging the marine. He'd found a neighbor! Then he decided it wouldn't be seemly for a major to go around hugging enlisted men, even neighborly ones. "The Tucker family were always good fishermen," he said, with the reserve he felt appropriate to his new rank.

The marine named Tucker, even if he was from the Outer Banks, didn't seem to be in the mood for reminiscing. "Major, there don't seem to be nobody in front of us," he advised. "I think the Japs figure they've killed everybody on this particular stretch of beach, and they have, pretty much. That's why we've been kind of sitting here, real quiet-like, hoping not to call attention to ourselves."

Ready nodded. "That makes sense."

One of the other marines gave Ready a semi-salute as if fearful of doing the wrong thing. "I'm Private Sampson, sir. New Jersey."

Ready semi-saluted him back. "Well, Private Sampson, what do you think we should do?"

"I guess we ought to invade this island, sir. That's what they sent us here to do. Do you think it would be all right if we got off this beach and killed us a few Japs?"

"I guess so," Ready answered after a short second of thought.

The marine who hadn't introduced himself picked up a rifle out of the sand and handed it to Ready. "Just give us the word, sir," he said, then added shyly, "My name's Private Garcia. I'm from McAllen, Texas. My daddy swam the Rio Grande, and look where it got me."

"A far piece from Texas," Ready agreed. Then, though he was thoroughly frightened, he said, "Let's go," and led the way across the seawall. No bullets greeted them, but there was an awful din not far away. After going forward for a while, he stopped at a shattered palm tree to regain his courage, then moved to the next one. Tucker, Sampson, and Garcia stayed close behind, their fingers on the triggers of their M-1 rifles. Sampson suddenly went down on one knee and fired into the top of a palm tree, and a Japanese soldier fell from it, landing hard on his back. When Ready ran over to him, the man looked up with a fierce expression, which then softened and, just before he died, turned childlike. The marines ran up and fell down beside Ready just as bullets ripped the air above their heads. "I think we found the Japs, sir," Garcia apprised him.

Ready supposed they had, and maybe something more. He thought he'd seen something unlikely, so unlikely it couldn't be real. He crawled forward and then up on a little mound of sand. Sure enough, his eyes hadn't been deceiving him. There, not more than fifty yards away, were a half-dozen Japanese officers, all tricked out in gold-braided dress uniforms and brandishing gleaming silvery swords. Standing outside a palm log bunker, they looked for all the world as if they were dressed up for a parade. When the trio of marines crawled up, Ready ducked back down behind the little dune. "Anybody know where I might find a radio?" he asked.

"There was one on a dead boy back there," Tucker said. "I'll go get it."

Tucker was as good as his word and was soon back carrying a pack radio. Ready halfway didn't expect it to work, but when he fired it up and said cautiously, "Uh, this is, uh, Major Deer. Anybody hear me?" there was an instant response.

"Loud and clear, Major. Who did you say you were?"

"Major Deer. I'm about fifty yards inland of Red Beach Three. Can you put me in touch with somebody what's got some big guns, like artillery and such?"

Within seconds, Ready found himself talking to a sailor aboard the destroyer *Ringgold*. Ready described the Japanese officers who were still standing in the open and where he thought they were.

"I think I know where that is," the *Ringgold* sailor said. "You want an airburst?"

"Sure thing!" Ready answered.

A few minutes later, Ready heard a series of distant thuds behind him followed by whistling screams overhead. The rounds from the destroyer proved to be long, but they burst high off the ground where Ready could see them. He told the sailor on the other end of his radio connection to shorten the next ones up a bit. The Japanese officers had looked over their shoulders with some surprise at the airbursts. One of them had subsequently walked inside the bunker, but the others apparently said something to him, and he walked back out. They were all looking around, as if wondering what to do. They didn't have to wonder long. Six more shells from the *Ringgold* came whistling in, this time bursting directly over them with massive boils of smoke and shrapnel. When the smoke cleared, all six Japanese officers were down.

"Let's go get their swords!" Tucker yelled, and before Ready could stop them, the three marines were up and running. He cautiously followed. The Japanese officers proved to be horribly shredded, their blood and guts splattered all over everything, and even the marines didn't have the heart to pick up their swords. With the stink of cordite still hanging heavy in the air, Ready ducked inside the bunker to see what was what. It proved empty of people but filled with maps and books and filing cabinets. On a table was a topographical map of Betio atoll. There were Japanese symbols all over it with arrows pointing this way and that. Tucker came up alongside. "What do you make of it, sir?"

Ready was a bit awestruck. "I think we just killed the officers in charge of this place," he said in amazement.

"So we done good?"

Ready supposed they had.

Outside the bunker, he called the *Ringgold* sailor. "Who did you say you was again, sir?" the voice asked.

"Major Deer," Ready answered, checking his name tape again just to be certain.

"'Sir, beg pardon, but your name is Reed," Sampson pointed out as gently as possible, and Ready realized he'd been looking at the name upside down. Sheepishly, he turned off the radio and looked at the three marines who were looking back at him.

"I just noticed you're wearing sailor pants," Tucker said.

"It's because they fit," Ready answered.

Tucker opened his mouth to say something else, but all of a sudden, a dozen Imperial marines appeared from behind the bunker and began to scream bloody murder over the bodies of their officers. They were clearly not pleased with the situation, and all Ready and the three marines could do was run for their lives.

So that was what they did.

7

At sea, there was a big explosion, and Josh saw a Higgins boat upended by a direct hit from a big artillery round. Nasty smoke boiled from a wound in its side, and then a dozen men crawled overboard, stood on the reef for a moment as if uncertain what to do, and then fell, cut down by an unseen machine gun. Josh finally came upon a marine fiddling with a pack radio. "Does it work?" he asked.

"No, sir," the radio operator answered. "It got wet coming in."

"Follow me," Josh said. "Bring the radio."

"What for? It's no good."

"Maybe we can fix it. Come on."

The marine reluctantly picked up the waterlogged radio and emulated Josh's low dash behind the seawall. It was tricky going because of all the dead marines. It was easier just to step on them, though Josh felt like apologizing each time he did it. Then Josh found what he was looking for, another radio operator, this one looking disconsolately at his battered set. Josh fell down beside him. "Does it work?"

"No, sir, and I don't know why," the second operator said, eyeing Josh's collar and his rank. "I kept it dry coming in." He raised his canteen. "You know where I can get some water? I can't keep this puke down, and I'm dry as dust."

"Get that radio working and I'll call for water."

The radio operator shrugged. "I'm a little short of spare parts."

The first radio operator arrived and laid his radio down beside the other one. "See if you can make one out of two," Josh told them. "And keep yourself alive if you can. We've got some important calls to make."

Fifty yards on, Josh finally found a live officer, a tall major with a fiery red mustache who was squatting in the sand and pondering a map. Crouched around him was a mixed group of exhausted amtrac drivers and riflemen. When Josh hailed the major, the man looked up and blinked. A Coast Guard captain in ship's khakis and brown shoes, armed only with a bloody K-bar, was apparently the last person he'd expected to encounter on the atoll of Betio. Josh quickly introduced himself, and the major said, "I'm Major Ryan, sir. Do you know you've been shot?"

"Three times, I think. You got a radio that works?"

Ryan shook his head, and Josh pointed behind him and said, "Send a runner that way. I left two operators putting one together."

Ryan tapped an amtrac driver on his shoulder. "Son, go up the beach and see if you can find us a radio."

The boy nodded and ran off, keeping low. A storm of bullets suddenly whipped the air above their heads. Ryan and Josh duckwalked to the seawall and crouched there, perusing the map together. Ryan pointed to where he thought they were, the extreme western end of the area designated as Red Beach One. Josh pondered the sandy peninsula that marked the right flank of the beach. On the other side of it was a shoreline that faced generally north. Josh put his finger on the map that identified that particular stretch of sand. "That's Green Beach, and it looks wide open. If the Sixth Marines landed there, they could roll up the Japanese *toot sweet*."

"The Sixth Marines are only supposed to be held in reserve," Ryan replied dubiously. He looked seaward. Dozens of Higgins boats were burning on the reef, amtracs were adrift and on fire, and the lagoon was filled with hundreds of dead, drifting marines. "Looks like they've stopped trying to land," he observed.

"The Second Marines are done," Josh said. "General Smith is going to have to send in the Sixth, and here's the place to do it."

Just then, the first radio operator Josh had met fell down beside them. "We got a rig going, sir," he said.

"Where's your buddy?"

"Dead."

"How about the runner we sent after you?"

"Dead, too."

"See if you can raise Battalion," Ryan ordered. "Tell them we're holding on to Red One and intend to move over and secure Green Beach."

"Which battalion, sir?"

Ryan shrugged. "Just contact anybody who'll answer."

"Aye, aye, sir," the operator replied and sat cross-legged in the sand and cranked the radio. After a few minutes, he looked up. "Sir, I got a Colonel Shoup. He said for us to take Green Beach if we can."

Ryan looked surprised. "Colonel Shoup? Did he say where he is?"

"Red Beach Three, sir."

Ryan rubbed his chin. "What the hell is Shoup doing on the beach? He's supposed to be in charge of the whole damned landing. He ought to be on the *Maryland*."

"Nothing's going as planned," Josh answered, raising his voice as the Japanese made a sudden assault on their position, screaming curses and firing their long rifles at the hip. The marines rose and shot them down. When Josh saw the attack was over, he continued. "Shoup probably decided to get in and see what he could salvage of the landing and his career."

Ryan called over two gunny sergeants. "Listen, gunnies, you don't know me, and you probably don't know many of these men, but put together a couple of rifle squads and get ready to move. We're going to take that beach over yonder."

"Aye, aye, Skipper," one of the gunnies responded, and the other one nodded, then asked, "What about water? It's hot as blazes, and the men can't drink this piss in their canteens."

"I'll see what I can do," Ryan promised, and off the gunnies went, yelling at the men or slapping them on the backs of their helmets to let them know they were still in the Marine Corps, didn't matter what their old unit was, or how thirsty they were, and now they had a clear mission, which was all a marine ever needed. Josh felt for the first time a little optimism. If they could secure Green Beach, the gate to victory on Betio might be forced open, though it would have to be done by men who had not expected to fight.

Hearing a low drone overhead, Josh looked up and saw a scout plane. "Let's hope that pilot will report back on Green Beach, too," he said, but it was to nobody. Ryan, the gunnies, and all the other marines had gone over the seawall and were busily raising hell with a pillbox, which shortly exploded in a ball of fire and sand.

Then Josh saw an amazing sight. On the reef, a Mike boat, a medium landing craft, was disgorging six M-4 Sherman tanks. They ground across the reef and into the shallow lagoon, blue smoke blowing from improvised exhaust pipes stuck like snorkels from their engines. Japanese artillery had spotted them, too, and were lashing out with so many rounds the sea around the tanks was whipped into a white froth. When the fire lifted, Josh saw only two tanks still grinding toward shore. When those two reached the beach, Japanese artillery concentrated on the lead tank, and it exploded, its turret flung into the sky, falling with a mighty crash into the sand. The second tank, the name *China Girl* stenciled on its turret, successfully climbed the seawall and waddled on, unscathed. Josh ran after it, finding the driver's hatch open. "Head for Green Beach!" Josh yelled to the driver, pointing the way, then hopping aboard.

Josh hugged the turret until Major Ryan came running up. Seeing Josh and the tank, a grin spread across his sweaty face. "Where'd you find the Sherman?"

"Went out in the lagoon and pulled her in," Josh replied, then hopped off while Ryan took his place to direct *China Girl* where it could do the most good.

Josh encountered the radioman. "Who you got on the line, son?" he asked.

"Colonel Shoup, sir. I already told him about the tank."

"Well, tell him one other thing," Josh said. "Tell him down here on Red Beach One we ain't winning yet, but we've about stopped losing."

The radioman rang up the line and announced Josh's message. He listened for a long second, then looked up. "He wants to know your name, sir."

"Tell him that was from Major Ryan," Josh answered with a grin, then snarled when a piece of whistling shrapnel caught him in the back, knocking the wind out of him and pitching him face first into the sand. Gasping and spitting grit from between his teeth, he pushed back onto his knees, then looked around and saw the gentle, lapping sea, and the pretty blue-white foam climbing all about the exposed yellow reef, and also the surprised, dead face of the radioman, who had taken a piece of shrapnel in his heart. "You were brave," Josh told him even though he was past hearing anything forever.

Josh carried the blood-spattered radio to Major Ryan and wordlessly dropped it in the sand. "It's busted," he said.

Ryan was digging in with his men behind Green Beach. "My God, Captain Thurlow. Now you've been hit in the back. Hang on."

Josh hung on. Ryan asked his troops if any of them had a pair of pliers. One of his engineers did, and after Josh had taken his shirt off, Ryan used them to pull a jagged sliver of steel from his back. "There's another big scar back here," Ryan noticed.

"Nazis off Killakeet gave me that one," Josh answered cryptically. "Is it bleeding much?"

"Not much. Cauterized itself, I guess."

"I think I'll go find Colonel Shoup," Josh said. "Just to make sure he knows Green Beach is open."

"You're going up that beach? You'll never make it."

Josh noticed the angle of the sun. It was already late afternoon. If he was going to find Shoup, he'd need to hurry. "Look, Major, there's not much light left," he said. "Most likely Jap will counterattack tonight, give you a big *banzai* scare. Just do whatever you can to keep this beach secure. The Japanese believe they're the best night-fighters in the world, but we skunked them on Guadalcanal and you can skunk them here. When it gets dark, send out a couple of your best men to cut some throats. That'll give them pause. Oh, and steal their water, too."

"Aye, aye, Skipper. Tell Colonel Shoup I'll hold the line here."

Josh headed up the beach, a depressing trek that took him past hundreds of bodies and great piles of wreckage and soggy gear, all spoiling in the terrible heat. When he crossed the boundary to Red Beach Two, he was astonished to come upon a big sergeant and several other marines tossing sticks of dynamite over the seawall. The sergeant took a look at Josh, and his jaw fell open. "My God, man, you're shot all to hell!"

"Where'd you get that dynamite?" Josh asked.

"Brought it in with us. We were just about to go over the top to take out some pillboxes. Want to come along? Looks like Jap couldn't do much more to you."

Josh thought it over and said, "Why not?"

"That's the spirit," the sergeant said and introduced himself. "Bill Bordelon. I'm a Texas boy."

Josh made a quick study of the man's open, honest face and instantly liked him. "Haven't we met?"

"You bet we have! I was on the Canal. I helped build the runway at Henderson. Ever so often, you'd land there in that junk heap of a PBY of yours. Your pilot made every landing fun to watch. They were always more like crashes than landings."

Josh smiled. "Mister Phimble taught himself how to fly. It ain't pretty the way he does it, but he generally gets us where we're going."

Bordelon gave Josh a quick rundown of the rest of his men. Every one of them was a sergeant. "We used to be navy Seabees," Bordelon confided, "but they decided to make us into marines for this foul-up. Since we were all technical, they had to make us sergeants. We're a whole company of sergeants, believe it or not, what's left of us. We got shot up pretty good coming in."

"You and everybody else. You got any water?"

"No, but we got plenty of oil in our canteens."

One of the sergeants silently handed Josh a utility shirt, and Josh put it on. It was a little tight but serviceable. He left it unbuttoned.

"You ready to go?" Bordelon asked.

Josh nodded, and Bordelon gave him a big grin, lit the fuse on a cluster of four dynamite sticks, and yelled, "Come on, all you sergeants! Let's make some noise!"

Over the wall they went, a cluster of ex-Seabee engineers made into marine sergeants carrying dynamite, along with one battered Coast Guard captain, armed only with a K-bar.

The Japanese were caught entirely by surprise.

8

Sister Mary Kathleen was young, very young, and she had about her a certain Irish farm girl beauty, but her habit covered all but her face and hands. Still, more than a few of the battle-begrimed *rikusentai* glanced avariciously in her direction and, as Soichi had predicted, snarled their intentions to rape her. Although she understood them very well, her response was to nod and smile as if she didn't. The wise captive always seeks to understand the language of her captors, and this was not the first time Sister Mary Kathleen had been imprisoned by the Japanese, or threatened by them. She even understood their curses when they descended into the slang of the streets. She knew gutter Japanese all too well. She also knew her only chance was to keep one of them from going over the edge and following through on his threat. It was the mentality of the pack. If one began his attack, the others, swept along by the frenzy, would follow. Then she and her fella boys would surely be torn to pieces.

A particularly loathsome brute with big yellow teeth reached toward her, only to have his hand slapped away by a defiant Tomoru. Seeing the confrontation, Captain Sakuri came up behind the Imperial marine and struck him on his head, bowling away his helmet. When the man bent over for it, Sakuri, screaming curses, further planted his boot on the man's hindquarters and pushed him to the floor. The Japanese marine crawled after his helmet and, after retrieving it, hastily departed the fortress. Sister Mary Kathleen mumbled her thanks to Sakuri in English, but the officer, in response, burned his eyes into hers, then slowly drew his finger across his throat, saying in Japanese, "Woman, you will not live through this day." Then he stalked outside.

Sister Mary Kathleen decided to take Lieutenant Soichi's advice and shepherded her fella boys behind the table that held Captain Sakuri's plans and maps and made them sit. "Be like the sea after a storm, me boys," she directed them. "Be strong but quiet. Heads down, that's it. Do not look at them."

Tomoru objected. "If a Japonee comes near us again, I will break his back."

"Nay, Tomoru," the nun counseled in his dialect. "We did not come here to fight the Japanese but to find the Americans. I think they are coming. You must be patient."

"Tomoru, you will heed Sister," Nango advised the young man, and Tomoru, though he frowned, nodded assent. Nango was, after all, the next great chief of their island.

The *rikusentai* kept rotating in and out of the sand fortress, coming inside to rest and eat and drink and resupply themselves with ammunition. The battle outside had only been noise to the nun. She had no idea what was happening, only that it must be a furious fight. She was surprised that no wounded Japanese were ever carried inside. Did that mean the Japanese were winning? Or were they leaving their wounded on the battlefield?

As the hours went by, the Japanese seemed to be losing control of themselves, becoming ever more hysterical as the battle got louder and apparently closed in on the fortress. Once, three of them came running inside and collapsed, breathing heavily and groaning. Then they rose to their knees and held one another and began to chant something that Sister Mary Kathleen could not understand. She concluded it was in an obscure Japanese dialect. Perhaps the men were all from the same remote village. Captain Sakuri came inside, saw the trio, and spoke to them. Immediately, they all nodded assent and, with shamed expressions on their faces, quietly gathered up ammunition and went back outside into the riotous tumult. Sister Mary Kathleen heard very clearly what the captain had said to them. "Do you expect to live? For shame! Your life is over! Today or tomorrow, you will die, either by the Americans or by suicide. These are my final orders."

She could not help but feel admiration for Sakuri and the *rikusentai* and marveled at the faith that allowed them to so willingly sacrifice themselves for their cause—but could they not see how foolish, and ultimately worthless, their deaths would be? Fight for your beliefs and your country, yes, but when the enemy is overwhelming, why deliberately die? To her, by everything her church had taught her, this was a mortal, unforgivable sin. Yet here were all these men, made by the same God as she, accepting death as long as it was glorious, and it didn't matter much if it was by the hand of the enemy or their own. She reflected that if she had stayed in Ireland, she would have never observed such strange beliefs. Giving it some thought, though, she wondered if that was really true. Her father, during his protracted war with the English, had adopted much the same philosophy, had he not? And if she allowed herself to look back, to trace the line of fate that had brought her to this terrible atoll, it was what her father had believed that had caused his death and therefore changed her life, ultimately bringing her into the sisterhood. And was that not good? Could mortal sin be the direct cause of goodness? She did not know. There was so *much* she did not know.

A sudden crash at one of the portals startled her from her contemplation. A gout of smoke blew inside, a choking sulfurous fog. As it condensed, she saw a Japanese marine staggering around the bunker, his quivering hands reaching out. She saw now that his face was gone, replaced by a gory mass of torn flesh. He swiveled his head hideously and helplessly trying to see, though all that remained was dripping scarlet eye sockets. Pitifully, he staggered to the table and put his hands on it, allowing it to take his weight. She saw now that he had no jaw; his upper teeth, the few of them left, exposed like pink pegs in the purple mush of his palate. Captain Sakuri came inside and wordlessly gripped the man by his shoulder and turned him around. Then the captain put a dagger in the man's hands and watched stoically as the Imperial marine plunged it hard into his stomach and jerked it once, then twice, his terrible face bubbling his agony. Though she knew it was sinful, she was grateful when the man fell. She rose to go to his side, to pray for his everlasting soul. Captain Sakuri roughly pushed her away. But then he looked at her, and for just an instant, she thought she saw no hate in his eyes but a kind of desperate sadness, a yearning for an end to the torture. She entered his eyes for a moment, to allow him to understand that she desired such a release herself. Startled by her silent honesty, he opened his mouth to speak, then closed it and walked swiftly to the portal and outside, leaving her and her fella boys alone once more. Now she knelt beside the faceless soldier, crossed herself, and said a prayer for him, and then one for herself:

Saint Monessa, as ye had such faith, ye chose to die upon baptism, let me have an equal faith in the mission God has visited upon me. In yer few short years on earth, ye acquired a marvelous humility and serenity. Teach me, Saint Monessa, and take me and me fella boys under yer protection.

When Sister Mary Kathleen finished her prayer, she waited with hope that she might receive a sign from the tiny saint. She looked up at the roof of palm logs and, though she knew full well it was but her imagination, saw a child in a robe, much like the habit she wore, except woven with gold thread. The little girl was alert, as if listening, and then she cocked her head, and Sister Mary Kathleen decided she was hearing her prayer. In an instant, the child was gone, climbing into a white nothingness toward the throne of heaven itself. *Run for me, little saint,* the nun silently urged, and then she thought she heard a small tinkle of joyful laughter even while the ground beneath her shook. Though she did not fear death, Sister Mary Kathleen feared pain, and her heart pounded in her chest. Something awful was coming now, something gigantic and wounded, and it was coming to maim and kill all that stood in its way.

9

Josh staggered along the beach. He still couldn't quite believe what he'd just seen. Sergeant Bordelon and the other sergeants of the Seabee-turned-marine outfit had crawled up next to a bunker and calmly tossed in spewing sticks of dynamite. The bunker exploded in a rain of logs and sand, and then they had sprinted to three more and dynamited them, too. When a blasting cap had gone off in Bordelon's hand, blowing away his thumb, he'd laughed and wrapped it up in a torn strip of his shirt. All the while, Japanese snipers were sniping away. Though wounded several times, Bordelon never stopped until a bullet caught him in the stomach. Finally, he sat down. "Helluva place to die," he remarked as Josh sat down beside him.

Josh didn't deny the man the truth. "I'll make sure nobody forgets what you did today, Sarge. You and all your sarges."

Bordelon laughed, frothy pink bubbles appearing on his lips. "That presumes you're going to get off this island alive, Josh!"

Josh waited until Bordelon died before walking back to the beach. Based on an ache he felt in his leg, he suspected he'd been hit again. Bullets snapped past his ears, but he didn't care. His back hurt too much to stay bent over, so he walked upright until he reached an amtrac with its bow pushed up against the seawall. Twenty or so marines were hunkered down around it. One of them was a colonel talking on a radio.

Josh felt a hand on his arm and looked at a navy corpsman holding a canvas medical kit. "You've been hit, sir," he said. "Sit down and let me take a look."

Josh shrugged him off. "You Colonel Shoup?" he asked the officer.

A pale, round-faced colonel eyed him. "I am. Who the hell are you?"

"Captain Josh Thurlow. You get the word on Green Beach?"

It took a moment for Shoup to get his thoughts wrapped around the bloody apparition that had appeared before him. "Josh Thurlow. You got to be kidding! I thought you were just a story the guys made up after a round of applejack. Green Beach, you say? Is it open?"

"Was the last time I saw it," Josh answered. "That's what I walked up here to tell you."

"Well, I appreciate it, Captain," Shoup said, "but there ain't a thing I can do about it until morning."

"You plan to get the Sixth Marines across it?"

"That's my plan. Whether it happens is up to General Smith. The Second Marines are too beat up to take this atoll, but I don't think he's reached that conclusion."

Josh suddenly felt like he needed to sit down. That was good, since he discovered he was already sitting down even though he didn't remember doing it. The medic was working on him, bandaging here, probing there, powdering him with sulfa. "I think I'll take a nap," Josh told Shoup. "I mean, if you don't mind . . ."

And that was the last thing Josh recalled until he awoke in Dosie Crossan's arms, or perhaps, after he'd thought about it and smelt the perfumed tropical air, it was Penelope, her glowing black skin so warm to his touch. A sudden scream in the night caused him to open his eyes, and then he noticed the lovely woman he was holding was actually a quilted camouflage cover. He felt around and his fingers dug into gritty sand and then it all came back as to where he was. He looked up and saw a million, trillion stars, glittering little remnants of the beginning of the universe, the vast, undulating belt of the Milky Way, illuminating the pale milky-white beach dotted with wreckage and dead men.

He heard now the low voice of Colonel Shoup, still talking into his radio. Josh crawled over to him. "You still alive?" he asked, clearly surprised.

"After a fashion," Josh answered. "Jap attack us yet?"

"No, and it's almost dawn. Don't know why they didn't. If they had, they might have pushed us into the sea. Either we were lucky or Jap was stupid, not sure which."

"It doesn't make sense," Josh said after a little thought. "Jap loves to fight at night. It's when he figures he has the advantage. What could have happened?"

Then an amazing, miraculous sight appeared from around the back of the amtrac. Barefooted, bare chested, wearing only his dungaree pants, Bosun Ready O'Neal appeared. "Captain Thurlow, you're alive!" Ready cried and made almost as if to hug Josh although he stopped short, such a display of affection between men not allowed even on that awful beach.

Ready plunked himself down in the sand beside Josh and rattled off everything that had happened until that very moment, except he gave all the credit to Major Reed for blowing up the Japanese officers. Josh and Colonel Shoup gaped at him. "I bet those officers included the admiral in charge," Shoup mused. "That's why we got through the night. By God, I'll see that Major Reed gets one hell of a big medal. Killed, you say?"

"Dead as a hammer, sir," Ready answered sorrowfully.

"Jap is one helluva fighting man," Josh said, "but when he loses his officers, he tends to get confused, even fold. It's a weakness."

Shoup grinned, then said, "Well, look there now! Ain't that a welcome sight!"

Shoup was referring to a typical gaudy Pacific morning that was busily being produced on the eastern horizon, a huge scarlet orb bobbing up from the sea, all the while tossing out yellowish-red streaks of the purest light anyone could imagine. Josh studied the reef in the morning light and saw that it was now submerged, the tide well in. "We should have invaded today. Man figures and studies, but God don't have to," he said and shook his head.

There came from inland a frightful big bang, and Shoup's radio soon crackled. He listened to whoever was on the other end and said, "Well, knock it out. Who've you got there to do it?" He looked around. "I need a runner to carry a radio and some batteries to Red Beach Three." Shoup's eyes lit on Ready. "Bosun, how about it? Could you put on some boots and make a run for me?"

"I guess so, Colonel," Ready answered and took the radio and a pouch of batteries from a radioman. Another marine handed him some boots. There was no shortage of them.

"Hold on, Bosun," Josh said. "Your mama's probably not ever going to forgive me for bringing you out here, but if I get you killed for a radio and some batteries, I'd never be able to go back to Killakeet. I'll go with you."

"But you're shot all to hell!" Ready protested.

"Just little holes," Josh said, though when he smacked his hand against the patch on his ribs to show how healthy he was, he nearly passed out from the pain. But he was a big man, and strong despite the loss of blood, and it wasn't long before he and Ready were heading down the beach toward Red Beach Three, a radio on Ready's back, a bag of batteries over Josh's shoulder.

Since the Japanese were no longer keeping up a steady fire, Josh and

Ready made good progress, although the stink of the corpses on the beach was nearly enough to knock them down. "So many men," Josh said.

"Americans will never forget this place!" Ready cried in a burst of misplaced patriotism.

"Yes, they will," Josh answered while feeling the hot sun burning against his cheek. It was going to be another scorcher. "Most folks will forget it by next month or the next island, whichever comes first. Oh, the families of the dead boys will recall for a while, but this spit of sand's too far away for Americans to bother with for long. Anyways, worse battles are yet to come."

Although he was always inclined to defer to his captain, Ready chose to argue. "There can't be any worse battles than this one, Skipper! The people won't stand for it!"

"Oh, they'll stand for it because they don't have much choice. You see, Ready, we're in the show now, us and Jap, and only one of us is going to be on our feet after it's all over. A lot of men will have to die or wish they were dead before it's done." Josh went on a few more steps. "But I hope you're right about there being no worse battles than this one."

A sudden storm of bullets flew in front of their faces, and Josh and Ready hit the sand, then looked out to sea when they heard the growl of engines. A line of Higgins boats was pushing straight at them, aiming for an opening between the dozens of empty boats still hung on the reef. Though the reef was underwater, it still snagged the boats, and seconds later, three of the landing craft were burning, one had sunk, and the rest were being pounded by big, unseen shore guns. Marines climbed out of the boats onto the reef, where they stood in waist-deep water, holding their rifles over their heads. "Get ashore!" Josh yelled, but snipers picked them off, and fresh bodies began to float alongside the ones from the day before. Only a few marines made it to shore, splashing in without packs or rifles and throwing themselves against the seawall. Josh and Ready looked at two of the marines who lay there gasping, their eyes wide with horror. "You boys got any water?" Josh asked, politely.

One of them, his eyes huge beneath his helmet, silently handed over his canteen, and Josh and Ready took a drink from it. "Still full of oil," Josh said, though he swallowed it anyway. He looked at the marine. "Are you Second Marines or Sixth?"

"Second, sir."

"Where's the Sixth?"

"I don't know, sir. I don't even know where *I* am."

Josh smiled and handed the man's canteen back. "You're on Tarawa, son."

"What should I do, sir?" the marine asked.

"Pick up a rifle," Josh said. "Then go one way or the other along the beach, it don't much matter. Find some marines. Join up, get into the war."

"Aye, aye, sir," he said and crawled off with his buddies, disappearing into the shimmering heat waves coming off the sun-drenched sand. Josh and Ready went on, trying not to look at the bloated dead floating in the lagoon. "I keep expecting them to raise their heads and take a breath," Ready said.

Then a big Japanese artillery shell fell short, striking the beach instead of the Higgins boat it was aimed at. The blow sent them both, senseless of thought or feeling, cartwheeling through the air.

1 0

Josh climbed back from wherever the artillery round had sent him. Apparently, the day had passed. It was dark, and there were screams and the terrible sounds of struggle—deep grunts, guttural swearing, random rifle shots, puking, gasping, and choking death rattles. Then a boot stomped his hand.

Josh was at least relieved to see, by the light of a flare, that the boot belonged to Ready O'Neal, who was too busy to notice, mainly because he was receiving a lunging Japanese soldier equipped with a long bayonet on a longer rifle. As Josh watched with interest, the two men fell away, and then there was a muffled sob followed by another muffled sob, the last from Ready, who was crying because he had been forced to kill a man.

"Don't feel bad, Bosun," Josh said from what seemed like a deep hole he'd fallen into. "You had to do it."

Ready abruptly stopped his sobbing. "You awake, sir?"

Josh tried to focus on one thing, to help him understand where he was. "Is it night or am I going blind?"

"Night, Skipper. They've been coming at us since the sun went down. Usually, the boys in the foxholes up front stop them, but now and again one or two slip through. Like this poor youngster I just murdered."

Josh absorbed the information, pausing long enough for a cogent thought to present itself. "You didn't murder him," he said at length. "You just killed him. It's war." He paused again. "Thanks for taking care of me while I was out."

"I wouldn't leave you, sir. You know that."

"Where are we?"

"Near the runway. At an aid station some corpsmen set up."

"Are we losing?"

"No. I heard Colonel Edson say we were winning."

"Red Mike's ashore? Thank God. Did you tell him about Green Beach?"

"Yeah, Skipper. Sixth Marines came ashore on Green Beach this afternoon."

While Ready was talking, Josh was silently allowing his mind to search his body. It ached like hell, pretty much like it did before he got knocked out, but at least he could move his fingers and toes, both good signs. Then a harsh thirst overcame him. "I need some water," he said. Ready silently handed him a canteen. Josh polished it off and, running his tongue through the oily residue left in his mouth, said, "Still foul."

"Yes, sir. Most of the marines can't keep it down and are running pretty dry. First priority ain't to land bullets, Red Mike said, but water."

Josh tried to piece it all together. "How many days have we been on this atoll?"

"Two days and two nights, sir."

"Seems like two weeks." Josh kept thinking. Likely, his bowels would be sliding that water through pretty quick. He just hoped his body would keep a little of it. When he next raised his head, he saw the sun rising, producing yet another spectacular gold and scarlet spectacle and lighting up a vast and terrible battlefield of dead men, ruined machines, shattered palm trees, sandy bomb craters, and a cracked concrete runway with heat waves already rising from its surface like wriggling, translucent worms. "I hate this place," Josh said and wasn't certain if he was talking about the atoll of Betio or the earth itself. At that moment, probably both were true.

Josh realized he was bare chested except for bloody bandages wrapped across his torso. He saw his khaki trousers were in shreds and he'd lost one of his shoes and his Coast Guard cap. He felt at his waist and was gratified that at least the K-bar was still there. "I'd better put on some utilities," he told Ready, "and some boots."

"I'll get you some," Ready said and went off, returning with two sets of utilities and a pair of boots, complete with socks. Ready pulled off his own bloody dungarees and drew on a camouflage uniform. Then he helped Josh put on utilities and socks and boots, all of which proved to be a fair fit. Ready allowed himself a moment of guilt, seeing as how he had stripped the clothing off dead marines.

Josh asked, "Where's Red Mike? I'd like to have a word with him."

"Don't know, sir," Ready answered as he finished tying the last knot on Josh's boots. "Well, would you look at that! I just thought it was a big old sand dune last night."

Josh looked where Ready was looking and saw the sun had lit up a big pyramid of sand and palm logs not more than a hundred yards away. From it, Japanese were busily firing machine guns and rifles in a constant clatter. Dead marines were littered around it. A pair of corpsmen carrying a stretcher came racing past and then tossed down the stretcher and threw themselves into the crater beside Josh and Ready, a stitch of machine-gun fire following them from the fort. One of the corpsmen groaned and grabbed his leg, and the other one stared incredulously at his left hand, where a bloody bullet hole had appeared. Other medics came running and helped the wounded corpsmen up and took them away.

"That big sand fort's got to go," Josh observed and raised his head a little higher out of the crater to get a better look at it. For his trouble, a bullet whipped past his head. He ducked down. Then a few marines ran past, going toward the fort. "Ready," Josh said, "let's go see if we can help these boys take that pile of sand."

"Sir, you're awful banged up," Ready objected. "You've broken out in a sweat, too. I think you've got fever coming on."

"But I can still walk," Josh answered.

Ready looked at his skipper's rough, whiskery face, the old broken nose, the livid scar on his chin, the sweat standing out on his grimy forehead. He looked a million years old, yet Ready knew Josh Thurlow was only thirty-three. "Let's just rest awhile," Ready suggested.

"I can't," Josh replied. "I've got to do something about that fort."

"Let other men do it."

"It's not my way."

Ready saw that his captain was bound and determined. "I'll help you up," he said. And he did.

1 1

A big-boned Southern gentleman, that's what he was. "Sandy Bonnyman," he introduced himself to Josh. Josh had found him lying on the shattered remnants of a palm log bunker, intently studying the Japanese fort.

Josh lay beside him and also studied the pyramid of sand and palm logs. It had several protruding pipes that were probably air vents. Sandbagged machine-gun positions were on its top and along its sides. There was also a wall of sandbags on both ends that probably masked entries. Josh identified himself, adding, "I'm just an observer."

Bonnyman laughed after noting Josh's wounds. "Observing ain't healthy the way you do it, Captain," he said.

"What's your take on that fort, Sandy?"

"You ever hear of a Forlorn Hope?"

"The British used that term in the Napoleonic wars. A direct frontal assault against a fortified position requiring major casualties."

"You're well read, sir. They used to hand out promotions and bonuses to any soldiers willing to join in. Of course, not many of them survived to collect."

"You think that fort requires a Forlorn Hope?"

"Yep. Bombs won't touch that thing, and neither will artillery. All that sand just absorbs the energy of the detonations. But I think I see a weakness in its design."

"Are you an engineer?" Josh asked.

Bonnyman grinned. "I'm a supply officer, but since supplies have been kind of pinched, I thought I'd come up here to see what I could do to help."

"I noticed the markings on your uniform," Josh said. "Those white stripes make you kind of stand out."

"Supply officers need to be seen so trucks on the beach won't run over them. But it don't much matter. Jap can see all of us just fine from atop that big old pile of sand. The way I see it, Josh, that fort is the only thing still holding the Japanese together on this atoll. We knock it out and this battle will be over."

Josh nodded, agreeing with Bonnyman's assessment. "What's the weakness you see?"

"The air vents. If we knock the Japs off the top, we can stop them up. Then it'll be our ball game."

"A tall order. You've got no supporting artillery, and all there is between you and the fort is open ground. The machine guns on top of it will chew you up."

"Crossing that field will be the hard part," Bonnyman acknowledged, "but once we get there, I think we can do what we have to do. Flamethrowers, they're the key. I've been watching this battle since I hit the beach. It's the one thing Jap can't stand up to. He sees them flames coming at him, he backs off."

"It would be bloody for our boys," Josh said.

"But quick, I think," Bonnyman replied.

Josh looked over his shoulder and saw around thirty marines, two of them equipped with flamethrowers. "Why not wait for more men?"

Bonnyman shrugged. "These marines have had enough. They're ready to get this thing over with."

Josh could feel his blood rising. "I am, too. I'll go with you."

Bonnyman stared. "Hell, Captain, you don't even have a sidearm!"

"I won't lack for a weapon," Josh answered, knowing there would be plenty to pick up along the way.

Bonnyman shrugged, then turned to his marines. "Gents, y'all ready to go?"

The marines nodded, their eyes hooded and determined beneath their steel helmets. Bonnyman looked at Josh—their eyes met for a long second—and then the supply officer said with a smile, "OK. Let's go."

And, just like that, they all went. Bonnyman's Forlorn Hope was on its way with every man in the assault running as hard as he could at the sand fort. The Japanese saw them coming and cut loose with all they had. Bullets blew by, grenades exploded, and some of the running marines grunted and fell. One of the men carrying a flamethrower sprawled into the sand, then got up and kept going, dragging a mangled foot. Josh put a hand under the man's arm and helped him along. The noise of rattling machine guns, whistling bullets, and exploding grenades and mortar shells was hideous, nearly paralyzing, but Josh kept dragging the marine with the flamethrower with him.

Bonnyman and three marines were the first to arrive at the base of the fort. They began tossing grenades as if they were baseball pitchers warming up. Two Japanese machine-gun emplacements blew up, sending pieces of the guns and chunks of flesh and flying sand raining down on the attackers. Josh and the marine with the flamethrower reached the base of the pyramid, and Bonnyman motioned them to get to work. The marine, gritting his teeth against the pain of his bloody foot, worked the device, and fiery yellow and red flames blossomed from the nozzle. "Put it right there!" Bonnyman yelled, pointing toward the top, and the marine did as he was told, and a roaring, orange liquid fire tunneled through the air with a horrible growl like a demented beast. The Japanese machine gunners on top of the fort were transformed into screaming, flailing torches.

Marines followed the arc of fire, racing up the slope of the fort. The Japanese defenders were screaming, shooting, slipping in the sand, and dying. Josh saw that Bonnyman had somehow come up with a satchel charge, tossing it over the top. A huge, shattering blast followed, and Bonnyman raced up through the sand with Josh close behind. They fell down together and looked to see the result of the explosion. The backside of the slope was covered with dead Japanese.

Josh looked at Bonnyman. "Well, Sandy, I think you've pulled it off."

"You think so?" Bonnyman asked, then died when a bullet slapped through his helmet and pierced his skull.

Josh wasn't aware that Bonnyman had been hit. He clapped the man on his back. "You're one hell of a marine. It's been a privilege and an honor."

Then Josh noticed Bonnyman was dead, and it was as if a plug were suddenly pulled from his body, releasing the last energy he had. He rolled over on his back and rested his head on the hot sand and looked up into the clear blue sky. The terrible noise of the assault faded, and all Josh could hear was his own ragged breathing. He noticed there was some sort of creature flying over him, and then he saw it was but a pelican. Strangely, though, it was looking down at him with interest, and to his astonishment, Josh recognized the bird. Its name was Purdy, and Josh had last seen it on Killakeet Island of the Outer Banks of North Carolina. Josh's grandfather had told stories of Purdy and said his grandfather had done the same. Purdy was so old, he had surely been there in the Cretaceous and maybe before. Now here he was on this terrible, mangled atoll, against all reason. "You old, old thing," Josh said, breathing quietly, watching with fascination as the pelican continued his infinite circles. "Why did you let this happen?"

Purdy, if it was Purdy, ignored Josh's question. Instead, he gained altitude, his mottled wings stretched against the wind, and before long he'd vanished and the noise of the battle came back and Josh found Ready lying beside him, looking concerned. "Skipper, you all right? The marines are going inside the bunker, sir."

"Then we'd best help them," Josh said and drew his K-bar from its scabbard with terrible resolve.

Ready looked at the big knife. "You don't have to, sir," he said in as gentle a tone as the awful noise of the battle would allow. "The marines, they've got it under control now."

Josh wiped the sweat from his eyes. "I saw Purdy," he said, blinking furiously.

Ready's expression was dubious, which Josh thought impertinent. "Purdy, sir? The pelican? We're an awful long way from Killakeet, sir."

"You can make that into a song, boy," Josh said, then stood up and walked down the hill of sand, each step reminding him of the great dunes of Killakeet and how he'd loved to play on them as a boy, running up, then running down, sinking in up to his knees, turning and climbing them again. A smile formed on his otherwise grim lips that seemed hideous under the circumstances. At the bottom of the fort, he heard sounds of struggle and screams coming from within. "Perhaps I might yet get in on the fun," he said and was quite surprised to hear himself say it. Then he noticed that he was burning up. "I wonder why I'm so hot?" he asked himself.

"Oh, sir, just stop," Ready cried, taking Josh's arm and turning him around. "Let the others do it. You've done so much already!"

Josh pulled away. "A man's work is never done, not on this atoll," he said in as odd a tone as Ready had ever heard his skipper use. His words were cheerful, yet filled with menace. Then Ready saw the copious sweat of fever break out, streaking down Josh's bearded cheeks to drip off his chin.

"The fever's on you, sir," he warned.

"Not to worry. It's an old friend," Josh replied, then pulled away and turned at the corner of stacked sandbags that led to the crooked entrance of the fort. He caught the scent of coppery sweat and foul breath that always seemed to accompany terrified and dying men. Marines, bayonets fixed, brushed past him, and he heard shrieks as Japanese defenders rose to meet them. "Now it all begins," he said and once more surprised himself with his own words. For was this not an ending rather than a beginning? How odd it is that sometimes a person knows more than he knows. He promised himself to think more on that, presuming he survived the next few minutes, which he sincerely doubted, though he didn't much care. Fever was odd that way.

It was dark inside the bunker, the room barely lit by light from the doorway, and it took a moment for Josh's eyes to adjust. Yet he easily dispatched a small Japanese marine who grappled with him briefly, then fell beneath a swipe of Josh's razor-sharp knife. Then Josh turned to meet a Japanese officer who was holding his sword like a lance and running straight at him. Before Josh could react, his shoulder was grabbed by a huge, powerful hand and he was shoved aside.

There was a grunt, a scream, and then Josh saw what appeared to be a native man, wearing but a lava-lava wrapped around his waist. He was doubled over the little Japanese officer's sword, which was stuck solidly into his stomach. The officer was shrieking at the top of his lungs, but Josh bashed him into silence with a big fist, then flung him aside. The native man, with terrible resolve, pulled the sword from his flesh and then fell to his knees.

Someone had brought a flashlight. It cut across the darkness and swept across the brown, tattooed man, who was looking up at Josh with a remarkably calm expression. The light also caught the awful wound in his stomach, the blood flowing from it like a scarlet river. Josh lifted the man, took his considerable weight, and half-carried him through dozens of churning individual battles until he had him outside in the sunlight where he laid him down. Josh saw better now the tattoos on the man's chest, blue and intricate, and the necklace of shells and shark's teeth around his neck. "Thank you," Josh said and then yelled for a corpsman and for Ready.

No corpsman came, nor did Ready. Bullets smacked into the sand beside Josh and the dying man, throwing up little puffs of grit. Josh pressed his hands on the terrible stomach wound in a vain attempt to staunch the bleeding. "Thank you," Josh said again, then put his ear close to the man's mouth and heard him say, "You are very welcome, my brother."

Josh impulsively took the man's hands into his. "Why did you do it?"

Before the man could answer, if he had an answer, he shivered once as if a cool breeze had washed over him, even in the terrible heat, and died. Josh stared at the new corpse. It had the handsome, fit, calm, confident look of a sleeping athlete. Josh, to his great astonishment, began to cry, thick tears making tributaries down his face through the grime of battle and the fresh sweat that was draining out of his every pore.

Then Josh sensed a presence, completely silent but somehow announced as if by trumpets and fluttering pennants. He looked up and discovered he was nearly falling into the eyes, the lagoon-blue eyes, of a freckle-faced girl dressed in a white robe with a white cap with white wings, folded like those of a dove, alongside her cherubic, pink-cheeked face. Around her neck, she wore a silver medallion, and engraved on it was a heart and a cross. Holding the medallion in her hands, the girl knelt beside the dead man. She looked at Josh for a long second, and then she said in a voice tinged with an Irish lilt that was as pure as milk and soft as whipped butter yet heard clearly over the whine and shatter of battle as if it were the only sound there was then or ever in all infinity: "On this day, ye will be with yer Savior."

Her words startled Josh, and he felt a sudden fear, but then he realized she was not speaking to him but to the young native man who was lying with the dignity of the dead. "Who was he?" Josh choked.

"His name was Tomoru. He was always very brave."

"He died to save my life."

"As Christ did," she replied.

Josh's mind was filled with turmoil. "But why would anyone die for me?" he asked in a plaintive voice that rang up and down his life.

"Because God is love, my dear," she answered beneath flying bullets, "and He is with us, even here."

"There is no God on this island!" Josh protested.

"Yer wrong," she answered. "He is everywhere."

"Then he is not a good God," Josh argued above the hideous screaming still coming from the sand bunker. "He is a stinking, ugly evil God."

"Nay, nay," she insisted as a bullet smacked into the side of the already dead man. She reached for the new wound and covered it with her hand. Blood oozed between her fingers. "God is peace. God is life."

Josh was very hot, so hot he thought his brain might boil and explode. *I have fever,* he told himself, *and I must drink water, cool down, or die.* Yet he could not tear his eyes from the woman, nor stop the debate. "God is war," he pronounced over the roar of a flamethrower and more screams. "God is death. He says so Himself in His awful Bible."

"God loves especially the sinner," she replied as a tracer flew a half inch past her ear. She did not flinch. "So He loves ye most of all. And me," she added mysteriously.

"You must lie down," he said, suddenly solicitous. "You'll be hit."

"Not today," she answered. "God is saving me for what I must do."

Josh could take a bullet, and shrapnel could rend his flesh, but such certainty of the supernatural before terrible reality was more than he could bear. "Get down!" he shouted at her as a marine gasped nearby and fell heavily across the legs of the dead native man.

"Don't be afraid," she answered while wicked bullets flitted past her like hornets. "God will protect you."

Now a horrible realization sank in. The girl was not human. She was an angel, or worse. "Go away," Josh told the apparition as she reached toward the dead marine and made the sign of the cross. "Be gone, I say!"

But the apparition did not go away. Instead, she gently peeled the dead man's bloody hands from Josh, hands that he didn't even realize he still clutched. Her lips moved in silent prayer, and then she folded the man's arms on his chest and leaned over and kissed him on his forehead, his nose, and his cheeks. Then she sat up and looked at Josh with a terrible sorrow that seemed to encompass all the world.

This was more than Josh could take. He stood and compulsively brushed the sand off his trousers while she looked up at him with her luminous eyes filled with love and goodness and all the things Josh couldn't abide, not on this stinking atoll. "Shall we pray?" she asked. "I shall do my best to comfort ye, absent a priest."

"I don't need comfort," Josh mumbled and backed away from her. "I need to get the blood off my K-bar." It was an odd thing for him to say, and he knew it, but he had said it, so he jabbed the awful knife into the sand, once, twice, and again, then inspected it. "It won't come off," he explained, his voice a croak, and then he noticed that his hand holding the knife was shaking so hard he couldn't control it. He threw the K-bar down and stared at it. Its blade shimmered back at him in the awful, torturous sun.

"Please, rest yourself," the girl said in velvet tones.

"I don't need to rest," Josh said and then, as he always did when he was confused or uncertain or frightened, abruptly made for the sea, walking hurriedly away from the girl or angel or whatever it was and the dead young man who had died for him.

The sweat kept pouring off Josh as he struggled across the sand. He felt as if he were walking through a blast furnace. To his considerable surprise, he came upon Sergeant Pinkerton, the gunny who'd led the charge off the Higgins boat. Pinkerton was sitting on a sand dune, his face white as cream, his lips gray and shriveled, and there was seaweed draped around his shoulders. "I thought you drowned," Josh told him, and Pinkerton grinned and a speckled eel climbed out of his shirt, waving its toothy head. Pinkerton said, "I did, Captain."

Josh blinked the drops of perspiration from his eyes and then saw that the brash lieutenant who'd jumped up on the seawall with a rallying cry was sitting under a shattered palm tree. His helmet was still on backward. With an anguished expression around the terrible holes in his face, he looked at Josh. "I'm sorry you were killed so quick," Josh told him. "Surely you would have won a medal otherwise."

The lieutenant shrugged and said, "Remember me."

"I will," Josh promised and went on, encountering the little Japanese soldier he'd killed when he first arrived on the beach. "You died honorably," Josh said to him, but after bowing politely, the Imperial marine turned away.

Then Josh saw the Seabee Bill Bordelon and the supply officer Sandy Bonnyman. They were sitting together on a palm log, engaged in a deep conversation. At his approach, they both turned to look at him. "How do, Josh?" Bill greeted, as Sandy smiled even though there was a bullet hole in his head.

"I'm sorry," Josh told them.

"What about?" Sandy asked.

"Your getting killed and all."

"It was our time," Bill replied.

"When is mine?" Josh was moved to ask.

"God knows," Sandy answered, which Josh took as either an answer or a question.

Josh walked on, past hundreds of sprawled bodies and piles of battlefield debris and smoking craters. He tripped over a dead marine and fell down. He felt as if he were suffocating and tore off his soggy shirt and then kicked off his boots and threw them away in sailing arcs and then also his socks. He stripped off his bloody pants and even his underwear and tossed them all into a crater filled with brown water and three goggle-eyed Japanese corpses who at least had the decency not to say anything.

Naked, Josh kept walking, leaving a pattern of sweat mixed with blood drops behind. He kept mumbling, reminding himself where he was going and why, to immerse himself in the good, clean ocean and rinse away the awful reek of combat and the blood of the young man who'd died for him and the vision of the odd little Irish girl who wore raiments of white. Josh now suspected she was a devil, for it was well known that sometimes devils sneaked onto battlefields. "I should have killed her," he said aloud. He looked over his shoulder, fearful that she might be following, but saw he was alone, not counting the dead men, all of whom were watching him.

When he reached the beach, Josh saw a Higgins boat coming through a shattered section of the reef. Then an amtrac shoved past it and rushed ashore, grinding up on the sand. It stopped, and out hopped none other than

Colonel Montague Singleton Burr and his staff of two majors, their pistols drawn as if they were the first men ashore. They ran past Josh, then stopped and turned around to gape at him. "My God, Thurlow," Burr bellowed. "Where are your clothes? Are you drunk? Pull yourself together, man!"

Josh looked at Burr and decided to do the world a favor and kill the bastard right then and there. It wasn't personal. Not at all. It was just that Burr needed killing, he really did, and now was as good a time to do it as ever there was. Josh felt at his waist for his K-bar, but all he felt was his own bare skin covered with cracked, dried blood. Burr pushed his face close and Josh got a whiff of Brown Mule chewing tobacco, sweet and disgusting. "You're a disgrace, Thurlow. Get off this beach before I clap you in irons!"

Josh's throat was dry as dust, but after swallowing several times he managed to strangle out a few tortured words. "Don't move, Colonel. Stay right there." He looked around, spied the nearby body of a dead marine, and crouched alongside, searching for a K-bar. When he didn't find one, he instead took the man's entrenching tool. Stripping off its canvas cover, he opened the small folding shovel and walked back to Burr, who, no surprise, defensively raised his pistol and aimed it at Josh's stomach.

It was a shot Burr could not possibly miss with a bullet that would leave a wide tunnel straight through and out Josh's back. "Don't make me do this, Thurlow," Burr warned, while his staff officers watched complacently, apparently not caring what happened next.

Josh raised the shovel and rasped, "Just remember, Montague. Through privation comes triumph and glory! Your words, sir, and the last you'll ever hear, God damn your soul!"

Then Josh swung his blow while Burr cheerfully pulled the trigger on his forty-five.

PART II

The Island of Dead Men

Welcome, happy morning!
Age to age shall say:
Hell today is vanquished,
Heaven is won today!

Lo! the dead is living,
God for evermore!
Him their true Creator,
All his works adore!

—VENANTIUS FORTUNATUS, A HYMN

1 2

Bosun Ready O'Neal, wilting beneath a flat, scalding sun, sat on a little hill of sand and watched men moving as if in a dream across the smoky, littered battleground. Their haunted eyes seemed to be seeing past one another, perhaps even into another world. The island of Betio had turned into a graveyard, and though the battle was essentially over, the dying was not.

Ready flinched at the familiar sharp crack of a Japanese rifle, but no bullet whipped past his head, and no marine fell or even paid attention. The *rikusentai* were committing suicide in holes and ditches all over the island. Ready had come across a Japanese soldier lying on his back in a ditch that ran through a grove of shattered palms. The Japanese had removed his boots, placed the muzzle of his rifle beneath his chin, and put one of his big toes on the trigger. For a moment, Ready and the young man had looked at one another, and somehow Ready knew he was in the company of a fellow fisherman. In that moment, an entire scenario developed in Ready's mind: The youth would remove his toe from the trigger and put his rifle down and rise up out of the ditch. Then he and Ready would commandeer a boat and go out past the reef, and there, in the rich, deep water, they would fish and talk about boats and bait and women and all the really important things of this world. But the man, even while he looked into Ready's eyes in a friendly and almost beseeching manner, jammed his toe against the trigger and the rifle bucked and the top of the man's head exploded, splattering Ready with blood and brains and skull fragments. After wiping himself off as best he could, Ready walked on through the grove of splintered trees before coming across another remarkable sight. A young woman, dressed all in white, was kneeling, and around her were marines who were also kneeling, their heads down in evident prayer. "Who is she?" he asked a marine who looked like he might know something.

The marine had his arms loaded with Japanese helmets. "She's a nun. What did you think she was? I heard somebody say the Japs had her prisoner. You want a Jap helmet? Five bucks."

Ready didn't want a helmet. He was too busy staring at the nun. When she lifted her head from her prayers, he noticed that she had a very sweet face, and he wondered why a woman with such a sweet face would be on this terrible island of dead men. He wanted to watch her for a little longer and maybe ask her that question and many others, but he needed to find his captain. He had last seen Josh Thurlow at the big sand fort in the swirl of battle, but afterward he had disappeared. Ready feared for him, afraid that he might be lying in a hole somewhere, dying or dead.

"Here, take one of these things anyway," the marine said, handing Ready a helmet. "You can owe me."

Ready took the helmet and then wandered on toward the beach, passing marines loaded with Japanese flags, swords, rifles, pistols, helmets, knives, and even boots. Then, to his joy, he chanced upon his captain. His joy was tempered, however, because Josh Thurlow was naked from head to toe and looked a bit deranged. He was also lifting a shovel as if to strike his old nemesis Colonel Burr, who, somewhat naturally, had drawn his pistol in self-defense. Instinctively, Ready heaved the Japanese helmet and struck Burr in the head. This had the result of knocking Burr to his knees and also deflecting the marine officer's aim just a tick, a tick that saved Josh Thurlow's life as the bullet slapped into the sand behind him. Seeing Ready, Josh checked the swing of his shovel. "A man died for me," he announced, "and he was the only innocent man on this island."

"Who would that be, Skipper?" Ready asked as he took the shovel from Josh's hands.

"An island man covered with tattoos," Josh answered distantly, then blinked, as if looking at something very far away. "Then a creature came, a terrible creature who spoke of the love of God, who, by the way, is a rank bastard or else the last three days on this atoll would never have occurred. The creature was dressed all in white and had a pretty face and talked Irish. Devils do that, you know, look like angels and talk Irish. It's supposed to throw you off."

Ready thought about all that for a moment, then perceived who Josh was talking about. "Oh, sir, you just talked to a nun, that's all. She's up in a grove of palm trees with some fellows, all praying to beat the band."

Streams of sweat carved through the dirt and grime and blood caked on Josh's body. His legs were trembling and it didn't look like he would stay upright for much longer. "I'm telling you she's Old Scratch!" he insisted. "It would be best if somebody killed the thing."

Ready smiled what he hoped was a comforting smile. "Aw, she ain't no devil, sir. Somebody said she was a prisoner of the Japanese."

"That's what I mean, Ready," Josh said eagerly. "She's a devil for sartain!"

While Ready puzzled over his captain's pronouncements, he noticed that even though Colonel Burr had been knocked to his knees, he still held his pistol. He also had rediscovered his voice. "You're going to the brig, Thurlow!" he growled, and then his terribly mean and coal-black eyes sought out Ready. "And you're going with him, Bosun. You assaulted me!"

Ready ignored the colonel and took Josh by the arm. "Let's have a corpsman look at you, Captain."

"You're a good man, Ready," Josh said. "As good as I am evil."

"You've just got the fever, sir," Ready answered. "You ain't much evil at all."

Burr struggled to his feet. "Somebody arrest those men!" he demanded.

"There, there, Colonel," one of the two majors said consolingly. "There, there."

Burr spat a brown stream of tobacco juice into the sand, then wiped his mouth while giving the major the evil eye. "You 'there, there' me one more time, Major Smith, and I'm going to kick your fucking 'there, there' butt across this miserable 'there, there' atoll!"

While Burr was preoccupied with instilling discipline into his staff, Ready led Josh, still naked, off the beach and across the battlefield until they reached a shell crater near the big sand bunker where medical corpsmen were at work on a dozen wounded marines. Without comment, the corpsmen took Josh in, disinfected and bandaged his wounds, forced aspirin down him for the fever, and then, because they had done all they could do, laid him on his back on the hot sand. Stretcher-bearers came and took the wounded marines away, and then the corpsmen left, too, though they promised Ready that other stretcher-bearers would be along to take care of his captain. Ready sat down, took off his shirt to fan Josh, and waited.

While he fanned and waited, Ready observed the situation around him, which was growing ever more chaotic. There were no officers in sight, and most of the marines seemed to be doing whatever came into their heads. Many of them were looting the Japanese dead; others were simply standing around, looking vacantly at nothing. A few were drinking from jerry cans, which had finally arrived with supposedly oil-free water. It didn't appear to be an improvement, however, because as soon as they'd drunk their fill, most of the marines fell to their hands and knees and puked it up. Still others squatted over shallow depressions they'd kicked in the sand, trying to get their bowels to move after three days of fear and dehydration. Occasionally, to punctuate the chaos, there was the crack of a Japanese rifle announcing another suicide.

Thousands of corpses on the tiny atoll were also putting up a powerful stink. Ready pressed a helmet camouflage cover to his mouth and nose, but it did little to filter the awful odor. There was not a breath of a breeze, and Ready thought he might suffocate from the stench. He was grateful when a Seabee bulldozer appeared and began shoving sand over a row of Japanese bodies lying in a ditch. Some marines were also digging graves for their dead buddies, the smell forcing them to get the bodies under the sand. Ready thought it was going to be one hell of a job to find out who had been put where. Then he heard an aircraft engine and observed a navy Corsair lazily descending toward the coral airstrip. It flew over another bulldozer busily pushing bodies and battle debris off the runway, then bumped down. A few marines cheered, but most ignored the fighter plane as it coasted along. It stopped at the end of the runway, sat for a moment, then turned around, fired up its engine, and took off again. The Betio airfield, for which so many had died, was open for business.

Then a marine who'd been watching the Corsair accidentally pulled the pin on a Japanese grenade he had plucked off a body and it detonated, with him going one way, his hand and a good part of his arm the other. His buddies ran out to him, picked him up, and brought him to the crater. Mistaking Ready for a corpsman, one of them said, "Fix him up, Doc," then left. Since all the real corpsmen had gone elsewhere and there was no one else to do it, Ready grabbed a bandage out of an abandoned medical bag and wrapped it tight around the man's bloody stump, stabbed a syrette of morphine into his shoulder, pinned the empty needle to his chest, and then watched and waited until he quieted down. Eyes open but apparently uncomprehending, Josh blinked up at the crystal-clear sky and occasionally groaned.

Ready took a moment to cast up a prayer that the stretcher-bearers would come, and no sooner had he said "Amen" than four men appeared, native men from the looks of them, with brown muscular bodies covered with various tattoos, red lava-lava breechcloths about their waists, and necklaces of cowrie shells and shark's teeth hanging in deep arcs across their hairless chests. They also bore stretchers. "We take," one of them said in a deep voice.

Ready didn't know what to make of that. He draped his shirt over Josh's privates and climbed out of the crater. "Take where?"

"We take," the man replied. "We say we help. Marine all say OK. We take."

Then Ready was roughly gripped on his shoulder and spun around, whereupon he found himself looking at a short gunnery sergeant with a stubby cigar stuck between his teeth. "Corpsman, you are now under my command," he said. "Get your stuff and come with me."

"I ain't no corpsman, Gunny," Ready replied, irritated at the presumptuousness of the little man. "I'm a Coast Guard bosun, and I probably outrank you. That's Captain Thurlow, my skipper, down in that crater. I'm looking after him. Now get away from me."

The gunny was unimpressed by Ready's explanation. "Stow it, Doc. My God, some of you boys will say or do anything to get out of a little work! Them ain't Coast Guard utilities you're wearin', and they ain't Coast Guard boots you got on, neither. Now load up your gear and come along like a good little corpsman. I got a detail and you're part of it whether you like it or not."

"I told you I ain't no corpsman!" Ready snapped, which so impressed the gunny that he slammed the butt of his rifle into Ready's stomach. Astonished more than hurt, though his breath was knocked clean away, Ready fell to his knees.

"I told you to get your stuff, Doc. I won't say it again."

As Ready struggled to breathe, a white cloth passed before his eyes. When he looked up, he realized it was the habit of the nun. She had stepped between him and the gunny. "Ye won't hit him again," the nun said.

The gunny was startled by her sudden appearance. "This ain't none of your business, ma'am," he said nervously.

"Nay, 'tisn't," she agreed, "but I could hardly stand by and watch ye whomp yer own man, now, could I?"

The gunny looked at his boots. "No, ma'am."

"I hope you're properly ashamed, then."

"Oh, yes, ma'am," the gunny said, looking out of the tops of his eyes at her. "I am. I surely am."

"Well, then get on with ye!" she demanded.

The gunny kept his head down. "I'm just going to walk over there beside that pile of dead Japs," he told her contritely. "You send Doc along to me next couple of minutes, it'll be good."

The nun glanced at the mound of rotting Japanese the gunny had mentioned, took on a wistful expression, then turned to Ready, who had managed to climb stiffly to his feet. "Are ye all right now, boyo?"

"Yes, ma'am," Ready answered, smiling crookedly at her pretty face peeking through her cowl, as pretty as any he'd ever seen. He especially admired her eyes, as blue as the Gulf Stream off Killakeet, and he liked the freckles sprinkled across her pert little nose, though he also read in her expression a certain steady resolve. Ready wished at that moment that he was a handsome man, even if the Irish girl was a nun, and surely uninterested in any man, handsome or not. He stepped down in the crater, picked up the corpsman's bag, inspected its contents, and climbed out.

Guessing his intentions, the nun was astonished. "Surely you're not going with that man!"

Ready shrugged. "I have to. That's a Marine Corps gunny, ma'am, and they don't know how to take no for an answer. Anyway, I'll go until I figure out how to get away. In the meantime, would you take care of my skipper? His name's Josh Thurlow, Captain Josh Thurlow. That's him, the big lug with nothing but my shirt across his privates. I'm sorry he's otherwise buck naked, but I guess he got tired of wearing his clothes. He needs to get out to a hospital ship. He's lost a bit of blood, you see, and he's real worn out. He's got fever, too, which he caught on Guadalcanal. Just see to him the best you can, that's all I'm asking."

"I will be pleased to take care of yer captain," the nun answered. "This is the second time today I have seen him. One of my fella boys even gave up his life for him."

"He told me a native man with tattoos died to save him!" Ready exclaimed.

"His name was Tomoru. He was a very good man, though a bit reckless. I shall miss him, but I know he is in heaven and will never know sorrow again."

"That's a good philosophy in these parts, for sartain," Ready allowed. "Captain Thurlow is a good man, too, except, well, he's got a few faults, I suppose . . ." Ready realized he was rambling and interrupted himself. "Well, that's neither here nor there, is it? When the captain comes awake, would you tell him I'll catch up soon as I can?" He hesitated, then asked, "And will I see you again, I wonder? I hope I will." When she frowned, Ready quickly added, "I'm sorry, ma'am. I don't mean to be familiar or nothing."

Her frown turned into a smile that warmed Ready's heart. "Nay, 'tis fine, Bosun. I was just thinking how to frame my answer, y'see." Then, after a moment's thought, she nodded. "I believe we will meet again. In the meantime I will pray for ye, if ye'll but tell me yer name."

"My name's Ready, ma'am," he answered eagerly. "Bosun Ready O'Neal of the Coast Guard."

A part of his answer clearly delighted her. "O'Neal! Ye don't mean it! The O'Neals are a fine family, as fine as ever walked an Irish road or plowed an Irish field. I am Sister Mary Kathleen, but once I was naught but Kathleen Shaughnessy, the tenth child of Liam and Maureen Shaughnessy of Ballysaggart in the county Tyrone. We Shaughnessys have always been partial to yer O'Neals." She looked at him carefully. "Are ye all right, Bosun? Ye look a bit unsteady. Are ye faint?"

"I am," he confessed. "It's been a few days since I got much sleep."

"Do ye need to sit down?"

"I wish I could," Ready answered and then impulsively stretched his hand out to her. After a moment's hesitation, she grasped it with both her hands, and he was surprised not only at their strength but at their roughness. A woman with such hands had not spent a life with them clasped in prayer. He released her hands and watched with regret as they disappeared within the shrouds of her deep sleeves. He ached to feel them again.

He was surprised when she asked, "Will ye help me now, Bosun O'Neal?"

"If I can, ma'am."

"I need to see a big man."

"A big man, ma'am?"

"Aye. A man who can order other men around."

"You mean like the gunny over there?"

She shifted her eyes suspiciously toward the little gunny, then shook her head. "Nay, someone much bigger, someone who could gather many men and put them in big boats and sail away with me and me fella boys to another place."

"What place would that be, ma'am?"

"To the Far Reaches. There are Japanese there. I want them to surrender, y'see."

Ready was allowing her odd pronouncement to sink in—the days and nights of combat had dulled his ability to think clearly—when the gunny started yelling at him, telling him to get his butt in gear. Ready said, "Look, Sister, when he wakes up, maybe Captain Thurlow can help you. He's got some clout. He even knows the secretary of the navy like a brother."

"Now that would be the first hopeful thing I've heard in a terrible long time," she answered, producing her wonderful smile once more. "Thanks be to God. Ye are a kind man, Bosun O'Neal. I knew that the first time I laid me eyes on ye."

"I'm glad I've said a hopeful thing," Ready answered, though he doubted it was much more than a thin hope, considering Josh's present condition.

"God go with ye, then," she said.

"God go with you, too, ma'am, for sartain, although I guess that happens, anyway, you being . . . well, who you are and all."

Her smile turned small and embarrassed. "Aye, Bosun O'Neal. God does look after me, though in His own mysterious way."

1 3

Ready broke away from the nun and trudged disconsolately to the gunny, who then waved him over to a knot of four sullen marines standing beside a palm tree. The arm of a dead Japanese sniper could be seen hanging from the tattered fronds of the tree, and the marines were standing so as to avoid the dripping blood slowly pattering off the sniper's fingers.

Ready was surprised to see Tucker the Hatteras boy, and beside him Sampson from New Jersey, and Garcia from Texas, the marines he'd led a century or more ago when he'd been Major Reed. The fourth marine introduced himself as Private Roger Harland. Tucker gave Ready the once-over. "You look familiar," he said, finally.

Ready answered, "I don't see how. I hardly know who I am myself."

"You got a corpsman's bag," Garcia said in an attempt to be helpful. "So you're a corpsman."

"That don't mean much," Ready replied. "Say a man has an ax, that don't make him a lumberjack."

"Don't make him not one, neither," Garcia answered, looking put out.

Ready looked over his shoulder and saw that the native men, the ones the nun had called her fella boys, had placed Captain Thurlow and the marine who'd lost most of his arm aboard stretchers and were toiling with them down a path toward the beach. She was following, looking small and vulnerable beneath the folds of her habit. She stumbled once, and his heart actually hurt to see it. He longed to rush to her and help her along, to hold her hands again and talk to her and hear her lilting voice and maybe find himself in her eyes.

"Hey, it's that nun," Tucker said, noticing where Ready was looking, though not noticing the longing with which he looked.

Garcia said, "I knelt down beside her while she was praying and got a good whiff of her. She smelled clean. *Dios mío!* I think I'm in love."

"That's about the sickest thing I've yet heard you say, Garcia," Sampson accused. "And that's going some."

"Knock it off," Ready snapped at the marines. With a sudden burst of clarity, he added, "You can't love a nun because she can't love you back."

Ready's statement puzzled Tucker. "Hell, I've loved women all my life who ain't loved me back. That's the usual case, ain't it?"

All the marines agreed with Tucker's assessment, and the conversation turned to women in general and how hard it was to find a good one. This degenerated inevitably to a discussion of the hourly price of love in Hawaii. Ten bucks seemed to be the average for enlisted marines, although the discussion included ways to get that knocked down a bit, mainly by begging, and then the gunny brayed for silence in the ranks. He went down on one knee and began to draw an outline of the atoll in the sand with his K-bar.

"Now, listen up! Battalion says there's still some Japs holding out on t'other end of this shithole. I been ordered to take a patrol up there, see what's what and kill the whole bunch of 'em if we can. You got five minutes to get your shit together. Make sure you got a full ammo load. Savvy?"

"Why us, Gunny?" Sampson demanded. "We already done our share. How about one of them newbies just got off the boat?"

"What's the Corps motto, son?"

"I got mine. How'd you make out?" Sampson answered.

The gunny stared bullets at him. "I'm gonna keep my eye on you. You try to slip off, I'll shoot you, don't think I won't."

"I ain't slipping off, Gunny," Sampson replied tiredly. "All I'm saying is it just ain't fair."

"Fair ain't got a thing to do with this lashup. You ought to have that much figgered out by now. Semper Fi, boy. Semper Fi. And don't you forget it."

"Christ on a crutch," Sampson groaned, then shut up.

"You better carry a rifle," Tucker said to Ready. "You might want to wear a shirt, too."

"I used my shirt to cover the skipper," Ready answered.

"Who's the skipper?"

"Captain Thurlow. We're both Killakeet boys like you're a Hatterasser."

Tucker was astonished. "How do you know I'm from Hatteras?"

Not wanting to let on that he'd once been Major Reed, Ready said, "I can hear it in your voice. You ever been on Killakeet?"

"Oncet. But I was just putting some barrels of mullet ashore at the fish plant."

"I might have seen you there," Ready lied. "I worked in the plant some."

"Let's go, ladies," the gunny barked, saving Ready further explanations and fibs.

The marines went, their training and discipline kicking in, and Ready slogged along with them, the corpsman's bag bumping against his hip. Though there was plenty else to occupy his thoughts, they kept returning to the little Irish nun. He wondered what she was doing, whether she and her "fella boys" had gotten the skipper and the wounded marine to the beach, and what they would find once they got there. He also wondered if Captain Thurlow would help her go to her faraway place, wherever it was, and send armed men along to make the Japanese surrender. He doubted it, seeing how poorly the skipper was doing, and also because the Japanese never surrendered anyway. Maybe there might be somebody who would explain all that to her. He hadn't the heart to do it. He felt a pang, a rather large pang, of regret that he might never see her again.

"Kill Japs, boys!" the gunny cheerfully sang. "Now, ain't the Marine Corps good to you, gives you a simple job like that? Don't have to think, just aim and pull the trigger. Get it done and then we'll all go to the isles of easy nooky, your Hawaiian Islands, which are just like heaven."

"It would have to be heaven before any easy nooky came your way, Gunny," Sampson jibed, and everybody laughed except Ready, who was thinking about the nun, and the gunny, who was thinking about living and dying and weighing the odds for each during the remainder of the day. He concluded the odds were better for dying, and it made him a bit melancholy. *I ain't getting out of this one alive,* he said to himself, although he kept walking forward, leading his men toward a hard fight, which is what marine gunnies are paid to do.

1 4

Sister Mary Kathleen walked across the atoll of Betio, and past all the dead men. Her chin was up, her shoulders back, and her expression serene, just as she'd been taught as a postulant. "Observe the sisters, notice the manner in which they walk, talk, and even eat," Sister Theresa, the mistress of postulants, told her covey of recent novices on their first day in the convent. "Ye will see an expression of humility and serene detachment in their posture as they move, sit, or even lie in their beds. Note as well the quiet but steady manner in which they address one another and others, and how they eat, never quickly, but slowly, without any apparent enjoyment, food but a means to live."

She picked her way over a line of bodies, careful not to tread on them with her soiled white slippers. They were a mixed lot of Japanese and Americans, the dead uncaring of their neighbors. She made the sign of the cross over them and then tucked her hands inside her sleeves, for such a gesture might be interpreted as self-important.

Self-importance and a lack of humility were two evils she struggled against. She had not been a postulant for more than a few days before she was called into the august presence of Sister Theresa for those very offenses. It had been reported that she had a tendency to walk faster than the others, and once she was observed looking at herself, presumably in an admiring manner, in the shiny curved surface of a teapot. For those transgressions, she was made to lie prostrate behind the Mother Superior's chair during chapel and afterward remain in that humiliating position until all the nuns and postulants had filed past while looking down at her.

The next morning, she was again called to the mistress's office, where she was bade to sit and then sternly corrected when she put her hands on her knees rather than folding them on her lap. For two hours or more—she had no way of determining the time—she sat with her spine straight as an arrow, never daring to touch the back of the chair, while the mistress recorded entries in her ledger. During the torturous silence, she had tried to show no interest in what Sister Theresa might be writing, nor curiosity about anything else. This was not entirely difficult since the mistress's office was barren except for her desk and a crucifix displayed on the wall beside a painting of the Blessed Virgin.

Finally, the mistress put down her pen, clasped her hands together, and looked at her. Sister Theresa had a round, ruddy face that was composed into the serenity of the perfect nun. "Kathleen," she said, "the path to humility is hard and not for the weak or the silly. Ye must work every day, every hour, every moment to humble yerself before all men, even the lowest and vilest of men, and women, too. Even children requiring discipline must sense yer willingness to sacrifice yerself for them. Learn to be truly humble, Kathleen, or else leave us."

"But what did I do, Mistress?" she asked, sincerely confused.

"Ye were observed again admiring yerself in the teapot."

"I was not admiring meself," she replied honestly. "I was just curious how I look in me new garb."

"Such curiosity reflects a lack of humility in yer person. It is the reason why there are no mirrors in the convent."

"Yes, Mistress," she replied and humbly hung her head, though she still did not understand.

Sister Theresa sighed. "We have much work to do with you, Kathleen. But together, we will get there, by and by."

Her fella boys stopped, staring at a Japanese corpse. She recognized him as Captain Sakuri, struck down by the big man carried now on the litter, but clearly not killed by that blow in the sand fortress. Instead, the captain had apparently fought on until he could sit atop a small sand dune and commit ritual suicide. His intestines, turned gray by the blistering sun and alive with flies, lay in a curved pile between his legs. "Oh, Captain," she said. "Such a waste!" Sakuri stared back at her, if such could be said of dead, dry eyes, and Sister Mary Kathleen knelt briefly beside him, then closed his eyelids. "Ye were not evil," she told him. "I know evil, ye see. It has a home in me heart." She rose, thinking once more of her progress toward sisterhood over the years and miles.

In the days that followed her initial counseling by Sister Theresa, she had done her best to learn humility and discipline. Looking back, it should not have been difficult, especially with the constant example of the other nuns. She had marveled at their orderly, motionless rows in the chapel, their heads bowed in faultless angularity. No matter their age or infirmity, she never saw one of them show any evidence of pain, nor heard even the smallest complaint. There was an interior silence to each of them, their personalities diminished to only their facial characteristics. She considered all of them beautiful, though some had soft, round, country faces and others more aristocratic features, which gave them, no matter how placid their expression, an intelligent aspect. She had secretly hoped she would also appear intelligent and be admired for that, if nothing else. Even though she said nothing of this wish, it was as if Sister Theresa could read her mind.

Once more she found herself sitting on the hard little chair before the mistress's desk and forced to meditate. Finally, a short lecture came, this one on false pride. Sister Theresa cocked her head and allowed a thin-lipped smile that diminished as she talked. " 'Tis the curse of the Irish, Kathleen, this desire to feel important and inflate one's opinion of oneself. But such has no place in our order, no more than envy or greed. Ye must clear yer mind of any sense of yerself as a person. If ye join us, ye will be but one of many, the same as all, no sister different from the next. Now, can ye do it or not, child?"

She had said yes, she could do it. She also said she would do it better than any of the other postulates. This had made Sister Theresa sigh and shake her head. " 'Tis not a contest, Kathleen. 'Tis a journey. Ye must allow God to enter yer very core, to seep inside ye and strip ye of anything other than His will. If ye are not willing, or able, t'would be better if ye left us. Now, what say ye?"

She had dutifully answered. "Please, Mistress. Give me another chance."

Sister Theresa nodded, then waved her away, though she stopped her at the door. "Perhaps ye could find a special saint to intercede for ye."

Sister Mary Kathleen confessed something then, something she had not even allowed herself to believe. "I have had dreams of a girl. She is dressed in gold. I believe she is a saint, but I know not who she might be."

The mistress's eyes turned bright with interest. "What does she do?"

"She smiles at me and captures me in her eyes."

"How old is she?"

"I believe she is around six years old."

Sister Theresa stood, and a rapturous expression formed on her round face.

"It is Saint Monessa. Do ye know her story? She was the child of an ancient Irish chieftain. Upon her baptism when she was but six, she died. Pray to that child, Kathleen. For no saint is so humble as she."

Sister Mary Kathleen recalled now how startled she was at this history. "Why did she die, Mistress?" she asked.

Sister Theresa shrugged. "No one knows, but ever since, a few especially blessed sisters have claimed to have been visited by her in their dreams. Ye are therefore blessed, Kathleen, more than you—and I—may know. Henceforth, I beseech ye, let Saint Monessa be yer guide."

Afterward, she began to pray almost exclusively to the little child-saint, and to her surprise, wisdom soon came. She began to understand she could not simply force change onto herself. She had to trade pride for humility through prayer and to exchange her Irish temper for detachment by believing that she had no right to anger, that only God could judge. She was all the more surprised when, just as she felt she was making progress, she came under even heavier criticism from Sister Theresa. "Ye seem humble," the mistress told her, taking her aside after chapel.

"Yes, Mistress," she answered with a secret, triumphant smile.

"But if ye believe ye are humble, then ye are not."

Stricken, she nearly cried out in despair. "I am sorry nothing I do pleases ye!"

Sister Theresa took her hands. "Please me, child? It does not matter if ye please me. Ye must please God by your total subjugation to His will! Will ye never understand?"

"But I am here, Sister," she argued. "Is that not enough? I have turned away from life outside. His will be done, I said!"

The mistress sadly shook her head. "I know why ye came, Kathleen. What? Such an expression on yer face! Did ye think it was a secret? Ye came because of yer father, he who murdered a priest and other men and never asked for forgiveness even while a rope was around his neck. A priest damned him as he died. Now ye hope to save his soul through yer own sacrifice. But a sister in this order is not allowed to be here other than for God's own purposes."

"God brought me here," she answered stubbornly. "This much I know."

This earned another smile from Sister Theresa. "Ah, Kathleen. Perhaps he has, indeed. Or perhaps not. Ye must meditate to discover God's truth. And keep praying to Saint Monessa. 'Tis her glow about ye I feel."

So she had meditated all the more and prayed until she thought that she could pray no more and that surely Saint Monessa was tired of hearing her pleas. Then, when she had all but lost hope, she made a surge of progress toward being a true and perfect nun. When she was dispatched to scrub the floor of the cell occupied by an ancient nun riddled with cancer and filled with constant pain, the nun had complained loudly from her bed that it was not being done properly. Though the floor was clean enough to eat off of, Kathleen silently bowed her head and did it all over again. And when Sister Claire, the choirmaster, told her that her voice was not good enough—never mind that everyone had always told her she sang like an angel—she did not argue but went to sit with the others who had also been rejected, her hands folded placidly on her lap, her eyes cast downward, her expression unconcerned, even though she felt as if her stomach had tied itself into a knot.

Then, one night, when she recited at the culpa a list of her most recent faults—walking too fast to chapel, reaching across the table for a biscuit without permission, paying more attention to a particularly colorful flower in the courtyard than her prayers during meditation—she lifted her head and for just a moment, a split second, no more, saw something in Sister Theresa's eyes that told her she had been accepted. Soon after, she took her final vows.

And now, even after she had been dispatched to a place beyond her imagination, to a group of islands on the other side of the world, she had continued to reach for the three unwritten goals of every sister in her order: subservient humility, a sense of detachment from the world, and a willingness, nay, eagerness, to bend to the will of God, even when such was harsh and unfair. And, after all that had happened, her terrible sins in the Far Reaches yet unforgiven, she still kept on with her unceasing quest to become a proper nun. *Even now,* she thought, forcing down the bitterness. *Saint Monessa,* she prayed, *ye know I am weak, so very weak, and afraid. I beg ye, give me strength and speed my presence before a priest.*

She listened for an answer, which she knew was also a reflection of her awful pride. For why would a saint in heaven, even one so ignored by the Church as this little girl, give her any thought at all? Instead, she heard in her head only her pap recounting some foolish joke. "I love ye, ye old poot," she said beneath her breath and felt so very lost at that moment with her vision of him dancing in the air on the gallows and her ma and her brothers and sisters so far away, so impossibly far away. Ah well, distance, both in miles and time, she supposed, was necessary and good. She prayed often in the darkness of the night when she couldn't sleep that all the folks of Ballysaggart of the

County Tyrone would believe she was dead. *I am, ye know,* she said to herself, for she had come to learn there were many ways to die.

So she walked on, following her fella boys and the stretcher that held Josh Thurlow, who, she sensed, held her salvation locked away in his shattered body and perhaps shriveled soul.

1 5

Led by the bandy-legged little gunny, the rump squad of four marines plus Ready O'Neal reluctantly slogged past shell craters and foxholes filled with dead Japanese. Ready kept averting his eyes, but the marines managed to make a joke out of each corpse according to the expression on its face or its death pose. There was also a great deal of griping about how hot it was and everything else in general. Sampson especially griped about his left foot. "I stepped on something. I don't know what," he told Ready. "It went right through the sole of my boot."

Sampson stopped and turned up his boot for Ready to examine what proved to be a small hole in the tread. "Looks like you stepped on a nail," Ready said.

"It hurts like hell," Sampson said, limping on. "Hey, gunny! I need to see a corpsman!"

"You're walking beside one," the gunny replied tiredly.

"Well, I need to see one that ain't walking, one that could sit down with me and take a look at my foot. I need to go back."

"Well, you ain't going back." The gunny stopped and arced his finger across his detail. "And if I hear another sorry word out of one of you jokers, I'm going to put a sorry bullet into your sorry skull just like these Japs. Savvy?"

Nobody claimed he savvied, seeing as how that would have required a sorry word, which might earn a sorry bullet, so the gunny spat out his tobacco, tucked in a fresh chaw, and took on as friendly an expression as his grizzled mug could manage. "Listen to me, boys. We got a simple job. All we got to do is to walk to the end of this island, which ain't all that far. If we run across any live Japs, we kill them. If we don't, and it don't look much like we're going to, we turn around and walk back. I know you're worn out. I am, too. It's too damn hot and I've forgotten what fresh water tastes like. Them's the facts. But let's just make it easy on ourselves and get this thing done and then we'll all get on back to the beach and off to the islands of nooky-nooky. What do you say?"

Ready thought the gunny had presented a sound argument, but it didn't much matter what Ready thought, because just as the gunny had finished his little speech, a Japanese bullet zipped through his back, punching right through his heart and out his chest in a cloud of dust and blood, whereupon the gunny fell dead without so much as a whimper. All the marines, and Ready, too, threw themselves face-first into the sand. Some pent-up cursing erupted, but then they all settled down and waited for the next thing to happen.

Since he was the medic, or as near to one as they had, Ready crawled up beside the gunny and looked for signs of life. Seeing none, he pondered the dead little sergeant, whose dirty face wore an expression of resignation. Ready rolled over on his back and thought of the nun and wondered what she was doing, if she was all right. *She was sure pretty, Gunny,* he said silently. *I bet you'd have liked her, too, if you hadn't been trying so hard to do your duty.*

Ready's unspoken conversation was interrupted by Tucker, who pulled his face out of the sand and asked, "Anybody see the Jap what shot Gunny?"

"Yeah, I seen him," Sampson answered, spitting sand. "He's behind that palm tree, that one, see where I'm pointing? Yeah, the one chopped halfway down. Look, you can see his rifle sticking out from behind it, the dumb moron."

Ready peered at the broken palm. Sure enough, he could see what appeared to be a rifle protruding from it. The marines shot at the tree; one of them managed to hit the rifle with a lucky shot, and it went flying. The Japanese soldier could be seen crawling after it, and then he was shot, too. Then everything got quiet and the marines plus Ready just lay in the sand for a while.

"Well, who's got the rank?" Sampson finally asked when Garcia started snoring. "Anybody got any stripes in this lash-up?"

"He probably does," Tucker said, nodding toward Ready. "The corpsman."

"I ain't no corpsman," Ready said. "I'm a Coast Guard bosun."

"Well, even if that's true, you still got the stripes," Tucker said. "So I guess that puts you in charge. What do we do, Bosun? Go back to the beach?"

That suggestion got an immediate chorus of agreement from all the marines, including Garcia, who woke up long enough to cast his vote. Bolstered by their enthusiasm, not to mention the awful heat and his thirst, Ready came close to ordering them all to jump up and run back to the airfield, quick as they could. There, they could all split up, find their outfits, pretend they'd never seen or heard of the gunny, and then loll around until it was time for the marines to load up for Hawaii. Ready could also find Josh Thurlow and, with luck, maybe even the pretty little Irish nun. It was perfect, just what they ought to do. Then Ready's awful sense of duty took over. He sighed and said, "Let's finish this detail."

"Well, shit," Tucker muttered, and every man said his own favorite curse word and spat sand. But then, because they were marines and knew a legitimate order when they heard it, even if it was from a Coast Guard bosun, they stood up, spread out, and walked forward, all the while straining their eyes for a live Japanese.

"Does anybody have a radio?" Ready asked after a few minutes.

Sampson answered. "I had one, but it got heavy, so I pitched it. It didn't work too good, anyway."

They kept trudging until at last they came to a beach before a glittering blue inlet, across which they could see another island that appeared as flat and ugly as Betio. "Look, Bosun," Garcia said, pointing to the island. "There's guys over there."

Ready looked and his heart sank. They weren't just guys. They were Japanese *rikusentai,* alive and well, who looked like they still had some fight in them. They waved a flag with the rising sun on it, pumped their rifles up and down, and yelled curses across the shallow water. Ready struggled once more with his sense of duty, then said, "I need a runner."

Private Harland spoke up and said he could run fast as the wind. Ready told him, "Go find an officer, Harland. Tell him we've reached the end of the island and it's all clear. Also tell him we found some live Japanese on the next island up. Looks like a bunch of them. We're going across to keep them running."

"The hell we are, Bosun!" Tucker erupted. "We done what we were supposed to do, just like the gunny said. He didn't say nothing about going on to no other island!"

Ready nodded agreement but said, "Those fellows over there are as worn out as we are, I reckon. But give them time to rest, they'll dig in and shoot up the marines who'll be ordered to go at them later today or tomorrow. We've got to keep them on the run."

"What if they don't run?" Tucker demanded.

Ready shrugged. "I don't know. Maybe they'll crawl in their holes and shoot themselves."

"Am I still supposed to go, Bosun?" Harland asked hopefully.

"Yes," Ready answered. "Tell the first officer you find it would be best if he got some folks up here, *toot sweet*."

Harland took off, leaving Ready in charge of only Tucker, Sampson, and Garcia. It was like old times.

"Now we got only us four against a whole damn army of Japs," Tucker complained.

Ready didn't reply since Tucker was correct, and he led the way into the shallows between the islands with as much hope as determination. He still had no weapon, no helmet, not even a shirt, only the corpsman's bag slung across his naked shoulder. After a spate of grumbling, the trio of marines followed him, their rifles held chest high. The Japanese troops watched them for a while, waved their flag again, then took off. Relieved they hadn't been shot at, Ready and the marines walked up on the beach, fanned out and found a few dead Japanese, suicides all, then threw themselves down when machine-gun fire whipped past them. "Knock that thing out!" Ready said, and the three marines crawled forward and tossed grenades on top of it until it disappeared in a rain of flame and smoke.

Disappointingly, another well-hidden machine gun opened up and then another. Ready reflected on his lack of training when it came to leading infantry. He realized they had walked into an ambush and were stuck. "Dig in," he said because it was all he knew to say.

"Well, ain't this pleasant?" Tucker muttered, lifting his entrenching tool off his back. "Bosun, this is surely a fine mess you've got us into."

Garcia defended Ready. "Hell, at least he didn't get us stuck on no coral reef. Takes a general and a couple of admirals to pull off that kind of fucked-up operation."

"You're right, Tucker. I messed up," Ready said. "You want to take over?"

"Hell no!" Tucker yelped, astonished to hear an officer, even a noncommissioned officer in the Coast Guard, admit that he was wrong about anything. It was a first in his short military career. "I ain't a leader, just a rifleman. Lead on, Bosun, lead on!"

"OK," Ready said. "Then you boys dig in, like I said."

The marines dug in, like Ready said. Tucker even dug a shallow depression for Ready. For two hours, they waited for something else to happen. The machine guns stayed silent. Then Tucker looked over his shoulder toward Betio. "Hey, here comes John Wayne!" he yelled, and Ready looked to see a marine tank coming across the inlet and a dozen or so marines coming along behind it.

"We're gonna make it after all!" Sampson yelled, waving his helmet.

But then the Japanese machine guns opened up, the tank stalled, and its crew abandoned it and retreated through the water back to Betio along with the riflemen. "Well, that weren't pretty," Sampson observed, plopping his helmet back aboard.

"Guess we're still the only Americans on this island," Tucker said. "Whimper Fi, y'all."

Ready peered at the blistering sun which wasn't quite so blistering now that it was drooping toward the horizon. "We'd better dig in a little deeper," he said.

Without argument this time, the marine trio hauled out their entrenching tools again and dug deeper. "Anybody got a spare K-bar?" Ready asked, and Garcia silently passed him one. "How about a pistol?" Garcia silently passed him a forty-five with two magazines and, before he could ask, three grenades.

"Somebody want to tell me why we're here?" Sampson griped.

"*Semper Fidelis,*" Ready answered, which made all three of the marines laugh.

"Hey, Bosun," Sampson called, "what's the Coast Guard motto?"

"*Semper Paratus,*" Ready proudly answered. "It means always prepared."

Sampson gave that some thought, then made a prediction. "Well, Mr. Coast Guard, get prepared for Mr. Jap to kick the everlasting crap out of us tonight."

1 6

Sister Mary Kathleen and her fella boys and their laden stretchers finally reached the beach, and there she focused her mind to the task at hand. She instructed the bearers to place the wounded men near a makeshift landing where boxy, slab-sided boats were putting in and out. Obediently, the fella boys lowered the stretchers and then sat down beside them, their expressions neutral and their minds apparently the same. She so admired their ability to not think when thinking was not required. Thinking was her curse, as it was for so many Europeans who came to the Pacific isles, for thinking led to a desire to change the way people were used to doing things in this world of vast blue seas, small green islands, and tropical rainbow abundance, a world that had over eons shaped a completely different approach to life, one that was at once leisurely and barbaric.

She looked around, hoping to find someone to help her with the wounded and also assist her in finding a big man. Before long, she took note of a short marine officer stomping up and down the beach, bellowing at everyone within the sound of his voice, which meant most of the atoll, and demanding that everything be done *toot sweet!* Before she could approach him, he abruptly marched up and stared at her. "Who and what the blue blazes are you?" he demanded and then, noting the cargo in the stretchers, put his hands on his hips and threw back his head in a frightful howl. "Look what you brung me! Josh Thurlow, brought low! Haw! Now ain't this rich! You boys! Get over here! Take a look at this!"

Two bare-chested marines came running and gawked at the men on the stretchers. "Take this wretched fool, the big naked one, and put him inside that pillbox," the officer demanded, pointing toward the ruin of a concrete

Japanese gun emplacement. "See if you can find some barbed wire. That's our new brig, and this is our first prisoner."

The marines approached the stretchers, but the fella boys jumped to their feet and barred their way. The marines tiredly pulled their K-bars. "Back off, you brown savages," one of them growled.

The stout little officer continued to gloat. "I have you now, Josh. Yes, indeedy, I do!"

Sister Mary Kathleen interrupted the man's strange glee. "Beggin' yer pardon, sor, I was told by a Bosun O'Neal to see both these men out to a hospital ship, especially this big fellow. He's frightful wounded, and he has fever, too. You men there. Put down yer knives. Me boys are just doing me bidding, don't ye see?"

"What should we do, Colonel?" one of the marines asked, swiping his blade near the stomach of one of the fella boys, who did not so much as flinch. In fact, he crossed his big arms as if challenging the marine to do his worst.

The little colonel looked the situation over, then said, "Oh, leave them savages alone, but go find that barbed wire and prepare the pillbox for our prisoner." He studied the nun with his awful, simian face. "You're Irish," he said, and it sounded as much accusation as observation.

"Indeed, I am, sor," she answered. "I am Sister Mary Kathleen, born in Ballysaggart of the county Tyrone, and a member of the Order of the Sacred Blood."

The officer raised his bushy eyebrows. "Well, I am Colonel Montague Singleton Burr, born in Hays of the state of Kansas, and a member of the order of the United States Marine Corps, which has expended its share of sacred blood. I am, I might add, in charge of this beach. As to Josh Thurlow, I've seen worse wounds, and fever's common enough out here. I've got a touch of it myself, even as we speak." He wiped his brow with the palm of his hand, then wiggled his fingers to show the drops of sweat that adhered to them. "You see? Some folks out here consider fever their best friend. Knocks you out, lets you sleep and dream of ice cream or women or De-Soto automobiles or whatever is your fancy. I can hardly wait until it puts me down. Now, that marine without his arm, he can go out to the navy docs, but Josh Thurlow ain't going nowhere but my new brig. I need to keep an eye on him because he's a killer, you savvy?"

Sister Mary Kathleen thought the colonel was so much like the men she'd once known in Ballysaggart, untalented men who had little but their pride, which they used like a club. For such men, a friendly and agreeable response was always best. "I do understand, sor," she answered. "Sure, he has killed many a man on this atoll, but then, wasn't that why he was sent here?"

Burr smirked. "That may be so, little sister, but lately Thurlow has become something of a nuisance. Say, what are you doing here? I had no intelligence there were missionaries on this atoll."

She drew herself up before forcing herself to subside, even allowing her shoulders to slump in deference. "Faith, sor, I am not a missionary, for they are grand, adventurous people in service to our Lord. My order's purpose is not to convert but to care. In the Forridges on the isle of Ruka, we operated a small clinic and also taught the children to read and write."

Burr was distracted by a young officer, heard his report with a sour expression, then sent him running, propelled by a following stream of foulmouthed invectives. "*Toot sweet,* you hear? *Toot sweet!* God damn these shavetails, Sister. They're as worthless as teats on a boar hog."

"Aye, sor," she replied brazenly. "Or as an English landlord, I'd wager." Internally, she berated herself for the snappy answer.

Burr squinted speculatively at her, chewed his cud of tobacco, spat, then grinned and said, "Or the nooky on a nun, eh?"

She looked the odd little marine officer in the eye to let him know she was not offended, as surely he'd meant for her to be. She'd heard far worse as a young girl whilst serving the men their malts and various liquors in the town's only pub. The colonel was testing her, just as they had. "As you say, sor," she answered, her eyes lowered.

Burr asked, "Where did you say you were from?"

Quietly, she admonished herself. "The Forridges, sor. Some call them the Far Reaches."

"Never heard of the place. A group of islands, I presume?"

Sister Mary Kathleen nodded, keeping her eyes downcast. "Yes, sor, that is correct, named for the Englishman Ansel Forridge by Captain Cook hisself. I think the captain owed him money or some such." She raised her eyes to see the colonel still grinning at her. "Anyways, three hundred or so miles nor-nor'east of here they are, sor. 'Tis the merchant sailors and yachtsmen who call them the Far Reaches. They're great green hills that push out of the bluest sea God in His mercy ever made, not like these nubs, these skinny flat atolls of Tarawa."

A trickle of tobacco juice escaped from the corner of Burr's mouth. He delicately wiped it away with a finger and said, "Thank you for the travelogue, Sister. So how was it you came to be here?"

"My fella boys and I sailed in outriggers. We heard the Americans were here. It was a bit of a surprise to find only Japanese."

"It's a relief to hear even the Catholic Church sometimes has lousy intelligence. I presume, therefore, you were made a prisoner by the Japanese?"

"Indeed, sor. For two days before ye landed."

"Did they abuse you, Sister?"

"Nay, sor. They were too busy getting ready to fight to bother much with me and me fella boys a'tall. They put us up in a big sand fort but scarcely said a word otherwise, except for a kind lieutenant who saw to our needs."

"I would have thought they would have at least raped you," Burr said, sounding disappointed. "What made you sail all this way? To find Americans, is that what you said? What for?"

She tried to speak with detachment, but her enthusiasm for the subject defeated her. "One of our islands—its name is Ruka—was taken over by the Japanese in February of '42. The commander is a man by the name of Colonel Yoshu. I came here to tell ye that if ye will send an armed force there, I think he will surrender."

Burr snickered. "I'll see if the Second Marines is available for the required negotiations." He shook his head. "Sister, what you're saying is nonsensical. The Japanese don't surrender."

"These might," she replied.

Burr frowned while he managed a quick calculation. "Did you say the Japanese occupied this Ruka in February of '42? That was nearly two years ago. Where have you been during all this time?"

"A prisoner of Colonel Yoshu."

He cocked his head and eyed her speculatively. "You seem to make a habit of being a prisoner of the Japs."

She was silent for a long second while she worked on a properly humble response, then, not finding one, said, "Perhaps I am talking to the wrong man. I need a big man, y'see."

Burr scowled. "It don't matter how big a man you talk to, Sister. No American's going to a cockamamie island to palaver with some crazy Japanese colonel. Tell you what. I'll talk to General Smith and see if he will give you a ride to Australia. There you can go about your business, praying and the like. You can leave the Japanese to us."

She worried with the rosary beads that hung from her cincture, then shook her head. "Beg yer pardon, sor, but I would like to talk to this General Smith. Not sometime later, neither. Now."

"It's not going to happen, Sister."

"But—"

"Just a minute," Burr interrupted and started yelling at the crew of a Higgins boat who had managed to snag their craft on the reef even though the opening through it was clearly marked with bobbing buoys. He snatched a passing marine by his collar. "Get out there and tell those idiots to rip off their stripes, boy! Ever last man jack of 'em, you hear me?"

Burr allowed a great, exaggerated sigh, then turned back to the nun. "What else can I do for you, Sister?" he asked, nearly politely. "As you can see, I'm a very busy man."

"This man," she said, nodding toward Josh, "pray let me care for him." *When he wakes up,* she thought, *he'll find me a big man and not give me yer guff.*

"You're a nurse?" Burr asked.

"Nay, sor, though I have attended to the sick."

Burr shook his head. "He don't need your care, Sister. What he needs is to be under lock and key. When he comes awake, I fear he might pick up a shovel and brain someone important and crucial to the war effort. Look, go to Australia, I tell you. There you can talk to your archbishops, subpopes, or whatever and wait out the war. The entire Pacific will be clear of the Japanese, given time."

"And how much time would that be?" she demanded, her eyes flashing before she forced her expression back toward one of deference.

Colonel Burr was happy to answer her, for he had recently given that question some thought. He had walked his mind up the various island chains and then contemplated the home islands of the Japanese and what it would take to beat them even with a good pounding of their cities by saturation bombing. "Eight years," he concluded. "Maybe a little more. We'll have to kill nearly all of them before this is done, but we'll get it done, with God's help. The United States Marine Corps, you see, is the right arm of God."

Sister Mary Kathleen looked around and saw all the dead marines bobbing in the sea or sprawled facedown on the sand. "Then it appears God's right arm is terrible hurt today, Colonel."

Burr's face clouded over at the perceived insult to his beloved Corps. "Is there anything else?" he demanded bitterly.

She raised her chin. "I could use a priest. An American one will do."

"A Cat-licker Holy Joe? There's got to be one or two landed by now. What do you need one for, if you don't mind me asking?"

"I have need to make me confession."

"Confession of what?"

"Me sins, of course."

Burr scratched his jaw. "I thought being a nun and all, you weren't allowed to sin."

"We are all sinners, sor," she replied. Then she added, all humility forgotten, "The priest, if ye please?"

"All right, Sister," Burr growled and then barked at his marines to move Thurlow into the pillbox and don't forget the barbed wire, by thunder, then collect all those men still floating in the sea and lying dead in the sand and, oh yes, go find the little nun here a fish-eating Holy Joe and he meant all that to be done right now *toot sweet!*

1 7

As soon as the sun expired into the Pacific with its usual gaudy display of pink spokes and scarlet-rimmed clouds normal to those latitudes, Ready made up his mind. He told his little band of marines they were going to move. "Move where?" Sampson demanded, brought awake by Ready's command.

"To the beach," Ready replied. "Jap knows where we are. Won't be long, he'll be sneaking in."

"My foot is killing me," Sampson complained. "I can't walk."

"You can walk," Ready said, "because nobody's going to carry you."

"You got that right, Bosun," Tucker said, "but you're wrong about the Japanese sneaking in. I figure it'll be a big *banzai* attack. They're probably out there drinking sake and stuff right now, getting themselves all worked up."

"Three riflemen and a fellow without a rifle or even a shirt ain't worth a *banzai* attack," Ready replied. "Them Imperial marines will just wait till dark and then come over here and cut our throats."

Tucker smirked. "Well, ain't you the optimist!"

Garcia withdrew his K-bar from its sheath and fondled it. "Let them come," he said menacingly. "I'll take a few with me."

Ready ignored both Tucker's sarcasm and Garcia's bravado. "Pick up your traps and let's go," he ordered. "You get one more round of griping and then I don't want a peep out of any of you until we get to the beach. And if you got a canteen that rattles or anything else, fix it so it don't make any noise. We got to be like shadows."

The three marines cheerfully accomplished the griping—none of them wanted to move out of their holes, and all of them said so—and then they grimly tore strips from the uniform of a nearby dead Japanese to muffle their gear. "Let's go," Ready said when he thought they were prepared.

"And that's the last word you'll hear out of me until we get to where we're going."

"Where *are* we going?" Sampson demanded.

"The beach," Ready answered.

"Why to the beach?"

"Because we may need to swim to save ourselves."

The moon was new, just a sliver of it showing, and therefore didn't cover the atoll with its usual Pacific silvery brilliance. It was dark as dirt, which Ready thought a good thing. He picked out a direction, easterly, and crept ahead. The marines followed, holding their bayonet-tipped rifles. Before it had gotten dark, Ready had calculated their course, one that would take them past a line of low scrub bushes of what he supposed was a type of sea grape. Now the shapes of those bushes, their dark darker than the rest of the dark, loomed very near. He stopped, and the marines behind him stopped, too. Ready strained his eyes toward a shadow off by itself, and then he saw, or thought he saw, it move.

Then he thought he saw another of the shadows move, just a nudge. Holding his breath, he looked so hard at the shadows that his eyes hurt. *There!* Now he was certain. The shadows were not bushes but men, a conjecture almost immediately proved when something hard and sharp pushed into Ready's bare right arm, which held his K-bar. It was a bayonet, tipped he supposed on a long Japanese rifle, and it slowly slid along his arm. Then the bayonet stopped, withdrew, sliding back across. Ready and the man holding the rifle were close enough now that Ready could hear the man breathing, and it had the smell of sake on it, too. Tucker had been right about the Japanese drinking their courage. Ready caught movement out of the corner of his eye and realized he and his marines were all mixed up with the Japanese who had probably been on their way to cut their throats. Coincidentally, they had chosen similar paths. Now each man, American and Japanese, was wondering what to do.

The *rikusentai* slowly nudged Ready's arm. Perhaps he still wasn't convinced he was facing a man—but then came a rifle shot, and the Japanese marine stepped back, and disappeared into the gloom. Then Ready heard a cacophony of grunts, spews, and shrieks until finally there was nothing but the sound of heavy breathing. "Marines?" Ready called, fearing the answer.

"I got mine, Bosun," Tucker replied from the ground.

"I got one," Garcia gasped, still catching his breath.

"I killed one and wounded another," Sampson answered. "I think he crawled off somewhere."

"Mine got away," Ready confessed. "I think there must be at least two more." Just as he spoke, he heard the scramble of boots on sand, then running sounds that gradually diminished.

"They're running back to their camp," Tucker said. "They'll tell the others where we're headed."

"Well, we're still headed there," Ready answered.

Nobody argued with him, so Ready led his marines off at a trot, leading them, like the good Killakeet boy he was, to the sea.

1 8

Colonel Montague Singleton Burr was having trouble getting to sleep. It was all the scheming that was keeping him awake, that and the terrible stink of the dead, not to mention all the awful popping and crackling of the gas escaping from their bloated bodies in the terrible heat that had not much dissipated after the sun had set. Burr had made his bed in a battered amtrac with the hope of getting away from the dreadful odors and sounds. Instead, the slap of the waves against the amtrac added to the general turmoil of his increasingly fever-ridden mind. There were many schemes playing through his head, but only one was insistent, and it had to do with Josh Thurlow. The idea made him chuckle under his breath when he thought about it, even though he kept telling himself no, he couldn't do it, and it would be so wrong. But then he would tell himself yes, he actually *could* do it, and it would be for the best, anyway. In fact, it was probably something that was meant to be, and he was only a cog in the wheels of fate that had begun turning the moment he'd laid eyes on the little Irish nun in her dirty habit. Wiping the burning sweat from his eyes, Burr finally gave in to it. What else could he do? *Kismet,* he said to himself, even though he halfway suspected that his rising fever might be disturbing his logic. He sat up on the hard deck of the amtrac and yelled for his clerk.

A gray-haired marine rose from the beach and wandered sleepily across the sand to the amtrac. "You bellowed, Colonel?"

"Private," Burr croaked, "how'd you like to get your stripes back?"

Burr's clerk was famously known for having sergeant's stripes one day and none the next, depending on the whims of his boss. "I'd admire my stripes back, sure, Colonel," he answered, stifling a yawn.

"Then, my man, get yourself a notebook and a pencil!"

The clerk already had a little notebook in his pocket and also a pencil. He showed them to the colonel, and Burr said, "I want you to write down all that is about to transpire for my daily log. You can type it up later. Savvy?"

"Savvy without doubt, sir."

Snatching up a flashlight, Burr climbed out of the amtrac and led the way to the blasted pillbox that was Josh Thurlow's prison. To Burr's distinct displeasure, which caused a spate of grumbled curses, he saw neither barbed wire surrounding it nor any guards. Half-expecting Thurlow to have escaped, he went inside and was relieved to see the man lying unconscious on the sand with flies and mosquitoes buzzing around his grimy and sweat-damp face. "Sit him up," Burr brusquely ordered.

Thurlow groaned as he was raised up, then sagged crookedly against the broken concrete, his chin resting on his dirt-caked chest. He was a sorry sight, which improved the colonel's mood. "Now, Captain Thurlow," Burr began in a condescending and syrupy tone, "some interesting intelligence has come my way that I think you should hear. Are you writing this down, Private?"

The clerk looked up from his pad. "Writing, aye, aye, sir."

Burr nodded, withdrew a red bandana from his hip pocket to wipe the sweat from his face, and then continued his one-way conversation. "Some interesting information, as I said, Thurlow, and I knew you were the one to hear it. For despite your denials, I know you are in fact an intelligence officer sent out here by the great power brokers of Washington, D.C. Am I not correct?"

Josh said nothing, mainly because he was unconscious, so Burr went on: "Well, says you, Colonel, you're in the right of it, for certain. I am sent out here to find out all I can, for how else, says he, can Secretary of the fucking Navy Frank Knox, and Chief of Staff George C. for Christ Marshall, and maybe even God, otherwise known as President Franklin Delano Roosevelt himself, know what they should do next? Says you, says I. Got that, Sergeant? Read back our conversation so far."

The clerk scratched his head with the eraser end of his pencil—and read: "And then Colonel Burr said, 'Well, says you, Colonel, you're in the right of it for certain. I am sent out here to find out all I can, for how else, says he, can Secretary of the fucking Navy—'"

"Hold it, Private!" Burr angrily snapped. "Are you an idiot, man? Write it down the way it's being said, not the way you hear it!"

The clerk looked stupidly at Burr for a long second, then licked the point of his pencil and smeared out what he had written. "You're right, Colonel," he apologized. "I guess I'm going a bit deaf. All these artillery rounds, I suppose." He scribbled a bit and then read, "Captain Thurlow replied, " 'You're in the right of it, Colonel Burr. I am sent out here to find out all I can, for how else can Secretary of the Navy—' "

"Very good, Sergeant," Burr interrupted. With a grim smile, he continued: "Now, Thurlow, this nun, this little snot-nosed Catholic sister, has come to me with a most interesting story. It seems the Japanese have occupied a group of islands known as the Forridges, a.k.a. the Far Reaches. That means we have the enemy placed in our rear, a terrible thing. Well, Colonel Burr, Josh replies, says you, says me, says he, that would be a terrible thing indeed. Perhaps I should go out there and take a look. Why, Captain Thurlow, says I, do you think so? I mean, after all, you are terribly wounded, man! Yet, (I'm shrugging, Sergeant, and most reluctant—take note of it) you know your duty better than I, of course. Says he, I tell you what, Colonel, where is that fucking common little nun? Does she have a boat? If she does, I'll ship along with her, take a run up to those islands, see what's what and be back here in a jiffy. Well, all right, Captain, says me, says I, if you think that's best. I'll call the little Irish creature over right away to talk about it. Read me that last line, Private."

The clerk stopped his scribbling and cleared his throat. Josh fell over on his side, and his breathing became even more labored. Both men ignored him. " 'I'll call the nun, God bless her," the clerk read from his notes, "to brief us on the situation in the Forridges immediately so that you can decide what you should do.' "

"Very good, Sergeant."

"Thank you, sir."

"The nun is obviously required at this point," Burr said. "Go get her."

"Where is she?"

"How the hell should I know? Find her!"

The clerk tucked his notebook and pencil in his shirt pocket and went off to find the nun, wherever she might be. She wasn't far, as it turned out. A marine trying to sleep on the beach pointed to where she and her savages had made camp, which was close by a shattered Higgins boat. Behind the Higgins, the clerk was surprised to find three large outrigger canoes. The nun was kneeling in the sand in front of them, not at her prayers but with an M-1 rifle in her hands. Beside her, in the light produced by a hissing kerosene lantern, was a towheaded and helmetless young marine. The marine was saying, "That's it, Sister. Now, try it again."

The astonished clerk watched as the nun disassembled the rifle, carefully placing the various parts on a palm frond mat beside her, then reassembling them all in the same order. She finished with the receiver slapping shut. "Was that done well enough?" she asked the marine.

"Yes, ma'am. They'd be proud of you on Parris Island."

"May I keep it?" she asked of the rifle. "And some ammunition?"

"Don't see why not. There ain't no shortage of rifles lying about. Here's a couple of clip bandoliers."

The clerk cleared his throat. "Sister? Colonel Montague Burr would have a word with you. Will you follow me?"

"Will ye follow Christ?" she retorted.

"If Christ will lead me off this atoll, ma'am, I'll follow him or any other damn god you name."

She looked at him with big, disappointed eyes, and the clerk mumbled, "Don't mean no disrespect, Sister. I'm just a bit tired." He paused to assess the situation. "What are you doing with that rifle?"

She ignored the question and turned to the marine beside her. "Would you please place my rifle and ammunition on that canoe? Yes, that one there. Thank you." The young marine carefully wrapped the rifle in the mat and then used the ammunition bandoliers to strap it all together. Sister Mary Kathleen turned to the clerk. "Will ye take me to Colonel Burr, then?"

"Yes, ma'am." Then someone, for no apparent reason, popped a flare over the atoll, and as it floated down, streaming smoke, the clerk saw in the dancing shadows naked men covered with tattoos crouched about what appeared to be a body. Their hands were busy with flashing knives. "What in God's name are they doing?" the clerk gasped.

The nun looked over her shoulder, then said, most serenely, "They are flaying one of their fella boys so that he might be carried home."

"Flaying? You mean removing the . . . the flesh?"

"Aye. Bones they can carry, but not the flesh. They will feed the meat to the fish. It is their way. Do not look if it bothers ye."

It did indeed bother the clerk, so he took her advice and didn't look anymore. Instead, he quickly led the nun away from the beach to the pillbox, where Burr was still contemplating, with some obvious satisfaction, the fallen, sweat-soaked, and thoroughly filthy Josh Thurlow, whose eyes had rolled back into his head. The nun knelt at Josh's side. "He is worse!" she said in an accusing tone. "Have ye not called a doctor for him as I asked, then?"

"He doesn't need a doctor," Burr archly replied. "A long sea voyage, that's what would revitalize our Captain Thurlow here, not the ministrations of some pill pusher."

The nun felt Josh's brow. It was scalding to her touch, and she also observed that his wounds were oozing yellow pus and watery blood. "He's dying!" she announced.

"Oh, now, Sister," Burr chuckled. "Hardly. Old Josh's asleep, that's all. But before he took his nap, he and I had the most interesting conversation. It seems he would like to accompany you to your Far Reaches, to scout out the situation, and then, at such time he is able to make it back to these waters, which I anticipate to be a very long time, if ever, he may lecture us about all that he has learned. For all I know, he will recommend we send marines in force to defeat the Japanese on your islands. Of course, I debated with him, saying how much he was required for the war effort right here at my side, but Thurlow is a stubborn fellow, you know, and I have reluctantly agreed to let him go. You may take him when you're ready, as long as it's pretty much *toot sweet*."

The nun seemed poised to argue but, after a long second of meditation, subsided. "May I at least have clean dressings and what medicines you might have for him?"

Burr wiped his forehead with his bandana, blew his nose, and then called out to his clerk. "Sergeant-Private? Go round up a corpsman. Tell him to help the good sister here with Captain Thurlow and to give her whatever she requires. Tell him I could use some aspirin and quinine, too. Fever's got me, and this one feels like a doozy."

The clerk charged off, and then Burr staggered a bit, before leaning against the pillbox wall. Fever when it came to him always came on padded feet, like a stealthy cat, but then it dug in its claws and drew blood. "I spoke with the Holy Joe priest you confessed to, Sister," he said, blinking through the sweat running down into his eyes. He dabbed his brow with his soggy bandana, then wrung it out, the sweat pattering around his boots. "The man seemed a little shaken to me. What did you tell him? Although I ordered him twice to confide in me, couching it in terms of helping the war effort, not to mention any future promotions for him, he still wouldn't do it. I will see him broken, of course, so you might as well tell me what sins you confessed that so stressed the poor padre."

"Why do ye care, Colonel?" Sister Mary Kathleen calmly inquired. "What are my sins to ye?"

Burr took a deep breath, desperate for oxygen, but there was only the foul air of dead men. "Sister, help me."

"How can I? Tell me what ye need."

"I need you."

She lifted her eyebrows. "In what manner?"

Burr's uniform was soaked with sweat. His knees were unhinged, near collapse. The fever was fully on him, its claws tearing away at his flesh. "I need you to explain to me the ways of heaven and earth," he croaked. "I sense you know everything."

Shocked, she snapped, "I know no such thing!"

"Please, Sister! I am in hell, don't you understand? Save me!"

"No!" she yelped. "I am not the one ye seek!"

"Help me, please God!" Burr gasped, then staggered out of the pillbox and disappeared into the darkness.

Trembling from fear and shock at the colonel's outburst, Sister Mary Kathleen waited until she regained her composure, then knelt beside the big, fever-wracked captain and placed her hands together in prayer. She prayed to Saint Monessa for all the dead men of Tarawa, and particularly for Josh Thurlow, and then she prayed for Colonel Burr. Finally and most fervently, she prayed for herself and asked the little saint to please intercede with God, who surely was otherwise too busy to notice her, and, *please, Saint Monessa,* help her complete her mission to recover the precious thing God had given her and, because of the weakness of her flesh and spirit, she had lost.

She expected no immediate reply to her prayers and therefore was all the more surprised when she got one. There was what seemed to be a child's voice in her head, and it said, *Go, and take Captain Thurlow with you.*

So she did.

1 9

Ready had come to believe that the world was going to stay dark forever and that the sun would never rise. Perhaps, he thought, when he heard the labored breaths and shuffling footsteps that told him the Japanese were coming again, he was already dead and hell was the absence of light. Then the K-bars and bayonets clashed, gunshots popped, there were shouts and cries and gurgles, and he knew he was still alive, though hanging on by the merest chance. The beach fell silent once more except for the whimpering of the sea against the sand and the last breaths of men. Ready called out, "Marines?" The answers came back: "Tucker here." "Sampson, Whimper Fi." Garcia hissed, "Still with you, Bosun!"

They had been assaulted three times by teams of four Japanese each, and those twelve men now lay dead in the sand around them. Another assault was surely on its way. Ready looked off to the east, willing the sun to rise, which it did, coincidentally. It was a brilliant sunrise, sudden as usual in those latitudes, a molten red ball flashing hot light across a sea that instantly turned from a sullen gray to a most glorious and transparent blue.

"Will you look at that that!" Ready exclaimed, and the three marines looked and saw three snowy white sails skimming with graceful purpose across what seemed the edge of the world. One detached from the others and glided toward the beach. Fearing for its safety, Ready jumped up and down and waved his arms. "Go back!" he yelled, but the little boat kept sailing toward them, and then it seemed the entire island exploded in a wash of fire and brimstone that sucked the very breath from Ready's lungs.

2 0

The sails were raised on the outriggers, and Sister Mary Kathleen, for the first time in days, took a deep breath without the accompanying stench of dead men. She silently thanked God for fresh air and freedom while her fella boys thanked the spirits of the sea with a song that rose and fell with the waves. The outriggers were all designed the same, built from the wood of the breadfruit tree and consisting of a hull, a sail, an outrigger float, a lee platform, and a small hut in the stern. Outriggers built in the Far Reaches were known throughout the Pacific as fast and durable. They did not so much sail on the sea as skim above it, their passage marked only by the hiss of spray. Now, to Sister Mary Kathleen's delight, the wind was propelling the outriggers as silently and quickly over the water as if the finger of God were pushing them.

God lived in the spray and the wind, she thought, as much as he lived in the ancient rites performed by priests. It was times such as these that she wondered if her church held all the answers as to the nature of God and the world he had made. Certainly, when she had first arrived in the Far Reaches, good Father Ballester had expressed those very doubts.

She recalled now her many conversations with the old priest, and the stories he'd told. Most of them were pleasant, given as the white-haired old man delicately sipped his whiskey—stories of his garden, and the geography of the islands, and his home back in Ireland, and how it would have been so much better for the world if the Irish had created a vast empire, rather than the English. But some of the things he'd said to her were unsettling. He had concluded, he confided, that some things in the catechism were contradictory, and other things simply made no sense. He believed, after much study, that many parts of the Bible were just so many fairy tales.

He even expressed doubts as to the divinity of Christ. "But what other religion is there, my dear," he had opined, "that can bring peace and love to the people around the world? Perhaps it is simply the best religion we have, and our duty to bring it to the heathens, even if it isn't true."

She had argued with him, gently, of course, for it was not proper for a young nun to confront an old, experienced priest, even if he was expressing heresy. Usually, she was able to lead him off into a tangent, easy to do as he loved to talk about the early days of the church in the Far Reaches. He could wax on for hours about how he and the other priests, all young then, of course, had coaxed the native people into wearing proper clothing rather than walking around naked, and how they had explained to them the righteousness of marriage before coitus, and the wrongness of ritualized war and the occasional bashing of heads for sport. "It is a terrible toil we have, Sister," he'd said. "These fella boys, they accept our baptism and our mass, they learn to cross themselves and say all the proper words, then they go right back to doing what they were doing before we came. I'd rather they resisted than the sham they show us."

"Why the sham?" she had asked in all innocence.

"Because they know we are persistent and they take the easy way," the priest replied with what was clearly a heavy and frustrated heart. "They know the English have the gunpowder to back us up, so giving in is the way they resist. They intend to outlast us, that's what I think, then go back to their heathen ways after we're gone."

"But we will never leave, will we?"

Father Ballester had shrugged and smiled a sad, tired smile. "We will grow old and then we will die, Sister. And naught will come to replace us. 'Tis our fate, I'm thinking, but never breathe a word of my opinion to the other priests or sisters, I pray."

Why Father Ballester chose her to share such doubts and heretical philosophies, she did not know. There was too much she didn't know or understand, except the one thing. She believed in God, and He had given her a test, a terrible test, and she had failed it. Now she supposed He had given her another, and this time she would not fail. She would die first.

But wasn't such thinking surely yet another aspect of her awful pride? She recalled Father Donnelly, the American priest on Tarawa sent to her by Colonel Burr, when she had confessed that particular little venial sin. He had smiled and said, "Well, we Irish have to be especially watchful against pride, don't we?"

"We do, Father," she'd replied humbly.

The priest, who was from Boston, had continued conversationally, "An Irish convent must be a tough place."

"Nay, it is a place to learn," she'd answered.

"What was an example of your penances?" he'd asked.

And so, because she was proud she had endured it, thus adding to her sins, she had told him of the penance of the begging of the soup, where she knelt at the knee of each nun in turn at the dinner table and, with her empty bowl, begged for a spoonful of soup, just one, until at last she had enough to eat. "The sisters had eaten from their bowls, and some of them had tooth decay or false teeth or bad gums," she explained. "Yet I took the bowl back to my place at the table, and I ate every drop."

"I would have puked," Father Donnelly vowed. "We don't do things like that in the United States."

"Then how can ye be strong enough to do all that is to be done?" she'd asked, a brazen question for a nun to a priest, even an American one.

He seemed to take no umbrage. "What other sins besides pride do you have for me, Sister? Let us have your confession."

And so she had told him her sins, including her greatest sin, and watched the blood drain from his shocked face, this from a priest who had spent the day roaming an island awash in blood and draped with thousands of dead men. "You are lost!" he'd cried at the end of her confession. "What penance could I possibly give you great enough to match this . . . *thing?*"

"This one, Father." Then she pressed upon him what she required.

The priest replied in a voice turned cold as ice that he would do what he could. Then she'd left him because she could no longer face the terrible loathing it was certain he had for her as a nun, a woman, and a human being.

And now all she could do was to penance herself in her own way, to lie prostrate upon the floor of life and beg for the soup of wisdom, to fix in her mind that she was of no importance except for what she had to do to save the gift given to her through pain and mortification. Within her hut, as the outriggers skimmed along, she said her prayers, her Our Fathers, her Hail Marys, and her Glorias, and, of course, her special prayers to little Saint Monessa. Then she climbed out of the hut and walked forward and looked toward the next island up from Betio. It was then she saw them, a little knot of men on the beach that included a new friend.

"Ply on, Nango, Moru, Kapura, Valuta!" Sister Mary Kathleen urged her fella boys as they sailed and paddled the outrigger toward a shore suddenly covered with flames and sulfurous smoke. "On, ye good fellas!"

The crew of the outrigger responded to the nun's urgings with deep, hearty grunts at each dip of their paddles while Nango, captain and navigator, minded the sail pumped full of wind. "Into thy hell we proceed, devil Satan," Sister Mary Kathleen exulted over the hiss of the sea spray and the tortured creak of the rigging. "Praise the Father, the Son, and the Holy Ghost! Mary, Mother of God, we beseech ye yer protection! In yer perfect hands, we are not afraid!" Then she put her hand to her mouth, realizing that she had reached a most inappropriate level of ecstasy, one denied her in her vocation. "Sail on, sweet canoe," she whispered, tamping down her enthusiasm as best she could.

A great wind came then, a mighty blow that swept the beach clear of smoke and seemed to lift the hull of the outrigger and send it flying ever faster. Now Sister Mary Kathleen saw many marines, their rifles held high, crossing the shallow water between the islands. There were more going ashore in their slab-sided vessels, the ramps dropping and men running out. Artillery rounds were falling in a crescendo, and a tank bellowed its cannon as it roared through the shallows past another tank that was stalled. Japanese soldiers were climbing out of their holes everywhere and were rushing to meet the invaders. Another complement of Japanese was racing down the beach. She willed calm, even in the turmoil of the approaching battle, and stood brazenly on the bow, an easy target.

2 1

Ready had done everything he could to keep the outrigger from coming so near, especially after he saw the nun aboard it. Surely the Japanese and maybe even the marines would shoot the native boat full of holes. Yet it came on, unscathed, sailing close to the beach, until its crew turned its sail to dump the wind.

"Is that boat here for us?" Sampson asked.

"It sure is!" Ready cried joyfully, "and look who's aboard it."

"Why, it's that nun!" Garcia said accurately.

"Let's swim, boys," Ready said. "It's our only chance."

The marines, however, seemed reluctant to swim. They slowly waded into the surf, their rifles held over their heads. Ready, halfway to the outrigger, turned and yelled at them. "Throw them rifles down and swim, you jarheads!"

This they promptly did, also tossing away their helmets, and dog-paddled to the outrigger, where they were hauled aboard. Then Ready lifted his hands and was pulled aloft by a big native man, who dropped him onto the mats lining the bottom of the hull. When he climbed to his feet, he saw the nun standing on the bow, completely vulnerable to shot and shell. "Sister, get down, please!" he said, and even as he said it, the sea fairly exploded all around with bullets from the Japanese on the beach.

The nun calmly turned to him and said, with a certain smile, "No worry-worry, Bosun O'Neal. I think today is not my day to die. Or yours." Then she spoke quietly to the big tattooed man holding the sheet that controlled the set of the sail. "Sail on, Nango, me old friend."

Nango grinned and made an adjustment, and instantly the outrigger's sail filled with wind, and the boat began to skim over the water, curving toward the open sea. Nango nodded to Ready, one sailor recognizing another.

Before long the noise of the battle dwindled and all that could be heard was the whispering of the sea and the spirited wind snapping the sail and thrumming the rigging. It was only then that Ready noticed the big naked man lying in the stern, his legs akimbo, his jaw slack, his face pale, and his eyes shot with blood. "Captain Thurlow!" he cried in disbelief and knelt beside him and touched his shoulder just to see if he was real or part of a dream.

The nun came then, kneeling on the mats. "Your captain is sore sick, Bosun. I fear for his life. His wounds are infected. I have salved them but to no avail."

"I have sulfa in my bag," Ready replied. "If it didn't get too wet, it should take care of these scrapes. Anyhow, Josh Thurlow's a tough bird, Sister, and make no mistake."

She smiled at him, a smile that made Ready's heart skip a delighted beat. "Yer devoted to yer captain," she observed approvingly.

Ready blushed. "We grew up in the same place, ma'am, on Killakeet Island off North Carolina. He's like my brother except when he's ordering me and everybody else around."

"Then, Bosun, you and me, we'll take care of yer brother, won't we?"

At that moment, Ready would have agreed to take care of the entire world as long as it was beside this beautiful little Irish girl who also happened to be a nun. "Yes we will, ma'am," he said and felt at that moment an odd, though quite pleasant, twinge in his heart, a twinge he had not felt in many a year, if ever.

PART III

The Voyage

When the mists have rolled in splendor
From the beauty of the hills,
And the sunlight falls in gladness
On the rivers and the rills,
We recall our Father's promise
In the rainbow of the spray:
We shall know each other better
When the mists have rolled away.

—ANNIE HERBERT, A HYMN

2 2

Three days passed and the outriggers sailed on, three tiny dots on an endless sea driven by an endless wind beneath an endless sky. In the oven of the sun, the occupants barely moved, and the outrigger captains dozed, the sheet controlling the sail tucked between their toes. At nightfall, when the stars spread above them like a snowy blanket, a fresh breeze flowed off the sea and into the hulls, bringing coolness and stirring life. It was then the fella boys sang songs of their home islands and the sea and of the dream-world that surely existed alongside the world that could be seen and felt. Sometimes they would bring out a small drum and thump against its hide cover to keep rhythm with the songs. It was a pleasant time, though Ready often wondered what the words in the songs meant. He wished he had his fiddle, for he was a consummate player, and sometimes imagined he was holding it and playing some sad Killakeet tune. He could almost hear its strains in his head, and the banjo and the jug and guitar the crew aboard the old *Maudie Jane* used to play, once so long ago when Ready and Captain Thurlow and the other boys of Killakeet were plying the great blue river of the Gulf Stream, out where the big fish danced their eternal dance of life and death, and German U-boats had sunk so many ships and killed so many men. Thoughts of Killakeet were joyful and painful all at once; though he tried not to be unmanly, he found himself on many a dark night wiping away tears when his memories came on too strong.

Days and nights passed, marked by songs and drums and memories and miles of sea, but, through it all, Josh Thurlow remained sealed inside a terrible sickness, shivering and sweating in turns, eyes fluttering, his lips trembling as he had conversations with unseen visitors. Once he yelled out, "Naanni!" and subsided with a groan. Ready told the nun that Naanni was the name of the captain's wife, who had been murdered in Alaska, though he knew little else of the story, other than there were rumors Captain Thurlow had killed the men who'd done it.

"Faith," Sister Mary Kathleen had replied, "'tis a story that sets me to thinking. How is it, Bosun, that love, our Father's greatest gift, can lead to murder? Do ye suppose yer captain was being tested by God? He was given love, then it was taken away. What should he have done? Turn the other cheek or seek revenge? Vengeance is God's, according to what the priests say, but would God fill a man with honor and pride and then tempt him in such a cruel manner? Tis all a quandary."

Ready supposed any response he might make to the nun's question would be inadequate, but he did his best. "I think maybe we don't know much of what God's about, ma'am," he offered. "We just see a few straws in the wind, you might say. I don't know. It's the province of preachers and, like you say, priests."

"Perhaps 'tis not for any of us mortals," she replied. Ready felt a failure for not being able to give her a better answer.

He often and surreptitiously watched her when she stood on the bow, her head down in prayer and her lips trembling in silent supplication. The fella boys all seemed to love her so; they watched her with adoration evident in their big brown eyes and gave her encouraging smiles whenever they could catch her eye. It seemed to Ready that the nun was a woman in torment and that the Polynesians were carrying around some kind of secret about her.

Ready kept offering Josh water. Some of it was taken, though much dripped from his slack mouth. Sister Mary Kathleen washed him with copra soap, and Ready dusted sulfa into his wounds, but still they did not heal. The miles flowed on beneath the hulls of the outriggers, and Josh did not wake or show improvement. Finally, the nun took Ready aside. "I think yer captain will surely die," she said.

"Is there anything more I can do?" Ready asked.

"Pray, Bosun," she answered. "'Tis all I know."

"I can do that, ma'am," he replied and bowed his head. She smiled at him and watched him with her sea-blue eyes. The bosun was a good man, she'd decided, and kind. She liked him and was pleased that he might like her back, though she feared he would loathe her when he discovered all that she had done. She considered telling all to him, but such revelation, she admonished herself, would only be another form of self-importance and pride.

Nay, she would keep her secrets until God revealed His plan for her punishment or salvation.

At night, when she took the air on the bow, listening to the chuckling of the sea being swept aside by the outrigger, Sister Mary Kathleen often prayed for Captain Thurlow, though any and all her prayers felt small and unheard beneath the great canopy of the sky. It was so easy to look up into its vastness and sense that God was not there but far away, that He had done His work on earth and left His creation to itself. Whether it prospered or not, whether men lived or died, whether they were joyful or suffered, He no longer cared. He had wound His eternal clock, and now it simply ticked on without interference. " 'Tis the sea," she told herself when she had such sinful contemplations. " 'Tis its great, endless self. Here God makes Himself small. I know not why."

In moments of uncertainty and doubt, Sister Theresa spoke to her across time and tide: "When ye take yer vows, Kathleen, yer life will be all for Jesus. Never forget that, even when ye are filled with the gravest doubts. Say it for me, now."

"All for Jesus," Sister Mary Kathleen whispered in the darkness of the great sea. She recalled saying the same words when she had turned away Desmond O'Rourke, the sweet young man who had professed his love to her the night before she'd taken her vows of sisterhood. He had slipped over the walls of the convent, crept down the dark corridors redolent with soap-scrubbed floors, and somehow found her cell. There, he had gone down on one knee. *Sweet Kathleen,* he'd begged, *come away. Be my wife, have children with me, help me raise a family. Ye are too good to be buried alive in a nun's shrouds.*

She had been tempted, but she loved Jesus, the perfect man beside whom all mortal men could not compare. She had gladly pledged herself to Him forever. But where, she asked now and then, had Jesus been during her ordeal on Ruka? *Sweet Jesus, why do Ye forsake me?* She had groaned those words to heaven as she lay in the filthy cell where Colonel Yoshu had put her all those months, a cell that seemed to shrink around her at night as she lay quaking in fear of being bitten by starving rats and giant cockroaches. Jesus was all powerful, wasn't He? Could He not have spared her the torture if He had cared enough? She concluded that if she suffered, it was because He desired it, perhaps to see if her faith was strong. It was the only explanation she could accept, not the one put forth by Father Ballester, that Jesus was a good example for the heathens but in reality a myth. Nay, Jesus was real, real as she, and real as Colonel Yoshu. But as a husband, she thought, Jesus was not as kind or gentle as perhaps Desmond O'Rourke might have been.

When the sun sank beneath the sea on the sixth day of the voyage, Ready, who was sleeping, felt something touch his foot and was astonished to discover it was Captain Thurlow's trembling fingers. Ready took his captain's big, sweaty hand while Josh looked up at him with raw pink eyes. "What is it, Skipper?" Ready asked. "Do you need a drink of water?"

Josh Thurlow, during those days of sailing, had often dreamt of many things, of many people and places. Now he thought he was still dreaming because he seemed to be aboard a kind of native canoe. The air was also fresh with the sea. "Is this heaven, Ready?" he asked in wonder.

Ready felt Josh's forehead, and to his joy, it felt cool. "No, sir, not heaven, but at least not hell, neither."

"Then we've left Tarawa," Josh mumbled. "There's a blessing."

"I'll change his dressings!" Sister Mary Kathleen cried. She began to work away on Josh with bandages and ointments, all the while telling him that he would soon be better, yes he would, and that he was a strong man, to be sure he was.

Josh stared at her. He had some vague memory of seeing this white-shrouded woman before. He allowed her to turn him this way and that, and raise and lower his arms and legs, and scrub him and rub him and paint ointment on him, but during all her ministrations, his eyes never left her face while he tried to recall who she might be.

"Is your captain a modest man?" she asked Ready, and when Ready shrugged, not certain what Josh Thurlow was when it came to being naked in front of nuns, she said to one of her fella boys, "Valuta, you have lava-lava for this one fella?"

Valuta, who was young, handsome, oiled, and tattooed like all the other native men, smiled fondly at her and unrolled a palm frond mat, which held, among other things, a bolt of cloth and a pair of scissors. He sized Josh up, then cut the cloth, which was red with a pattern of green flowers, and Sister Mary Kathleen wrapped it around Josh's waist. "There," she said, finishing the knot that held it in place. "Yer in fashion for these latitudes."

Josh had not been much concerned about his nakedness, but he was very hungry and said so. Sister Mary Kathleen brought him chunks of fish, which the fella boys caught in copious numbers simply by tossing out a string and a baited hook. The fish was grilled on a little kerosene stove, which was also used to boil rice in a tin pot. Josh ate it all, fish and rice, and drank water and felt renewed. For the remainder of the evening, he ate, then slept, then woke, and ate and drank again. Come morning, he was capable of voicing two questions, both to the nun: "What is my condition?" and "Who are you?"

She leaned against the thwart opposite him, her white cotton habit rustling in the breeze, and considered his questions, answering the second first. "Well, Captain, I am Sister Mary Kathleen, of the Order of the Sacred Blood. We are an Irish order, dedicated to the sustenance of mankind, and have outposts in the Pacific."

"Is this the first time we've met, Sister?"

"Nay. I first met ye on Betio, beside a sand fortress. One of me fella boys died saving yer life. Do ye recall such?"

Josh nodded that he did recall such, indeed. "I regret your fella boy took that sword for me. He said I was his brother."

"Tomoru was a brave man," she replied.

"But I also recall you and I argued. I thought you were a devil."

She held out the sides of her habit, then raised the rosary on her cincture. "As you can see, I am but a wee Irish nun."

He squinted at her. "Not more than nineteen years old, neither."

"I'm twenty-four, but thank ye," she answered, smiling shyly. "As to yer injuries, here is an accounting: Ye have a terrible bruised rib on yer left side with a bad scrape, yer left bicep has an infected wound, quite deep, and there would be a three-inch gash in yer back, also infected. Yer right knee is swollen, I think there's a piece of jagged metal in it, and there's another small wound on the back of yer neck, which is healing, thank God. And this and that, here and there, else. To be honest, though yer fever has broke, I still give ye no better than an even chance to live, considering the infections and your general health."

"An honest assessment. I'll take them odds," Josh said and then pushed up on his elbows to have a look about. "Did we win?" he asked, grimacing due to his bruised ribs. "At Tarawa, I mean?"

Ready moved so his captain could see him. "I'm pretty sure we did, sir. The Japanese were all about dead when we left. A lot of them killed themselves."

Josh took on a grim aspect. "They are brave soldiers, but too brave in my estimation. They indulge in frontal assaults, and when those fail, as they invariably do, they kill themselves. Let us hope they keep the same philosophy throughout the war, for if they do, we shall surely win it."

"I came across one of them, just before he blew his head off," Ready advised. "I think he was a fisherman."

"A double waste, then." Josh made to look about but failed since his neck was stiff. "Are we alone?"

"There are four outriggers, including ourselves," the nun answered, "with four of my fella boys on each, although 'tis but the bones of Tomoru on one of them. We are carrying him home for burial."

"Where's home?"

"The Forridges. Some call them the Far Reaches."

Josh absorbed that information, then asked, "Why am I here?"

"Because Colonel Burr sent you."

Josh was sure he must have heard the nun wrong. "Colonel Burr sent me? Why?"

"Because he knew I needed a big man who could convince the Japanese to surrender."

"What Japanese?"

"The ones in the Far Reaches, of course," she answered, her eyes honest and wide.

Josh feared he was still in one of his fever-addled dreams. He eyed the tattooed man who was managing the sheet with his big toe. "You there. Captain of the outrigger. What name belong you?"

Nango, startled by the sudden demand, frowned at Josh but answered, "Nango. What name belong you?"

"Josh Thurlow. But you might know me as Jahtalo."

"Jahtalo," Nango mused, then nodded. "Yes. I know Jahtalo. Cabum boy *Bad-sheba*."

Josh smiled. "Nango, tell me, is this a dream?"

Nango laughed. "No, Jahtalo. This belong here-now, not spirit place."

Sister Mary Kathleen was astonished at the exchange. "You and Nango have met before?"

Josh arranged his thoughts, then told his story. "When I was just a pup, I spent a year in these waters as cabin boy on a two-masted trading schooner named the *Bathsheba*. The old girl often visited the Forridges. Nango's daddy, as I recall, is chief of Ruka. Namu, that were his name. Right, Nango?"

Nango's mouth turned down and tears flooded his big brown eyes. "Daddy Namu all finish. Japonee all finish daddy Namu."

"Colonel Yoshu murdered all the native leaders on Ruka," Sister Mary Kathleen explained.

"Colonel Yoshu?"

"The commander of the Japanese."

Josh shook his head. "Sister, let me catch up. Do the Japanese occupy the Far Reaches?"

"Only Ruka," she answered, "which is the seat of government, as I suppose you know."

"And pray tell me again what you want me to do?"

"I want you to tell Colonel Yoshu to surrender."

"Sister, no Japanese commander is going to surrender."

"That's what Colonel Burr said, but if you told Colonel Yoshu the situation, that the Americans had taken Tarawa, I think he might listen."

"How would I tell him anything? Go in with a white flag? He'd have my head off in an instant."

"I will go with you if you're afraid," she said with her chin up.

Josh studied the little nun, then said, "You're damn right I'm afraid, Sister. Anybody in their right mind would be afraid!"

She lowered her chin and struggled with her temper. "We can talk about this later, perhaps." She rose and moved to the bow, where dolphins were playing.

Josh looked after the nun, then groaned when he tried to move.

"Can I do anything for you, sir?" Ready inquired.

"Yes, turn this boat around. I recall now that I tried to murder Colonel Burr. I need to go back and finish the job."

"I can't do that, sir. Only Sister can, I reckon."

"Nango, good fella boy!" Josh called. "Take me back to Tarawa. I pay you many Yankee dollah."

Nango smiled. "No, Jahtalo. We go Far Reaches."

Josh, too tired to press an argument he knew he was going to lose, lay back and squinted into the cloudless sky. He felt a sudden wave of sadness wash over him, and he saw anew the faces of the dead men on Tarawa. "I could use that drink of water, Bosun," he said to Ready, "if it wouldn't be too much trouble."

"No trouble at all, sir," Ready answered and went to the water barrel while Josh kept studying the sky until he realized who or what he was looking for. He had recalled seeing an ancient bird, the Killakeet pelican named Purdy, floating above a sand fort on Tarawa. Surely that had been a feverish dream, but dreams and truth seemed to be mixed up in his mind. All he knew was that he was very tired. When Ready brought a wooden cup to him, Josh drank the cool water and then sank back on his mat, determined to think things through and figure it all out. Instead, he was very nearly instantly into a dreamless sleep, resting up for what he did not know or could scarce imagine.

2 3

Just as Colonel Burr had predicted, the sea air proved to be something of a tonic for Josh, although Ready's sulfa might have had something to do with it, along with the nun's tender care. Soon Josh's wounds had ceased festering and the yellow pus drained away, though his ribs still ached and the scabs across his body were itchy and his right knee was stiff. He felt something hard moving beneath the skin at the base of the knee and suspected the nun was right—there was a piece of shrapnel lodged there. He decided to leave it alone in the hope that it might work itself out over time. If people left most hard and difficult things alone, he thought, they might all work themselves out. Josh, however, could not take his own advice. He borrowed Nango's knife and, at night when most were asleep, dug out the piece of steel, which proved to be a fragment oddly shaped like the hull of a boat. In fact, it reminded him of his old cutter, the *Maudie Jane*. Nango wrapped a turn of wire about it and fashioned a necklace for Josh. The nun admonished him for his surgery and said his digging around his knee with a dirty knife was surely the final blow to his health, but the wound healed quickly, though the knee remained stiff.

Josh turned to fishing. With only a hand line, he caught a tuna and an albacore, both of which Ready chopped up for him, and he ate them raw while smacking his lips and rubbing his belly to the amusement of Nango and the fella boys. "You boys wouldn't happen to have any Mount Gay rum in this rig, would you?" he asked, making them laugh all the more.

"Jahtalo fine fella," Nango announced, and all the fella boys nodded their heads in agreement. They thought the big white man was a fine fella, indeed, since he could catch fish, which was the measurement of any man in the Far Reaches.

Josh's recovery was further expressed in his interest in the outrigged ca-noe that was carrying them across the great emptiness. "These outriggers are marvelous boats!" he exclaimed to Ready. "They go out on the open water for hundreds of miles and through mighty storms even though all they are is just tree limbs and grass. They ain't sturdy, you see, so much as they give and take with the sea."

Hearing Josh's comment, Sister Mary Kathleen came near and said, "I have seem them build one, and, faith, they are all atwitter, with gangs of men come round to offer advice and lend a hand and drink kava. 'Tis a grand social occasion, it is."

"I'm sure you were all agog at the sight, Sister," Josh replied, suddenly in a foul mood. He was irritated that the nun had interrupted him while he was trying to educate Bosun O'Neal, and he also resented her for kidnap-ping him. "Tell me again why you're taking me to the Far Reaches," he de-manded.

She sat beside Nango, who smiled affectionately at her. "As I explained, sor, I need a big man to convince the Japanese on Ruka island to surrender."

"Did Colonel Burr understand this idiocy to be the case?"

"Faith, I'm not certain what he understood! All I know is that he seemed to have something against ye, though he never said what it was."

Josh replied, "I guess his latest reason is because I tried to kill him, though it was only with a little shovel. Now, Sister, here's what I have to say. Turn this outrigger around and take me back to Tarawa. You have shang-haied me, which is against international law. Otherwise, I shall see you stood up in a proper court and sent to prison."

The nun produced a faint smile. "That I cannot do, Captain. Nango, all my fella boys, are anxious to return home and *toot sweet.*"

"You should be careful using that expression, ma'am," Josh growled. "It reminds me too much of Montague Burr. Now, do you have a plan for sur-vival when we reach the Far Reaches? Or shall we simply turn ourselves in to the Japanese and lay our heads on the chopping block?"

Sister Mary Kathleen knew she was being baited and remained calm. "I had hoped for enough Americans to simply march ashore on Ruka and make Colonel Yoshu surrender. Since I only have you, Bosun O'Neal, and three marines, a different approach is required. I think we will first go to Burubu, some thirty miles west of Ruka. There is a village there that will take us in. Then I will send one of my fella boys to Ruka, and under the cover of darkness, he will tack a message on Colonel Yoshu's door. It will tell him the Americans have taken Tarawa and also inform him that you, an

American official, are in the islands to negotiate his surrender. If he agrees, he will lower the flag in front of his headquarters. My fella boy can bring us his answer. What do you think?"

"I think his more likely reaction will be to track me down and cut out my liver."

"Colonel Yoshu isn't like other Japanese. At heart, he is a coward."

"How do you know that?"

"I was his prisoner for over a year. So were me fella boys. We escaped together."

Josh absorbed that information. "Well, Sister," he said, "your plan has more holes in it than Swiss cheese. Let's look at things another way. Maybe the best course is to do nothing."

"Nothing is not a course at all," she pointed out.

Josh shrugged, which hurt his ribs, and he visibly winced. "In this case, I think it is. Now that we've taken Tarawa, the Far Reaches will be within range of our bombers. My guess is Colonel Yoshu will be ordered to evacuate. All you have to do is wait until he leaves, which shouldn't be all that long."

"But if he leaves . . ." she began, then pressed her lips together, sealing a thought.

"Yes?"

"I was hoping . . ." But then she looked away and said nothing.

Josh pondered the nun for a long second, then said, "Sister, I can't figure you out." He turned to Ready. "Did I just hear Sister say there are three marines with us?"

"Three marines, yes, sir."

"You should have informed me, Bosun. I'm surprised at your inattention to detail."

"I guess I had other things on my mind."

Josh allowed a sigh, then turned to the nun. "You're dismissed, ma'am. The bosun and I have military affairs to discuss. I'll let you know if I need to talk to you further."

"I will not be shooed away with a wave of yer big hand, Captain," Sister replied. "I lead this expedition, after all."

"I thought pride was a big sin in your religion," Josh teased.

"Clearly, 'tisn't in yers," she snapped before rising and going forward, her habit billowing in the breeze, to lean on the stem and glare at the sea.

"God save me from all women," Josh muttered, then wished for just a sip of Mount Gay rum, as he always did when he'd been rattled by a female.

"That was disrespectful, sir," Ready said. "The way you talked to the sister."

"Stop taking her side, Bosun. That's an order."

"She saved my life, Captain. Yours, too."

Josh snorted, which hurt his ribs again. He put his hand on them, which made them hurt all the more. Bruised ribs were a terrible nuisance. "She shanghaied me, that's what she did," he said after the pain subsided. "Some women think they can presume control over the affairs of men, but that's not the way the world is set up, Bosun, not by a long shot, and thank God for it. That little Irish nun needs to be set back a pace, in my opinion. And didn't I tell you to bring me those marines?"

"You did, sir."

"Well?"

"I was waiting for you to finish your pissing and moaning." He waited a disrespectful second before adding, "Sir."

Josh glared at Ready, then said tightly, "I'm finished. Now get me those leathernecks, son. And *toot sweet*, you hear?"

2 4

Toot sweet, as quickly as possible, the captains moved their outriggers along-side, and the marines were transferred aboard Nango's boat. Although Garcia wore his utilities, proper for reporting, Tucker and Sampson brazenly wore lava-lavas, though they still had on their combat boots. Josh made no comment on their dress but asked the marines to tell him their outfits, which they did, and their experiences on Tarawa, which caused them to hem and haw just a bit before Tucker told it, only exaggerating a little.

"That Major Reed was surely a hero," Josh replied with some astonishment after Tucker finished describing how the officer called in naval artillery on what was apparently a Japanese admiral. "He might have won us the battle right there. What became of him?"

"I dunno, sir," Tucker said while Ready hid his blush and looked off into the distance. "He just kind of disappeared. Likely got killed."

Then Tucker told how they'd been grabbed by the gunny and all that transpired until Sister Mary Kathleen had rescued them, just in the nick of time. "We're surely glad to be off them pohunky islands," he said, to wrap up his tale.

Josh said, "Tucker, I do believe you're a Hatteras boy. Am I right?"

"Yes, sir. And I know you're the Killakeet Keeper's son. My daddy is a fisherman, of course. Works mostly on the *Cathy Dove,* which is a right fine shad boat."

"I know her," Josh acknowledged. "A bit weak in the braces but otherwise a fine sailer."

"That would be her, for sartain."

"Well, you boys did a swell job, and I know the Corps is justly proud of you."

"Mostly, they probably wonder where we are," Garcia piped up. "Where are we, sir?"

"We're northeast of Tarawa, though how far out I don't know, and I doubt these fella boys know, either. They don't navigate like white men, wondering about miles and such. They use the stars and the sun to keep going in generally the right direction, figuring sooner or later they'll get where they're headed, which in this case is an island group known as the Forridges. Some call them the Far Reaches, and justly so. They ain't on normal trading routes. I guess you could say they're on the far end of nowhere."

"But why are we going there, sir?" Tucker asked. "Shouldn't we go back to Tarawa?"

"Indeed we should. But that little nun there on the bow pretending not to be listening has kidnapped us."

The three marines stared at Sister Mary Kathleen. "How come?" Sampson demanded.

Josh considered an answer, dismissed one that was sarcastic, then said, "She has a good reason, I suppose. The Japanese have occupied Ruka, which is the capital of those islands. She wants us to make them surrender."

"Surrender? That don't make sense. If they're anything like those bastards on Tarawa, giving up ain't in their nature."

"Indeed," Josh said, nodding agreement.

"Are we deserters?" Sampson asked. "When they call the roll and we don't answer, they're going to think we're deserters, ain't they?"

"Maybe. But as long as you stay with me and do exactly what I tell you when I tell you to do it, they likely won't hang you."

The marines looked at each other, and Tucker spoke for all. "But you're Coast Guard, ain't you, sir? Marines don't usually take orders from the toy boat navy, beg pardon, sir."

"Didn't you take orders from Bosun O'Neal?"

"That was different. We knew him."

"Well, now you know me. Take my orders or I'll toss you overboard and let the sharks have you."

The marines gave Josh's eloquent argument some thought, noticed his big ham hands and bulging arm muscles, and then said, nearly in unison, "Happy to be aboard, sir!"

"Good. To celebrate your joining the toy boat navy, you're all promoted one rank."

Sampson perked up. "Thanks, sir. I could use the extra pay."

"This kind of promotion don't come with extra pay, son. You've got a brevet rank, which means it's only good for as long as you're with me."

Sampson frowned. "Well, hell, sir, why don't you make me a general, then?"

Josh smiled. "Let's see how you do as a corporal first."

After the marines were transferred back to their respective outriggers, Josh thought things over some more, then asked the nun to join him. "Sister, I suppose I should know a few things. For instance, how many Japanese do you think are on Ruka?"

"I believe about a hundred, Captain."

"A full company, then. How are they armed?"

"Rifles and pistols. Some machine guns, I think."

"Boats?"

"They have two vessels that look like your box-shaped landing craft, only bigger. I believe they called them *daihatsu*."

"They're called barges, Sister. Used to transport their soldiers and supplies. Daihatsu is the company that manufactures them. By the way, how good is your Japanese?"

"Fair, I would say. The fella boys know a few words as well. It is natural to learn the language of one's captors."

Josh nodded. "All right, Sister. Thank you. Now, here is my decision. You have carried me off on a suicide mission, but I have decided not to participate. As soon as we get to the Far Reaches and let you and your fella boys off, I intend to take one of these outriggers, load up my marines and Bosun O'Neal, and head back to Tarawa." When she opened her mouth to argue, he snapped, "That's all, Sister!"

Sister Mary Kathleen struggled with her temper, her face flushed with the effort, then said, with her eyes downcast, "As you wish, Captain." She gathered her habit and climbed inside the hut on the stern.

Ready started to protest, but Josh held up his finger. "Not a word, Bosun. She needed a dose of reality. Maybe you do, too, eh?"

Inside the hut, Sister Mary Kathleen knelt before the statue of the Virgin and kissed the medal of her order and then sat down, cross-legged beneath the folds of her habit. Her lips pursed petulantly and she thought several dark thoughts about Captain Josh Thurlow in sequence; then she heard the man laugh his crude laugh. She poked her head outside and saw that he'd taken Nango's seat and was controlling the sail, a great grin creasing what seemed to her now a mostly apelike face. *Who does he think he is, this grand Josh Thurlow?* she thought. Then she closed the hatch on her hut and shut her eyes tight against the bright light filtering through the bamboo lattice and begged forgiveness to Saint Monessa for allowing her anger to overcome her studied humility. She gave herself a penance, and it was to humble herself in some way to Captain Thurlow, *even if he is a big, foolish gorilla, excuse me, Saint Monessa!*

Then she heard Nango call out something in an excited voice. She popped out to see what it was and saw that the mighty, great Captain Thurlow had handed the sheet back to Nango and was now on the bow, peering forward. Bosun O'Neal was with him, also staring intently. "What is it?" she demanded.

"It's the marine, Sampson," Bosun O'Neal said. "He's gotten himself eaten by a shark."

2 5

It was a small tiger shark, Josh was fairly certain, probably a loner just out to see if he could find an easy meal. Through Josh's mind ran the number of times he'd caught sharks off Killakeet. They had once been a cash catch on the island, the cannery processing vitamin A from their livers, but around 1932, synthetic vitamins began to be produced, and the demand for sharks collapsed. Afterward, they were considered trash fish that competed with the fishermen for their catch. But Josh had always respected them. He recalled a lemon shark he'd hooked down by Ocracoke Shoals. When he'd reeled it in close to the transom, it had suddenly gone berserk, frantically twisting and turning its body and rolling its baleful eyes toward Josh until finally he'd cut the line. With a single flick of its tail, the shark was gone, just vanished with scarcely a swirl of bubbles left behind. Sharks were powerful and wild and free and always hungry, and until they were dead, they were going to do whatever they wanted to do, which meant, when they weren't making baby sharks, devouring anything edible they encountered.

Sampson had been trailing his foot in the water. It seemed he had been hiding a puncture in the sole of his left foot. When it had gotten so swollen he had to take off his boot, he had been astonished at how awful the wound looked and felt. Thinking to clean it, he hung off the side of the outrigger and immersed his gory foot in the sea. Within seconds, the shark had come up and taken a bite out of it, removing several toes and shredding the flesh, leaving the metatarsals exposed.

"Does it hurt much, Sampson?" Josh asked, as tenderly as he was able.

"Like it's on fire, sir. But I can take the pain."

"Aye, sure, 'tis a given for a marine," Sister Mary Kathleen said.

Josh got down to cases. "It would have been better if the shark had bitten off more than it did. In any case, it did you a favor, because now we can see what you've been hiding. You have gangrene, son."

Sampson gulped. "Am I to lose my foot, Captain?"

"No, my boy. If you are to live, we'll have to take off your leg."

Sampson stared at Josh, then lay back. After a long second, he asked, "Sister, is the captain telling the truth?"

"Aye, Sampson," she answered. " 'Tis true. Ye'll die otherwise."

"My whole leg?"

"I think a few inches below the knee will suffice."

"Isn't there another way?"

"Nay, Sampson. I'm sorry."

"How about just my foot?" he begged.

She gave it some thought. "Maybe. 'Twould be risky. Better to cut too high than too low."

Josh barged in. "For God's sake, stop coddling him, Sister! Now, look, Sampson. You brought this all on yourself. You let your foot fester in your boot, kept it to yourself, and it took a shark to call it to our attention. This ain't up for a vote. We're going to take off everything up to a couple inches below your knee and you're going to lie there and take it like a marine. That's an order."

"Oh, do be quiet, Captain Thurlow!" Sister Mary Kathleen snapped. " 'Tis Sampson's leg, not yers!" She touched the marine's cheek. "Choose, me boy. Open your heart to God and He will tell ye what to do."

"I'm Jewish, Sister," Sampson said.

"God doesn't care what ye are, lad. Choose!"

Sampson nodded, then closed his eyes, his brow furrowed in thought. "Sampson," Josh said, "I think you and God should hurry up and decide, else we'll lose the light."

"Will you do the cutting, Sister?" Sampson asked, opening his eyes.

"I'll do it," Josh said.

Sister Mary Kathleen raised her head as if to argue, then nodded her consent. She knew such surgery, considering the tools available, required more physical strength than she had.

"Ready, let me see your K-bar," Josh said. The bosun complied, and Josh considered its edge. "Nango? Do you have a whetstone on board? Sharpee? Whoosh! Whoosh!"

Nango searched among the canoe's various dilly bags until he produced a thoroughly worn whetstone. Josh handed him the knife. "Sharpen it up, Nango. Savvy? I need an edge like a razor. Then boil it good. Ten minutes at least with a hard boil. Sister, needle and thread, there's surely some aboard. You have such for your habit? Very good. And Ready? I'll want some sulfa powder from your medical kit, if you have any left."

"I used all I had on you, sir."

"How about morphine?" Josh demanded. "I'll need two syrettes at least."

"Those I have, sir," Ready replied.

"So you're really to do it, sir?" Sampson asked, gulping back his fear.

"Ease your mind, son," Josh said with a confident smile. "Back when you were a pup, I did the odd amputation of legs now and again on the Bering Sea Patrol, and nearly every one of my patients survived. Hell, somebody had to do it when the doc wasn't around, and as the lowest-ranking officer, it fell to me. But I'm not going to lie to you, Sampson. I ain't no New York surgeon. It may come out looking a little rough, but I promise to do my best."

"Then say me a prayer, Sister," Sampson said. "Say me a *big* prayer."

She smiled at him. "I will say many prayers for ye, Sampson."

"Will you say one now, I mean out loud? I'd like to hear it."

After a bit of thinking, she nodded, and all on board lowered their heads, except Ready, who took the opportunity to push a syrette of morphine into Sampson's shoulder. The sea and air murmured a quiet song syncopated by the steady rhythm of Nango polishing the edge of the K-bar blade as Sister Mary Kathleen prayed, "God of all things, great and small. Hear me prayer for your servant, Sampson. Though we sail through the tempest, even to the far reaches, keep our wits about us as we engage in this surgery. Let Captain Thurlow's mind be clear, his hand strong. Let him do that which must be done with skill and care. And please give Corporal Sampson the strength and resilience of his youth and the courage of his assembly, the United States Marine Corps. Do these things, we ask, in thy Son's name. Amen."

"Right pretty, Sister," Sampson said as if from far away.

"Jesus was a Jew," she said. "He came to fulfill yer people's destiny."

"That was good of him," Sampson replied sleepily, his veins coursing with morphine.

"Sampson, I'll ask you again," Josh said. "What's it to be? Below the knee or just the foot?"

"Just the foot, sir. Thank you."

Josh took Sister Mary Kathleen, Ready, and Nango aside. "A knife like a K-bar, even with an edge, is barely useful as a cutting tool. It's going to be tough getting it through the bone, and I fear all the crunching might bring the boy awake. He must be held down."

Nango said, "Fella boys hold. No worry-worry, Jahtalo."

The fella boys placed two sturdy breadfruit planks (the outrigger was astonishingly well supplied with odds and ends) across the gunwales, shoving them together to make a makeshift table. Sampson was laid across it; then Sister Mary Kathleen washed the marine's infected foot and leg, using the copra soap Nango produced from yet another dilly bag.

Josh studied the afflicted foot from several angles. "What's your opinion, Sister?"

"Me opinion is that a Coast Guard officer has no business cutting off a man's foot, but here we are and there ye are."

Josh laughed. "I told a little lie, Sister. I never cut a man's leg off before, although I did have to amputate a man's arm once upon a time. It was one of Colonel Burr's marines on the old *Comanche*."

"Is that what started yer argument with the colonel?"

"It didn't help it. But our main contention was we fell in love with the same woman, the fairest maiden ever to walk across the tundra. God, how I loved her. I even married her."

"Faith. The poor girl. What became of her?"

Josh looked away, into the emptiness of life and its equal fullness. "She was murdered. It's a long story."

"I should be pleased to hear it, though I suspect 'tis not the time."

"No, Sister," Josh answered forthrightly. " 'Tis the time to cut off a man's leg."

"His foot only, if ye please."

"Aye, aye, ma'am. His foot only it is, and God help Sampson for having such a poor surgeon."

"Well, at least he will have a good nurse," she answered with a shy smile. "Now raise yer knife, Captain, and let us get about today's work."

And so they did.

Sampson came awake in the night, and Sister Mary Kathleen held the lamp so Josh could inspect him while Ready watched from the shadows. "All's well, Sampson," Josh told the boy, who was staring at him with owl's eyes, still dilated from the morphine.

"How much did you take off, sir?"

"Just the foot, as you said."

"I hope it wasn't too much trouble."

"No trouble at all. You have soft bones, Private. It's all that easy living you marines practice."

Sampson blinked a couple of times. "I thought I was a corporal," he noted.

"I demoted you for letting yourself get gangrene."

"I'm glad. The responsibility of rank was wearing me down." Sampson looked up at the nun, whose expression, by the light of the lantern, was one of quiet joy. "Thank you, Sister. I know you had a big part in this mess."

"I just mopped up a bit. Now, sleep a bit more, why don't ye?"

"Aye, aye, ma'am. I feel like I could sleep a hundred years."

Josh and the nun watched over Sampson until he began to breathe easier and they knew he was asleep. "You did well, Sister," Josh said in honest admiration.

Sister Mary Kathleen was tired but pleased at the result of their labors. She smiled up at Josh, thanking him with her smile and her eyes. Hidden in the shadows, Ready was astonished when she said, "Ye are a good man, Captain Thurlow, at least when ye put yer mind to it."

"Why, thank you, ma'am. I've always loved a backhanded compliment."

"Sampson not finish?" Nango asked from his steering position at the mast.

"Sampson not finish," Josh replied proudly.

"Sampson not finish," Ready muttered under his breath in mockery. "Ye are a good man, Captain Thurlow," he added, also mocking the nun. His expression hardened into petulant outrage. During the surgery, he had been given nothing to do besides being a spectator. Once he'd asked if he could help, but neither Josh nor Sister Mary Kathleen had even given him the courtesy of a reply. They were too busy, not with the surgery, in Ready's opinion, but flirting with each other. She had oh so tenderly mopped Josh's brow, then encouraged him when he'd hesitated, the big lug claiming to be nearly worn out from cutting through bone with the K-bar. In Ready's opinion, it had been nothing but butchery, and if Sampson lived, it wasn't anything the captain or the nun had done.

Nango was in high spirits. "Ah. Good fella Jahtalo!" he exclaimed. "You swoop swoop blade tumas good."

Josh nodded, accepting the compliment, then cocked his head to peer approvingly at the nun. Under his attention, she smiled at him again, and he responded with a big, thoroughly delighted grin. "All right, Nango," he said grandly. "Let us proceed now to the Far Reaches. Does that suit you, Sister?"

"Aye, it does, Captain, surely it does."

He laughed aloud. "Then, Nango, let's fly!"

And fly they did, Sister Mary Kathleen laughing gaily as the outrigger bounded crisply from wave to wave, and Josh grinning broadly beneath the great sail, his sandy brown hair ruffled by an eager breeze. Nango and the fella boys even broke into song, while Ready, having fallen asleep, was startled awake as he felt the first stirring of an awful jealousy.

PART IV

The Far Reaches

Out of the deep I call
To thee, O Lord, to thee.
Before thy throne of grace I fall;
Be merciful to me.

Out of the deep I cry,
The woeful deep of sin,
Of evil done in days gone by,
Of evil now within.

—HENRY WILLIAMS BAKER, A HYMN

2 6

It was seen two hours before dawn, a flickering glow that meant something was burning on the distant edge of the coal-black sea. Josh studied the trembling sliver of light while Nango worked the sails and called quietly to his fella boys to pull taut the lines and to move back from the bow and mind the pontoon. They complied, their wide eyes never leaving the thin glimmer toward which the outrigger was aimed. "Far Reaches belong this way," Nango said in a low voice meant for Josh.

"What think you?" Josh asked, his eyes riveted on the fire.

Nango wiped his face with his big hand and then peered at the quivering ember. "Island Burubu," he said reluctantly. "She burn."

Josh kept studying the yellow streak, trying to discern the size of the fire and what might be fueling it. It was not unknown for villages and the bush on Pacific islands to fall prey to accidental fire. An overturned kerosene lantern, a celebratory fire built too high during a kava-drenched ceremony, the jungle being burned off for farmland, there were any number of possibilities. Josh recalled now that when he'd been cabin boy on the trading schooner *Bathsheba,* he'd seen such glimmers in the night, and that had been in these very waters. More often than not, Captain Fairplay bypassed the burning islands and Josh never discovered what caused the flames. But he recalled the *Bathsheba* once anchoring in a lagoon before the smoking remnants of a village and the captain oddly chuckling at the sight. "Damn fools have burned themselves down again," he'd sworn. Josh, new to the Pacific then, had stared wide-eyed at the destruction, not a hut, house, or chicken coop left standing, and thought surely the village was doomed. But after going ashore, he saw that reconstruction was already well along, the people cheerfully working together to rebuild. "Like a phoenix rising from the ashes," Captain Fairplay had remarked, grinning and shaking his head at the foolishness of mankind in general.

Josh recalled those days, those comparatively untroubled, halcyon days, when he'd sailed aboard the *Bathsheba*. It was his father, Keeper Jack, who'd sent Josh to the Pacific to work for Fairplay, an old friend of the family. In the Keeper's opinion, such would provide his eldest son an opportunity to understand there was more to the sea, much more, than the Atlantic off the Outer Banks of North Carolina. Josh hadn't wanted to go, couldn't imagine being that far from Killakeet, but the Keeper wouldn't hear his objections and ordered him off on his adventure. It had proved to be a wondrous year even though it had ultimately seen Josh a victim of shipwreck. He'd survived, of course, and even though he'd been scared more than a few times during his stint along that tropical sea, he'd always been grateful to his father for making him go.

Josh rubbed his eyes, willing that the fire would prove to be an illusion, but when he looked again, the amber smear was still there with all its unhappy implications. Here he was, back in the waters of his youth, and he was older, but was he wiser? He had learned to kill and was immersed mentally and physically in a great war, but Josh doubted he had gained much wisdom in the process. He wished now, while studying that fire in the darkness, that he might have alongside him the mentors of his life, Captain Fairplay, Captain Falcon, and, of course, his father, the Keeper, so that he could ask them what he should do. *But perhaps,* he thought further, *they are here, and they are telling me their opinion, if I but listen.* Josh considered a truism that someone had told him somewhere, maybe even in a bar: that a good teacher never left his pupil, not really, and that the lessons were embedded, just waiting until they were required. Those old men, Josh thought with a sad smile, they had been the best teachers there were. *So what would you do?* he asked them, and sure enough, they answered, each in turn, Captains Fairplay and Falcon and the Keeper. Josh took a breath, fancying that he caught a whiff of smoke, then made his decision. "Pull down your sail, Nango," he said. "Whistle up the others to do the same. We'll wait for dawn before getting any closer."

"You're thinking Jap, sir?" Ready asked, hearing Josh's order and coming forward.

There was something in the bosun's tone that irritated Josh, perhaps because he'd just séanced with the great men of his life. "Well, Bosun," he growled, "I ain't thinking Germans or Italians."

Ready was thus rebuked, and it stung. Without comment, he helped the fella boys lower the sail, then sat down, his mind swamped with righteous indignation. Then he took stock. Ready was an honest man, usually, and recognized that Captain Thurlow was merely being his normal self, that is to say with his common tendency toward arrogance. So why, Ready asked himself, was the captain so bothersome? Ready searched for the source of his annoyance and then confessed to himself that it was surely jealousy. Ready was jealous that the nun seemed to be in awe of Josh Thurlow, even with all his dictatorial ways, while she had never expressed the slightest admiration for Ready himself. Ready's anger therefore crept toward the nun, for what was clearly bad judgment on her part. Not only did she have them all on a fool's errand, but she esteemed Captain Thurlow, who was, after all, nothing but a big bully, always had been, not to mention (*though somebody should!*) a lecher with a tendency toward drunkenness. Ready decided his best course was to be through with the both of them. They could admire each other, do anything together they wanted! Henceforth, he would do only what he was told, and the nun, well, she could go to hell! *I wish I was home,* Ready determined at the end of his internal rant. *If I ever make it back to Killakeet, I'll never leave it again.* Then he pulled up his knees and lowered his head onto them and tried to recall his mother's sweet face and forget Sister Mary Kathleen's pretty (but foolish) Irish mug.

Nango's whistles soon had the other outriggers to their bare poles, and the sea, free to exert its will, pushed them slowly down-current, away from the burning smear. With nothing to do, the fella boys sensibly laid themselves down and went to sleep. There was no sound from the nun's hut, so Josh assumed she slept as well. Ready apparently was also dozing, his head on his knees. Josh sat down and soon was fast asleep himself. Some hours later, he was wakened by a flying fish that had flung itself into the outrigger like a silver knife, landing at Ready's bare feet. The bosun awoke, picked up the fish, inspected it, and tossed it over his shoulder into the sea. Then he rose and came forward, yawning and stretching.

"I wonder what was chasing it?" Josh mused.

"Tuna maybe," Ready answered. "Good water for tuna, this."

"You were always the best fisherman of any of the boys," Josh said. "I recall it was almost like you could feel the fish in the water. It's a gift only a few men have." When Ready made no reply, just stood there, Josh briefly wondered if he had done or said anything to upset the bosun. He quickly concluded it was unlikely, Ready being the most sensible of fellows, and himself typically so evenhanded. So he asked, "What's your opinion of that fire, Bosun?"

"You want my opinion, sir? Maybe they're cooking copra. Or maybe there's a big celebration and that's their dancing fires."

"If that's your opinion," Josh replied, "you're dead wrong."

Ready shrugged. "Nothing new there, Captain. I can hardly remember when I was right, especially in your opinion."

Josh noted the bosun's grumpy reply and was moved to explain his position. "Those fires ain't right for copra. They'd be burning lower and more of a yellow coloration. I doubt anybody's dancing around them, neither. Too big. It's the war, and I don't see why you would say it's something else."

Ready was silent for a long second, then replied, "Maybe it's because this war don't make sense to me no more."

Josh was astonished at the bosun's declaration. "Have you forgotten Pearl Harbor?"

"No, sir. I haven't forgotten it, but I guess it's been cleaned up by now."

"Three thousand of our boys killed, a lot of them trapped underwater. There's no way that can ever be cleaned up."

"We just got a thousand more killed on Tarawa, sir, and I guess a couple of thousand bad wounded. Tell me what sense that makes."

"Don't be simple," Josh growled, then struggled to find a proper metaphor. "Say a man knocks down your door, shoots your kids, rapes your wife, loots your house. What do you do? Shake his hand? No, you fight and kill him even if you get knocked around doing it. That's what we're doing out here, fighting and killing the men who attacked us without warning. Sure, we're taking our lumps, but war makes as much sense as anything else when it needs to be done. So what's really going through your head, Bosun? Let's hear it."

"There's nothing in my head," Ready answered. "Nothing at all."

"Don't play the fool!" Josh snapped. He discovered he was truly angry. *Imagine! The war being questioned!*

"Captain, the problem with you is—oh, never mind. It's like talking to that flying fish I threw overboard."

Josh started to unleash a sharp rebuke, reminding Ready of his manners before a superior officer, but Nango interrupted the arguing Americans with a warning: "Jahtalo! Bo! Look-see!"

Josh and Ready looked and saw. A moving light, now two, appeared from the flaming glimmer, then moved steadily eastward. "Japanese barges heading to Ruka," Josh said. "I'd stake my life on it."

"We go Burubu now, Jahtalo?"

"No, Nango. We wait. If those are Japonee, I want to give them time to sail far away." Josh watched the moving lights a little longer, then turned to Ready to continue the argument, which he intended to turn into instruction and the bosun's return to discipline. He was disappointed when he saw that the bosun had gone to his sleeping place, pulled up his knees, and rested his head on them again. Josh watched him and tried to imagine what might be causing his ill humor. *It's that nun,* Josh concluded. *I think he wants her, but he'll never have her, so it's tearing him up inside.*

Satisfied that he had identified Ready's problem, Josh sat down to give it all a good think, to see if he could find a solution that would make the bosun happy and keep the peace between them. Six seconds later, he was fast asleep.

2 7

The sun bolted from the sea, startling Josh when it bore into his face like a white-hot barb. Shielding his eyes and rising with a deep ache in his right knee while unsuccessfully trying to recall what he'd been thinking about before he went to sleep, he looked at the sea, which stretched out before him, undulating and endless. The glow of the flames on the horizon he recalled now had vanished in the furious glare of the morning sun, replaced by a column of blue-gray smoke that rose crookedly against the clear sky. Josh was pleased to see that all the outriggers were still on their bare poles. Nango, dozing at the masthead, came suddenly awake, raising his big head and calling out, "We go Burubu now, Jahtalo?"

"Not yet," Josh answered, wishing with all his might for a cup of coffee. His mouth tasted like putty and his mind was befogged, surely a job for a fresh cup of java. Without hope, he asked Nango if he had any that he'd kept hidden.

"No, Jahtalo," Nango replied, grieving for the American in obvious need. "But I have tea."

Josh sighed. "Could you brew me a cup, then? Make it strong."

The other outrigger captains, hearing the voices, beseechingly began to hail: "Burubu, she burn! We go, Jahtalo!"

"Not yet!" Josh yelled at them as Nango busied himself with the little kerosene stove. Before long, the pot was bubbling, and not too many minutes afterward, Nango handed Josh a tin cup filled with tea, which proved to be hot and bitter but just the ticket.

"Nango!" the outrigger captains cried at random. "Jahtalo wrong! We go! We go!"

Nango turned away from them, his arms crossed, though his eyebrows were lifted significantly in Josh's direction. Then the captains started to call the nun, who had surreptitiously emptied her bedpan into the sea and then made her way to the bow. "Sister, we go! Sister, we go!"

From his position slumped before her hut, Ready, coming awake, watched Sister Mary Kathleen go by. *Who cares about you?* he thought, even while his heart was crying, *I do! I do!* His heart wailed a little more when he saw her smile at Captain Thurlow. He allowed himself to slide ever deeper into a jealous stew. The two fella boys sitting across from him nodded and smiled, polite young men that they were, and the one named Vanu wished him "a berry good morn." Ready replied "Good morning," and since he was a Kil-lakeeter, and it was the custom there, went on to comment on the weather. "A fine day, an easy breeze, a blue sky."

"Too much good, Bosun," Vanu replied. His smile broadened into a toothy grin, matching the one owned by the fella boy Kanu beside him. Ready discovered he was pleased to be in their company, though outwardly there could not be more differences between him and them. For he was pale and ugly, and they were brown-skinned, tattooed, uniformly handsome men with long, glistening black hair. Still, they were sailing men, just as he. For a moment, basking in their good natures, he managed to forget all about the nun and the ache in his heart.

On the bow, Sister Mary Kathleen sipped from the cup of tea Nango had handed her and asked, "Why do we wait, Captain?"

Josh explained his reasoning to her, pointed out the smoke that probably marked Burubu island, and said that the Japanese had possibly been sighted leaving and he wanted to give them plenty of time to be miles away. When the outrigger captains began to beg anew to let them put up their sails, she called in a sharp rebuke that it was necessary to wait. In response, they began to chant something ancient and not Christian, though they performed fer-vent signs of the cross across their tattooed chests. "They're surely worked up," Josh marveled.

"Everyone in the Far Reaches knows everyone else," she explained. "Though my fella boys are from Ruka, outriggers constantly go back and forth between the islands. There are also many celebrations throughout the year that cause all the people to gather as one."

"Yes, I remember," Josh replied. "There were no hungry people or or-phans in the Far Reaches. They shared what they had and took care of one and all."

She nodded toward the plume of smoke. "What do ye think we'll find on Burubu, Captain?"

"War, Sister."

"Aye," she replied sadly. "I fear yer right."

"This mad Colonel Yoshu you spoke of?"

"Faith, it's likely. You must make him surrender, Captain, I beg ye."

"You keep saying that. But, Sister, must I tell you again that the Japanese don't surrender? They prefer suicide before such dishonor."

She was not swayed. "I think Colonel Yoshu is cut from a different bolt of cloth."

Josh gave the nun's words some thought while he tapped his cup on the heavy breadfruit stem of the bow. "Maybe," he concluded, "but even if he's a coward, I doubt if he would surrender to a half-naked Coast Guard captain, a heartsick bosun, and three marines, one of them with but one foot. No, Sister. I pray your Colonel Yoshu doesn't catch us before I convince you to gather the people of the Far Reaches and evacuate to the Gilberts."

"I scarcely know what to pray for these days!" she suddenly confessed.

Josh's reply was immediate. "That the Americans beat Jap, and soon, Sister. Then all your problems will be solved."

She looked at him thoughtfully. "Not all," she said after a moment.

Then she started to say something else, and Josh could almost see the wheels turning in her head, but at the end of her internal argument, whatever it was, she chose to stay silent. It seemed to Josh she had just come close to revealing a secret, though it was a secret he chose not to pursue, a greater matter taking precedence. For now he had an island to visit, and perhaps another battle to fight, and men he might yet have to kill. Captain Falcon rose in his mind to speak and chose a battle cry: *Strive into battle, boys! Strive and bludgeon, and heaven be damned.* It was the shout the captain gave his men just before he drove his cutter alongside a pirate whaler. "So be it," Josh said to his old skipper, who grinned his rough grin down the years.

"What did ye say, Captain?" the nun asked.

"Nothing, Sister," Josh replied, though he tipped the wink to the captain's spirit. "Nothing at all."

2 8

Past noon and, having failed to see anything further of the Japanese barges if, indeed, that's what the moving lights were, Josh told Nango to raise his sail and head toward the island. As soon as the other outrigger captains saw Nango's sail go up on the poles, they quickly raised their sails, too. The breeze, a spirited one, fluffed out the patched canvas, and soon the outriggers were skimming across a tossing sea.

Sister Mary Kathleen stood beside Nango, her habit filled with the wind like an extra sail. Ready, unable to restrain himself, stepped up beside her. "Good morning, Sister," he said, nearly simpering. "Are you well this morning?"

"Well enough, Bosun," she replied, "though I long to put me feet on the sweet sand of the Far Reaches. I do love these islands so. The people here have lovely souls, y'see."

"It's you who has the lovely soul," Ready said before he could stop himself.

"'Tis kind of ye to think so," she said in an uncertain tone.

Though he knew he should have left well enough alone, Ready barged on. "Ma'am, what's your opinion of Captain Thurlow?"

She smiled into the wind, and her cheeks flushed pink. "I think he is a rough surgeon."

"You like him, is that it?" he demanded.

The threatening tone of his voice surprised her. "I like him well enough. So do ye, I presume. When we first met, he was yer only concern. Bosun, are ye angry with your captain, for some reason?"

"No, ma'am," Ready replied before slinking off to the stern to mope. "A fool often speaks foolishness, that's all."

Confused but with more important matters at hand, Sister Mary Kathleen sent up a prayer for the bosun, then turned toward Burubu.

Another hour passed, the sun climbing higher in the sky, and the island, its silhouette low and rounded like a loaf of bread, could be better discerned through the smoky haze. A mile closer and Josh could make out that some trees on it were burning, but the main fire, the one that was producing the crooked column of greasy black smoke, was coming from the western tip, where Nango said the main village was located. Then people, many people, were seen lying on the beach, and Josh's heart sank. "Anchor in the shallows," Josh advised Nango. "No need to rough up the bottoms of your outriggers. We can wade in and see what's what."

Nango ignored Josh and kept the sail of his outrigger filled. His fella boys even took up their paddles and drew vigorously at the sea, grunting with each stroke, until the outrigger plowed into the beach. The two other outriggers landed hard beside it, their crews already wailing in anguish at what awaited them. Josh estimated that about fifty men, women, and children lay in the sand. After a quick inspection, the fella boys began to slap themselves on their chests and faces. A few stomped on shells and used the resulting broken edges to cut themselves along their hairlines until blood ran down their faces. "Stop that!" Josh yelled at them, but they would not be stayed. A couple of them even began to scream, and if their wails were meant to wake the dead, Josh thought they might succeed.

"Stay on board," Josh told Sister Mary Kathleen, and she responded by pulling up the hem of her habit and swinging nimbly over the side of the outrigger and splashing ashore. Josh reflected that he might command this odd company, but certainly he was not much in control of it.

"Come now," the nun called to Nango and the others, staying an arm holding a sharp shell here and a fist pounding a chest there. "Help me to look them all over. Perhaps someone is alive. Perhaps a child . . ."

Her fella boys, their eyes pleading to the nun, stopped torturing themselves long enough to accomplish her bidding. They knelt in the sand and touched the bodies with great tenderness, placing their ears to silent lips and unbeating hearts, then wailing anew as each death was confirmed. They even took some of the bodies into their arms and pressed them close, rocking with them while weeping torrents of tears.

Ready, Tucker, and Garcia came up on the beach and stood beside Josh, watching the proceedings with various expressions of astonishment and compassion. "How's Sampson?" Josh asked, just to change the subject.

"He's OK, sir," Tucker replied, "but he said his stump itches something awful."

"That means it's healing. Tell him not to scratch it, no matter how much it itches. Now, listen, boys, while these fella boys are distracted, I want you to go into the outriggers and search around under the mats and tucked up under the thwarts and take off any rifles, pistols, grenades, and ammunition you find. I think they took quite a lot of ordnance off Tarawa. Bundle it all up and put it in Nango's canoe where I can keep an eye on it. Take Sampson off, too. Lay him out on the beach just down there, away from these poor souls. Place him on a mat and tell him to let his stump air out a bit. After you do all that, arm yourselves and report back to me. We'll have a look around. And be on guard. The gents who did this might still be here. They could be watching us, even now."

Ready and the marines went off to do his bidding, and Josh approached Sister Mary Kathleen. "A terrible thing, Sister," he said.

"Aye," she answered, "but God says he knows when even a sparrow falls. I trust these people are with Him in paradise."

"Do you really believe that?"

"Yes, I believe it. Whether it is true or not, only God knows."

There was little Josh could reply to that, so, with the fella boys, he helped to gather the bodies, placing them together in a long row on the grass behind the beach. "They will dig a common grave," she told Josh, nodding toward Nango and the others. "I would imagine there are shovels in the village."

"There's likely to be more bodies, too," Josh replied, and she nodded sad agreement.

Tucker, Garcia, and Ready returned from their chores, the marines with Japanese rifles and Ready carrying an M-1 Garand. They were back in their utilities and boots. Grenades hung from their belts, and their pockets were stuffed with ammunition. They nearly looked like proper American fighting men. "We stowed a few rifles in Nango's outrigger," Ready reported, "but we couldn't put everything in there. You wouldn't believe all the weaponry in those canoes. These fella boys policed up a ton of stuff, that's for sartain. They even packed up some Jap machine guns and a pile of ammo to go with them. It's a miracle the outriggers haven't sunk under all that gear."

"Don't let them play with any of it," Josh replied. "They'll only get themselves hurt. Now, let's scout the village. Tucker and Garcia, you take up the flanks. Ready, you wait down here on the beach with the sister and the fella boys and try to keep them out of trouble, best you can."

"Aye, aye, Skipper," the marines chorused, and off they went with Josh toward the village while Ready waited protectively beside Sister Mary Kathleen as she silently prayed over a dead baby. The bosun cleared his throat and said, "Maybe you ought to wait at the boats, Sister. It'll be safer if there are any Japanese about."

She raised her head. "And why would I care to be safe?" she demanded. "And where are Captain Thurlow and the marines off to without me?"

"The village," Ready replied, ignoring her harsh tone. "You are to wait here until they return."

"I must see what I must see," she said, rising.

"It might not be pretty," Ready advised, taking her arm.

She roughly pulled away. "Unhand me! I did not take up my vocation to see pretty things!"

He reached out for her again. "I know that, but—"

"Bosun O'Neal!" she snapped. "It is not right for ye to touch me. Surely ye must know that!"

Ready felt his heart tearing itself to pieces. "I was just trying to help."

"Ye'll help most by remembering always who and what I am!"

With a flip of her habit, Sister Mary Kathleen turned away and walked up the path to the village. Ready followed her at a discreet distance, his mind in turmoil and sorrow.

Along the path, nothing moved, nothing lived. All was death. Five more bodies were found, three without their heads. Mary Kathleen knelt and said a prayer over each. In the village, there was more devastation and murder. Every house was burned, every pot shattered, every canoe stove in. Bodies lay strewn about. Some of the people were shot, most bayoneted, and their frozen postures told individual stories of horror. Terrible bruising of the women's genitalia indicated many of them had been repeatedly raped, and their purpled throats showed they'd been strangled. Some of the men were found beside the raped women with their hands tied behind them, perhaps indicating they'd been forced to watch their wives and daughters being violated. Even corpses of dogs and cats littered the village, and a dozen fat pigs were found in a pen, all killed by gunshot. The hot stink was all but unbearable, and no breeze came to lessen it. It was as if tragedy had carried away the wind along with everything good and decent.

"This was more than a raid," Josh muttered as the nun and her bodyguard

Ready came up beside him. "It was a deliberate and utterly evil act. But why, beyond mere cruelty? What was the need?"

"Colonel Yoshu needs no excuse for murder, Captain," Sister Mary Kathleen said. " 'Tis his way."

Tucker and Garcia came in from the flanks. "No Japs, dead or alive, sir," Tucker reported, "but we found something else." He glanced at the nun. "Maybe you'd better have a look. I mean just you, sir."

"What is it?" Sister Mary Kathleen asked.

"It's pretty rough, ma'am. I don't think you should see it."

She began an angry retort but stopped herself, for she accepted that the marine was only trying to be kind. "I thank ye, Corporal Tucker, for being such a gentleman. But ye must know I have seen many a rough thing since I came out here."

"She can come along," Josh said, and it was settled. He ordered Ready to stay with the fella boys, to keep gathering the dead, preparatory to burial. Then, Tucker and Garcia led Josh and Sister Mary Kathleen back to the beach, then along a path that passed through a phalanx of low, thorny bushes, and thence into a grove of palms backed by a stand of thick bamboo. After that, the path ran along a little stream. It was there, in a flat of mud, that Josh saw boot prints going to and fro. He knelt to inspect their tread pattern. "Jap army boots," he concluded, pondering the implication. "I recognize the tread pattern. A bit of a surprise."

"How come, sir?" Garcia asked.

"The Japanese navy is assigned the eastern Pacific, the army the west. That's why there were *rikusentai* at Tarawa, and we were up against Imperial army in the Solomons." Josh thought it over. "Garrison troops," he concluded. "Bottom of the Japanese barrel. No good for anything but occupation of some near-worthless islands."

"It is what I have been trying to tell ye," Sister Mary Kathleen said. "A show of force, and Colonel Yoshu will surrender."

"It's up there, sir," Tucker interrupted, pointing to where the path continued, along a steady rise that led to a headland covered with deep bush.

"Do you think you can climb it, Sister?" Garcia asked.

" 'Tis no problem, Corporal," she said, then proved it by nimbly picking her way all the way to the top. Impressed, the marines followed, leaving Josh behind. He took a breath, then started after them.

Halfway up, he was winded. His knee also predictably hurt, sweat poured off him in buckets, and he gasped for breath in the thick, sultry air. He wished he were wearing more than a lava-lava, because flies and mosquitoes were biting his legs. Since he'd stubbed his toe, he also wished he were wearing boots, rather than the pig-leather sandals Nango had loaned him. Finally, thoroughly chewed by insects, and aching in more places than he could count, Josh pulled on a thick root and crawled onto the ridge. There he stretched out on his back, and wheezed.

"You OK, Captain?" Garcia asked.

"No, I'm dying," Josh said. "Help me up." He took the marine's hand and was pulled to his feet.

Though he was still wheezing, Josh squared his shoulders and walked ahead. The path continued along the ridge toward the sea. It was well worn and lined by gardenia, the vibrant perfume of its white flowers nearly over-whelming. When they passed a small stack of rocks and shells, Garcia puzzled over them. "What are these for?"

"Shrines for the gods," Josh explained, taking the opportunity to stop and suck in more air. After a few breaths, he said, "The people of the Far Reaches believe there are many, many gods. Their big god is the sea, but it don't rule the roost, either. Their gods are always bickering and getting humans mixed up in their fights, so they build shrines to this god and that, asking them to calm down."

"But ain't these people Christians, sir?"

"They allow the missionaries to think so, but their Christianity is only an inch deep. Maybe less."

"Well, the fella boys sure love the sister."

"She seems to have a way with them," Josh acknowledged. "She has a way with all men."

"Including you, Captain?"

Josh gave that interesting observation some thought and was shocked to discover that, indeed, it did include him. "She's a right fair package," he confessed, "but it's Bosun O'Neal I'm worried about. I think that idiot has himself believing he's in love with her."

Garcia frowned. "That's probably not a good idea, her being a nun and all, but I understand it. She's a pretty girl. I wonder why she chose to shut herself off from life?"

"As far as I can tell, she's got enough life for three women."

Garcia looked at the nun. She and Tucker had stopped, pretending to admire a gardenia bush, while waiting for Josh to catch his breath. "Sir, you ever wonder what she'd look like out of that habit?"

Josh shook his head. "If I wasn't so tired, Garcia, I'd knock your block off for that."

"But ain't you wondered, Captain?"

"No!" he hissed, though he knew full well it was a lie. "Just leave it be, Garcia, and let's go!"

Garcia shrugged, and he and Josh continued on, catching up with Tucker and Sister Mary Kathleen. Finally, they reached the end of the path, at the tip of a headland over the sea, where stood an impressively large wooden cross. Its base was solidly buried, and it faced the sea. "Here's what we wanted to show you, sir," Tucker said.

Josh had seen many such crosses erected on prominent points on South Pacific islands. They acted as billboards to any passing missionaries, ones that said, in effect: *Go away. This island already converted, thank you very much.* "Well, what of it, Corporal?" Josh asked.

"You have to go around to the front, sir," the marine answered. He glanced at the nun. "Ma'am, maybe you'd better wait, let the captain have the first look."

A faint breeze blew off the sea, and Josh caught the whiff of death. Though he hoped he was wrong, he suspected now he knew what was on the other side of the cross. "Wait here, Sister."

"Nay, Captain. I'll see it with you," she answered, and so together they walked to the front of the cross. Sister Mary Kathleen crossed herself and knelt while Josh, to his dismay, found himself trembling, whether from fear or suddenly overwrought nerves or mere exhaustion, he could not discern. He steadied himself and forced himself to look, and to absorb what hate and evil could do.

Though this was a shrine surely erected by the natives of Burubu, it had been put to use by the Japanese. A native man, horribly scoured by hundreds of slashes, was attached to the cross by big rusty iron nails pounded through his wrists and ankles. Above his sagging head was nailed a small plank about two feet long and six inches wide, and a message was carved on it. There was also a design scratched into the dark mahogany vertical timber of the cross, just below the crucified man's feet. Josh read the message on the sign and then studied the design. He noticed Sister Mary Kathleen was also pondering the symbol, her lips moving in silent prayer. "What do you make of it, Sister?" he croaked, but she chose not to reply.

When Nango arrived, he picked up a stone and struck himself in the forehead. "Chief Moruno!" he cried in recognition. Blood running down his face, he made to hit himself again.

Josh sprang to stay the second blow. "Nango, take it easy!" He pried the stone out of the man's hand and tossed it away. "Now look-see, Nango. You must stop hitting yourself, you and your fella boys. It does no good and is probably not healthy in the long run."

Nango was not convinced. He struck himself on the side of his head with the flat of his big hand, then cried, "Chief Moruno good fella boy, good chief! Now all finish! Damn all Japonee!"

Tucker walked around the cross to stand beside Josh. "What does it mean, sir?" he asked.

Josh shook his head, then walked out onto the point to get away from the smell of the dead chief, and to think. Other fella boys soon arrived and took the island chief down; Sister Mary Kathleen stayed on her knees, her head bowed, her lips still moving in silent prayer. Josh wondered what kind of man would commit such an atrocity. And what did he want?

At least there was a partial answer to that, and it put an icy grip on Josh's heart. For Colonel Yoshu had communicated one desire quite clearly. It was a message the colonel had sent to the people of the Far Reaches, transmitted through the example of a murdered village and a tortured chief nailed to a cross, plus four simple words engraved on a rude plank:

GIVE ME THE NUN

2 9

As soon as the villagers were properly buried and the fella boys had finally beaten themselves enough according to custom, Josh gathered everyone at the outriggers. "We should head back to Tarawa," he declared. "There is nothing worthwhile that can be done on these islands. And Sister, there is no doubt now that this place is not safe for you."

"Do not concern yerself about me, Captain," she retorted. "Colonel Yoshu is far away, back on Ruka. He has made his foray, a terrible one to be sure, but now he will rest."

"How do you know?"

"Because I know the man."

"Far Reaches home for fella boys, Jahtalo," Nango said. "We stay."

Tucker spoke up. "Well, I'm with Captain Thurlow. We need to get while the getting's good."

"I'm with the captain, too," Garcia put in. "My outfit's probably halfway to Honolulu by now. I need to catch up."

"How about you, Bosun?" Josh asked, when Ready didn't say anything.

Ready's face was a neutral mask, as was his response. "Whatever you say, Captain."

Josh frowned at Ready, sad that the man was so obviously lovelorn, then turned to the nun. "Well, Sister?"

"Tahila is twenty miles west. Let us sail there and allow a short rest. Then, if you and the marines and Bosun O'Neal still want to leave, you can take an outrigger and go, and blessings be on ye."

"We need to talk," Josh said.

"I believe we are talking, sor."

"Just you and me," Josh replied and nodded down the beach.

She inclined her head in agreement, and together they walked away from the others, along the booming surf. Josh was quickly winded and had to stop to catch his breath. "What's wrong, Captain?"

"Nothing," he growled.

"Faith, it does not appear to be nothing. You need a long rest, I'm thinking."

"I said it's nothing. Anyway, it isn't me you should be worried about. It's yourself. Why does Colonel Yoshu want you enough to slaughter an island and crucify a chief?"

Her response was bitter. "Do you think he needs any pretext, Captain? I have told you he is cruel beyond measure." She looked eastward, toward the island of Ruka, then said in a small voice, "I was a possession. He does not like to lose his possessions."

"What did he do to you, Sister?"

"Use your imagination."

"I have, but there's a world of possibilities. What does that symbol carved on the cross mean?"

"Snow," she answered after a moment.

"Snow? Here, so near the equator? That don't make sense."

"Perhaps the colonel meant it as a joke. Now, Captain Thurlow, the others are waiting for us beneath a blazing sun. The fella boys believe the recent dead stalk the night for three days, and they will not care to stay here past sunset. We will speak on this matter again, that I promise ye, but now we must go to Tahila."

Josh pondered her, then said, "How about this? Me, Bosun O'Neal, and the marines take one of the outriggers right now and head back to Tarawa. You and your fella boys go on to Tahila."

"No," she replied.

"What do you mean, no?"

"No, it is an empty threat. I know ye wouldn't abandon me or me boys."

"What makes you so sure?"

"Because we are friends." She raised her eyebrows. "Tell me I'm wrong."

He mulled over her accusation. "Yes, we're friends," he grudgingly confessed. "But sometimes friends have to hurt friends, to get them to see the light."

"I shall be happy to see the light. In Tahila."

Josh hung his head. He *was* tired, they were all tired, and perhaps a brief stop was in order. With a little sleep, maybe he could argue out of his head the emotions storming around in it. "All right, Sister," he relented. "You win. We'll go to Tahila and hope the Japanese aren't there. Then my boys and I will head back to Tarawa after a couple of days. I hope you'll go with us, but if you won't, I'll have done my best."

"Thank ye, Captain." She cupped her hands to her mouth and yelled to Nango and the fella boys in their dialect. They cheered in response.

"What did you tell them?" Josh asked as he followed her back to the outriggers.

"Never ye mind, Captain, darling," she said over her shoulder. "All is well, for God almighty is with us."

"That don't mean He gets a say in our affairs," Josh griped.

"Oh, Captain, of all the things ye have uttered since we've met, that is the most foolish!"

Josh would have argued except he believed she was right. He decided he needed a drink, that's what. Maybe two or even three.

3 0

The navigation was accomplished, the easy sail made, and Tahila loomed before the orphans of the sea as the sun disappeared in a splash of crimson and gold, and the blue-white stars popped out, twinkling brilliantly in a wash across the sky. All was serene, but it was hard to tell in the darkness what or who waited for them on the island. "Let's wait for morning to go ashore," Josh proposed to the nun.

"But the Japanese are not there," she argued. "If they were, the village would be burning."

"You are probably right, Sister," Josh sighed, "but let's wait until first light, and then we can be certain."

"I'm already certain."

During the voyage to Tahila, Josh had turned restless and edgy, and he knew if he wasn't careful he might explode in ways unpleasant to all. "Please, Sister," he said through gritted teeth. "Just this once. Don't argue with me."

"Faith, Captain. I don't mean to be disagreeable."

He relented, tamping down his anger. "I know you don't. I don't, either. Get some rest, Sister. Let me rest as well. Here, on the outrigger."

She started to argue further but then caught his expression, which was dangerous, and lowered her eyes and nodded agreement. Relieved, Josh had a word with Nango, who whistled up to the other captains to lower their sails. Though they could be heard complaining, such was accomplished, and the outriggers were adrift on their bare poles once more. There was little current, and the breeze was gentle, and so they kept their position throughout the night, aided occasionally by a little paddling by the fella boys. Giving up sleep, which would not come in any case, Josh watched the island. A few small fires could be discerned, and snatches of voices heard between the swish of fronds of the tall palms lining the shore. All remained peaceful except for Josh's mind, which would not turn off. He felt odd, and his mind roamed on to discover why, but no answer came. *Simple exhaustion,* he muttered inwardly, but he feared it was more, that he was becoming unhinged. He thought again of drink. Surely this island would have rum! A real man needs a good drink now and again, he told himself, especially one who had been so grievously wounded!

Sunrise, purple and gold and dazzling, was accompanied by the eruption of what sounded like a hundred crowing roosters. A village crystallized in the fresh light, and Josh saw a number of big outriggers pulled up on the beach along with dozens of smaller lagoon canoes. Several bamboo frames on the beach were apparently for drying fish, and a street of sand stretched into the interior, along which were built houses of bamboo and thatch with artful designs woven into their walls. All in all, it seemed a prosperous village, and at peace. Sister Mary Kathleen emerged from her hut to stand beside him. "What say you, Captain?" she asked.

"It looks safe, though the Japanese are masters of camouflage."

"Colonel Yoshu's way is simple mayhem. Nay, if he was there, we'd know it. Let us go in."

Josh nodded his agreement and told Nango to whistle up the other captains. "Bosun, I'd like to see a rifle in your hands," he called over his shoulder.

"Aye, aye, Skipper," Ready answered and retrieved an M-1 from the stash of rifles brought from Tarawa. He locked and loaded a clip and prepared his mind for battle.

Paddles quickly filled the hands of the fella boys, the island being too near to bother with sails, and the outrigger captains, obviously familiar with the approach to the village, threaded their way through coral heads. The beach that fronted the village curved around almost in a half-circle, creating a lagoon that ended at rocky headlands on both points. The reef forced any boat entering the lagoon into a narrow slot between the headlands and then broadside to the beach before a final turn to land. Josh thought it was the perfect place to be ambushed, and he was relieved when he saw the people of Tahila emerge from their homes, and no evidence of the Japanese.

A big man, wearing a bright red lava-lava, emerged from the onlookers and gravely watched as the outriggers pushed up onto the sand. Josh stepped out and walked up to him, followed by Nango, Sister Mary Kathleen, and all the others. The man looked Josh over, his flat nose flaring as if trying to catch his scent, then inspected Sister Mary Kathleen, the marines, Ready, and, last, the fella boys. A great grin spread across his wide, tattooed face, and he and Nango embraced. Nango said, "This fella boy Chief Kalapa."

The chief walked up to Josh. "My word, you Jahtalo, cabum boy with old *Bad-sheba*," he said. "You savvy me?"

Josh recalled a long-ago visit to Tahila and a spindly youth, the son of a chief, who had swum out to the *Bathsheba* and demonstrated his diving skills when Captain Fairplay tossed out coins. Clearly, that had been many years and meals ago. "Chief Kalapa, good fella," Josh greeted him, just before he was enveloped in the huge arms of the chief, followed by ritualized sniffing of the air on both sides of his face. Josh reciprocated.

"Jahtalo, good fella," Chief Kalapa replied fondly. He held Josh by his shoulders, searching his eyes, and then said something in the island dialect.

"He said he saw you returning to this island in a dream," Sister Mary Kathleen translated. "He says he hopes you have come to chase away the Japanese."

Before Josh could respond, little boys and girls rushed to the nun, draping her neck with garlands of flowers and tugging at her habit for attention. Then they turned to the other visitors, who were soon also festooned with flowers and children.

Chief Kalapa and Josh were shortly joined by a white man attired in a white suit. He wore a Panama hat and carried a folded black umbrella, which he was using as a cane. His face was thin, adorned with a neatly trimmed salt-and-pepper beard and mustache, and his eyes were gray-blue and crisp. He held out his hand to Josh. "The Honorable Robert Bucknell, representing the interests of His Royal Majesty's Colonial Government, such as they are these days. And who might you be, sir?"

"Captain Josh Thurlow," Josh answered. "United States Coast Guard."

"Jahtalo old hand these parts," Chief Kalapa apprised the diplomat. "He cabum boy on old *Bad-sheba*."

Bucknell raised his silvery eyebrows. "A homecoming, then, Captain? Bloody odd time to play the tourist, isn't it?"

"I ain't on a vacation, Mister Bucknell. I'm here because . . . well, it's complicated."

Bucknell frowned. "I see. Actually, I don't see at all, but I expect I shall." Then Bucknell peered along his thin nose at the nun, who was still being sung to by the people. She was now so thoroughly draped with garlands, her mouth and nearly her nose had disappeared beneath them. "I recognize her," he said. "Though I never saw her before that she didn't have a broom or mop in her hand. Served as a maid for the other three nuns on Ruka, best I could tell. She reminded me of Cinderella, a pretty girl the old hags enjoyed ordering about."

Josh called over Ready and the two marines and introduced them to the chief and Mr. Bucknell. Tucker and Garcia had both developed grins, perhaps brought on by the number of quite shapely and bare-breasted young women in the crowd. "Bosun, take charge," Josh ordered. "First thing, haul the ordnance ashore." He turned to the chief and the diplomat. "We brought along rifles and a couple of machine guns plus a considerable amount of ammunition. Where can we secure it?"

Chief Kalapa nodded toward a large house on stilts by the beach. "Go along boathouse," he said.

"Boathouse it is. See to it, Ready. Also bring Sampson ashore and fashion him a crutch. He needs to move around, avoid clots in his stump. Now, gentlemen, shall we have a quiet word?"

"Certainly," Bucknell answered while the chief inclined his head in agreement. "May I suggest we retire to the temporary government house of the Far Reaches? My woman will prepare a breakfast. No use discussing important matters on an empty stomach."

"Lead the way," Josh said, grinning, pleased that perhaps a meal of something other than fish and rice was in the offing. And where there was a British diplomat, surely strong drink would be available, too. His mouth suddenly felt very dry, and in great need to be made wet.

Sister Mary Kathleen, observing the men leaving, broke away from the children to intercept them. "Mr. Bucknell, how do ye do? Do ye recall me at all?"

Bucknell bowed. "Of course, Sister. I am pleased to see you still alive. May I present Chief Kalapa?"

"Faith, the chief and I know one another. I visited Tahila twice with the other sisters on medical missions."

"Sister," Chief Kalapa grunted as they accomplished the ritual sniffing of their respective faces.

"If ye are meeting to discuss the situation," she said, "I believe I should be in on it."

"I think not, Sister," Josh replied. "I am in charge of this expedition and will do all the talking required."

Surprised at Josh's sudden swagger, she took a moment to understand it, concluding it was because he was in the company of big men, rather than men he could order about. "I don't know that you're in charge, any more than I am," she stubbornly replied.

Bucknell and the chief shared a glance; then Bucknell said, "Let us hear from the captain first, my dear. I assure you we will consult with you after we better understand the situation."

"Very well," she said, after an apparent internal struggle. She looked at Josh. "But I'm surprised at your mendacity, Captain."

Josh jutted out his scarred chin. "I don't care to argue with you on the street, Sister. Mendacity? If that means a man has to do what a man has to do, I plead guilty."

"Posh!" she snapped, then gladly went back to the children, who quickly gathered around her with their shy smiles. At least they were not afflicted with false and foolish pride as were so many adults, especially big American captains.

"She's a spirited thing," Josh said, watching after Sister Mary Kathleen, "but she's often wrongheaded."

"We will be pleased to hear all about that and more, Captain," Mr. Bucknell replied as diplomatically as his post required. Then he led the way toward food and words.

31

The "temporary government house of the Far Reaches" proved to be a board shack with a tin roof. Waiting inside was a young woman who wore a high-neck gown and had a flower in her long and shimmering black hair. She was apparently expecting visitors, as she had already set out on a rude table several plates of diced coconut, banana slices, and other succulent fruits. While Josh and the chief ate, Bucknell explained the shack had been built by an Australian named Old Burt who had tried to make a go of raising coconuts for copra. "This was his plantation house," Bucknell said as he set three tumblers on a makeshift bar consisting of a plank laid between two barrels. "His grave is out back. Died of fever, which is not common here. He was an old Solomon Islands hand. Caught it there, most likely."

The chief provided a little more background. "Old Burt belong many wimmins. Old Burt sick. All wimmins go. Nobody come. He die."

Bucknell smiled. "Precisely. Now, although it is still morning, may I propose a gin and tonic for a round of toasts prior to our conference?"

"You wouldn't happen to have any rum on you?" Josh asked.

"Sorry, old man. Gin is the preferred anesthetic of the white man in these islands."

Bucknell retrieved an unlabeled bottle of clear liquid from a termite-riddled hutch, as well as a jar of liquid Josh supposed was tonic, then mixed them in another jar and poured the contents into the only slightly dirty tumblers. "We take it neat in the Far Reaches, of course," Bucknell said. "I haven't seen an ice cube since the war began. Come to think of it, I haven't seen ice since I've been here, which is going on eleven years, save a bucket on a yacht sailed by a trio of American millionaires who bumbled out this way back in '35." He handed the drinks over, then proposed a toast. "To the king, God save him, the president, God bless him, and our friend the chief, God have him."

"*Salut,*" Josh toasted, raising his tumbler.

Chief Kalapa also raised his tumbler, then downed its contents in a single gulp. "My word! Good fella gin!" He belched and smacked his lips in the island style.

Josh took a swallow and felt the liquid burn all the way down his gullet. Then he followed Chief Kalapa's example and finished it off. "Fine stuff, Mr. Bucknell," he rasped.

"I managed to escape with a good stock from Ruka," Bucknell said after an appreciative sip. "What I will do when it runs out, I have no idea. Probably kill myself, I shouldn't wonder."

They had another drink and exchanged more pleasantries, in the course of which Josh discovered that Mr. Bucknell had inherited a pile of money, then lost it due to a combination of the Depression and gambling, and that his posting to the Far Reaches was to get rid of him when his poverty had become an embarrassment to his peers. "In other words," Bucknell concluded, "I'm an Englishman, down on his luck, but fortunate to have an opportunity to serve my king and country."

Josh said, "A good story, and I like it. As for me, I am the son of a lighthouse keeper, grew up on the island of Killakeet on the Outer Banks of North Carolina, and am now a professional coast guard officer."

Bucknell's eyes sparkled impishly. "And sent amongst us savages for what purpose, Captain?"

Josh pondered the question, then said, "I was shanghaied by that nun." Then Josh explained how she'd accomplished it, becoming angry as he told the story and letting his repressed resentment boil over.

Bucknell and Chief Kalapa shared a glance, and then Bucknell said, "I confess when I first saw you I hoped you had come to send the Japanese packing."

"With two sound marines and a bosun? No, Mr. Bucknell. I fear not."

Chief Kalapa said, "We know you go along Burubu. One Tahila fella boy fish Burubu. See Japonee come along. Too much smoke, too much peoples cry, Burubu peoples all finish, he think. Then Japonee go, you come along, and Tahila fella boy come along here, say all same."

"That about sums it up, Chief," Josh said.

"Tell us what you found on Burubu, Captain," Bucknell said.

Josh described the massacre, and upon his conclusion, Chief Kalapa struck himself in the face to demonstrate his grief.

"Please don't do that, Chief," Josh begged.

Bucknell said, "It is most odd, Captain, that suddenly we see Colonel Yoshu on the move. He has been content to stay on Ruka and leave the outlying islands alone. Now, for whatever reason, he's become active. We assume this island will be next."

"And I assume you're correct," Josh said, "and when he comes, he will do the same thing here he did on Burubu. So here's my proposal, gentlemen: Let us load the outriggers with everyone on Tahila and clear out."

The chief frowned. "No many marine come along Far Reaches?"

"No, Chief. No many marines. No Americans at all, other than us."

"Why is that, old man?" Bucknell asked.

"I'll draw you a picture, Mr. Bucknell. Could I borrow your umbrella? Thank you."

Josh used the tip of the umbrella to draw on the sand floor of the shack. "Here's Australia—see that, Chief?—you savvy Australia? Now, just to the east are the Solomons—Guadalcanal, New Georgia, and so forth. We finally took the Solomons . . ."

"I didn't know that!" Bucknell exclaimed. "Good show! How are my fellow colonialists there? I knew more than a few of the plantation owners."

Bucknell's question stirred up a few painful memories for Josh, who had fought for so long in the Solomons. "Most of the British left before the Japanese arrived," he informed the diplomat. "Those that didn't, for the most part, I'm sorry to tell you, were murdered. A few men served as coastwatchers or formed irregular forces using loyal natives. When the Japanese started building an airfield on Guadalcanal, our marines landed, followed by regular army and National Guard troops. I was there, too, on an inspection trip for the secretary of the navy. We were all raw, and it was a close-run thing for nearly a year as we fought up through the chain of the Solomons. But finally, though we lost a bunch of fine men, we beat them. New Guinea and Tarawa were next. They were bloody, awful battles, but we beat them there, too. I'm sorry, Mr. Bucknell, but on all the islands, the old plantations have been abandoned. Most of the British colonists have decamped for home or Australia."

"I fear this war will spell the end of our empire," Bucknell said after absorbing Josh's story. "Perhaps all empires."

"I don't know, Mr. Bucknell. You could be right. First we got to win the blamed thing, then sort out the results." Josh went back to his sand cartoon. "Now, look here. Up here to the north of the Solomons is New Guinea, and then way up here the Philippines. General MacArthur with mostly army troops plans to sweep up this line. He wants to free the Philippines before moving on to Japan."

Chief Kalapa stared at Josh's drawing, tugged at his chin, then shrugged. "Wrong way," he said.

"Yes, Chief. It's the wrong way, at least for clearing the Japanese from this part of the Pacific. But the United States Navy, under Admiral Nimitz, has a different idea." Josh sketched on. "Here's Tarawa over here. See where I'm dotting the sand, Chief? North are the Marshalls about here, then the Marianas, the Volcanos, Okinawa about here, then Japan. You see? That's the way Admiral Nimitz is going to go with his navy and his marines. All the way to Japan. The Army Air Force likes this plan since it will allow their bombers to get closer to the cities. They plan on pounding them into dust."

"How long do you think victory will take?" Bucknell asked.

"Depends on who you talk to. I figure the army and the navy will get to Okinawa about the same time and then join up. That will take about two years. Then it'll take another three to beat the Japanese in their home islands."

Bucknell's face fell. "Five more years of war?"

"At least. Unless somebody has a big secret weapon up their sleeves. From what I saw on the Solomons and Tarawa, we'll have to pretty much kill every man, woman, and child in Japan to beat them. I don't know if we have the stomach for that. Anyway, Chief, look here. About here is the Far Reaches. See how they're way off by themselves? See the two arrows I've drawn pointing toward Japan, one going up the left and the other the right? You ain't on either one of those tracks. So killing Japonee here won't help the Americans get up to Tokyo. Savvy?"

"Many Japonee belong this place," Chief Kalapa insisted.

Josh handed him Bucknell's umbrella. "Show me your islands, would you, Chief? I don't quite recall how they're laid out."

Chief Kalapa looked doubtfully at the umbrella, then poked its snout into the sand. "What I do?"

"Draw the Far Reaches."

Chief Kalapa stared at the sand, stirred it with the point of the umbrella, then handed the implement to Bucknell. "Far Reaches belong here," he said, touching a finger to his head. "Me see all land. Me see all ocean water. Me see village here, there. Me see all. No see nothing in sand."

Bucknell stirred Josh's war cartoon into oblivion and started drawing. "I can show you, Captain. The Forridges include many small islands, some inhabited, some not. The main islands run along an east-to-west arc. The biggest is Ruka, over here to the east. It is the seat of government. Then, going westward, Burubu and Tahila. Tahila is the far reaches of the Far Reaches."

Josh studied the map. "Tell me what happened when Jap arrived on Ruka, Mr. Bucknell."

"Certainly. Though we knew the Japanese had bombed Pearl Harbor and attacked across the Pacific, we hoped for a time we might be spared their attention, though their aircraft flew across us several times. Then, one fine day, they waltzed in aboard two barges, marched into town, tore down the Union Jack, ran up the Rising Sun, and gave a big *banzai!* After that, they proceeded to round up any Europeans they could find. That included me, the priests and nuns, and an Irish-American barkeep named Carl Spurlock plus his wife Gertie and his other wife Tilly. We were herded inside the government house, and there we waited, for what we did not know."

Bucknell frowned at what was an obviously unpleasant memory. "We were made to squat on the floor of the library, our hands tied at our backs, until a tall, handsome Nip all trumped up in braids and brass strutted in as if he owned the place, which, I suppose, he did. This proved to be Colonel Hideo Yoshu, a charming monster, who harangued us for a while, not that any of us could understand him, and then a young officer put it all into English. The upshot of it was that we were beneath the good colonel's interest but if we had any money or gold or jewels or anything of value, and if we turned it over to him forthwith, he might decide not to execute us. Father Ballester, as brave an Irishman as I've ever known, stood up and argued that we were all civilian noncombatants and that the colonel had no right to keep us prisoners or take our worldly goods. Yoshu conceded that the priest had presented a most excellent argument, and to demonstrate his appreciation, he had one of his bully boys thank the good father with a rifle butt. After that, several of them stomped on Father Ballester until they'd broken both his arms and a good number of his ribs, which must have punctured a lung, as he began to spit up gobs of blood. The rest of us, to our shame, did nothing. Some of us even looked away."

"How about Sister Mary Kathleen?"

Bucknell gave the question some thought. "Quite honestly, I don't recall that she was there. She might have been. She was always such a little mouse, maybe I missed her. Anyway, the priests and nuns were praying incessantly, and I guess you might say they called up a miracle. An airplane flew over and dropped a single bomb in the harbor. This made Colonel Yoshu and his troops panic and run for the hills, leaving us unguarded. Funny thing is, I believe the bomb was accidentally dropped by a Japanese bomber. Anyhoo, we got ourselves untied; then Spurlock, his two wives, and I slipped down to the harbor and thence aboard Spurlock's launch. Long story short, we ended up here. I made common cause with Chief Kalapa and set up shop—someone must run the empire's bureaucracy, after all. Carl and his girls now live on the northern shore of the island. After you've rested, I'll take you to visit. I think he'd enjoy meeting a fellow Yank."

Josh absorbed the story, then asked, "What happened to the priests and nuns?"

"I begged them to come with us, but even with the offer of free booze, which, believe me, had to be a considerable attraction to Father O'Toole, they refused. The Mother Superior said Father Ballester was too injured to travel and, in any case, she and the others could not abandon the people of Ruka. In effect, they were signing their own death warrants, but I think they knew that."

"So how was it . . . ?" Josh began, then stopped his question when a shadow fell across the sand cartoon of the Far Reaches. "What is it, Ready?"

"Beg pardon, sir, but we got all the ordnance unloaded and I put the marines to guarding it. Should we build ourselves a hut or something?"

"A hut? What are you thinking, Bosun? We're only going to be here a couple of days at most. We'll sleep on the beach."

Ready shrugged. "On the beach it is, sir. I'm certain the sand fleas will enjoy our company. Sorry to interrupt."

Josh shook his head at Ready's near-insubordination but let it pass. "Go away," he told him, "and don't come back to talk to me about anything, unless the Japanese are attacking. Clear?"

"Very clear, sir."

Ready left, and Bucknell said, "You were hard on that man, Captain."

"Yes, I was, because he requires discipline. He is in love, you see, an unrequited love, and it has muddled his mind."

"Unrequited love is a difficult burden," Bucknell acknowledged. "Such is rare on this island, the women being too kind to allow it. If a man loves a woman, she will at least make certain he isn't sexually frustrated, even if she doesn't love him enough to marry him, a most civilized tradition, I must say. But back to cases. Captain, I should like to formally request that you reconsider your plan to abandon us." He nodded toward Chief Kalapa. "I know the chief and I know his people. They will not go. This is their home and they would die if they had to leave. Nor will I go, for I have a duty to represent His Majesty's government here. Will you not stay and help defend us?"

"Me stay," Chief Kalapa confirmed. "You stay along, Jahtalo. Fight Japonee."

Josh was incredulous. "It would be past foolishness to even think about it. You see, there is a further consideration." Then Josh told the diplomat and the chief about the message nailed to the cross. "Colonel Yoshu wants that nun, though I don't know why. He probably has no idea she headed to Tarawa and collected me up. He likely thinks she's been hiding on one island or another and he's been searching them, big and small. Tahila is surely in his sights. He's coming, and he'll likely kill everyone on Tahila when he does."

Bucknell frowned. "But you brought rifles and machine guns with you. Why did you do that if you didn't plan to fight?"

"That was Sister Mary Kathleen's idea, not mine. If you are bound and determined to stay, I'll leave all that ordnance with you. My boys and I will just take what we need for the voyage."

Bucknell sighed after a short ponder. "Your advice is sound, Captain. Chief Kalapa and I will discuss it." He gave the chief the eye, nodding toward the door. "For now, duty calls us both. Please make yourself at home here in my office. We shall talk more later."

Bucknell and the chief rose, gravely shook Josh's hand in turn, and went out the door. "You have a day to make up your mind, no more than two!" Josh called after them.

"We understand, old man," Bucknell answered over his shoulder. Then he and the chief walked on down the common road, their heads close as they conversed.

Josh shrugged, told himself he'd done his best, and then, as invited, made himself at home.

He was still making himself at home an hour later, mainly by drinking a great deal of the Britisher's gin, when Sister Mary Kathleen found him. "A word, Captain?" she asked, then knew instantly by his crooked smile that he was inebriated.

"Sure, Sister," Josh said. "How about a gin and tonic?"

"Faith, I am not an imbiber of alcoholic spirits."

"Why not? Nothing in the Bible against it. Jesus drank wine. Even made some for his ma, best I recall."

"Many men in my village were drunks," she answered. "I chose to avoid the curse."

"Oh, come on, Sister. A little booze can soften a long day."

"The sun has only recently risen," she pointed out. "Nay, Captain. I will not drink and I beg ye to stop."

Josh laughed and refilled his tumbler with gin, neglecting the tonic. "What do you want?"

She crossed her arms and tapped her slippered foot. "You had the bosun and the marines put away the rifles and machine guns. I think they should be handed out to the people so they can be ready if Colonel Yoshu attacks."

Josh lifted his eyebrows. "Give weapons to untrained islanders? I might as well throw them into the lagoon."

"Then I ask ye to teach at least me fella boys how to use them."

"Sister, when will you see the light? When Colonel Yoshu comes, which he will, he'll roll right over us."

"No, 'tis you who cannot see the light, Captain." She puffed out an exasperated breath. "How can I make ye understand? If we put up any kind of defense, Colonel Yoshu will turn and run. I know this man. Why don't ye trust me?"

"Trust you? I don't even know who you are!"

She was startled. "What do ye mean? Ye know who I am."

"I don't know that I do," he answered, squinting at her, as if perhaps he could see into her mind, even though, in truth, his vision had become a bit blurred. "There are things left out about you. For instance, I have no clear idea how you spent your time on Ruka before your escape. It's also not clear to me how you escaped and who exactly your fella boys are and why they are so devoted to you. And, of course, I don't understand why Colonel Yoshu is so bound and determined to get you back."

"This is neither the time nor place to talk about that," she retorted.

Josh laughed again, which made her wave her hand in front of her nose, so strong were the gin fumes.

"Well, that's fine, Sister. On the voyage back to Tarawa, you can tell me everything. I've pretty much convinced Mr. Bucknell and Chief Kalapa to gather up the people on this island and come along." He drank up, then refilled the tumbler, thus emptying the bottle. "What do you think of that?"

"I think you've had enough gin," Sister Mary Kathleen answered.

"Do you? Well, I shall take your opinion under advisement." Then Josh tossed the gin down his throat and happily smacked his lips, island style. He lifted his eyebrows at her and grinned, though it was not a friendly grin, more a baring of his teeth.

She stared at him in disgust, then bit her lip and forced an expression of calm and outward humility. "I'll take me leave now," she said.

Josh shrugged. "*Vaya con Dios*, Sister."

"I usually do, Captain," she snapped, then left.

Josh frowned after her. "God save me from all women!" he swore, then took another bottle of gin from the cabinet, unscrewed the cap, tossed it away, and discovered he was in a mind to get good and soused. He deserved it, after all, considering all he'd been through. The problem was gin had never been a friendly drink for him. He recalled hitting it a little hard in Alaska, in the little frontier town of Petersburg, and wandering around half out of his mind for two days. Also, if he got drunk, how would the bosun and the marines get along without his sure and certain leadership? *They'd be in one pohunky stew,* he concluded, and poured himself just one last drink and, soon thereafter, another.

3 2

It was nearly midnight before Sister Mary Kathleen sank to her knees in the little house that belonged to the two widows who had invited her to spend the night beneath their thatched roof. Both were asleep, snoring peacefully, and so she prayed silently for guidance, grace, strength, and, most of all, forgiveness, though her heart told her such was not possible. She crossed herself at the end of her prayers, including in them even Josh Thurlow, the big lout, and kissed the medallion of her order and wiped the inevitable tear of regret and sadness that always came to her at the end of each day. For it was only then she allowed her thoughts to drift toward Ruka and the unbearable joy and disgrace that was there. *I will find a way,* she swore, even as she accepted that for some days or weeks, Tahila would be her home.

After removing the corona, veil, and wimple of her habit, she placed them carefully aside and lay down on the large straw mat that served as a sleeping area for her and the two women. Lying there, staring into the darkness, she felt dirty, tired, and ugly and wished she had insisted on washing both her garments and her filthy body before taking to bed. But everyone in the village, it seemed, wanted her to visit, and no time had been allowed for anything else other than the sociable. She had found the homes of Tahila kept neat and clean, and the ladies of each were eager to show off their various treasures. This one had a Bible to show, though it was in Spanish, which no one in the village could read, and that one had fashioned artistic fired clay pots, which Sister Mary Kathleen admired too much, it seemed, as the woman had pressed on her several. Other women showed her their gardens and even their chickens, dogs, cats, and pigs. Sadly, none of them introduced her to their children, since they were considered too low to be brought forth to a holy person. So she contented herself with sidelong glances at them, almost always rewarded by shy smiles. She so longed to swoop them up and hold them in her arms, but she resisted the urge and instead cooed over everything shown to her, all the while allowing her smiles to seep out to the boys and girls hiding in the shadows of their houses or peeping out from behind trees and bushes.

The evening had brought a meal with Chief Kalapa and his several wives. It was a sumptuous meal of rice and yams and chunks of boiled chicken and fish. She had eaten appreciatively, then wiped her mouth with the back of her hand, then belched delicately, all in the island style, and pronounced everything more than satisfactory.

Although the chief started to speak to her in pidgin, she apprised him of her knowledge of the dialect, and he inclined his head, accepting her offer to speak in his language. "I understand Captain Thurlow has convinced you to leave Tahila," she said.

"That is not true," he answered. "Mr. Bucknell and I heard the captain out, but we are still thinking the best course."

"I am pleased to hear it. If you agree, I should like to stay here."

"Nango and the Ruka fella boys are welcome, but it is my understanding you are coveted by the Japanese colonel. Perhaps it would be better for Tahila if you went elsewhere."

"I have nowhere else to go."

"You could go back to Tarawa with Captain Thurlow."

"I cannot, sor. I must find a way to force the Japanese to leave Ruka."

"Why?"

"The people there suffer terribly under their rule."

"I am certain that is true. Our fishermen encounter Ruka fishermen. They say their families are kept hostage so they will bring fish back to the Japonee. They say many, many have been killed. They say they are treated as slaves." Chief Kalapa thought for a while, then said, "Still, I confess I do not entirely understand your position. Why have you taken such a responsibility upon yourself? Could it be, like most Europeans, you look upon us as your children and therefore you must save us?"

" 'Tisn't that! I just think . . ." She hesitated before saying, "I regret much of what we Europeans have brought to yer islands. Except the word of God, of course."

The chief nodded, noticing that she had changed the subject, then tossed a chicken bone over his shoulder and licked his fingers. "Well, Sister, the first white men who came here brought both good and bad. I think we were ripe for change, anyway. It didn't take long before we wanted to be as much like them as we could."

"You thought their way of life was best?"

"Best? What is best? We knew no other way than our own, that's all. When we found ourselves rubbing up against a different people, we were bound to change. Once, we had an American woman stay with us for a year. She was a student, she said, and we were her teachers. But if we were her teachers, why did she keep asking us things we had not put into words before or did not know? Where did your people come from? How do you travel without maps? Why do you build your boats this way? Why do you have sex without shame? She bedeviled us with her incessant and rude questions about things we had always taken for granted. She forced us to put into words these things and made our most cherished customs seem silly. At the end of her year, we were happy to see her leave, but it was too late. She had already changed us by making us answer her questions."

Chief Kalapa thought a bit more, then added slyly, "You Europeans reject our religion as fairy tales but say Christianity is all true. This is strange, because Christianity does not match most of your thinking. It is an ancient religion, filled with impossible things such as men raised from the dead, Jesus walking on water, the lame throwing away their crutches, and God Himself plotting the terrible torture and death of His own son. It does not square with your otherwise logical beliefs. Can you explain this?"

Sister Mary Kathleen leaned forward. "Faith is not easy to explain, 'tis true, but if a man does not believe in miracles, how else does he explain himself? Is it not a miracle that a man exists at all? If there is a watch, is this not evidence of a watchmaker? We are the best proof of the hand of God."

Chief Kalapa nodded understanding, if not agreement, then looked at his three wives, who had been pretending not to be listening. "What do you women think of these things?" he asked. When none answered save with a shrug, he smiled with satisfaction. "You see? Here is a strange thing. The women of the Far Reaches are satisfied to be wives and mothers and cooks and gardeners. They do not think the deep thoughts such as I and the other men do. Yet you European women, you think like men. How did that come about?"

"I cannot believe your women don't have deep thoughts," Sister Mary Kathleen answered. Then she spoke to Mori, the wife who seemed to be the first among the three. "Mori, do ye ever think why things are as they are? Why ye as a woman can never be a chief, for instance?"

Mori, who had a streak of silver in her long ebony hair and was maturely beautiful, pondered the question, then replied, "It is true we women do not exercise authority, but we are allowed to own land. When we are married, we carry our land into the marriage but retain control of it. This is the way it has always been and allows a balance between men and women in our affairs. It also causes the best lands to be mixed around the various families, never always and forever in the hands of one." She glanced meaningfully at Chief Kalapa and added, "I am quite capable of thinking deep thoughts, husband, though I choose to let them run toward family, such as when our sons should be allowed to go out to sea on the outriggers, or when our daughters are ready for sex. You have no inkling of these things."

Chief Kalapa grunted dismissively at his wife's pronouncements, but Sister Mary Kathleen noticed he chose not to argue with them, either. Instead, this time it was he who changed the subject. "Sister, our children need a school. Would you be their teacher?"

She was as pleased as she was astonished at the proposal. "Faith! It has always been a dream of mine, to be a teacher."

"Yet you became a nun."

"I did, yes, sor, but I hoped some day I would also be able to teach. I love children."

"I noticed that you were enjoying their company," Chief Kalapa said approvingly. "Since the missionaries left two years ago, the children's education has suffered. They need to learn to read and write, as well as our language, our history, the history of the world, English, and arithmetic."

She could hardly breathe, so pleasurable was the idea to her. "I would do me best, Chief Kalapa. I thank ye!"

"But none of your religion," he cautioned. "We have no use for your plaster saints. We are Christian, but we also love our old gods. You must not interfere with our beliefs."

"I understand," she said. "Where will me school be located?"

"I shall have a suitable structure built for you beside the boathouse."

" 'Tis a fine chief ye are," she said, "to care about the children's education."

"What he cares about is that they not make too much noise while he is trying to sleep," Mori said, as the other wives tittered.

Chief Kalapa frowned. "First wife, you should speak only when spoken to."

"I shall try to remember that, husband," Mori answered, smiling triumphantly.

After the meal, as the wives were taking up the plates and cups and feeding the dogs and cats with the leftovers, Chief Kalapa leaned forward with his hands on his bare knees and contemplated Sister Mary Kathleen for so long that she began to feel uncomfortable. Finally, he said, "I should like very much to speak with you further, but not here. Would you join me on the beach?"

She agreed, and so they strolled down the common road toward the lagoon. "You should pray, Sister," the chief said. "Make a show of it. It is not seemly for an unmarried woman to be walking alongside a married man after dark, even you. It will be believed that we are going somewhere to have sex. If you pray, and loudly, they will assume you are trying to make me into a good Catholic, you see."

Sister Mary Kathleen complied, praying an Our Father while taking note of the eyes watching them from the huts as they passed. At the beach, before the shimmering lagoon, the chief said, "I have talked to Nango and the other young gentlemen who came with you. Of course, I know them all very well. They are of royal blood from the house of Ruka. Nango, as I'm certain you know, is the first son of Chief Namu, who he said died at the hands of the Japanese. By the way, I have given them permission to bury Tomoru's bones on this island until he can be moved to Ruka."

"Thank you," she replied. "As for Nango, I saw his father murdered. Colonel Yoshu used a sword to take off his head. Chief Namu died bravely with the name of his people on his last breath."

"Is that so? Nango did not provide that detail."

"That is because he was not there. What else did Nango tell you?" she asked, fearing the answer.

Chief Kalapa waved his hands dismissively. "Very little. He said everything I wanted to know was better told by you. Now, Sister, I bid you tell me what happened to the royal fella boys, and to you at the hands of the Japonee. As chief, these are things I should know."

She took off her slippers and walked ankle-deep into the surf, letting the clean sea water flush across her bare feet and drag at her tattered, grimy habit. "Nango and the other young men of the royal families were rounded up by Colonel Yoshu. He wished to humiliate, disgrace, and dishonor them so that his authority would be unquestioned. He turned them over to his troops who . . . wanted them."

"Ah," the chief said and went directly to the heart of the matter. "Nango and the others were the object of debased sexual practices, then. I feared as much. And what of you?"

"What of me? I am a nun."

"Does that mean you are immune from being debased by others so inclined?"

"They left me alone."

"Why?"

"Because Colonel Yoshu so ordered."

"You were not tortured? Not at all?"

"Not in the same way."

"Why would he show any kindness toward you? Did he not order the other nuns to be killed?"

"Yes."

"But not you? I do not understand."

"It is not decent for me to say more."

"How did you escape?" Chief Kalapa pressed.

She studied the lagoon and then looked up to the stars. There were millions lying athwart the edge of the galaxy, a river of light. She wished she could rise into the sky and dance along the celestial stream. But such was the playground of angels and, she hoped, her sweet Saint Monessa. The sea washed heavily against her knees, the tide inexorably coming in. She backed out of the water and stood in the dry sand. "One day," she said, "Nango secretly visited me and told me that he and the other fella boys planned to take some outriggers and leave, even though it was under the penalty of instant death if caught."

"That was brave of him, was it not?"

"Yes. Very brave. When he offered to take me with him, I agreed."

"Had you tried to escape before?"

"I had no opportunity."

"You were in prison?"

"I was in Colonel Yoshu's house when Nango offered escape."

"What did you do in his house?"

"Existed. I was locked in my room much of the time."

Chief Kalapa frowned. "Your story is odd. I think there is something wrong with it. But what I need most is to know why Colonel Yoshu is chasing you."

She said nothing, her lips pressed together, and kept studying the lagoon and the black, star-strewn sky above it.

"Do you have nothing more to say?" Chief Kalapa demanded.

Her reply was a sad whisper. "What does it matter, after all? I am here now. What is, is."

Chief Kalapa pressed a finger against his lips, an expression of frustration, and said, "I do not know if I should let you teach our children. You harbor a terrible secret, of that I am certain. I shall have to think on it. Now, Sister, I must bid you a very good night. Here are Nanura and Palula. They are widows without children and have room for you in their house."

The two women, who had obviously waited in the shadows for the chief to give them a signal, appeared and urged her to follow them, and this she had done.

Now Sister Mary Kathleen lay on the mat beside the sleeping sisters, and tried to stop thinking, to let sleep take her into the oblivion she desired. She was suffering, and it occurred to her that perhaps that was what God wanted from her most of all. *Would you ask Him why, Saint Monessa?* she prayed, and, as if in response, she heard somewhere, far into the jungle and the night, a creature screaming, whether in pain or fright, she did not know. She prayed for that creature, and for all the creatures on earth who were in pain or frightened, and then, unwillingly, she allowed a prayer to escape from her lips for a man she was certain was also suffering, though he was evil and corrupted and had taken from her that which she wanted more than life itself.

3 3

She woke at sunrise to the crowing of the roosters that stalked the village, all seeking dominance over everything they encountered, and sometimes losing their heads at the hands of disgusted villagers as a result. Sister Mary Kathleen arose, noted that the two widows were still asleep, and poked her head outside. Pale blue smoke from the remnants of the evening cooking fires, mixed with a steamy mist off the lagoon, gave the village the washed-out quality of a faded photograph. She smelled a smoky, woodsy perfume and found herself inexplicably enchanted with the little town.

She also decided she could no longer stand being dirty. She studied the items scattered about the house and discovered a little pot that was filled with a soft white jelly redolent of coconuts. She dipped her finger in it and put it to her lips and was rewarded with the sharp taste of raw copra soap. Thrilled at the thought of a bath, she drew on the headdress of her habit, then slipped through the village. No one challenged her save the roosters and hens, which clucked in fright and scurried away on their stiff legs, and the dogs who growled low. One of the dogs, a small brown mutt, came up to her with its tail tucked between its legs but its nose raised in apparent hope of a little kindness. She stroked the offered snout, and its tail came out wagging. "Come with me, laddy," she said. "Pertect me from the roosters." He did, and she had herself a dog.

At the stream, she found herself momentarily perplexed as to how to wash herself and her clothes. She decided she had to get farther from the village and so took a path that paralleled the stream until she came to a small dam of piled-up rocks. Behind it was a pretty little pond, and hanging over it, reminding her of worshipping nuns, were heavy-limbed candlenut trees. On the far end of the pond, there was a little waterfall that gushed in a torrent between two boulders high on a rocky cliff. The water struck stones as it fell, producing a shower of rainbow drops that played musical notes on the surface of the lake. " 'Tis a fine place for a wash, Laddy," she said to the pup, who now had a name.

She set the pot of soap on the shore and then stripped until she wore only her undergarments. Multicolored birds twittered and hopped in the trees overhead as she dipped her hand into the pot of soap, then vigorously scrubbed the multiple pieces of her habit in the pond and afterward wrung them out and spread them on the rocks of the dam to dry. Then, though she felt most brazen doing it, she took off her undergarments and washed them, too. She looked all around again, still seeing nothing but the little birds and hearing nothing except their singing and the small, singsong notes of the waterfall spray. She scooped a handful of the jelly soap from the pot and carried it to the little waterfall, and there she raised her face to the stream of gushing water and turned and stretched beneath it until the accumulated grime of the voyage was washed away. As she washed her hair, she reveled in the way it squeaked so clean between her fingers. She felt almost as if she were in heaven. *For surely, if ever there was,* she thought, *this is God's own place.*

She swam and allowed the sun to do its work, then dressed in her nearly dry habit, clucking her tongue at the bloodstains that permanently stained the scapular and the ring of grime that would forever burnish the hem. Then she studied her reflection in the pond, as she had once done in the silver teapot at the convent in Ballysaggart. She smiled at herself, grateful that Sister Theresa was not on Tahila to fuss at her for her vanity. "Sister Theresa would be displeased with me filthy garment," she said to her pup. "But what else can I do but what I have done?"

Laddy had no answer except to nuzzle her hand. Then her stomach growled, and she turned back toward the village, though she and the pup had no sooner emerged onto the path than she encountered the two widows. Smiling, they escorted her back to the still-dozing village and thence to their house, where they offered her slices of fresh coconut and juicy, sweet pineapple.

She shared her meal with Laddy; then the widows led her to a house she had not yet visited. This was the Women's House, they explained. Inside the octagonal-shaped structure, she was shown an ancient treadle sewing machine and various bolts of cloth, including one of pure white cotton. It was hers, they said, and she was thrilled. "Thank ye, me darlings," she said, and both widows replied that she was more than welcome and that they would gladly help her make more of her holy clothes.

They left her then, and Sister Mary Kathleen sat for a while in the Women's House, breathing in the aroma of the clean bolts of cloth and the sweet scent of the bamboo walls and palm-thatched roof. She called for Laddy, who had stationed himself at the doorway, and the pup came inside and crawled into her lap. She stroked his head, cooing to him, telling him what a nice and handsome dog he was, and for just a moment, Sister Mary Kathleen was happy.

"Sister?" It was Mori, Chief Kalapa's first wife, at the doorway. "Would you come with me, please?"

Sister Mary Kathleen followed the woman to the shack that served as Mr. Bucknell's headquarters and there discovered Josh Thurlow, unconscious and lying on a mat. Vapors of gin emanated from his open mouth.

Mori gestured toward the captain. "I overheard my husband and Mr. Bucknell discussing this man. They said he planned on leaving us and taking his marines with him. They said if that was so, we would surely all die. They also said it was because of you. Before now, the Japonee have left us alone. But *Give me the nun,* the sign said on Burubu. By coming here, you have selfishly put this village in danger."

Sister Mary Kathleen absorbed the accusation, then contritely confessed, "Yer right."

Mori was not finished. "The symbol carved at the base of the cross. My husband said Nango described it but could not tell more. What is its meaning?"

"The symbol is Japanese for snow," Sister Mary Kathleen answered. "Do you know what snow is?"

"I have heard of it. It is white and pure. As you are, Sister. Why did this Japanese colonel carve this symbol on Burubu's cross? And why does he desire you so much?"

Sister Mary Kathleen's hand went to the medal around her neck. "I spoke to your husband about this already, Missus Mori."

"He told me what you said, but I believe you must have left a few things out."

"If I did, it was only because there are things it is not decent to tell."

Mori lifted her eyebrows. "You must tell me, for if you do not, I assure you the women of Tahila will drive you off this island and will not care if you drown. We may do so anyway if your reason for being here is not great enough. Besides, there is nothing so indecent that a woman cannot tell another woman."

The nun dropped her face into her hands. "I cannot!"

"You must. Take what I am offering to you. At least unburden your soul."

Sister Mary Kathleen raised her head and looked into the uncompromising eyes of the first wife. "I have already unburdened my soul to a priest, and to God."

"What did the priest say?"

"He said I was lost."

"And your God? What does He tell you?"

"He remains silent."

Mori smiled knowingly. "The priest is a man, and so, you believe, is your God. Tell me, Sister. Tell me everything and let me understand what you have done."

"You won't understand," Sister Mary Kathleen predicted miserably. "Ye will detest me, and then ye will force me to leave. But I cannot go, you see. I must stay and somehow devise a plan to make the Japanese leave Ruka."

"How is such a thing possible?"

"I do not know, yet I must try," she answered. "I must."

The nun's pain was terrible to see, and Mori's heart went out to her, but it was not enough. Her children, all of Tahila's children, were at stake. "I will ask you one more time. If you want to stay on Tahila another day, tell me everything."

So Sister Mary Kathleen, seeing that she had no choice, told Mori everything except her greatest sin, the one she could never voice to anyone save a priest, no matter if she was driven into the sea. After she had told the part that could be told, Mori wept. Then, beside a gin-soaked Josh Thurlow, the first wife of Tahila, tears rolling down her cheeks, knelt before the Irish nun and took her hands and kissed them and asked for forgiveness, and then she took her in her arms and held her tenderly, as a mother holds a child. "You may stay, my dear," she whispered as Sister Mary Kathleen wept bitter tears. "I will help you, for now I understand. And if any man says otherwise, especially this big drunkard, I will defend you. Of this, you may be certain."

3 4

Mr. Bucknell left Chief Kalapa's house, where he had been summoned to speak with the chief and his first wife. He carefully placed his wide-brimmed Panama hat aboard his head and walked down the common road to the boathouse, where he knew Bosun O'Neal and the marines had spent the night. They were sitting cross-legged on the porch and cradling their rifles. "Good day to you, gentlemen," he greeted them. "I trust you had a pleasant evening."

"Have you seen Captain Thurlow, Mr. Bucknell?" Ready asked.

"He is asleep in my headquarters," Bucknell replied. "I think he might have had a little too much gin. Chief Kalapa's first wife has been tending to him."

Ready absorbed the information and picked out the part that was most interesting. "How many wives does Chief Kalapa have?"

"Three, at last count. Anyhoo, I fear your captain will probably be a bit drowsy for the rest of the day. I shouldn't bother him."

Ready shrugged. "He said he didn't want to talk to me unless the Japanese were attacking, which they don't seem to be doing."

Bucknell smiled. "No, not yet—but from what I understand, they may. The nun, you know. Mad Colonel Yoshu seems to have it in his head to retrieve her."

"We know that, Mr. Bucknell. We saw that sign on the cross, too. I guess the captain is right. We should leave before we get attacked, but I'm afraid Sister won't go with us."

"No. I dare say she will not," Bucknell said. "A question, Bosun. Would you leave without her?"

"I took an oath to follow orders, sir. But would I be happy about it? No, I wouldn't."

"I wouldn't like it, neither," Garcia said. "But then I ain't too thrilled about getting massacred. I think we should leave, Bosun."

Tucker said, "It's nice of these folks to let us stay even overnight. I mean, considering what happened on Burubu and all. If I was them, I'd chase us off."

"The people of Tahila are by nature quite hospitable," Bucknell agreed.

"Well, it don't much matter since we're leaving pretty soon," Garcia said.

Bucknell nodded, then offered a small shrug. "I'm not so certain of that. When Captain Thurlow wakes, Chief Kalapa and I will try to persuade him to stay. I think you should make yourself at home in the meantime."

The marines looked at each other. "Does that include fraternizing with the women, sir?" Tucker asked.

"If one should take a fancy to you, of course. Tahila is very open to liaisons before marriage. The people here believe practice makes perfect."

"What a fine belief!" Sampson enthused. He was standing, leaning on a crude wooden crutch.

"How is your foot, young man?" Bucknell asked.

"Missing, sir," Sampson replied, "but Nango brought me this crutch, and it works pretty well." He touched his stomach. "Mr. Bucknell, you got any chow? I guess we're all pretty hungry."

Bucknell did have chow, indeed, and so invited Ready and the marines to breakfast with him beneath the shade of the spreading monkeypod tree that stood beside the boathouse. Various women brought baskets of fruit and jugs of fresh, cool water. "Now, gentlemen," Bucknell said, after they'd eaten, "I have a proposition for you. How would you like to have an adventure? There's an American with two wives who lives across yon mountain. Would you like to visit them?"

"Sure!" Tucker answered. "Sounds like fun."

"I don't know, Mr. Bucknell," Ready said. "What if the Japanese come today?"

"I don't think they will, Bosun. According to the sister, she knows this colonel very well. She is certain he has gone back to his lair, at least for now."

Sampson was also doubtful. "I don't know if I can climb a mountain yet, Mr. Bucknell."

Bucknell thought it over, then raised a finger, and a pretty girl swung by. Bucknell spoke to her, and she smiled enticingly at Sampson. "Valua has agreed to show you the nearby sights, Private. Would that do as a substitute?"

Sampson stared at the girl in openmouthed wonder. "Yes, sir!"

"Pick a girl out for me, too, Mr. Bucknell," Tucker said.

"And me!" Garcia volunteered.

Bucknell chuckled. "Patience, gentlemen. I'm certain your charms will not go unnoticed for long. But for now, I'd like for you to see the island and meet the American. Our adventure, yes?"

Their adventure, yes, and no more than an hour later, Mr. Bucknell, his umbrella laid on his shoulder, led Ready, Tucker, and Garcia up the mountain that rose behind the village. The path they followed led through a thick, luxurious tropical forest of mahogany and banyan trees, their thick limbs draped with hairy vines. Squawking and fussing exotic birds hopped among the branches. Along the path, mats of passion flowers draped rock outcroppings, and plants with slick green leaves as big as an elephant's ear waved in the slight breeze. It was a glorious jungle, filled with a million sweet scents. After the flat ugliness of Tarawa and the bloody mess of Burubu, Ready and the marines were awestruck by its beauty.

When the crest of the mountain was reached, Bucknell told them to take a moment and enjoy the view. Though the others looked ahead, down into a pretty lowland valley, Ready instead looked back to the village. Somewhere down there was Sister Mary Kathleen, and he wondered what she was doing. He wished more than anything he were with her.

"Glorious, isn't it?" Bucknell asked him.

Ready nodded. "Sure is, sir. The people seem nice, too."

"You might want to think how to defend them. Let me make a proposition to you. I have discussed this idea with Chief Kalapa. We think you should take charge of defending us from the Japanese."

Ready was astonished. "Me, sir? But we're not staying. Even if we were, such would better be handled by Captain Thurlow!"

"Captain Thurlow is drunk. Or sick. Or both."

"He's been drunk before. Sick, too. But when he wakes up, I'm sure he will want to leave."

"Perhaps or perhaps not. Let's worry about that later, shall we? Come now, what do you say to our proposal?"

Ready scratched his head. "You're talking about mutiny, sir."

"Nonsense. Your captain is in a stupor. The situation is dire. It is your duty to step up to defend yourself and us."

"I don't know . . ."

"Look, I think you're the perfect man for the job."

"You do?"

"Of course. Your leadership is unquestioned. I've noticed how the marines defer to you."

"Well, I led them for a while back on Tarawa."

"Then it's settled."

Ready was flattered. It was the first time in many days someone of the stature of Mr. Bucknell had said something nice about him. Certainly he'd heard nothing good out of Captain Thurlow for more than a long while. He nodded, saying, "Well, all right. At least until Captain Thurlow tells me otherwise."

"Splendid! I feel safer already. Now, let us continue our adventure."

Bucknell led them down the mountain and through a bamboo grove, behind which they found a large hole in the ground surrounded by various machinery, orange with rust. "The gold mine, gentlemen," Bucknell said. "And there is Mr. Spurlock, who appears to be waiting for us. Halloo, Carl! How did you know we were coming?"

"You bloody bastards make more noise than a herd of elephants!" a man in khaki shorts standing on the edge of the hole roared. He pointed at a little green bush covered with pretty lavender blossoms. "Skirt around that violeta bush there and then walk straight at me. Take care. I've got traps about."

"What kind of traps?" Bucknell called over.

"Camouflaged traps, holes in the ground with sharpened bamboo stakes, in case Colonel Yoshu comes by for an unannounced visit. Now, look sharp, come the way I told you, and you'll be fine."

Take care they did, walking as required near the violeta bush, and made it safely. Spurlock was a tall, weathered man with a square face, fringed by a trim gray beard, and a pugilist's broken nose. Shockingly, he also had only one ear, the other but a hole in the side of his head. He shook hands with Bucknell and then Ready and the marines, who did their best not to stare at the awful orifice. "American boys! Who'da thunk it?" Spurlock boomed. "Glad to meetcha. The girls are proper excited to receive visitors. Come on, but don't wander. You don't want bamboo stakes in your arse!"

Spurlock led the retinue along a path that led up a heavily forested knoll to a happy little stream. "Here is our home," Spurlock proudly announced.

Ready saw no home until he looked up and saw a most remarkable tree-house, sitting in the crook of a giant banyan tree. Spurlock pulled what looked like nothing more than a hairy vine and down fell a rope ladder. "Gentlemen, follow me," he said grandly, and up they climbed into a world Ready had never imagined.

Spurlock was pleased to play tour guide. The treehouse, built nearly entirely from bamboo, consisted of a living area, a bedroom, and a kitchen. The
living area was decorated with scattered pillows. "We read a lot in here,"
Spurlock said, nodding toward several shelves loaded with books. "Found all
them old novels at the gold mine. Read most of them. Some good, some
bad. Don't matter. Just like to read. Let's have a look at the bedroom."

Three individual mattresses lay on the floor of the bedroom, draped
with a single mosquito net hanging from a hook attached to the vaulted
roof. "The mattresses are filled with chicken down and kapok, and they're
soft as a bunk in a San Francisco whorehouse." Spurlock tapped the bamboo floor with his boot, then grinned. "Springy, you'll note? This gives us a
little fun when the girls are frisky, which is often, as you may imagine in
these tropical climes."

Spurlock led the tour into the kitchen, which was decorated with pretty
little painted pots and bowls. A variety of carved wooden utensils were
hung on pegs. "The girls do the cooking in a stone oven on the forest floor,
and the food is raised on a pulley system. Hark! I hear my ladies now.
They've been out gamboling." Spurlock stuck his head through a window
and yelled down. "Tilly! Gertie! We got guests. Come on up!"

The two women clambered up the ladder. "Gents, meet my girls. This
one's Tilly," he said, nodding toward a brown, plump young woman with
ample breasts. "And this one's Gertie."

Gertie was striking, and Ready and the marines frankly gaped. She was
tall, dignified, black as ebony, with short, curly hair.

"Pretty, ain't they?" Spurlock grinned. "Gertie, whiskey, if you please.
Now, Tilly there, shaking her delights for your edification, is from the island
of Yap where they have money made out of round stones big as tractor
wheels. You want to buy a loaf of bread, you roll your money to the store!
Haw! Tilly—you can stop tossing your stuff around now, sweetheart—was a
stowaway. I was trading on her island at the time, and she snuck aboard. Guess
she liked me. I married her first preacher-man I found. At least, he claimed he
was a preacher-man. Hard to say, considering I was in a gin shop."

"And Gertie, sir?" Tucker asked while enjoying the view of the breasts
of the half-naked black woman as she set tumblers out, then poured them
full of whiskey.

"Be careful admiring a man's wife, young man," Spurlock warned, then
chuckled. "Give us a smile, Gertie! No? Oh, well. You know what she is?
I'll tell you. She's an Aborigine. You ever hear of them? They're the native

stock of Australia and wild as any animal in the forest. I was prospecting in the Outback, you see, and got took in by her tribe when I ran out of food and water. Despite their reputation as warlike, I found them to be the most hospitable of people. In fact, Gertie's husband lent her to me on the odd cold night."

"Percentage of truth, Spurlock?" Bucknell asked.

"One hundred percent, you doubting Thomas of a limey! Anyway, when I decided to leave, I bought her from her husband for a bone-handle knife he'd admired. In town, I washed her from head to toe, then got one of the town fancy ladies to teach her how to dress and go to the toilet and such. By and by, as you can see, she turned out to be quite the lovely lady, though she will eat about any bug known to man. Show 'em, Gertie. Get that treat you been saving. Yes, you can have it now."

Gertie nodded and went to a jar, unscrewed the cap, and plucked something from within. It proved to be a big brown hairy spider wriggling between her fingers. She put it in her mouth, chewed it up, and swallowed the whole thing, running her pink tongue across her lips with unalloyed pleasure.

Bucknell chuckled. "How long have you and Gertie practiced this trick, Carl? Just waiting for the right guests to disgust, eh?"

Spurlock laughed, then scratched the hole that was his awful ear, prompting Ready's curiosity. "How'd you lose your ear, Mr. Spurlock, if you don't mind me asking?"

"Not at all. It was in Yokohama. That's right. In old Japan itself. I was married to a Jap maiden at the time. Sweetest little girl you ever saw. It were her brother what did this to me, stole into our bedroom one night and cut it off. He was *Yakuza,* you see. That means he was a Japanese mobster. Yes, just like Baby Face Nelson, only a thousand times worse. You can always tell Jap mobsters, usually got a finger or two chopped off. That's their way of showing loyalty to their boss. Boss says cut that off and they do it with a smile. Anyway, my honorable brother-in-law took umbrage that a white man might marry his exalted little sis and sliced off my ear while I was sleeping. Of course, I gave more than I got when I tracked him down." Spurlock grinned with satisfaction. "Ah, that was a sweet death. My wife, God bless her—her name was Miki—left me after that, though I never understood why. I barely got out of the country with all them chopped-finger bastards after me. I trust it wasn't she who set them after me."

"Percentage of truth, Spurlock?" Bucknell asked tiredly.

"One hundred percent, you rat bastard!" Spurlock roared, "and I'll thank you not to insult me in my own house! What the hell are you doing here, anyway?"

Bucknell smiled. "I have news of Colonel Yoshu, Carl," he said and then told him what had been discovered on Burubu.

Spurlock rubbed his beard and, after a moment of frowning, shrugged and winked. "Well, then, we're next."

"What's your take on the Japanese around here, sir?" Ready asked.

Spurlock gave the question some thought, then answered. "Colonel Yoshu's a gangster, just like I was talking about. He's got two truncated fingers, the little ones on each hand. I don't think he got those chopped off in Sunday school, nor even a Shinto shrine. No, he's likely a boss mobster back in Japan. He definitely ain't one of those 'die for the emperor' types. I doubt if any of his men are, either. *Sumiyoshi Rengo Kai,* I'm thinking is what Yoshu is. That's a Tokyo offshoot of the *Yakuza,* very dangerous and ruthless. They control every little gaming parlor in town, act as loan sharks to the poor people, run prostitution rings and every dodge you can name. Little Miki's brother was part of a rival gang, and I recall he was terrified of the *Sumiyoshi* bunch."

"I hate to think Sister Mary Kathleen lived with them for over a year," Ready said. "She must have been really scared."

"You know her, Carl," Bucknell interjected. "The little Irish nun the other nuns treated like a slave."

Spurlock raised an eyebrow. "She's here? I figured her for dead. How did that come about?"

Ready explained. He began with the first time he'd seen her on Tarawa, then backed up and told about the battle there, then the voyage across the sea and Sampson's surgery. He finished with his interpretation of the tragic discovery on Burubu, including the sign on the cross, and finally their decision to come to Tahila.

Throughout it all, Spurlock leaned forward with interest. At the end of Ready's discourse, he sat back and said, "So the wrath of Yoshu will soon be on this island. Well, it was only a matter of time, nun or no nun."

Bucknell nodded toward Ready and the marines. "Fortunately, Bosun O'Neal and these young fighting men have consented to help defend us."

"Actually, Captain Thurlow may decide to leave in a few days, sir," Ready said quickly.

Bucknell smiled. "We hope to change his mind, Bosun."

"Yes, sir." Then Ready spotted a most interesting artifact on a shelf. "Is that a violin case, Mr. Spurlock?"

Spurlock nodded. "Sure enough, and there's a violin inside. I found it in the shack at the old mine. Guess one of the miners left it behind. Or maybe he died. Do you play, Bosun?"

"Not the violin, no, sir, but I can saw on the fiddle a bit."

"Is there a difference?"

"Not much. Just the way you hold the instrument and place the bow. And the music played, of course."

"You're welcome to take it," Spurlock said. "Ain't no use to me."

Ready opened the case and found the violin wrapped in newspaper. Gently he pulled the knot holding the twine around it and then carefully unfolded the newspaper, which, it turned out, was Australian. Within, he found a violin with its bow. Ready sniffed the violin and said, "Whoever owned it loved it, so I reckon he's dead or he'd never have left it behind. It's been worked with wax and oils. That's why it's not falling apart with dry rot."

"Can it be played?" Spurlock asked.

Ready ran his thumb along the strings, feeling only a few marbles of corrosion, easily worked off. "Well, let's just see," he said and cradled the violin along his collarbone, an inch below his chin, and drew the bow across it. The note was sour, so he adjusted the strings and tried again. This time, the note was sweet.

So Ready played, and Tilly and Gertie threw themselves down on the floor, ecstatic at being entertained. The tune was the first thing that came to Ready's mind, a favorite on Killakeet Island, an old ditty called "Buffalo Girls." Then he played one of his own tunes, which he called "Killakeet Heaven." Spurlock sat cross-legged with his wives, immersed in the music, while the marines admired the women and Mr. Bucknell read from Spurlock's library of moldy novels. Of special interest was a Jack London novel titled *Adventure,* which he devoured, turning page after page with obvious delight.

On the hike back to the village, Mr. Bucknell kept going on and on about the famous, prolific, and colorful author. He concluded with "Jack London lived large, wrote well, and died young. What better can be said of any man?"

Ready wasn't certain that he had an opinion about authors, but he did have one concerning the fiddle he was carrying. "I don't feel right, taking this from Mr. Spurlock," he said.

"You paid for it with your tunes," Mr. Bucknell replied. "Spurlock will be especially pleased as I think you put Gertie and Tilly into a romantic mood."

"I think I saw Gertie smile."

"When you make an Aborigine woman smile, my boy, you have accomplished no mean feat. Be content with that."

At the village, the marines were met by women who clearly fancied them. After introductions from Mr. Bucknell, they were taken in hand and were led off toward the beach for a "swim-swim." There was a woman, a very lovely woman, who took Ready by his hand as well, but he pulled back. "No, me work-work," he said. Disappointed, she pressed her hands to her eyes, an expression of sadness, then trailed after the others.

"The women of the village are most democratic," Bucknell advised. "While you were gone, they gathered together, discussed which of them wanted the new men for romance, debated, then came to an agreement as to who would get whom. The young woman who took your hand, Bosun, is one of Chief Kalapa's daughters. A very intelligent and beautiful young woman, indeed. The chief will be disappointed you rejected her."

Ready handed Bucknell the violin. "Would you keep it for me, sir?"

"Of course. It will be right here any time you care to play it. And Bosun? Perhaps you might consider building yourself a house. The boathouse, you see, is a village center and often used for ceremonies. Though he is always hospitable, I think the chief would prefer you were elsewhere."

Ready nodded, then said, "I'd like to build a house like Mr. Spurlock's."

"Splendid idea. Perhaps one for the nun, too."

Ready lit up at the prospect. "That would be fine."

"You like her, do you not?"

"Very much, sir. But don't give me a hard time about it, please, like Captain Thurlow."

"Wouldn't think of it, dear boy. You are a grown man and surely know what is best for yourself. But the maidens here are comely, and they will continue to entice you."

"You've asked me to take a job, sir, and I intend to do it. That comes first."

Bucknell smiled. "And if, when he comes around, Captain Thurlow objects to your new job?"

Ready pondered his question. "Are you certain the villagers won't leave?"

"They will not leave, Bosun. Chief Kalapa has made that clear to me. This is their home and they will defend it, although I fear they are not warriors by nature. They will need a great deal of training."

Ready nodded. "Then I'll stay here for a little while, Mr. Bucknell, and help set up a defense. Don't matter what the captain wants."

"You are indeed a brave man. I know this must be difficult."

Ready considered the charge. "You know what, sir? It ain't difficult at all." Then he went on down to the beach, there to begin organizing the defense of the island of Tahila.

PART V

The Family Man

O voice of the Beloved!
Thy bride hath heard Thee say,
"Rise up, My love, My fair one,
Arise and come away.
For lo, 'tis past, the winter,
The winter of thy year,
The rain is past and over,
The flowers on earth appear."

—JACKSON MASON, A HYMN

3 5

One eye slowly opened, a very raw, dry eye, pink on the inside and out, fogged over, though clearing until Josh Thurlow could discern his surroundings, which included a curve, the very definite, curvaceous curve of a young woman lying beside him. The young woman appeared to be naked, which, no matter the man or his scratchy eyes, is always at least an interesting view. Josh's other eye now opened, and he blinked both of them in an attempt to improve his focus. Then he slid his gaze down the curve of the woman's back to the curve of her hip and the curves of her legs. Then he slept some more. When he woke, he discovered the woman had moved, though she was still with him. She was crouched at his feet and appeared to be studying him. Lifting his head, which hurt very much, he carefully observed her, at least as much as he could in the scant light that filtered through the bamboo walls of the house. He could see well enough to note that she had an oval face, full lips, a small nose, and large brown eyes. A classic Polynesian woman. She had very long and straight black hair, an attribute Josh had always admired. Her hair also happened to frame an intelligent expression on her pretty face. "Do you live, husband?" she asked.

Josh considered her question. "I am not your husband," was the answer he finally provided, each word an effort since his skull felt as if it might explode with each consonant and vowel.

"You *are* my husband," she replied and continued in a conversational tone in remarkably good English. "I asked you to marry me, you said yes, and Chief Kalapa performed the ceremony. Therefore, I am your wife and you are my husband."

"Let me guess," Josh replied, then waited with gritted eyes until the little hand grenades in his head quit exploding. "You attended missionary school, and this accounts for your excellent English."

"In New Zealand," she confirmed. "Every year before the war, the missionaries selected a child to be sent away for schooling. I was sent when I was six and allowed to return when I was fourteen."

Josh slowly propped himself on his elbows, then managed to sit up, though it hurt his head terribly. He rubbed his temples and allowed a short whimper. "How long have I been like this?"

"Two days."

Josh was certain he hadn't heard her quite right. "Two days? I've been unconscious for two days?"

"Not at all. For instance, you attended our marriage ceremony."

Josh held his face in his hands, vaguely remembering a crazy ceremony he'd taken as a joke. Chief Kalapa was there, and Mr. Bucknell, and Ready and the marines. He'd seen this woman before, too. He recalled ogling her breasts and acting the fool. But, no, that was all a dream fueled by the gin, wasn't it? He spoke through his fingers. "I must have gone off my gourd. That damned fever, then all that gin. Not a good combination. Though I fear the answer, how is it that we came to be married?"

Her reply was to the point. "It was determined that you required assistance since you insisted on drinking all of Mr. Bucknell's gin, and also because of all your injuries from the war. Since I of all the women speak English the best, and since I am a widow with two children, it was also determined that it would be to our mutual benefit to be married. You readily agreed to the arrangement."

"I did?"

"Yes."

"Who did all this determining?"

"Chief Kalapa, his first wife, Mori, and Mr. Bucknell approached me."

Josh rubbed his temples again, the only thing that seemed to help alleviate the pain, and did some rapid thinking. "I presume you have a name."

"Ranumu, although my English name is Rose."

"Well, Rose, what if I am already married?"

"You are not. I asked one of your men, and he said you were a single man."

"Which of my men did you ask?"

"Bosun O'Neal."

"I'll have to remember to thank Bosun O'Neal for his honest answer," Josh replied. Then, still thinking as quickly as he was presently able, which was similar to dragging his thoughts through molasses, he countered, "I am not a citizen of these islands and therefore not bound by your traditions or laws."

"That is true," she calmly replied. "You may ignore the requirements of our society, but if you do, I shall have no recourse but to commit suicide, considering the dishonor."

"Suicide? But what of your children?"

"They will be parceled out to more deserving women."

Josh knew he'd met his match, at least as far as he could play it while still nursing what was apparently the gin hangover of all time. "We'll talk more later," he suggested.

"So we shall, husband. May I provide you with breakfast?"

"Is there a possibility, any possibility at all, in which you might provide me with a gallon of coffee?"

She smiled, and he noted she had a very pretty and radiant smile with very white teeth. "A nice species of coffee grows on this island," she said, "though, as British subjects, we prefer tea, which also grows here."

"Are you saying there is no coffee?"

"I am saying I do not have any."

"Ask Bosun O'Neal. I trust he will have picked some beans by now. Please also ask him to visit me at his first opportunity."

"Of course. As your wife, I will be happy to accomplish this and other chores. You will find there is no more obedient woman anywhere in the Pacific than a woman of the Far Reaches."

"Well, hooray for that," Josh murmured, although he supposed she hadn't heard him since she was off like a shot.

Ready found Josh sitting cross-legged on the sleeping mat inside Rose's house. In one of Ready's hands was a steaming mug of black coffee and in the other a coffeepot. Without preamble, Josh snatched the mug and poured the scalding coffee down his throat. Ignoring the pain, he wiped his mouth with the back of his hand and held out the mug. "More, much more," he croaked.

Ready refilled Josh's mug, then set down the pot and sat beside it. "How are you feeling, sir?" he asked solicitously.

Josh didn't answer because he sensed Ready had asked the question with a certain amount of obtuse satisfaction. "Tell me the latest," he growled.

"Yes, sir. I have agreed to take over the defense of the island."

"What do you mean?"

"Mr. Bucknell asked me if I would command here, and I said I would."

"You command?" Josh cocked his head, squinted a bit, and then said, "Let's hear it all. What else?"

"The marines and I have decided to stay on Tahila. I guess you will, too, now that you have a wife."

Josh absorbed the information and desired to yell at the bosun but refrained, fearing it might blow the top off his skull. "You know, of course, this is mutiny," he said quietly, though menacingly, "and she is not my wife."

"Chief Kalapa says she is."

Josh's voice was low and dangerous. "Chief Kalapa ain't no preacher or priest, last time I looked."

"No, sir, but he's a chief, which, I guess, is sort of like the captain of a boat. He married you. I know. I was there. Besides, you said you wanted to be married."

"I was under the influence. Why didn't you stop me?"

"I tried, sir, but you said you knew what you were doing. At least, I think that's what you said. You were as drunk a man as I've ever seen."

"I never could drink gin. It is a failing."

"Yes, sir. I could see that."

Josh tossed back the coffee, draining every drop, then put the mug to his forehead, its smoothness somehow comforting. He gave Ready a careful eye and said, "You better get back on my side, boy."

"I am on your side, sir, but somebody had to step up to the plate when you couldn't. Or wouldn't."

Josh gave the bosun his best glare, though he could sense it wasn't having much effect. "Already planning your defense at the court-martial, is that it?"

"No, sir. Not at all."

Josh's mind wandered. He was still very tired. "Where did you get the coffeepot?"

"From Mr. Spurlock."

"Don't make me ask you a bunch of questions, Bosun O'Neal. I ain't in the mood. Who the hell's Mr. Spurlock?"

"He's an American Irishman who lives across the mountain near an abandoned gold mine. He's got two wives."

Josh gave that some thought, then said, "Keep going."

"Well, sir, just that this is a nice place to live. The men fish when they want to, and the women do everything else like gardening and picking coconuts or killing the occasional pig or chicken or odd dog for supper. Me and the marines are pretty happy, except for the dog meat."

"The marines are happy?" Josh asked, dismayed. "I suppose this means they have women."

"Yes, sir."

Josh frowned, though it hurt his face. "It's a good thing I am getting back to normal," he said. "Things are clearly out of control. Do you still have the weapons or have the marines traded them for nooky?"

"All secure, sir, and I taught the women how to shoot."

Josh thought he'd heard the bosun wrong. "You did what?"

"Taught the women how to shoot the rifles, sir. Even Sister Mary Kathleen. These Tahila fella boys weren't interested. When we tried to teach them, they just acted silly, yipping and running around. They prefer to use their spears and machetes, which ain't likely to be much good against the Japanese. So I got the idea to teach the women, like Amazons. They do all the work around here anyway. We trained twenty of them all day yesterday, and they did pretty good."

Josh hung his head. "Any sign of the Japanese?" he sighed.

"Nothing. All quiet."

"Well, at least that. How about the nun? What's she up to besides shooting at targets?"

"She's teaching the children."

"Teaching them what?"

"Reading. Writing. Arithmetic. That kind of stuff."

"I thought she wanted to gear up an assault on Ruka. What happened to that idea?"

"She's still got it, sir. Of course, I told her there ain't no way that can get done."

"That's the one thing you've said that makes sense."

"Thank you, sir."

After a long ponder, Josh said, "All right, Bosun, here's my orders. I want you and the marines to gather up your traps, including a rifle apiece and appropriate ammunition, and pack it all on an outrigger. Don't matter which one. We will leave for Tarawa in the morning."

"No, sir," Ready said.

Josh's eyes narrowed. "Surely I did not hear you correctly."

"I don't think you're in condition to travel, Captain."

"It is not up to you to determine my condition, Bosun. By the way, you're busted down to basic seaman."

"Thank you, sir. And thank you for not yelling at me. I figured you'd bust a gut."

"If I raised my voice, my head would surely detonate," Josh replied. "Will you follow my orders?"

"Not those orders, sir."

"Then go away. The sight of a mutineer makes me sick."

"Yes, sir."

Ready left, and Josh drank more coffee while a white-hot anger mounted him. Then Rose reappeared, dipping inside the low doorway of her house. "Did you miss me, husband?"

Josh took a moment to study her anew. All in all, he reflected regretfully, she was indeed pretty, as was his first impression. She had very nice, round breasts and wide shoulders and good legs. Her most attractive feature was her skin, which was so smooth and golden it appeared to have been poured on her from a honey jar. Josh also noted, with some dismay, that the intelligent expression on her face he had earlier discerned seemed even more intelligent now that he could see her more clearly. This meant trouble since Josh had always been a fool for bright and pretty women, a predilection inherited from his father and likely the entire line of Thurlow men in his family tree. If, as he reflected further, he allowed his natural proclivity to proceed, it wouldn't be long before this intelligent lovely with two children would have her legs wrapped around him, and that wouldn't be all she had wrapped around him, no, not by a long shot. *Here before me, in a honey-skinned package,* he thought with sudden clarity, *is nothing but trouble.* He congratulated himself for recognizing this irrefutable fact and then, uncharacteristically, proceeded with caution. "Now, Rose," he began.

"Yes, husband? Do you wish food?"

"Yes, in a bit. But first, we need to establish some rules."

"Of course. May I sit in your presence?"

"Yes. You may do anything you like in my presence."

"Very good. I should like to embrace you."

Which she did, in the Forridges style, holding his shoulders while nuzzling first one side of his face, then the other, and sniffing his cheeks. "You smell just a bit," she said disapprovingly, "and your whiskers are prickly. A bath is in order and a shave. I suggest the pond. I have Australian soap, and I will borrow Mr. Bucknell's razor."

Josh had taken the opportunity to smell her, too, and she did not smell, at least in a negative way. Quite the contrary, she seemed to have the perfume of roses about her, though he did not recall that they grew in the Far Reaches. In any case, her appropriate scent, considering her name, had taken his breath completely away. He worked to regain it, then said, "Yes.

Thank you. I will bathe shortly as well as shave. But first, you see, although you are a very pretty woman, and intelligent, for sartain, and any man would be lucky to have you, I'm afraid it's my duty to tell you that I'm in no position to have a wife. I'm in the Pacific to wage war and only war, you see, not take up a family. Do you understand?"

"Then why did you marry me, husband?" she asked, lowering her eyes.

"I was clearly out of my head," he said. "Why in God's name would you marry me? Surely you saw how deranged I was!"

"That is a good word. You were indeed deranged. Chief Kalapa and his first wife, Mori, said your only chance was to be cared for, night and day, and that the best way I could do that was to be your wife. So I agreed."

"That was very something of you. I can't think of the word."

"Altruistic?"

"Maybe. Now, Rose, here's the thing. I shan't stay in the Far Reaches long, and therefore it would be unfair to you and your children to have the likes of me, as a husband and father. So what I'm getting to is asking how divorcements are accomplished here, that is, without any form of sadness or hysteria, I mean whereby everybody is left happy."

Even as Josh spoke, he sensed his words were not being well received. In fact, Rose's expression had darkened completely, and her eyes had become a bit damp, and there was a subtle trembling of her lower (and undeniably luscious) lip. "It is not credible, that which you ask," she said, "unless you abandon me for at least a year."

"Well, there you have it, then!" Josh said, grasping at the straw. "Let the abandonment begin! Although," he was quick to add, "if there is anything I can do for you and your children, don't hesitate to ask."

"How can you do anything for me if you are not here?"

"Well, I don't guess I'm going to leave right away. First, I have to bring that idiot Bosun O'Neal and the marines back under my command. Until then, I'll still be around if you need anything."

Her expression changed to one of confusion. "But abandonment requires actually leaving. As long as you are in the village, and certainly if you offer me assistance, that is not abandonment."

Josh thought a bit. "Look. How did Chief Kalapa marry us with me unconscious?"

"You were not unconscious! You were singing. Something about Spanish ladies. And when Chief Kalapa asked you if you were willing to take on your responsibilities as my husband, you said, 'Oh, for sartain!' I remember you saying it exactly that way in your peculiar accent."

"It was the gin talking," Josh supposed.

"The bottle in your hand was quite silent as I recall, although you were not. 'Farewell and adieu, ye fair Spanish ladies,' that was part of the song you kept singing. Then, to everything Chief Kalapa said, you said, 'Oh, for sartain!' Ask Bosun O'Neal if you don't believe me. He was standing beside you."

I shall murder Bosun O'Neal, Josh swore silently, forgetting that he'd busted the man to basic seaman, then made another attempt to convince the woman what the situation was. "Perhaps," he said, "it has worked out that we are married, at least according to your customs, but isn't there a younger and better man you're attracted to?"

"Oh, well played, sir," Rose answered sarcastically. "You at once reject me and try to fob me off on someone else. Perhaps you *should* abandon me. There are, of course, many other men who would be pleased to marry me."

For the first time, Josh saw a glimmer of hope, a sliver of opportunity, and a slice of possible salvation. "If such a man pleased you, would it be possible for you to divorce me through some procedure and marry him?"

"Yes, if I loved this hypothetical man more than you," she said forthrightly. "At this moment, I think I would love a pig more."

"Very well!" Josh cried with great satisfaction. "Then while we look for a better man, one that you will love, our marriage will be one of convenience and formality and not consummated." Josh stuck out his big ham hand. "Is it a deal?"

Rose looked askance at the big hand, then answered, "I suppose so. But before I touch you again, even to shake your hand, I wish you to bathe."

Josh smiled. He would have laughed, but he feared it would split his skull. "Then we are in agreement. Take me for a scrubbing. And bring along that Australian soap."

And so Josh and Rose, husband and wife, ventured to the lagoon, there to bathe him with the Australian soap. Rose also provided Josh with a straight razor borrowed from Mr. Bucknell and a toothbrush a missionary had given her long ago. She smiled at him as he washed and shaved and brushed. She thought he was a bit rough but salvageable, and so set her course to snare the man she had already married.

3 6

Once he had cleaned up to Rose's satisfaction and was fed and rested, Josh sat on the mat outside Rose's hut and worried about all the things he had to worry about. The mutiny of Bosun Ready O'Neal and the marines, he decided, had to be his first priority. He called to Rose. "Do you have paper and pen?"

She stood in the doorway, her hands on her hips. "I do, of course, since I am literate."

"Might I borrow such? I will pay you back."

"What is mine is yours, husband," she replied in a tone that made it sound like a rebuke, then disappeared inside only to quickly reappear with a stubby pencil and a tattered spiral-bound notebook. "Will this do?" she asked.

Josh took the items, inspected them, noted that the notebook, besides being tattered, was only faintly mildewed, and said, "Yes, it will do very well. Thank you." Then he began writing down a list of charges against the bosun and the marines, ones he figured to scare them with, although he was a bit distracted by Rose, who was standing very close, so close the hem on her lava-lava brushed his arm.

Josh deliberately moved his arm, frowning and clearing his throat to indicate that he was preoccupied. Rose, taking the hint, went back inside her house, where the sounds of housekeeping continued. Josh jotted a few more words, then stood and, ducking low through the doorway, went inside to see what Rose was doing. He saw that she was rearranging her few simple sticks of furniture—a battered trunk and several wooden boxes with kitchen supplies—to place a large mat on the floor. "What's this?" he asked.

Rose pushed the hair out of her eyes. "It is customary that a just-married man and woman sleep on a new mat. I purchased this one from Malua, who lives four houses toward the beach from us on the second row. She is a fine weaver."

"It is very nice," Josh said. He stood for a moment, trying to think what else he should say, but after nothing came to mind said, "I am going to see Chief Kalapa."

"Please feel free to go where you wish without asking my permission," she said.

"I wasn't asking permission, just telling you. It is the polite thing to do, you see."

She smiled and then got down on her hands and knees to smooth out the mat. "You need not do even that," she answered from that position. "It is not customary for a man in this village to concern himself with his wife's feelings."

"I will keep that in mind." He watched her for a moment longer, her fetching hips wiggling as she worked over the mat, then said, "Even though we sleep on the same mat, we will not sleep together, if you get my meaning."

She sat up, again pushing her long hair from her eyes. "I do get your meaning very well, but it does not matter. Who in this village, who indeed of your men, will believe that we do not ficky-ficky?"

"Ficky-ficky? What kind of word is that?"

"The women say the marines taught it to them. It means coupling."

"It is not a word, even in the marine lexicon. They made it up."

"That does not change that you and I know what it means. Nor does it change the fact that everyone will assume we are engaged in it."

"*We* will know we aren't, and that is what is important," he said and walked out of the house, bumping his head on the doorway as he went. He thought he heard her laugh, then decided it was his imagination. He walked down the common road until he reached the chief's hut. One of Kalapa's wives was grinding up a root of some sort, and he asked her to relay his wish to speak to the chief. She pointed. "Chief along boathouse."

Josh tipped an imaginary cap, his being lost on Betio, then walked down the sandy road, where he encountered a new structure, a simple thatched roof covering a few rows of benches, which were filled with children. In front of them stood Sister Mary Kathleen pointing at a chalkboard, no doubt left behind by the missionaries. Apparently she was teaching the children, and then Josh recalled Bosun O'Neal had mentioned that fact. Marveling at how quickly everything had changed in just a few short days, he climbed inside the boathouse, where he found Chief Kalapa seated on a log bench and looking thoughtful. "What-what?" the chief demanded.

Josh opened the conversation casually. "Good morning to you, Chief. A great day, is it not?"

The chief inclined his head in agreement but squinted suspiciously since he doubted this was a friendly call. "How is it, Jahtalo? No more drink gin?"

"No more drink gin, Chief," Josh agreed. "It made me do things I wish I hadn't. For instance, marrying that woman."

Chief Kalapa smiled. "Ah. Too much pretty, that Rose. She make you happy man, Jahtalo."

"No, she won't," Josh said. "She's put me in a pickle, that's what she's done."

"Pickle I no savvy."

"She's trouble. You savvy that well enough, don't you?"

Chief Kalapa was all surprise and innocence. "What-what? But Rose too much good woman. She make baby belong you."

"I don't want baby belong me. I want to leave Tahila, go back to Tarawa."

"No baby?" Chief Kalapa shook his head slowly from side to side, as if unable to bear the news.

Then Mr. Bucknell entered the boathouse, bowing first as was the custom to the totem at the entrance, which, Josh reflected, he had failed to do. "May I enter this house?"

"Come," Chief Kalapa answered gruffly.

Bucknell greeted Josh. "It's good to see you up, Captain." Then he sensed the tension in the room. "Am I interrupting something?"

"I'm trying to make the chief understand why I can't be married," Josh replied, tamping down his irritation. "I suppose I'm not explaining it well. Maybe if I used the local dialect I could do it better. I used to know it but I've forgotten it over the years."

"Perhaps your wife could help you learn it again," Bucknell proposed with a bit of a smirk.

Josh glared at the diplomat, then gave up on that particular subject. He had bigger fish to fry. "Yes, perhaps she can," he agreed. "Now, Mr. Bucknell, Chief. I need to let you know something. Bosun O'Neal and the marines are engaged in a mutiny. I intend to put it down."

"Mutiny?" Bucknell breathed. "I'm stunned."

Josh regarded him and doubted that the Britisher was stunned at all. "You and Chief Kalapa must not interfere," he said. "This is a matter of the United States, which I represent as ranking officer."

"Chief Kalapa and I would never think to interfere, of course," Bucknell replied, "but, from my observation, Bosun O'Neal and the marines simply agreed to help us while you were sodden with gin. That is scarcely grounds for a charge of mutiny."

"Perhaps, but now I am recovered, and yet Bosun O'Neal refuses my orders."

"What orders would that be?"

"To gather up our things and leave."

"You mean abandon us? Including your wife?"

Josh glowered, and he clenched his big fists. "You know what I mean."

Bucknell shrugged. "Captain Thurlow, the way I see it is you lost control of your men by abandoning them for gin. Perhaps you can regain their trust, but it may take a while. In the meantime, it is obvious you are still exhausted and perhaps inclined to drink again, although I must tell you I have locked up my remaining stock of gin. Anyhoo, Bosun O'Neal told me all that you did on Tarawa, or, more properly, the atoll of Betio, and it is no wonder you require rest."

"I don't require rest, you Brit lackey!" Josh thundered, then staggered a little when he thought surely his head was going to tear itself right off his neck.

"Dear me," Bucknell said. "Captain, I implore you. Rest up, then you may take charge of your men. Until then, let them defend us."

Chief Kalapa rose and put his hand on Josh's shoulder. "Jahtalo no fight. Jahtalo sleep much. Ficky-ficky Rose. Be happy."

Josh saw now he was outnumbered, and his show of weakness had also mortified him. Holding his head, he turned and marched out of the boathouse and past the school and up the common road to sit on the mat in front of Rose's house. There he sat for a long time. Pink clouds floated over the headland where the sun was falling, and the breeze rustled the fronds of a nearby palm and also the tiny leaves of the candlewood tree that shaded the house. Many things passed through Josh's mind, but he was unable to make much sense of them. Finally, he latched onto the one thing he understood to be true, though he could scarcely believe it. He said it to himself: *I have no responsibilities.*

He must have said it aloud since Rose replied from within the house. "What responsibilities do you wish, husband?"

"I don't know," he answered absently. He continued to sit as the giant red orb of the sun slid down and then sank behind the headland with a spray of purple and gold. Josh suddenly thought that perhaps tomorrow he would climb that hill and watch the sun fall into the sea. Perhaps, he considered, he might even see the green flash, an optical spectacle the sun in those latitudes sometimes managed to produce. Maybe, he also thought, Rose might want to see it, too.

"Yes, I would like to see it with you," Rose replied from within her house, and Josh realized that he had expressed this thought aloud as well.

After darkness spread across the village, Rose came outside and sat beside him. She said nothing, just helped him look at the stars. Finally, after a long while, she asked, "Do you fear not having anything to do?"

"Yes," he confessed. "A man needs to work, else he loses his sense of worth."

"Then why did you choose to drink when you came here? Surely you knew there was much to be done."

Josh thought about that, then said, "I was sick. Not sick like with fever or with wounds, but sick up here." He tapped his head. "I thought drinking would fix things. It didn't, of course. It only made me drunk."

"Why were you sick, husband?" Rose asked after what she considered a suitable time.

Josh answered, with sudden insight, "I don't think I've been right since I was on top of that big sand fort on Tarawa."

"Tarawa?"

"It is a group of islands in the Gilberts. There was a big battle there on a Tarawa atoll called Betio."

"Tell me about this big sand fort. I want to hear it, and I think you want to tell it."

Josh looked at her in surprise, then knew she was right, he wanted to tell it very much. "It was one of the last obstacles we had to take. There was this man I met there. His name was Sandy. He didn't have to be there but he was, because he felt obligated to help out. He organized an attack against the fort and, against all odds, it succeeded. After it was pretty much over, Sandy and I were atop the fort and I was talking to him when he was struck in the head with a bullet, though I didn't know it at first. When I realized he was dead, I looked up at the sky and a bird flew over me. The thing is, I knew this bird, Rose. It was a pelican and its name was Purdy. It lives on Killakeet and is very old."

"Killakeet? Is that an island in the Gilberts?"

"No. It's where I grew up. It's half a world away from the Gilberts."

"Then how did this pelican from Killakeet get to Tarawa?"

Josh blinked a few times, his mind aswirl, then shook his head. "You see, that's just it. I don't know. All I know is that I'm sure it was him. After that,

I felt like reason was slipping away from me. I took fever but then came out of it long enough to hold myself together on the voyage here. I even performed surgery on a man with the help of Sister Mary Kathleen. But then we arrived on Burubu . . ." He shook his head. "The people there were murdered, Rose. It was not easy to see."

"Did you see the pelican there?"

"No. Just a crucified chief and a cry from a crazy man who wants Sister Mary Kathleen for a reason I can't figure, and she won't tell."

"You like her, don't you, husband?"

Josh sorted through his mind. "Yes, I like her. She is a remarkable woman."

"Do you love her?"

"Bosun O'Neal loves her."

"Yes, I know. Every woman on Tahila has figured that out. But do *you* love her? That was my question."

Josh considered it. "I think I was falling in love with her. You know, until this second, I didn't know that. Maybe that's why I wanted to get drunk." He looked at Rose and saw her stricken expression. "Oh, Rose. It was only because I was so tired. On reflection, I don't love her, not in the way you mean."

"That pleases me, husband," Rose answered. "It would be most foolish of you to love a woman who cannot ficky-ficky."

"I wish you wouldn't use that term," Josh admonished.

"But I like it. It is a good word."

"As you wish," Josh said, giving in.

"What else would you like to talk about?"

Josh found that he enjoyed talking to Rose, and it seemed to be helping him figure out a few things. He therefore continued with his litany. "I guess you know I have been cast adrift by my men. This troubles me, I confess."

She put her hand on his shoulder. "You have been through much. A man deserves every so often to simply rest and recuperate."

"But I have lost my leadership position."

"What does it matter? As long as those things that must be done are done, is it important that you are the one to do them? I do not understand why you fret so! From what I was told by Bosun O'Neal, you are a man who has fought in many battles and killed many men. You see? He was proud of you, even while you were drunk. He said the big men of your country look up to you. So why not let it go for a little while? Rest while you can, I say. You may even want to dream a little."

Josh let his mind wander across the things Rose had said and found no fault in them. "You are an intelligent woman, Rose."

"Yes, I am."

"I've been wondering something. You said you have two children. Where are they?"

"They stay presently with my sister. I have a boy of ten, and a daughter of six. They are not far away, three houses toward the lagoon. Would you like to meet them?"

"Perhaps tomorrow."

"What would you like to do now?"

Josh wasn't certain what he wanted to do now except to continue to talk, to unburden himself of all the things that had worn him down. This included clearing the air between him and his new wife. "I must confess two things to you, Rose," he said. "First, I am possibly engaged to be married, depending on my memory, which isn't so good right now. She lives on Killakeet, and her name is Dosie Crossan. I think I am in love with her. There is also another woman, a Melanesian of the Solomon Islands who goes by the name of Penelope although her name is actually Kimba. I might have impregnated her just recently."

Rose's hand remained in place on Josh's shoulder. "I see. Well, I think it is possible for a man to love more than one woman. I see nothing wrong with that. But a man has to choose between them, else there is trouble, much trouble, and only trouble."

"I know," Josh replied.

"Which shall you choose of these two women?"

"I don't know. For one thing, I'm not positive I will ever see either of them again."

"Why not?"

"I don't figure to survive this war. I say that not for your sympathy, Rose, but because I have seen so many other men die out here who never thought it was their time. My number will surely come up. It's simple arithmetic."

Rose was silent for a while, then said, "I believe your situation has come to this: On this day, this night, and perhaps for the remainder of your life, it seems you have only me."

Josh nodded. "It is possible."

"With that in mind, I think we should ficky-ficky."

Astonished, Josh stared at her. "After what I have told you of the other women, and confessed that I am a miserable failure?"

"Why not? You sense death is near. I do as well, to be honest. I understand you do not love me, but here we are. It is night. My children are elsewhere and safe. The air is warm and the breeze gentle, and if you will but use your nose, you will catch the scent of the night-blooming jasmine, which the gods put on these islands to remind us to love one another, and often. I believe it is a perfect time for a man and a woman to couple." She added, "And very sweetly."

Rose's hand left Josh's shoulder and slid down, trailing through his chest hair. Then she took his hand and held it. He looked into her eyes for what seemed to both of them a very long time. Then Josh detected the night-blooming jasmine. "It is most sweet," he acknowledged.

"Yes," she whispered. "It is."

Then Rose stood and Josh stood with her. He touched her hair, then kissed her lips and smelled her fragrance, that of her namesake. "But you are sweeter," he said while she smiled beneath his chin. "Don't we have a new sleeping mat?" he asked as if it had suddenly occurred to him.

"We do. Might you care to rest on it?"

Josh thought he might, indeed.

3 7

Two weeks went by, then another. Time on the island of Tahila was fluid and passed like water through a man's hands. During those days, as the sun rose and set, and the stars streamed overhead, and the sun rose and set again, Ready O'Neal's stature kept rising until he was among the most respected men on Tahila. Among his accomplishments was the organization of the defense of the island. He ordered stacks of firewood placed at observation points around Tahila, then created a rotating roster of watchmen to light them if the enemy was spotted. He established emplacements for the two machine guns brought from Tarawa, giving them good fields of fire to batter any Japanese barges that might try to enter the lagoon. Once a week, he called the militia of women out to go over their response to an invasion. Everyone was impressed with what Ready O'Neal had accomplished in a very short time.

The people of Tahila also took positive note of the determined but thoughtful manner in which Ready built his house. After mulling over its location and consulting with Chief Kalapa for available properties, he picked a rise overlooking the village and the lagoon. The property, coincidentally, belonged to the chief, who, as payment for leading the defense, ceded it to him for a hundred years. Mr. Bucknell drew up the papers and stamped them at least a dozen times with his big official stamp, and the bargain was sealed. Then Ready drew his plan, wrote out his materials list, and set himself to clearing the site and gathering all that he needed. The marines helped and turned into fair island carpenters.

The houses in the village were simple designs, constructed with a floor of earth, walls of bamboo, and a thatched roof. Ready, however, after studying the situation, raised his floor three feet off the ground, supported by thick palm stilts. The floor was constructed of thin bamboo struts lapped horizontally, then laced with hemp strands at the ends. With a woven palm frond mat over it, the result was a surface that was soft, springy, sweet-smelling, and infinitely pleasing to the bare foot.

The walls of Ready's house were built from lengths of thick bamboo. He contracted with a woman to weave geometric patterns in the walls with vines. This broke the verticality of the many bamboo pieces and therefore was pleasing to the eye.

The roof of the house, which became known as the Bosun House, was thatched with tightly knitted palm fronds on a bamboo frame reinforced by more hemp. Just as the last sheet of hemp was pulled tight and knotted, a big thunderstorm dropped a deluge of rain, and the Bosun House did not leak so much as a drop.

Put all together, Ready's house was open, airy, comfortable, liable to creak when blown hard by the wind, but undeniably sturdy. To finish the construction, a cooking house, a miniature version of the first structure, was built alongside it with a lava rock oven installed in the center. Without a doubt, it was the finest house on the island.

One day, Chief Kalapa called Ready to the boathouse. Why it was called the boathouse, since it was mostly used for meetings and ceremonies, no one could say, except that hemp line and other outrigger equipment was stored there. Ready bowed to the totem on the porch and entered to find the chief with a sour expression. "Bosun," he asked without preamble, "you build too much good house."

"Thank you, Chief."

"Good house need good woman. Why you no belong woman?"

"I don't know, Chief."

"Many wimmins come along me. They say we cook, clean, make house, ficky-ficky along Bosun. But Bosun, he no care. Bosun, he belong work-work too much."

Ready thought about the women who had come around while he'd built his house, beautiful women who had "accidentally" pressed their soft breasts against his arm as they leaned in with offered bowls of mashed taro root or fried plantains sprinkled with cane sugar or even the odd boiled chicken egg. He thought of their winsome smiles, their big brown fluttering eyes, and their skin that was so smooth. He was stirred by them, make no mistake, yet he'd held himself back.

"Bosun no happy," Chief Kalapa keenly observed. "You need ficky-ficky woman. Chief Kalapa send woman ficky-ficky Bosun."

"No, Chief," Ready answered. "Too much work-work, just as you say."

Chief Kalapa shook his head. "Bosun numbah one 'merican belong Tahila. Bosun no like Tahila woman. Tahila people too much sad."

"I like Tahila women very much, Chief."

"Then you go along one Tahila woman."

Ready realized he had offended the chief, and all the people of Tahila, because of his steady rejection of the women who had come around. "Please tell everybody I think the women here are wonderful," he said.

"Bosun love Sister," the chief accused.

Ready responded with a halfhearted chuckle. "No, Chief."

"Yes. No good Bosun love Sister. You go along Tahila woman."

Ready nodded. "I will. Just give me a little time."

Chief Kalapa frowned. "You go along Tahila woman," he said, just in case the bosun wasn't clear on what was required of him, and the meeting was over.

It was on a Sunday, while the villagers were napping during the hottest part of the day, that Sister Mary Kathleen came to the Bosun House with a housewarming gift, a jar of sweet copra soap. Her dog, Laddy, accompanied her. "Thank ye, Bosun," she said, as she was shown a seat on the floor by the ever courteous Ready. "'Tis a fine house ye have built. Will the marines live here with you?"

"They will stay with their women, Sister," he answered, sitting cross-legged before her.

"The mores of the women are of concern to me," Sister Mary Kathleen confided. "They are free with their bodies from about twelve until sixteen, and then they attempt with every manner afterwards to snare a man into marriage, including pregnancy."

"Getting pregnant to snare a husband is not unknown in America," he replied.

"Nor in Ireland," she confessed. "Several of me classmates used the same tactic, although it sometimes resulted in one less boy in the village, himself run off to America."

"Well, thank you for the soap," Ready said in an attempt to close the visit. She was making him uncomfortable since he kept wanting to tell her how pretty she was.

"I must say," she said, not taking the hint, "that living with the two widows has been most enjoyable. Though they do not keep a clean house, and they snore terribly loud, they have allowed me to sweep and scrub to my satisfaction, plus prepare their meals and look after them in nearly every other way. It is what a good nun does, ye know, be subservient to all who need her."

"I think the widows may be taking advantage of your kindness," Ready suggested. "Perhaps you should ask them to do the cooking, at least."

"Why? Do ye think I'm not a good cook?"

"I didn't say that. I suppose you're a very good cook, although I have never tasted anything you've prepared."

She nodded, mollified. "Of course, yer right." She patted her dog, which was lying on the mat beside her.

"Laddy seems a polite dog, and friendlier than most in the village," Ready observed, just to have something to say.

"That is because he knows he will not be eaten," Sister Mary Kathleen replied with a tender smile toward the dog. Then she studied the interior of the house, from corner to corner. "Aye, this is a grand house ye've built, Bosun, 'tis, it 'tis."

Ready didn't reply, because he still wanted her to leave. His heart stayed in his throat any time he was around her, and he was tired of it. He had been thinking about other women, the ones who wanted him, the ones with the soft breasts and the soft skin. But she did not leave, and they sat silently until she said, "Have ye considered building another one? A house such as this, I mean?"

Ready finally understood the purpose of her visit. "Would you like me to build you a house, Sister?"

"A house for me? But what would me widows do? They depend on me!"

"I see. Well, it was just a thought."

"I saw more bamboo piled on the beach, that was all."

Ready smiled. "Sister, I have a confession to make. The bamboo is for your house. I planned on surprising you."

She smiled back. "I will make a confession, too. As much as I love me widows, I won't mind being quit of them. 'T'would be nice to have me own digs, as it were. If I might compensate ye in some way . . ."

"No charge, Sister. Call it a gift."

She frowned. "I would prefer to pay you, in some manner. I have no money, but I would be willing to come here, to do housework for ye."

"No. I don't think that would be a good idea. Just be my friend, that's all."

"I am pleased to be yer friend, Bosun," she replied sternly, "but if ye build this house for me, I will be grateful to a friend, but a friend only. Ye understand this, do ye not?"

"Of course, Sister." His smile turned crooked.

"Yer sure?"

"Yes, of course."

"Splendid!" She was silent for a moment and then said, "There's one thing you must understand. I am happy here, never doubt it, and enjoy so much teaching the children. But somehow, I still must find a way to chase the Japanese from Ruka. That is my passion. After a suitable while, will ye help me do that, Bosun O'Neal?"

"Sister, you know I want to," Ready replied, wanting so much to take her hands in his, "but Captain Thurlow was right. We just don't have enough marines to chase ten Japanese away, much less a hundred. And from what I saw written on the cross, it looks like your colonel will come here first."

Her expression closed, and her voice turned cold. "He is not my colonel, as you say."

"Well, I didn't mean anything by that."

She rose and tucked her hands in her sleeves. "I do not expect ye to build me a house," she said.

"Sister, forgive me. I'm sorry for any upset I caused you. Let me build you a house. It would give me much happiness."

"No, Bosun. Put it out of yer mind. I'm sorry I agreed to it. I no longer agree to it at all."

She left, walking with her dog down a path lined with stones Ready had built with the hope she might one day walk along it. He watched her go, while leaning in his doorway, until she disappeared beneath the big candle-wood tree beside the boathouse. "That Japanese colonel wants you," he said to himself, "and, though I know it is past foolishness to insanity, so do I."

Then he went back inside his fine new house, and there one of the most respected men on Tahila sat alone.

3 8

Another week passed, plus a few days, and Josh Thurlow used the time to try to figure out a few more things. About himself, mostly, but other things, too. One afternoon, he found himself sitting in a chair in front of his wife's house. It was a sturdy chair. He'd fashioned it from the limbs of a breadfruit tree and bound it tightly with hemp twine. Rose had further provided kapok-filled cushions for it, and, sitting there in the warm sun, he supposed he was nearly happy, even as he was also frustrated. While Bosun O'Neal had risen in stature on Tahila, Josh had no stature at all, other than that of a former chief, now disgraced and discarded. When the marines saw him, they usually looked the other way. When Bosun O'Neal crossed his path, he would smartly salute, but Josh never saluted him back. Instead, he would growl, "I don't salute mutineers!" Chief Kalapa and Mr. Bucknell did everything they could to avoid Josh altogether, which they usually managed.

Gradually, over the days, Josh had come to accept that he was no longer in charge of anything and, with Rose's help, sometimes even like it. But since he was a dynamic man, such could not last, and that is why he became the charcoal man of Tahila.

From the first, Josh was surprised to see that Rose cooked on an open wood fire, which was, Josh suspected, inefficient. After some study, he saw that indeed there was a constant requirement to build the fire up, which meant frequent trips to the woodpile, and the heat it delivered was unsteady. As a result, the food was sometimes undercooked and sometimes overcooked. Since Josh looked forward to his meals, he pondered on how to make the cooking easier and better. Charcoal, he decided, was the solution. While on hiking trips with his father in the North Carolina mountains, he had observed charcoal kilns and, being an engineer, had paid attention to their design. He recalled that one of the mountaineers had used an oil drum to make charcoal, and that was the direction Josh decided to go. He hiked across the mountain, pleased that his strength had returned and even his knee didn't hurt much, and poked around the old gold mine until he found a steel drum that wasn't too rusty. With the help of Nango and another fella boy, he hauled it to a site just above the village and there prepared his kiln.

After scouting the forest, he chopped down a diseased monkeypod tree and began his tests. It took many tries, but finally Josh figured out how to use the exotic wood to make charcoal. Rose tried it, was delighted with the results, and showed it off to her relatives. Immediately they wanted charcoal of their own, and Josh was more than happy to supply it.

Since the output of his barrel kiln was limited, he thought about how to build a kiln from local materials. It turned out one of the fella boys knew how to make mud bricks, and the problem was solved. Josh built a kiln out of bricks, produced charcoal, and gave away his patent to anyone who wanted it. Soon many women were making charcoal in their own kilns. Josh, the charcoal man of Tahila, was pleased that he had introduced a new technology.

While Josh scoured the forest for diseased trees to use for charcoal, it also allowed him to inspect the lookout points Bosun O'Neal had established. He took the opportunity to check the fields of fire of the machine guns, and, from a distance, hidden in the bush, observe the weekly maneuvers of the women's militia and the nun's fella boys. Although he was averse to approving anything a mutineer might accomplish, his observations confirmed that Bosun O'Neal had done a good job. He studied the various beaches around the island to determine if the Japanese could use them for a landing. He was relieved to find that there were none that were suitable, due to high cliffs, save a small one on the northern side of the island. When the Japanese came, Josh believed they would come straight at the village. He also had no doubt that their landing would be successful—and tragic.

He was worrying about all this, sitting in the sun on his breadfruit chair, when Rose came outside and stood beside him to wait for the children after school. Turu and Manda raced up and flung themselves into her arms, laughing and chattering, and then, with pure abandon, threw themselves at Josh, too. He picked them both up, allowing Manda to climb up behind his neck and drop her little legs around it to dangle along his chest, and Turu to be held in one of his big arms.

"Jahtalo," Turu said, "I learned today of a place called Ireland. The nun read about it to us. I would like to go there someday. Do you think I could?"

"I think you could go anywhere and do anything you want," Josh answered and then, wanting to study the lagoon with an eye on how to stop the Japanese, said, "Why don't we go fishing?"

"I should like that very much, Jahtalo!"

"Let's take your mother along. What do you say?"

"Oh, yes!"

"No!" Rose yelped. "Tahila women have enough work to do. We do not go out on boats, unless it to visit relatives on the other islands, and we do not fish. Fishing is reserved for the men, who otherwise just play and sleep."

"Oh, come on, Rose," Josh pleaded. "Just go out with us today for a little while. We'll leave Manda with your sister. It'll be fun."

Manda was not pleased with this idea. "I want to fish, too," she said.

"I will take you next time, dear," Josh promised, "but this time, I think I want to take just your brother and your mother. It is not because I don't love your company, which I do, but because I think you would have more fun with your cousins."

"Yes," Manda answered sagely, "you are probably right."

Josh reached up and gave Manda an appreciative squeeze, causing her to giggle. His heart swelled at the sound of it. He thought it might even break.

A little later, Josh, with Rose and Turu aboard, paddled their canoe into the lagoon. He'd bought the canoe for only two bags of charcoal. Rose, sitting at the centerboard, looked decidedly uncomfortable. "It will be fine, Rose," he told her.

"But I've told you I do not want to fish," she insisted. "It is not proper."

"Of course it is. Where I grew up, all the women fished."

"Does your woman named Dosie fish?" she demanded. "I asked Bosun O'Neal, and he said she was a fine lady."

"Stop talking to Bosun O'Neal."

"Does she fish, husband?"

"No, but she wasn't born and raised on Killakeet. She is from a different tribe, you might say."

"A better tribe, one that doesn't make its women fish?"

"Well, it was the Yankee tribe, and I think some of its women fished, too. But not Dosie."

"I think I like your Dosie," Rose declared. "Bring her here. She can be your second wife and help me with the housework and cooking."

"I will think about that," Josh said, smiling.

Josh threaded the canoe through the coral heads until they reached deeper water. He baited a bone hook with a small chunk of parrotfish, which was called locally a *papu-papu,* and then, using a length of thin bamboo as a pole and hemp for the line, made his cast. Turu also baited a hook and tossed it in, using a traditional hand line. Josh admired the boy who, though small in stature, was wiry and strong.

It didn't take long before Josh got a bite. *Oh, how lovely it would be to have a reel,* he thought, although he expertly hooked the fish and dragged it in hand over hand. It proved to be a nice grouper, which the locals called a *lapa-lapa.* "Supper, I do declare!" Josh grinned and hauled in the flopping fish. He cracked it on the head with the butt of his K-bar and then deftly gutted and filleted it, presenting a juicy morsel to Turu and Rose. Both of them ate and, as was the custom, smacked their lips in appreciation.

"Oh, so!" Turu exclaimed, then pulled in a plump tilapia, which, oddly enough, was also called *tilapia* by the locals. Following Josh's lead, Turu stunned the fish with the butt of his bone-handled knife, then just as expertly gutted it and cut chunks of meat from it, proudly giving Josh and his mother each a morsel.

Ah, now ain't this living! Josh thought to himself. "Are you ready for a turn at fishing, Rose?"

"I dare not, husband. It is not proper, as I have explained to you."

"Oh, come on. I won't tell anybody, and neither will Turu. Will you, son?"

Turu shook his head, but Josh wasn't paying attention since he was reflecting, with some satisfaction, that he had called the boy "son." He looked at Rose and saw that she was smiling tenderly in his direction. She had heard him say it, too. She reached for the bamboo pole.

Josh flung her hook out across the water, and it didn't take long before Rose was rewarded with a jerk on the line. "Set the hook!" Josh cried and reached for the line. Rose pulled the pole in one direction as the hooked fish swerved in another, and Josh found himself reaching for nothing but air and tipping beyond his capability to correct. Knowing he was going in anyway, he dived in headfirst and came up spewing water. Rose was laughing so hard she dropped the pole, and Josh became entangled in the line. Climbing back into the canoe, no mean feat, Josh sat down, dragged in the rod, and proceeded to untangle himself. Then an idea popped into his head. He studied the lagoon, from headland to headland. "I know what to do," he said.

"You don't act like it, husband," Rose said, still laughing.

Josh laughed, too, and kept untangling himself. "I mean I know how to stop the Japanese, Rose," he said.

"You fill me with pride, Jahtalo," she answered. "Now, teach me to fish. I have decided this is fun."

The next cast saw Rose hook a fish and pull it in. It proved to be a small barracuda, which she called an *ogo*. But Josh cut the line and let the toothy fish go.

"Why did you do that?" she demanded. "It was mine, not yours."

"My apologies, Rose. I should have told you my reason before acting. My father, Keeper Jack, turned me against eating barracuda. He said it was the smartest fish in the sea. He also said it could make you sick, that a type of poison built up inside it. Gives you tremors, makes you unbalanced."

"You must have eaten some *ogo* before you fell into the sea!" Rose said, turning to laughter once more.

Josh smiled, but then he spotted something floating in the water. He paddled the canoe over to it and plucked it out. It was a greasy lump, and it stank. "Throw that away," Rose said, wrinkling her nose. "That is *kakulu*, the spit of a whale."

"Actually, it is formed in the gut of the sperm whale," Josh informed her. "It's called ambergris in English, although I think it was originally a French word. It's used in perfume that fancy ladies wear."

"Perfume? But it has an awful odor."

Josh gave the lump a sniff and was reminded of a musty basement. "It's a bit strong, I'll warrant. Too bad there's not more of it around, though. It's worth quite a lot of money."

"Oh, I know where there is a great deal of it," Rose said archly. "On the beach of dead whales."

"What are you talking about, woman?"

Turu spoke up. "It is a hard paddle by canoe but an easy hike, taking but a day. It is there the whales come to die."

"I should very much like to see this place," Josh said, eagerly anticipating an adventure, not to mention becoming rich.

"Then I will guide you," Turu said.

"Will you go, Rose?" Josh asked.

"Of course. I could use a day off. So could the children."

"What about school?" Josh asked.

"What about it? Is it wrong for children to miss school to have an adventure with their father? I think not!"

"If every mother were like you, Rose," Josh admired, "there would be no unhappy children."

Rose smiled at Josh's sentiment, though she did not entirely understand what he meant by it. Would any mother in the whole world deny her children an adventure? She sincerely doubted it.

The fishing continued and several plump snappers, called *huma*, were caught to add to the larder, and finally a nice tuna, called *matu*. "After we dry them, we'll have enough fish to last us a week," Josh said, pleased. "And we've only been out for about an hour. These are some of the richest waters I've ever known. It's heaven for a fisherman."

"Then you like living on Tahila, husband?" Rose asked.

Josh nodded, then allowed a contented sigh. "I like living on Tahila very much, Rose. Very much, indeed."

Josh and Turu paddled back around the headland, and it was then that Josh caught sight of something white and rectangular just beneath the surface of the lagoon. He directed the canoe to it, then leaned over and plucked it out, discovering that it was a waterlogged scrap of paper covered with printed Japanese characters. A page from a book. Then, a rainbow stain floating on the surface caught his eye, and his blood turned cold.

3 9

Josh found Bosun O'Neal at the site of the nun's house, which he was determined to build, whether she liked it or not. It was a property with a huge
banyan tree and a sweeping view of the lagoon. To pay for it, he had promised Chief Kalapa to take a Tahila woman as a wife. More than a few had
since paraded by, bringing gifts of food and drink. He'd tried to be interested,
but though he knew he would have to do it, and though many had stirred his
libido, none so far had stirred his heart. Now he stared at the scrap of sea-
soaked paper Josh held out to him, then shrugged. "What does it mean?"

"What do you think it means? It means the Japanese are scouting us."

Ready took the soggy scrap, turned it over, then shrugged again. "It
could have been floating around in the ocean for a long time."

"Japanese paper is made of rice," Josh explained, "and it doesn't take
long before it dissolves in seawater. I also saw an oil stain on the water. Japanese barges tend to leak oil."

"Assuming this means anything," Ready said dubiously, "what do you
want me to do about it? I've already posted lookouts."

Josh, even though he had been turned into the charcoal man of Tahila,
was still not used to being questioned by lower-ranking personnel over such
matters. His annoyance showed. "Use your head, Bosun! You've got to ratchet
up everything. Tell your lookouts to be on the alert and stop sleeping on the
job. How do I know they sleep? Because I've gone out and caught them.
That's something you should have done. You can't just post lookouts and expect them to do their jobs. They get stale and need a kick in the butt every so
often. You also need to put the marines under some kind of discipline. I
haven't seen them take a turn on the machine guns in weeks."

Ready continued to look dubious, which made Josh even more annoyed.

Finally, the bosun said, "I guess I could tell everybody your concerns, Captain. And I've asked the marines to go down to the guns every so often and check them, make sure they're ready to go. But they have responsibilities now with their women."

Josh glared at Ready, wanting to knock him down and kick him for good measure, but, knowing such would do no good, he lowered himself to explain. "Look, Bosun, if you are going to command, then command. That means telling the marines what to do and not worrying about what they want. You also must discern the enemy's mind. The Japanese are here, but they haven't waltzed right in. That likely means they've spotted us or heard that we're here via the coconut telegraph. These local fella boys go out and fish. Likely they've run across fishermen from Ruka, too, and they gossip, and that gets back to Colonel Yoshu."

"So?" Ready demanded. "That's good, isn't it? Maybe he won't attack if he knows we're here."

"Maybe it will make him cautious, but he will come anyway. Remember that plank on the cross? 'Give me the nun,' it said. He murdered an island to send that message, Bosun. He ain't gonna stop for a few white men with guns."

Ready, chafing under Josh's uninvited advice, answered, "I'll give it some thought." Then he gestured over his shoulder and asked, "What do you think of my treehouse? I'm nearly done. It's for Sister."

"Bosun, your priorities are all wrong. You need to defend this island, not play the architect for that nun."

"I have seen to the defense of this island, Captain," Ready asserted. "Mr. Bucknell and Chief Kalapa think I've done a first-class job. And I did it without your help, I might add. Now, I promised Sister Mary Kathleen a house of her own, and I intend to build it."

"I hoped you had gotten past your infatuation with her."

"Don't worry about me, Captain," Ready replied. "I know what I'm doing."

"Not if you're harboring any kind of hope you'll yet win her over. She's a nun, Ready. A nun! Doesn't that mean anything to you?"

"She's my friend," Ready answered, "and that's all she is."

"Oh, I'm certain of it," Josh replied sardonically.

"Is there anything else you have to say, sir?" Ready demanded. "Otherwise, I'm pretty busy. And I'm sure you've got some charcoal to make."

Josh absorbed the insult, because he had to. "All right, Bosun. Have it your way. But here's an idea to perhaps win the battle that's coming, and soon, whether you believe it or not. Stretch a thick hemp cable across the lagoon and secure both ends to palm trees. Put weights on the cable to keep it a few feet underwater, and the outriggers and canoes will glide right over it but a barge won't. Its prop will snag. Your guns could tear it to pieces before the Japs could get it free."

Ready rubbed the back of his neck, giving the idea some thought. "I don't know, Captain. It would take a lot of work."

"No, it won't. There's a ton of hemp line in the boathouse. The women know how to wrap it to make it thicker. Two inches thick is all you'll need. Look, Bosun, it's the only chance you've got. If the Japanese get on shore, you're done for."

Ready studied Josh. "How come you're not arguing with me to pack up an outrigger and leave?"

"Because I don't care what happens to you. You and your mutinous marines can stay here and rot, for all I care. But Rose won't go, so I'm stuck. You have my idea. If you don't do it, well, piss on you."

Ready nodded. "We'll stretch a cable across the lagoon, Captain. It's a good idea. Thank you."

"You're welcome. Anything else you'd like to say? An apology? Coming back under my command?"

"No, sir. You were drunk. I took your job. Reckon I'll keep it."

Josh's temper boiled over. "You know the cause of all our trouble? That damned nun!"

"How can you blame her, Captain?" Ready asked quietly. "She would never hurt anybody on purpose."

"I've had time to think about it, Ready. Something stinks here to high heaven. Ask her to tell you why Colonel Yoshu wants her so bad. She's got a nasty secret, for sartain."

Ready looked away, to the treehouse he was building for the woman he loved. "Good evening, Captain. If you have any other ideas, I'll be glad to hear them."

"Why would I have any ideas?" Josh demanded. "I'm just the charcoal man." Then he stalked away.

4 0

The next morning saw Josh and his family off on their adventure to the Beach of the Dead Whales. He was still angry over his encounter with Bosun O'Neal, and he'd almost decided not to go. No, he told Rose, he would go down to the beach and make sure the worthless wretch of a mutineer stretched the cable across the lagoon as he'd promised. But Rose instantly set him straight. "The children were scarcely able to sleep last night," she admonished. "You promised them an adventure, and an adventure they will have."

"But, Rose, this is important!"

"Yes, but it's Bosun's job, not yours. Your job is with your family."

Josh could see clearly by the set of his wife's expression that any other argument he might advance would be to no avail. So he strapped on the forty-five pistol he'd retrieved from the boathouse when no one was paying attention, and off he went with Rose, Turu, and Manda for a day of adventure. He would, he swore to himself, check on the cable when he got back.

It was a nice hike, during which Josh and Rose discussed many matters, including the gods, brought on when she told him the mountain they were crossing was named Panua, after the Tahila goddess of ill fortune.

Josh stopped to help Manda step across the thick roots of a ceiba tree and then followed close behind, to ensure she didn't trip on anything else. She was a cute little girl, and respectful and polite, too. Josh had never met as sweet a child. In fact, he loved her and was, according to everyone who mattered, her father. Josh would have gladly died for her, for all his new family. "Why would you name a mountain after a goddess of ill fortune?" he asked Rose.

"Why, to appease her, of course," Rose replied, astonished at the ignorance Josh displayed. "She is a jealous god, jealous of all the other gods as well as some humans. She is therefore often unhappy and compelled to cause trouble."

Josh scratched up under his cap, which he noticed, once again, wasn't there. He missed the damned old thing and wondered briefly if some marine had picked it up on Betio. "Why would a god be jealous of a human?" he asked after his moment of cap distraction.

"Because some gods are not loved, only feared," Rose answered. "Poor Panua is one of those, and her feelings are constantly hurt. It is why I often pray to her, to thank her for being a goddess, and to ask her to forgive me for finding the love she cannot have."

"You told me you were a Christian. Why worry about the old gods?"

"Because the old gods are also real, of course," Rose replied. "The Christian God is just as real, but He is the most jealous god of all. He is so jealous He tries to make his followers believe that none of the other gods exist. We, who know better, are amused by Him, poor thing."

Josh decided to carry Manda and swung her up on his back. She held onto his shoulders with her strong little hands and nuzzled along his ear. He felt her warm breath along his cheek and was seized with a profound and inexplicable joy.

"You and Manda make a very nice couple," Rose teased.

"Quiet, woman," Josh said. "I am thinking about your last comment. So God almighty, the great Jehovah, is pathetic in your eyes?"

"Yes, husband, He is quite a sullen god. In contrast, His son Jesus is a good and gentle god, much nicer than his father. We believe, in fact, that his father caused this war."

"What?" Josh demanded. "How can you say such a thing?"

"I suppose we could be wrong, but that's what we believe," she said. "The father of Jesus started this war because He knows we will never stop believing in our other gods."

"You think God is punishing the people of the Far Reaches with the Second World War?"

"Not just us. Everyone. He's trying to scare the whole world so people will turn to Him, and only Him."

Josh gave the proposition some thought, then shook his head. "I don't see why He's killing us Americans, then. We mostly have no other gods except old Jehovah."

"Are you certain, husband? No other gods?"

Josh thought it over, then said, "I see what you're getting at. Our other gods are money and power."

Bored with the talk between her parents, Manda became restless on his shoulders. Josh swung her down and watched as she clambered over rocks and roots to catch up with her brother. "She is a good girl," he said. "Who was her father?"

"A fine man. In fact, he was Chief Kalapa's brother. He drowned with several other men while sailing to Ruka."

"How long ago was that?"

She thought for a moment, then said, "Just over three years. There was a storm. He and his crew mates were found on a Ruka beach."

"Was he also Turu's father?"

"Yes, of course."

"And since Chief Kalapa only has daughters, does this mean Turu may be the future chief of Tahila?"

"There is no doubt. Even if Chief Kalapa has a dozen sons, Turu will be the choice of the village. Everyone knows this. There is none brighter than he."

"I'm sorry. I don't mean to ask impertinent questions."

"You may ask me any question you like, husband."

The question escaped his mouth before he could stop it. "Do you love me?"

"Yes," she answered.

"I love you, too," he replied with some awe. "And I love our children."

"Then," she said, "it is good we are together."

They walked on, the great vengeful, bloody-minded big God of the missionaries and the unhappy little gods of the Far Reaches forgotten. When they reached the crest of Panua's mountain, the family stood together, holding hands, and admired the glorious green island below. Then, with the sun resting warmly on their shoulders, they began the long climb down toward the waiting sea. The descent to the beach was a scramble. From high above, Josh saw that the stretch of otherwise barren sand was dotted with white, oddly shaped formations, some like huge ice cubes, others like long curved plaster rods, and some like picket fences protruding from the sand.

Though it had the appearance of a playground for giants, the beach was a graveyard, covered with the bones of huge creatures. Josh noted a great jaw, the narrow bones swung open as if anticipating a meal, and several towering brattices of ribs. Teeth, as big as his fist, were scattered like snowballs. Vertebrae the size of footlockers sat alone or were still attached, forming a portion of huge, segmented backbones. A few hardy beach vines had secured holds on some of the ribs and backbones, draping them with masses of strange hairy red and green tendrils. Also colonizing the whale graveyard was beach morning glory, its green, glossy leaves brave and bright and covered with white blossoms just starting to close against the rising heat. There were also hundreds of coconuts, strewn around like cannonballs left on some ancient battleground. It was an eerie and somber place, yet somehow thrilling and beautiful.

The sun bore down like a great, hot hand, and Josh leaned against a tall rib that offered shade and studied the remarkable sight, a cemetery of whale bones, and of a particular kind of whale that he recognized at once. "Sperm whales," he marveled to Rose while the children frolicked among the skeletons. "Just like Moby Dick. Who'da thunk it?"

The children were playing with a giant vertebra, rolling it like a thick wheel along the hard-packed sand. Rose took a seat on a backbone that supported a double row of towering ribs. "What is your impression, husband?" she asked.

"Fantastic is the only way to describe it!"

"You are pleased I brought you here?"

Josh grinned and wiped the sweat from his eyes. "You bet I am."

"Then I am pleased as well." She smiled and shaded her eyes with her hand to watch after the children. Then she spotted something lying in the sand. It was a lagoon canoe paddle. "This paddle belongs to Kando, the father of Mori, Chief Kalapa's first wife. I recognize his mark on the handle. When I have been here before, I always find lost things from the village."

"I think there is a powerful current that sweeps into this cove," Josh observed, "but the skeletons are still a mystery. There are too many of them to imagine they're here only because of the current. They must come nearby to die. But why?"

"Only the whales know," Rose answered. "They have their ways, and they are not ours."

Josh decided to go exploring for ambergris while Rose went off to play with the children. He allowed himself to admire her for a moment, smiling at how she could so easily become childlike herself. He saw her waiting below while Manda climbed one of the great ribs. The girl threw herself off into her mother's arms, and then Rose, still holding Manda, twirled around and around with excited laughter. Turu came running up with a tooth, so large he had to use both his hands to hold it, and Rose went down on her knees to marvel at it. Then Manda picked up another tooth and tossed it into the hollow center of a particularly large vertebra, which started a game of throwing teeth into the hole, accompanied by much good-natured jeering when a toss was missed.

Josh walked among the magnificent yet sad remnants of creatures that had once ruled the sea. He knew sperm whales were not gentle souls. They were voracious feeders, diving into great, sunless depths to eat the masses of squid that could be found there. When Josh had been a cabin boy aboard the *Bathsheba,* he'd heard tales from whalers about sperm whales they'd found floating dead on the surface, their slick gray skin mottled by the wagon wheel–sized suction cups of giant squids. It was said that the big bulls especially liked to battle the giant squids, sought them out even, just to show them who was boss of the sea. How the old whalers knew that, Josh wasn't certain, but he liked to believe it was true. What he knew for certain was that ambergris seemed to be the result of the sperm whale's diet, since usually the gunk was found wrapped around squid beaks. The theory went that ambergris was a protective coating formed in the whale's guts.

Josh observed a towering mass of bones stacked up inside sea-carved rock alcoves. Storms had flushed them there, he supposed. He approached one of the towers and marveled at its height, at least sixty feet. The bones were jumbled but fixed perfectly against one another so they created a rigid structure. Josh touched a long rib that protruded from the base, discreetly pulled on it, and found it solidly wedged. He peered into the mix of bones, to see if ambergris had perhaps collected in the sand below. Seeing nothing, Josh walked around the edge of the tower. He found only teeth, sprinkled like seeds from a ghostly tree of bones.

He walked along the cliff that formed the beach until he came to a second alcove of bones. This stack wasn't as high as the first one, but still impressive. It seemed to have attracted jaw and skull bones. His nose caught a dank odor, and he looked behind a vertebra and spied what he'd been looking for, a fist-sized lump of ambergris. An arm's reach inside the base of the stack, just below a jawbone empty of teeth, he saw another. He carefully inserted his arm under it and clutched the spongy stuff, slowly withdrawing both lumps. But when his arm accidentally touched a bone, he felt the entire structure shudder, then begin to wobble. A huge skull fell from the top, and he barely dodged it. Then another bone fell, and Josh knew the whole impossible structure was going to topple. Clutching his treasure, he ran for safety, all the while yelling at Rose and the children to get clear.

The tower of bones swayed, then fell over, hitting the sand with a tremendous clatter. Bones flew in all directions, ricocheting off one another and hurtling into the air. Finally, when the last bone had struck the beach and tumbled to a stop, Josh picked his way through the skeletal parts and saw, with some relief, Rose, huddled with the children, standing in the water some distance away. "What are you doing, husband?" she demanded.

"Look!" Josh said, holding up his lumps of ambergris. He hurried over and thrust them toward her.

Rose turned up her nose. "More whale spit."

"Do you know what these are worth?" Josh demanded. "I bet I could get a thousand dollars for each of them."

Rose's nose remained in the air. "And what would you do with these two thousand dollars?"

"Why, I would buy—" Josh stopped and thought about what he could buy and concluded there wasn't much he wanted or needed, other than what he already had. "I don't know. Something," he said. "I mean if you ever needed anything, or the kids."

Rose frowned, then shook her head. "Silly man. We don't need anything. Throw that away. Let the gods have it to roll around on the beach."

Josh looked at the ambergris and then, shrugging, tossed the two lumps aside. "You're right, Rose. Anyway, we've had ourselves a splendid adventure."

She released the children, who raced to the scattered bones of the fallen tower, shrieking with laughter. Soon they were tossing teeth around, bouncing them off the ribs with glee. Josh and Rose sat down and watched the children and listened to the wind play a song through the bones of the great whales. "This is good," he said, pondering the empty line of the far horizon. "This is very good."

"Yes," Rose answered.

"I'm a happy man, Rose."

"Of course," she said as if to be otherwise were the most foolish thing in the world.

It was on the way back, halfway up the path that took them to the top of the cliff, that Josh, sensing something amiss, scanned the sea. In a moment, he saw it. "Dammitohell," he breathed.

"What is it?" she asked nervously.

"A Japanese barge, Rose. Likely out of Ruka. I told Bosun O'Neal they were here and he wouldn't believe me. Now here's proof."

"Are they here to attack us?" she asked, pulling the children close.

Josh peered at the barge, tiny and gray in the distance. "I don't think so. They're going away from the village. Probably just sniffing around, maybe looking for an alternative landing site. They won't find a good one."

"What shall we do?"

Josh put his hand on Rose's arm, then patted Manda's head, and next pretended to cuff Turu on his ear. The boy grinned up at him. "We'll go back to the village and let Bosun O'Neal know what we've seen. I just hope he's got that cable strung."

And so they did, although along the way Josh studied some rocks on the final ridge before entering the last leg of the path to the village. He climbed up to them and, as he hoped, was gratified to find a cave. It was small and a bit damp, but it would serve his purpose. He called Rose up to inspect it. "This is a good place for you to hide should the Japanese attack. I will stock dried fish and water here."

"I would not run away without you, husband," Rose declared.

"You will do as I tell you," Josh insisted. Then he softened his tone. "I only want what's best for you and your children."

"*Our* children," she replied in a firm voice.

When Josh nodded, she slipped into his arms. He felt her shudder and wondered if she had a premonition of what lay before them. "It's going to be all right, Rose," he whispered.

She pulled away. "It is a good idea, this cave," she said, and then, to-gether, they went back to their children.

4 1

"Here it is," Ready said, his open hand toward the big tree. "Your house, Sister."

Sister Mary Kathleen, who was well aware that Bosun O'Neal had continued to build even after she forbade it, and who had even sneaked around at night beneath the bright moon to see what he was building, followed his gesture to a lovely treehouse. Even though she was theoretically against the enterprise, she could not help the pure delight that suffused her at the sight of it. But then she forced her expression to change and deliberately turned down her mouth. "But why, when I told ye not to, did ye still build it?" she demanded. She shook her head. "I am not worthy of yer feelings for me, Bosun. I keep telling ye that. When will ye understand?"

Ready forced a laugh. "Oh, Sister, that's not the situation at all. In fact, I think I will very soon take up with a local woman."

Her expression registered the shock she felt. "Oh? And who would that be, now?"

Ready maintained a crooked smile. "Well, I don't know. I guess I haven't decided yet. But don't fret about me being in love with you or anything like that. That's all past, Sister. I just built this house for the fun of it, don't you see? Every boy dreams of building a treehouse. I didn't get a chance when I grew up on Killakeet, and now I have! I hope you like it. It's crude, just a bunch of bamboo and boards, but maybe you can spend some happy time here. I mean to accomplish your prayers and your teaching plans, say."

Sister Mary Kathleen considered Ready's little speech. She wanted to accept the little house in the tree, she really did, for it was truly lovely, but what would the bosun think if she accepted his house? Would it only reinforce his hopeless cause, the one she knew he had not truly put aside, that of winning her heart? "Thank ye, Bosun, but I cannot accept it," she firmly answered and turned away.

"Then it will remain empty," Ready replied with a hint of anger. "Or one of the islanders can have it. I don't care."

When she said nothing, he summoned his courage, and then asked, "Sister, what happened to you on Ruka?"

She faced him. "Why do ye want to know?"

"Because I must defend this island."

"Then defend it. I saw you today with the fella boys putting in place a cable across the lagoon. I knew instantly it was to stop a large boat from entering. What a fine idea!"

"It was Captain Thurlow's."

"Then it is a surprisingly intelligent one. Is he still angry with ye?"

"Yes. In fact, I think he'd like to kill me."

"Ready, ye have done a wonderful job. The captain knows that, deep in his heart. He will forgive ye. I'm certain of it."

Ready realized she had changed the subject. "Sister, if we are attacked, it is because Colonel Yoshu wants you. And, the way I see it, he must want you because of something that took place on Ruka. Don't you see it's only fair I know what happened? It might help me to figure out the way he thinks and better prepare for him."

She shook her head. "Colonel Yoshu needs no excuse to murder. That's all ye need to know."

"Let me tell you what I think," Ready said. "Tell me if I'm wrong. I think this mad colonel wants you back simply because he is angry that you got away. That is what I think."

She studied him. "I cannot stop you from thinking."

"Am I near the truth?" he asked.

"Near enough," she answered.

"Then it's settled. I will never ask you about it again. May I show you your house?"

"I have already said I cannot accept it."

"Yes, you can. And you will."

She smiled. "Ye are a true O'Neal. A stubborn people ye are."

She allowed Ready to lead her toward the stairs that wound around the tree. "Ladies first, if you please," he bowed.

"I will look at it, no more," she conceded, but her voice betrayed her, filled as it was with the delight she felt.

As he escorted her up the staircase, the bosun was like an excited boy, jabbering about all that he'd accomplished. She put her hands to her mouth as she looked at the beautiful, spacious living area. Then Ready, a little embarrassed, showed her the bed he'd constructed for her of breadfruit wood and hemp, and the mattress he'd stuffed with feathers and kapok.

" 'Tis a wonder," she told him, sitting on the bed and feeling its softness. She had not slept on a soft bed since . . . well, she did not like to think about that.

"I think you would be happy here, Sister," Ready said.

She shook her head. "Such a gift. Ye understand that if I accept, Bosun, I must pay ye somehow."

"Just call me Ready instead of Bosun. That's my only price."

"Yes, of course. Ready O'Neal. 'Tis a fine name. For a fine man."

Then he left her, left her in *her* house, left her to lean against the ledge of her window that faced the sea and toward the other islands, Ruka somewhere in the distance, obscured by the clouds on the horizon, and the miles, and time itself. Yet nothing could obscure what was there. "Are ye there?" she asked over the miles and time. "Are ye really still there?"

Then she heard the scrape of Ready's fiddle. The song he played was winsome and lonely and sad. "What is it?" she called, for she knew he could hear her. His house was not far away.

The music stopped. " 'Shenandoah,' " he called back, his voice like an echo.

" 'Tis a glorious tune. Was it written by an Irishman? It must be, so sad and beautiful as it is."

"I don't know, Sister, but it's being played by one."

And so Ready played on, and Sister Mary Kathleen, enchanted, sat down in her house, her lovely little house in the arms of the great tree, and was happy.

Her happiness didn't last long. The fiddle scraped its last note, and then she heard Captain Thurlow's booming voice, and then Bosun O'Neal said something, clearly an angry retort. The men argued on, and though she couldn't hear what was said, she knew instinctively it was about Colonel Yoshu and the danger he represented to the captain's family and to the village. She looked to heaven, then dropped her face into her hands. Would the nightmare never end?

" 'Tis a party we need, Laddy," she told the pup, which was resting across her feet. " 'Tis a party, to bring at least a little joy into our lives, especially now, as the day of the birth of our dear Lord and Savior approaches." And, though she knew it was foolish, an indulgence of the first order in the face of death and danger, a birthday party for Jesus was what Sister Mary Kathleen would have.

PART VI

The Perfect Nun

Break, day of God, Oh break!
The night has lingered long;
Our hearts with sighing wake,
We weep for sin and wrong:
O Bright and Morning Star, draw near;
O Sun of Righteousness, appear.

Break, day of God, Oh break!
The earth with strife is worn;
The hills with thunder shake,
Hearts of the people mourn;
Break, day of God, sweet day of peace,
And bid the shout of warriors cease!

—HENRY BURTON, A HYMN

4 2

Chief Kalapa was adamant. "I fear not, Sister," he said, speaking in the Far Reaches dialect. "I will not let you convert my people to your Catholic God. They have enough trouble."

"Faith!" Sister Mary Kathleen exclaimed in English, then changed to his language. "I do not wish to convert anyone. I asked to use the boathouse only to mark the birth of our Savior in a proper manner."

"The missionaries who came before you used the boathouse to preach their gospel, too," Chief Kalapa declared. "They yelled at us, told us we were all going to hell, and then sang their strange songs with harsh melodies. When we sang with them, we had to pretty their songs up as best we could. But no matter how hard we tried to make them welcome, the missionaries kept saying we were doomed to an afterlife of pain and misery. Their number one minister even pointed at me—*the chief!*—and said I was leading my people down the path of damnation. I asked him what I could do to change our path, and he said I had to rid myself of all but one wife. I instantly agreed, of course. We always agreed to everything they demanded. Of course, such agreement was only to make them stop yelling at us. Whenever a missionary came around to visit me, for instance, only Mori served food and drink while my other wives hid. Those white men were always so certain of everything. To them, it was all one way or the other."

"I have known many Protestant missionaries," Sister Mary Kathleen replied. "They do good work out here. Their doctors and nurses are first-rate."

"They are sorcerers. As, I suspect, you are, too."

"Sorcerers! Really, Chief Kalapa. That is silly. Those missionaries are just dedicated men and women, eager to bring the word of God to this place. As for me, I am a simple nun, put here to serve in any way I can."

"Perhaps you are, but how else other than magic could those missionaries have sustained themselves with their bleak outlook on life? Consider: They do not drink intoxicating beverages, they do not ficky-ficky except with their one wife, who is invariably ugly, they do not dance, they do not tell jokes or laugh. They do not even smile very much. When one of them took a village girl for a wife, I saw the union as a very good thing, that perhaps at least this one missionary might help the others to understand the way we live."

Chief Kalapa sighed and shook his head, his mane of lustrous black hair draping itself around his neck. "It only caused him to be cast out by his fellows. This man later drowned, and the number one missionary said it was God who drowned him. This made us fear his God all the more, and so we converted. But now that the missionaries are gone, run away at the first whiff of the Japanese, I think we are much happier. We have their big god and our little gods. It is good to know all the gods. But no, Sister, a thousand times no. I have allowed you to teach our children, and you have done a fine job, but preach your Catholic faith? Never!"

"Ye must believe me, Chief," Sister Mary Kathleen quietly insisted, "nothing like what ye fear will happen. I respect the way yer people live. Do I not bow to the totem before I enter the boathouse? Do I not let yer subchiefs come and tell the stories of yer island gods in the school? Ye say yer people converted to Christianity. Well, shouldn't everyone be allowed to celebrate the birth of Jesus on Christmas Day? Is it so much to ask?"

"It is very much to ask," Chief Kalapa grumpily answered, though he recognized she had logic on her side. He rolled his eyes and sighed heavily. "Let us say I agree. You will not berate us for drinking kava during the celebration?"

"Of course not. Ye may drink all ye want. I would imagine the marines will have their mangojack. I have gotten a whiff of their still, and it almost brings me to me knees."

"How about ficky-ficky? Will you make us feel guilty that sometimes we do it without marriage? And may even do it that very night as a result of drinking kava and mangojack and because sometimes young women tempt us otherwise innocent men?"

She blushed even through her deep tan, accentuated all the more by her white corona and veil. "No, Chief. I am not here to judge anyone."

"You are an odd missionary," Chief Kalapa observed.

"Oh, Chief Kalapa!" she cried with exasperation. "I would hope by now ye would understand I am not a missionary at all! My order is dedicated to the service of others, no matter who they are or what religion they practice. Preaching and proselytizing, we leave to the priests and preachers!"

Chief Kalapa gave it all a good think, then lapsed into pidgin to give his approval. "My word, then. I think more better peoples go along your Christmas jump-jump. Now you happy fella girl, Sister?"

Sister Mary Kathleen grinned. "Oh, I am, indeed. Thank ye, Chief!" She went down on one knee and kissed the chief's hand just as if he were a bishop, pope, or king, which he recognized at once to be a special honor from a nun.

She bowed her way out, leaving Chief Kalapa feeling charitable and benevolent, not to mention unburdened. But then Mori came to stand before him. "Why did you do this thing, husband?" she demanded in the cold voice she reserved for when he had done something irredeemable.

"What-what?" he demanded, for he had no idea what she was talking about.

"You gave the nun permission to celebrate on the eve of Christmas, did you not?"

"Yes, I most certainly did," Chief Kalapa replied. "I thought it the proper thing to do, all in all. Why do you ask?"

Mori's face was stern, her lips pressed tight and her chin up, the expression she wore that Chief Kalapa dreaded the most. He knew he had blundered, though he still didn't know how. Mori was pleased to explain. "I ask because I wonder what kind of celebration you think she might manage. Does she own even a single chicken or pig? Does she know how to make kava? Can she dance the celebratory dances? Does she know how to invite the people and to let them know what is expected? There is much more to a celebration, husband, than to give permission to have one. It is called work, sir, and it is work that will surely fall on me and your other wives. So I ask you, what were you thinking?"

Chief Kalapa worried with his hands and licked his big lips. "I suppose I was not thinking at all," he concluded.

"Indeed you were not," Mori replied heavily. "So now I and the other wives must begin the work, the very detailed work, in order that you and Sister can have this celebration. For your wise decision, we thank you, husband."

Chief Kalapa chose not to reply, though he began to consider what gifts he might give to Mori and his other wives on Christmas Day. He no longer felt charitable and benevolent, and certainly not unburdened. Instead, he felt somewhat silly, which, he mused, was the effect wives often had on their husbands, even when that husband was the chief and respected and adored by everyone else. He wondered, not for the first time, why he had collected three of the creatures and swore never to gain another, no matter how comely the girls or the fine gifts offered up by their fathers who wanted to be rid of them.

4 3

The celebration began on Christmas Eve with a rhythmic thumping on the traditional drums. Six men sat over the drums outside the boathouse and beat out an ancient cadence that started simply and built over the course of an hour to a crescendo of complex syncopation. Then, with the setting sun as a spectacular backdrop, a choir of women and then of men came to stand in front of the drummers. The singing was simple but glorious, the soprano trills of the women punctuated by the deep, velvety counterpoint of the men.

Aromatic smoke drifted past the choir and the drummers. It was produced by a spitted pig, basted with various lime and mango sauces, its dripping fat spattering into a bed of furiously glowing charcoal. Throughout the village, women were busily bringing to fruition various dishes including steamed *moi-moi,* boiled octopus, and lobster plus a kind of squash, roasted in stone ovens. There was also steamed chicken, dipped in coconut milk and wrapped in taro leaf. Whipped, sugared breadfruit mixed with morsels of fresh avocado was on hand for dessert.

When all the people were gathered, the songs sung, and the food prepared, Chief Kalapa came out on the porch of the boathouse. The drums ended abruptly. He waved his arms, called everyone in attendance his children (more than a few actually were), and then introduced Sister Mary Kathleen, though he said she needed no introduction except to remind everyone that she was a bride of Christ and therefore might be a sorcerer.

Sister Mary Kathleen put a hand to her heart. "Faith, Chief Kalapa," she lightly scolded, "I am no sorcerer. I am but a simple Irish girl. But there was once another simple woman, this one of Israel, who was given a great honor by God and his angels, and that was to bear a divine living being who would grow up to be our Jesus the Christ and Savior." She made the sign of the cross and kissed her medallion and then, to accede to Chief Kalapa's demand for no preaching or proselytizing, handed the proceedings over to the presumably secular Mr. Bucknell. The British diplomat, reading from his Bible, intoned, in his crisp British accent, the ancient story from Luke while beside him a dancing girl in a red and green lava-lava acted out some of the parts, mainly the angels: "And it came to pass in those days . . ."

As Mr. Bucknell read the old story, the circle of watchers widened below, and a woman, a very fetching woman in a white lava-lava, was seen kneeling on a woven mat and cradling a sleeping baby. A muscular, tattooed, half-naked man stood protectively over her with his arms crossed. His chin was raised proudly and belligerently.

Josh, standing on the edge of the crowd with his family, sourly thought to himself, *If these fella boys could fight as well as they strut, we'd have no trouble with the Japanese.* The marines and their women were in attendance, and Josh searched through the crowd until he could see them. He wanted to make sure he knew where they were, if needed. The Ruka fella boys were also there, looking already a bit glassy-eyed from kava. Ready O'Neal was there as well with his fiddle, his eyes never leaving the nun. *Poor man,* Josh thought.

Mr. Bucknell continued telling the story, which seemed at first to have something to do with taxes, a concept alien to the people of the village, though they suspected it was nothing that they would like, nor would anyone else. The dancing girl changed her expression to one of sadness and placed her hands on her hips to indicate her displeasure.

"Husband," Rose whispered into Josh's ear, "why do you Europeans put up with taxes?"

"It's our way of paying off the crooks we elect, Rose," Josh explained. "Sometimes, they even do good things with our money, such as build roads, but not usually. One way or the other, it ends up in their pockets."

"All right, then. Why do you elect crooks?"

"Because it's better to elect them than to have them try to take over. You see, in our world, crooks always end up running things, one way or the other. So we have elections to pretend we agree they should be in charge."

"I find it odd the manner in which you rule yourself," she said.

"Me, too," he replied while thinking what he ought to do was to go over and politely ask the marines, the rotten mutineers, to at least carry around their rifles, although such might seem a bit strange at a Christmas celebration.

He worriedly looked up at the moonless sky. It was a perfect night for an invasion.

"And this shall be a sign unto you," Mr. Bucknell went on, remarking about the shepherds above Bethlehem, another alien concept since none of the villagers had ever seen a sheep, although there were wild goats on the leeward side of the island. "Ye shall find the babe wrapped in swaddling clothes, lying in a manger. And suddenly there was with the angel a multitude of the heavenly host praising God, and . . ." The dancing girls started swiveling their hips most provocatively and raised their hands to the sky. The villagers cheered, glad that at least the angels knew how to dance.

Mr. Bucknell read on until he got to the visitors from the East, which the villagers especially liked since they figured they might be island folk. From the crowd came three fella boys, each carrying presents. One of them had a basket of mangos, one bore a monkeypod carving of Juki (who was the main goddess of Tahila), and the last fella boy held a boar's tooth necklace. They placed these most reverently at the knees of the woman holding the babe, then backed off to receive congratulatory bowls of mangojack from the marines. They knocked the drink back instantly.

With this accomplished, the choir and the drums went back to work, and Mr. Bucknell, accepting his own bowl of mangojack, was obliged to quit the story and descend to join the great feast. Using palmetto leaves for plates, the people of the village queued up at tables groaning with food. Just inside the shadows of the bush behind the boathouse, kava was also being dispensed, as well as more mangojack. Some of the men drank both, and it wasn't long before they were lying wherever their knees chose to buckle.

"This is a good party, Sister," Josh said to Sister Mary Kathleen, who, he noted with surprise, held a cup of mangojack. "I thought you never touched that stuff."

"I am merely sipping it, sor, to be sociable," she answered with a wink that astonished Josh, who reckoned she was close to being drunk. She had the Christmas spirit, all right, and so did the Ruka fella boys, who were barely able to stand. At least the women militia were probably not drunk, since most of the women were too busy as food servers to imbibe. Still, the village was undefended. Josh guessed even the lookouts had sneaked in to join the party.

Josh was worrying about the Japanese and watching the crowd and sipping a little mangojack himself when he caught a movement out of the corner of his eye and saw that it was his very own Turu rushing breathlessly into the light of the torches. The boy's eyes were huge, and he was looking all around. Josh called out to him, and he ran over. "Jahtalo, four men in a rubber boat just came ashore!"

Josh allowed the all-encompassing Marine Corps curse to escape his lips before he knelt and clutched Turu's bare shoulders. "Where did they go?"

"Behind those houses. Over there!" Turu pointed across the common road.

Josh peered at the houses and saw nothing unusual, though behind them was a bush-covered hillside, an excellent place to hide and observe the celebration. "Find your mother and Manda. Tell them to go home, and if they hear gunshots, head up the path to the cave. Then, bring me two rifles. You know where they are. That's an order, soldier."

"Yes, sir!" Turu saluted and scampered off.

Josh scanned the celebrators and saw Ready sawing away on his fiddle while people danced around him, including, he was amazed to note, Sister Mary Kathleen. She had apparently gotten more thoroughly into the mangojack. Then he spotted Mr. Bucknell, who looked reasonably sober. "We have company," he said after pulling the diplomat aside.

"What do you mean, old man?"

Josh gestured over his shoulder. "My boy said a landing party just came ashore."

"We must send the marines to the machine guns!" he yelped.

"Put drunks behind machine guns? I don't think so. Not yet, anyway. Apparently there are only four intruders. Most likely a scouting party."

"But perhaps more are coming behind."

"I sent Turu after rifles and ammunition. One for you and one for me."

"Good show, my boy. Four chaps, eh? We'll show our mettle."

"I just want to chase them away, Mr. Bucknell. No heroics."

It only took a long minute before Turu raced back carrying the two Japanese rifles and bandoliers of ammunition that Josh had stolen from the boathouse and hidden. A few of the celebrators looked at Turu but then went right back to their fun.

Josh and Mr. Bucknell crept down to the lagoon, seeing nothing. Behind them the drums were booming, and gales of laughter floated across the village and the lagoon. "There could be an aircraft carrier out there and we wouldn't hear it," Josh fretted.

"Where is the boat they used?" Mr. Bucknell wondered.

"Good question. But first . . ." Josh was going to say that they should first check behind the row of houses, but then he saw someone move there in the shadows. It was certainly a man, and he had taken a deliberate sideways step to keep from being seen. "Get down!" Josh hissed. Then Josh noticed that it wasn't Mr. Bucknell beside him. "Turu! Go home!"

"No, father, I will fight the Japanese with you."

"Stay down and stay back," Josh growled; no time to argue with the boy. "Mr. Bucknell?"

"Yes, Captain?"

"I'm going to get closer. If I draw their fire and you see a muzzle flash, shoot at it."

Josh didn't wait for Mr. Bucknell to respond. He threw himself forward, dashing all the way to the side of the house where he'd seen the figure. He put his back to the bamboo wall. Mr. Bucknell soon joined him, then Turu, breathless with excitement.

Josh knelt and peered around the house. The torches allowed a little light, as did the partial moon, though it was obscured by a passing cloud. The dense bush swayed in the breeze off the lagoon, and the shadows danced. Josh heard a thump in the darkness, as if someone had fallen, and then a man muttering angrily.

"I believe they have managed to get themselves tangled in the devil vine," Mr. Bucknell mused. "Beastly stuff."

"Do you know enough Japanese to tell them to surrender?" Josh asked.

Mr. Bucknell took an inordinately long time, in Josh's opinion, to answer, but finally he did. "No."

"Do you know any at all?"

"A little."

"Well, give it a try, anyway."

Mr. Bucknell shrugged and threw out a few Japanese words, one of which was *sayonara*. "What was that?" Josh hissed.

"I think I said, 'Pretty girls, we have had a delightful evening, but now I must really tell you good bye.' "

Josh shook his head. "That ought to do it."

There was no reply, in any case, no gunshot, nothing but silence from the shadows. "Perhaps they have run away," Mr. Bucknell suggested.

"Or died laughing at your Japanese," Josh said. "If they're in that devil vine and tried to move, we'd hear them."

Josh was pondering what to do next when Turu crawled up to the edge of the hut and called out in the Far Reaches dialect. "Come out, fella boys! Do not fear!"

There was no response to his call, either. "Maybe they speak European, Jahtalo," Turu suggested.

Josh called out in English. "All right, boys. We know you're in there. Come out with your hands up!" They were lines right out of a Gene Autry movie.

A voice in the darkness called back. "Is that you, Josh?"

Josh hesitated while surprise and not a little consternation washed across his mind. "It's me, all right! And you sound like . . ." He stopped, unwilling to get the name out of his mouth lest it be proved true.

But it was true. The bush parted, and a man emerged, a short, stubby man dragging a scrap of devil vine behind him. Cursing, he kicked at it, then stomped on it. The triumphant weed still clung tenaciously. Another dark figure emerged, then two more. Josh and Mr. Bucknell and Turu came out into the clearing behind the house. "Tell me you're not who I think you are," Josh said.

"Oh, it's me, all right, Thurlow," the man with the devil vine on his leg replied. "Come to make amends."

"Who is it?" Mr. Bucknell asked.

Josh didn't know whether to laugh or cry, so he did neither. Instead, he did a proper though reluctant introduction. "Mr. Bucknell, meet a United States Marine Corps legend, at least in his own mind: Colonel Montague Singleton Burr."

4 4

"Why, Thurlow, such a greeting," Burr said, finally kicking off the vine, which flew over to stick to one of the men standing beside him. "Who are these two fellows with you? Did that one call out in Japanese? I nearly told my crew to fire off a fusillade when I heard him."

"Mr. Bucknell is the representative of His Majesty's government in these islands, Montague. The boy is, well, my boy, name of Turu. It's a bit of a story. Now come out into the road where we can see each other better by the light of the torches."

This was accomplished, and Josh got a look at the colonel and his companions, three sailors wearing dungarees, denim shirts, and tub caps, gripping pistols and looking a bit frightened. "Gentlemen," Josh said, nodding to them. "You can put your sidearms away. This is a friendly village. Now, Montague, I'd surely like to hear how you got here, and why."

Burr holstered his pistol as did the sailors. "We're off a submarine, Josh, the *Scorpionfish,* commanded by Captain Taylor Wells. His sub sits out there, maybe a half mile off." Burr gestured toward the lagoon. "These sailor boy volunteers and I decided we'd paddle ashore to see what was up. Our raft is right over there, hidden amongst those canoes."

"How did you know where to find me?"

"It was that nun we knew where to find, old son," Burr replied. "She gave detailed instructions to a Cat-licker Holy Joe who's also aboard the sub and can't wait to see her."

Josh was dubious. "It must have been in a dream, because she didn't know we'd end up on this island."

"She told him to look on an island named Burubu or perhaps here or perhaps Ruka, though to be careful because Ruka was occupied by the

Japanese. Since Tahila was closest to Captain Wells's planned patrol, we started here."

"It was a good choice. No one lives on Burubu now, and as far as I know, Ruka's still occupied. The question is, why did you come at all?"

Burr took off his helmet and ran his hand through his sandy hair, then plopped it back aboard. "To make amends, Josh, like I already said. I shipped you out here and I regret it. In my defense, I had fever at the time, not to mention I was aggravated that you tried to murder me."

"I was beginning to think that was a dream," Josh confessed.

"Not at all. You tried to brain me with an entrenching tool. You were buck naked at the time."

"But didn't you try to shoot me with a pistol?"

"Yes, I did," Burr said, then shrugged. "Anyway, it turns out some folks up the chain of command was wondering where you were."

"Frank Knox?"

Burr sighed. "Yes, Josh, the high and mighty secretary of the navy himself still looks after you."

"So in other words, you were ordered to get your butt in gear and find me."

Burr smiled grimly. "That's one way of looking at it, I suppose. Now, if you'll get your traps, we'll paddle you out to the sub. After the priest sees the nun, we'll be on our way."

"I'm not going anywhere, Colonel. This island is my home now."

Burr did not appear surprised. "You always turn Turk, don't you, Josh? It was that way from the first I knew you, way up there in the Bering Sea. Captain Falcon recognized that about you. Even admired it, I think, though God knows why. But it don't matter. Knox wants you back, and I'm bound to bring you, willing or no."

"I'm not going without my family, Colonel."

"Your family?"

"I'm married, got a boy and a girl."

"My goodness. You do work fast, don't you?"

Burr rested his palm on the butt of his holstered pistol, and his fingers played across it as if he were contemplating a display of force. But he didn't, mainly because Josh held a Japanese rifle. "Well, Josh, we'll talk it over after we've all calmed down a bit," he said. "Anyhoo, the Holy Joe came all this way to talk to the little sister. I think I saw her dancing over there. Boys, paddle out to the sub, wait for morning, then bring the good priest ashore."

"Captain says we shove off at dawn, Colonel," one of the sailors said.

"You tell him there's some talking has to be done first. As a matter of fact, ask him to come in with that priest. All kinds of talking needs to be done, I expect. Josh, can you put an old pal up for the night?"

Josh could, although reluctantly. "Would you like some mangojack, Montague?" he asked as hospitably as he could manage. "It's like applejack, only made from mangos. Turned out three marines came along with me, and they're the brewmasters. I suspect you'd like to have a word and a drink with your fellow frat boys."

Burr's bushy eyebrows furrowed. "Are they deserters?"

"No. They were shanghaied, just like me." He decided to leave out that they were also mutineers, at least for now.

Burr, however, sniffed out Josh's evasion. "Let me guess," he said as the sailors crept off to their raft. "They've been good marines, meaning they've taken up with the native women and thrown off all discipline."

"Yes on the former, but sort of mixed on the latter, Colonel. They are the mainstays of our defense. They even trained a cadre of Amazons."

"Then I should very much like to discuss the situation with them."

"Tomorrow morning would probably be a better time. I think they're a little busy right now."

"Oh, I can wait. I expect when they see me, it'll be a shock to their systems."

"Oh, I'm certain it will," Josh answered, relishing the moment when the mutinous marines encountered Colonel Montague Burr.

4 5

Sister Mary Kathleen woke in her beloved treehouse at the first glimmer of dawn, then climbed from her bed to her knees to say her morning prayers. This was Christmas Day, and for this she gave special thanks and made a decision to burn celebration candles along the ledge of the windows that overlooked the lagoon. She had three votive candles, a gift of Mr. Bucknell, given some weeks ago and kept for a special occasion. She would burn them for ten minutes, maybe fifteen, but no more, so they would be available for other special days. As she carefully placed them on the ledge of the window at the foot of her bed, she saw the submarine.

At first, she thought her eyes deceived her, that what she saw was a school of fish, or perhaps just a passing shadow of a cloud drifting by. Then she accepted that it was indeed a submarine lying just outside the entrance to the lagoon. She also saw two rubber rafts being paddled toward the beach.

As the rafts drew nearer, she recognized one of the passengers. "Dear Mary, Mother of God, pray for me," she whispered. For now it had come to this, the answer she had given up hope of ever hearing, the answer she had lately decided she didn't want to hear, the answer that would finally make her account for the terrible sin she had committed on Ruka.

Nervously dressing, she willed her slippered feet to move across the matted floor, noticing with distracted joy the pleasing creak of the bamboo so carefully laid down by Bosun O'Neal. She gave thanks to God once more for giving her such a friend. Then, taking a deep breath, down the winding staircase she went, and thence along the stone-lined path that went past Bosun O'Neal's house, which was silent. She kept going until she reached the village and then the beach. A United States Marine Corps chaplain in utilities and helmet, the priest she had confessed to so many weeks ago on a bloody Tarawa beach, watched her approach. "A joyful Christmas to ye, Father," she said as brightly as she could manage. "Thanks be to God. Ye have come. Ye have come at last."

"Sister," he said, his tone cold and formal. His granite features were arranged in a grim visage, not angry but stern, as if he were a headmaster and she an unruly student requiring punishment. He held a manila envelope in his hand. Without further preamble, he lifted it toward her, though it was clear he had no intention of immediately handing it over. "Is there somewhere we might go for privacy?"

"Merry Christmas, Sister!" came a booming voice behind her.

She whirled about and saw to her astonishment Colonel Burr striding toward her, a big grin on his wicked face. "Colonel," she replied coolly, before remembering her humility. "It is so good to see you."

Burr opened his arms as if to envelop her, but her rigid posture dissuaded him and he dropped them. Josh followed with Turu, both nodding a greeting. Burr said, "Your instructions to the Holy Joe here were enough for me to find you, Sister. I am distressed to hear, however, the Japanese have not yet surrendered in these islands, even with Captain Thurlow's august presence."

"Perhaps you will persuade them, sor," she answered, her courage, shaken by the priest, returning.

Burr turned up his hands. "Sorry, Sister. Much as I hate to admit it, and in this one instance, I agree with Thurlow. I'd need the Second Marines behind me before I'd even think of asking a Jap officer to surrender. Even then, I doubt he'd do it. At least I've brought Father Donnelly for you. So please get your business done, and quickly. Yon sub will be going back on patrol this very day, I expect. I will go with it, and Father Donnelly, too. Josh will also join us."

"I will not, Montague," Josh replied.

"That's still open for debate, my friend," Burr purred. "Now, Sister, you and the cleric have church business to attend to. What it is, he would not say, but let's have it done. Thurlow, are we ever to have breakfast?"

"Rose will soon have eggs on the griddle," Josh answered, "and the coffee's boiling."

Burr looked about with quiet satisfaction. "This is a lovely island. I can see how a man might fall in love with it." He touched his stomach. "But breakfast now, Thurlow, then I'll see my three marines and get them back to discipline, and then all the rest, eh?"

Josh and Burr and Turu walked back up the common road, and Sister Mary Kathleen and Father Donnelly were left alone, not counting the sailors who had come across the lagoon on the raft, plus a dozen or so sleepy-eyed villagers. Chief Kalapa was among them. He looked as if he had been dragged through the dirt upside down. Such was the effect of combining kava and mangojack.

"Well, Sister, where shall we do this?" Father Donnelly asked. It was more of a demand.

"Chief Kalapa, good morning to ye," Sister Mary Kathleen greeted the clearly ailing chief. His eyes were nearly swollen shut, and his stomach sagged over his poorly tied lava-lava. He managed to raise a hand, though it trembled. She switched to the local dialect. "Could this priest and I use the boathouse for a short meeting? We require privacy."

"You may," Chief Kalapa answered. His head felt like a split coconut. "Only please no sorcery. It is too early in the morning."

"No sorcery, Chief. I promise."

Chief Kalapa nodded, then trudged toward home, being careful to step over a fella boy passed out on the road.

Sister Mary Kathleen led Father Donnelly inside the boathouse, after first bowing to the totem. The priest did not bow but clutched the envelope as if it were a club, following her to the front of the house, where she bade him sit on a palm log bench. He elected to stand. "I have your answer," he said tautly. "I thought your case demanded extra effort, so I caught a lift to Australia, where I sought out the bishop in Cairns."

Though her heart was beating fiercely, she worked for inner serenity. "Get on with it, Father, if ye please."

More curious villagers gathered outside the boathouse, including Mr. Bucknell, who sat down on one of the nearby school benches. He idly began to draw in the sand with the tip of his umbrella, waiting with everyone else, though for what he had no idea. The only word was that Sister Mary Kathleen was closeted with an official of her church, surely a sorcerer who had brought a missive from the high sorcerer of the Catholics on this the holy birthday of the god Jesus.

Shortly the priest appeared on the boathouse porch, looking about until he spied Mr. Bucknell. "Sir, would you do something for me?" he asked.

Mr. Bucknell approached and introduced himself. "If there is anything a representative of His Majesty's government can do, I shall certainly comply."

"The woman within requires assistance. She has asked for two women, one named Mori and one named Rose."

"The woman within?"

"The nun," he answered coldly.

"I shall see to it immediately," Bucknell said and told one of the fella boys in the crowd to go after Jahtalo's wife and Chief Kalapa's first wife. "Is she all right, Captain?" Bucknell inquired after squinting to see the man's Marine Corps rank pinned to the collar of his utilities.

The priest-captain did not reply. He stood on the porch with a stern expression while the silent crowd studied him. Some of the villagers were wondering if he was going to perform magic. To their infinite disappointment, he didn't, and it wasn't long before Rose and Mori, both a little breathless, appeared and went inside the boathouse. A few minutes later, Mori came out and ran back up the common road. There was much discussion of this event among the onlookers, which increased in volume when the first wife came back, this time carrying a package tied with a hemp string. She disappeared inside the boathouse, Father Donnelly all the while maintaining his aloof expression.

It was then that Ready, hearing the commotion, wandered down from his house. He was shirtless and, from his heavily lidded eyes, clearly in a bad way from the previous evening's festivities. "Merry Christmas, Mr. Bucknell," he said, shading his eyes, even though he was in shadow. "What gives?"

Mr. Bucknell gave Ready a rundown of the proceedings to the minute. Ready became instantly alert and pushed through the crowd to the porch. "Is there something wrong with Sister?" he politely asked the priest.

"It does not concern you," Father Donnelly sternly replied.

"If it concerns Sister Mary Kathleen, it concerns me," Ready answered. "What have you done to her?"

After a moment of deliberation, the priest intoned, "It is a matter of the Church, my son. Do not interfere."

"Tell me or I'll climb up there and knock your block off!" Ready barked.

But Ready didn't knock the priest's block off because Sister Mary Kathleen appeared at that moment at the doorway of the boathouse. It took Ready a moment to recognize her, as she was not wearing her habit but a loose gown made of blue lava-lava cloth that went from her neck to her ankles. Rose and Mori came behind and gave everyone a look of warning. Then the three women descended the steps from the porch and hurried along the path that led back to the treehouse. Ready made to follow, but Mr. Bucknell stopped him. "It would appear Sister wishes some privacy, my boy. Why don't you give it to her?"

"But I don't understand what's happened!" Ready cried.

"Neither do I, but it will come out. Patience, lad. Patience."

Father Donnelly stepped down from the porch. "What did you do to her?" Ready demanded anew. "Tell me, please!"

"Only what her sins required," came the priest's haughty response.

This was the last thing the priest would say for some minutes, mainly because Ready cocked back his fist and let fly, the punch sending the marine Holy Joe sprawling on his back. He stared up with unfocused eyes, a bloody nose, and a groan.

"So much for a troublesome priest," Mr. Bucknell chuckled, then bent down to see the damage. "Come on, Father. Snap out of it! I think you must have a glass jaw."

Ready started up the path to the treehouse, then stopped and reconsidered. Mr. Bucknell was right. Sister wanted privacy. So he headed toward Captain Thurlow's house, finding him sitting in a chair with Colonel Burr in another, both drinking coffee and having a genial conversation. The colonel's presence was a shock, but he was not Ready's priority. Ready nodded to Burr, then blurted a description to Josh of what had transpired at the boathouse. "I don't know what to do," Ready concluded.

"Why come to me? You're in charge of everything."

Ready ran his hand through his hair. "Because I don't know what to do, and I'm tired of being in charge. You take it back, sir. I'll do whatever you say!"

Josh, pleased beyond measure over this turnabout, advised Ready to have a seat and poured the unsettled young man a cup of coffee. "Something awful's happened to her, I know it!" Ready wailed.

"Remain calm, Bosun," Josh said.

"Is this man under discipline, Josh?" Burr demanded. "It appears he's forgotten how to properly report to a superior officer."

Josh shrugged. "Never mind that, Montague. We do things a little different here in the Far Reaches. Now, Bosun, look here. I don't know what's happened, but it can't be all that bad. She ain't hurt, the little Sister, is she? No. She's taken off her habit. Well, perhaps she was outside uniform regulations or some such since she's had to stitch her own. The Catholic Church is just like the military, has its rules and regulations, and if you don't follow them, then you have to walk off your demerits. Sister once told me that humility above all else was what a nun worked toward and humiliation was sometimes required, even invited. Maybe that priest came to bring her under discipline like the colonel here will do his marines."

"That reminds me," Burr growled. "When do I get to see my wayward boys?"

"They're still asleep, sir," Ready answered.

Burr's eyes turned cold, and he gestured toward Ready with his cup. "Listen to me, son. Go wake up my marines and tell them to get their butts here and I mean *toot sweet!*"

"Calm down, Montague," Josh said. "Your boys will be along by and by. And what do you know? The navy has arrived."

Josh stood and held out his hand to a naval officer who had walked up the road from the beach. "Captain Josh Thurlow, United States Coast Guard," he greeted.

"Captain Taylor Wells," the handsome young man in crisp khakis said, taking Josh's hand. "It's good to meet you at last, Captain Thurlow. You're a legend out here. The hero of Wilton's Ridge."

Josh waved the compliment aside and poured the submarine skipper a cup of coffee. He was enjoying playing the proper host. "Wish I could warm that up with some Mount Gay rum, but we're all out."

Wells took the cup, drank a healthy slug, and smiled. "Good stuff. Best I've had in a very long while."

"Locally grown," Josh said proudly. "I expect this island could grow a commercial crop, given some investment."

"See here, Josh," Burr snapped. "We didn't come here to talk about coffee beans. Captain Wells has a schedule and we've already disrupted it. Isn't that right, Captain?"

Wells nodded, then shrugged. "A commander has to roll with the punches. But I would like to get going." He looked at Josh over the rim of his cup. "Anytime you're ready, sir."

"I won't be going with you," Josh answered, then added, "This is not a point of discussion or argument." When Burr started to discuss and argue, Josh raised his hand for silence. "Now, Montague, hold on. You, I, and the skipper here are all of equivalent rank. Admittedly, you have me by your date of rank, but I am still not in your chain of command. In fact, I'm not in anybody's chain of command, except maybe Frank Knox's since I am out here by his invitation. But he told me to use my initiative and see what I could see. Well, I've seen it, and now I'm going to stay right here, at least until I can convince my family to leave."

"Rationalize it any way you want, Josh, but it's still desertion," Burr pointed out. "When Admiral Halsey hears about it, he'll likely order you captured, then trussed up on a stake and shot."

"I'll take my chances with Bull Halsey," Josh growled.

"Is there anything I can do for you, Captain Thurlow?" Wells asked.

Josh nodded gratefully. "There is, Captain Wells. I'd appreciate a full sweep of the area before you go back on patrol. There are at least two Jap barges that work out of Ruka. They need to be sunk."

Wells shook his head. "I'd like to help out, but Ruka's out of my way. You see, I need to get up north as soon as I can. There's convoys coming down from Tokyo to resupply the Marianas, and I've been ordered to stop them." Wells leaned toward Josh. "Look, Captain. What can I do to convince you to go with me?"

Josh shook his head. "Nothing. Since I've been here, I have tried to convince my wife and Chief Kalapa and all the others to evacuate down to the Gilberts for the duration of the war. I'll keep doing that, but if they won't go, I'm not going to abandon them."

Wells smiled. "I understand. I've seen your wife. A marine pointed her out to me on the beach."

Burr growled, "Well, I ain't leaving here without you, Josh."

Josh, oft surprised since he'd been in the Far Reaches, was surprised once more. "Why, Montague. I didn't know you cared!"

Burr frowned one of his deeper frowns. "I don't give a rat's rear end about you. Never have and never will. But I have my orders, and they were clear. I am to bring you back to Halsey. I've half a mind to get Captain Wells here to send a contingent of his sailor boys to tie you up and drag you aboard. Then again, as much as I hate to say it, you've made some sense. You've taken on a responsibility here, and I guess you can't sail away from it. Therefore, I've decided to stay and help you convince these people to escape while they still can."

Josh was shocked by the offer. "Thanks but no thanks, Montague! You go on with Captain Wells. I'll be along by and by."

"No dice, Josh. You're stuck with me."

Josh lowered his head into his hands. "I can't believe it."

Burr grinned. "Believe it, old son."

Wells finished his coffee and put down his cup. "Tell you what. After my patrol, I'll try to get back here, check on both of you, see if there's anything I can do. I'll also try to save a few torps to sink your barges."

They stood and shook hands. "Good hunting, Captain," Josh said.

"Same to you, Captain. By the way, I talked to an intelligence officer when I received my orders to come here. He'd heard of Colonel Yoshu. Said he was a violent, nasty customer."

"How long will your patrol last?" Josh asked.

"Hard to say. Matter of weeks, I would imagine. Say, Josh, would you like some khakis? That lava-lava looks like the perfect thing for these islands, but maybe you might like to put on the uniform for special occasions."

Josh nodded in gratitude. "I could also use some boots, large ones, if you have them. An officer's cap, too, if you don't mind. I don't imagine you've got one with the Coast Guard stiff eagle attached, but I'll be pleased to wear the navy bird, too."

Wells grinned. "I'll have two sets of khakis, a pair of large boots, and one cap sent to you immediately."

The khakis were sent along with the boots and the cap, and then Captain Wells waved from the conning tower of his sub as it curved out to sea. Josh stood with Rose and Colonel Burr and watched it go. "Well, Montague," Josh said, "your fat's in the fire now, I reckon."

Burr rubbed his hands. "Truth be known, Thurlow, I was ready for an adventure. Now, where's my marines? Discipline. That's the ticket for those leathernecks. I can't wait to get started!"

Josh chuckled. "I'm certain they feel the same, Montague. Yes, I'm certain they do."

4 6

Two days after Christmas, she announced through Rose that she was ready to be visited. First was Nango and the other Ruka fella boys, then Chief Kalapa. Afterward came Mori, Mr. Bucknell, and Josh Thurlow. Each left the treehouse and, to the astonishment of the people of the village, refused to gossip about what was discussed. The last to visit her was Ready. His face was a grim mask, a lump in his throat as big as his fist, as he climbed the winding stairs. He found her dressed in the blue lava-lava gown. Nothing covered her hair. It was, Ready discovered, brown and cropped short, giving her a surprisingly boyish appearance.

"Please sit, Bosun," she said, indicating a chair built of breadfruit wood that Ready had constructed for her, in which he'd used not a single nail but wooden pegs, and polished it lovingly until it glowed.

She sat opposite him in the other breadfruit chair he'd built, then leaned forward with her elbows on her knees. Her eyes were filled with meaning and brimming with tears. Before she could speak, Ready said, "You promised to call me Ready, Sister."

She nodded. "So I shall, Ready, but you must never call me Sister, no, not ever again. This is why I have asked ye here. I am no longer a sister of me order. I am back in the world, as the sisterhood calls it. Kathleen, that is me name. That is what I ask ye call me henceforth."

Ready nodded slowly, then asked, "Can you tell me why?"

She took a breath, then used a finger to wipe away a tear that trickled across her cheek. "I loved my vocation, Ready. I loved it more than life, though the other sisters often remarked that I was a worldly nun. They said I lacked humility. It was true, though I longed to be as devoted to the Church as they were, and to attain their serenity, no matter what the challenge. When

I told them this was my greatest wish, they said such longing only reflected pride, that I had to let go of all desire, but even then, there was no such thing as a perfect nun."

She smiled a sad smile. "But Ready, ye should have seen them when they faced death! They were perfect, indeed. They knelt with their eyes gleaming in trust that they would soon be in paradise. Ye see, I was there, in the same room. Father Ballester meant to save me, and so he hid me from the Japanese. But I was found and brought out into the chapel, there to observe Colonel Yoshu's vengeance against the priests and the sisters for their disobedience. That they tried to save me was their disobedience, Ready. Do ye understand?"

"Yes," Ready answered quietly. "I understand you were forced to do everything that you did."

She shook her head. "No. Not everything. I did not protest when Colonel Yoshu did not kill me. This was me first sin, though far from me greatest. I was led to me prison, a small concrete cell that had been used as a storage room in the chapel. There I was kept for months with little to eat but bread and water. My habit was taken away. I was kept naked and not allowed to wash. I lost track of time. Gradually, Ready, I fell into filth and self-loathing. I would have done anything for freedom. Finally, I even begged the guards to kill me, or take me and use me for their pleasure. Anything, to get out of that cage. They laughed, of course, and left me where I was. I was too grotesque even for them, y'see. It was a shameful thing and me next sin. But it was still not my greatest."

Ready pressed his lips together hard, then said, "Anyone would have done the same."

"Anyone but a nun! We have special duties!" she snapped. "Please just listen and try to understand. Then the guards came and dragged me from me cell. They held their noses, I stunk so awful, but I was allowed to bathe and given a clean robe to wear. Then I was moved to Colonel Yoshu's quarters, which had been Mr. Bucknell's house. Colonel Yoshu was not there, and for some days I was allowed to move about freely as long as I didn't try to leave. I met Nango there, and the other fella boys. They were kept as servants, and the soldiers, the most sinful, used them in terrible ways. We talked—it wasn't forbidden—and he told me he and the others had decided on suicide.

"I thought of escape, but there were so many guards, it was impossible. Then the colonel returned, though he made no attempt to speak to me or acknowledge my presence, even when I was ushered in to sit quietly in his office. He sat at his desk and issued orders to his officers as they came to see him. Or he met with native delegations, to whom he also issued orders. Then, one day, he called me again to his office and, through a translator, asked me for me advice. On the floor of his office was a native man, horribly beaten. Because his children were hungry, this man had refused to give food to a Japanese soldier when it was demanded. What, Colonel Yoshu asked, should he do with this man? I replied that a father's first responsibility was to his children and that he should be released. Colonel Yoshu clapped his hands and it was done. Then he complimented me and said I had been a great help to him. He inquired if I might be willing to help him again. And so I did. I ate well the nights I gave him advice." She shook her head. "More sin, but still far from me greatest."

"But you were trying to help the natives!" Ready protested. "There is no sin in that!"

She continued, her steady eyes silencing him. "No. To me shame, I helped this monster so that I could eat and so that I wouldn't be thrown back into that horrible cell. I began to learn Japanese, and I sat beside him each day, like some terrible white queen, and gave him advice. Some he took, some he didn't, but I hoped I was softening his rule. At night, when I whispered me prayers, it came to me how wrong I was. When I suggested to Colonel Yoshu it was no longer proper for me to assist him, he said he would simply go back to his old ways of cutting off heads whenever it suited him. Then he raped me."

Ready sucked in a breath and knotted his fists. Yet he said nothing. He waited because he knew there was more to come.

"He raped me over a period of three weeks. Day and night."

Ready released his breath. Still he waited, though it felt as if she had reached inside him and torn out his guts.

"I fought back, but he beat me until I was covered with bruises. He broke both me wrists and cracked me ribs. He bit me on my shoulders until they bled. Afterwards, while I lay weeping on the bloody sheets, he would speak softly to me. He told me he had received a dream that he would return to Japan and I would go with him, that together we would build a dynasty that would control the country. He said that I would therefore learn Japanese even better. I agreed, sin on top of sin, and a young soldier was provided as a tutor. When I didn't learn fast enough, Yoshu cut off one of the young man's fingers. The rapes stopped soon afterwards. I was pregnant, y'see."

Ready's face had turned into a mask of repressed pain and rage. Still he held his words back.

"My daughter is eight months old. She was born in April. I named her Monessa."

She allowed herself a quiet smile and went on.

"I was allowed to stay with her for a little while. Then she was taken away from me and a wet nurse supplied. It was only when I begged Yoshu that I was allowed to see her, and then for only a few minutes at a time."

Now, finally, the tears came, streaming across her round, flushed cheeks. She waited until they subsided, then wiped them away with the back of her hand, then continued as if they'd never occurred.

"I was desperate. I went to Yoshu, begging him to let me see Monessa. He agreed, but the price was total obedience to him. And so I entered his household and went to his bed. It was some time later that a revelation came to me, and I'm certain it was a provision of the Holy Mother. My humiliation was complete, y'see. I could go no lower. I had finally reached the goal that had been mine since I'd become a nun. I was victorious because of me degradation! One night, while Yoshu was atop me—I beg yer forgiveness for such rawness, but I wish ye to understand—I began to laugh. I could not stop. It frightened Yoshu, and he ran from his chambers. I sought out Monessa, took her into me arms, and cradled her and sang to her until Yoshu set his soldiers on me. I was dragged away, thrown back into the cell where I'd spent those first awful months. And there I was until Nango and his fella boys came to me rescue, killing the guards. Before we went to the outriggers, I insisted on going to the chapel to retrieve a habit. I was still a nun, no matter me sins, and I felt the need to look like one, may God have mercy on me. So we put to sea, though we didn't know where to go. Then we happened upon a fishing canoe from the Gilberts. The men in it said they thought the Americans were coming to those islands, so we headed there. You know what happened after that."

Ready waited, and when she said nothing else, he said, very simply, "I love you."

She studied him, and he could feel her in his eyes and in his mind. When she seemed satisfied with her inspection, however it was meant, she said, "I know. That is why I am asking ye to do something for me, something that will be terrible hard for ye. Me fella boys won't do it, nor will Chief Kalapa, or Mr. Bucknell, or even Captain Thurlow. They do not love me enough, y'see."

"I love you enough, whatever it may be," Ready replied staunchly.

"I do not love ye, Ready O'Neal," she said. "This ye must know."

"Love can grow."

"Yes, when there is room enough in one's heart, it may. But this has nothing to do with love, but with what is practical, and best for everyone. I am asking ye with all me heart to do this thing for me. Take me to Ruka, slip in at night, and I will go ashore, there to give meself up to Colonel Yoshu."

"No!" Ready cried. It was a howl of released pain.

She knelt before him and took his hands. "I should have never left him. That he would try to find me, and murder innocents to do it, was certain. I was blind not to see it."

Ready steadied himself. He had to be strong with her. He knew she was under a terrible strain. He had to lend her his strength. "I will not do it," he said and took his hands away.

"Ye must," she replied softly. "If ye love me, this ye must do. And it must be done in secret, lest others try to stop us. Therefore, I have decided we should be married."

Ready blinked. "Married?"

"Aye, so that our being together and our leaving together will not raise suspicion."

"You ask too much!"

"I ask only what should be done. Nothing more. Do ye not wish to marry me?"

"Of course! I want nothing more."

"Then cast aside yer doubts. Marry me and make me yer wife."

"And then hand you over to a monster?"

"Yes. So that I may protect Monessa."

"But he will . . ."

"Kill me? Rape me again? I don't think so. I can control him long enough."

"Long enough for what?"

"Until I can kill him. Then I will escape with Monessa."

Ready was incredulous. "I do not believe you could kill anyone."

"A mother will do anything for her child."

"No, Kathleen. Maybe I don't love you enough, either. Not enough to let you commit certain suicide. But maybe . . ." He trailed off, frowning, thinking.

"Maybe what?"

He took a deep breath, let it out. "Maybe if I went with you, we could steal Monessa away and bring her back. I don't know how, not yet, but maybe there's a way to do that. At night, perhaps . . ."

She moved into his arms. Then she kissed him full on the mouth. He tasted her and nothing mattered, nothing save her taste, her touch. Forever and ever. He knew then he would do anything for this woman . . . nearly anything.

"Marry me, Ready O'Neal. Marry me, and together, we will rescue Monessa."

He took her hands, and his face was wreathed with joy. "Yes! We will!"

Then he took her again into his arms, and Kathleen placed her head against his strong shoulder and knew she would get her wish. She would marry, and her husband, besotted with love, would carry her to Ruka. The hand of Colonel Yoshu was extended, and she knew now God wanted her to take it, evil to evil, sin to sin, and damnation to them both.

4 7

It was the saddest marriage ceremony Josh reckoned he had ever seen, or ever would see. The former nun was lovely, as always, though shrouded from neck to ankle in her terrible loose gown. Kathleen, as she called herself now, was not radiant. She was downcast throughout, and Josh's heart went out to her, almost as much as it did to Ready, who stood there in his old, ragged utilities. He looked stricken, as if possessed by some terrible spirit.

Chief Kalapa presided over the ritual, placing their hands together and knotting them with hemp twine, signifying that they were forever joined. Mr. Bucknell then read from the Bible and, as a representative of His Majesty's government, asked the couple if they agreed to follow the traditional Anglican formalities.

"Aye," she answered. " 'Tis near enough to me own."

"Yes. All right," Ready answered miserably.

Their heads bowed, they made their vows.

"Who gives this woman to be married to this man?" Bucknell asked in a quiet voice.

"I do," Josh answered, stepping up beside her. He was wearing his fresh khakis from the submarine.

Bucknell adjusted his half-glasses on the tip of his nose, scanned the Anglican text, and then said, "I see no reason to continue reading the ceremony. Chief Kalapa has already properly married you according to the beliefs of this island, and your hands are tied with the hemp. You've answered my 'wilt thous' with your 'I wills.' Certainly, you take one another for better and for worse. As far as His Majesty's government is concerned, I pronounce you man and wife."

She raised her head and said, in a small voice, "I have a ring."

Mr. Bucknell did not hear her clearly. "What did you say, dear?"

She opened her left hand, revealing a simple silver ring lying in her palm. "I have a ring," she said again. Bucknell recognized it as the one she had worn as a nun.

"Help us, Josh," Ready said, the first time he'd ever called his captain by his first name.

Josh untied the hemp twine from their hands, allowing Ready to take the ring. Wearing a crooked smile, Ready looked into her eyes and said, "I love you."

"Thank ye," she answered as he slipped the ring on her finger. She turned to the assembly, which was everyone in the village. "Thank ye all for coming."

Chief Kalapa smiled, though not broadly, and announced a feast. It would prove to be a pathetic one. No pigs were roasted, although several chickens were grilled. No kava was drunk, and only a little mangojack. People stood about listlessly and ate the meager fare, then wandered home or to dig in their gardens or wherever the evening took them. For their part, Ready and Kathleen proposed a few toasts with the marines and Colonel Burr, who, oddly enough, had shed a few tears during the ceremony. Then they walked down the path to the treehouse.

Josh went to sit in his chair in front of his house, and there he sat, drinking mangojack, wishing he might get drunk and swearing to himself not to. Rose came and sat alongside him. "You are sad, husband."

"I am sad for Ready and I am sad for Sister. Kathleen, I mean. I am also frightened for them."

"You? Frightened?" She smiled and touched his hand. "I cannot imagine such a thing."

"Do you know she asked me to take her in a canoe to Ruka and give her to Colonel Yoshu?"

"Yes. She also asked Nango, Mr. Bucknell, and Chief Kalapa. I also have no doubt that she asked Bosun O'Neal, and perhaps he has agreed. That is why she married him. If so, it is a good thing. I wish you and the others would have done it."

Josh was astonished. "You would have me turn her over to a monster?"

"Before anything else, I wish for the safety of my family."

Josh nodded agreement but said, "Nothing, not even Kathleen killing herself, would stop Colonel Yoshu from coming here. The colonel has had

a long time to get thoroughly annoyed with this island. You can bet the coconut telegraph let him know early on she was here. And he'll come, no
matter what, to teach us a lesson for sheltering her."

"Perhaps you are right. I will change my mind to match your opinion."

"I have never known a finer woman than you," Josh swore, taking
Rose's hand. Then he said, from a part of his heart he scarcely knew was
there, "Will you marry me?"

She laughed. "We are already married."

"So we are." And Josh Thurlow was content, at least as much as any man
whose family was in terrible danger.

She burned her candles, three brave flickering lights against the darkness.
Ready sat in the breadfruit chair, a cup of mangojack in his fist. He was
staring at nothing. Kathleen sat on the bed, fearful of the intimacy to come.
She steeled herself for it and tried to act as any bride might on her wedding
night. "Ready," she said and patted the mattress, just once, and lightly. "Are
ye not tired? Come to bed."

He looked at her, then put the cup down and took off his boots and then
stripped off his utilities. Tossing them aside, not bothering to hide his
nakedness and therefore his clear lack of excitement, he heavily sat down
beside her. She touched his shoulder. "Why are ye troubled?"

"It is because I don't know who or what I am. I haven't known it since
the moment I met you."

"What can I do to help?"

His tone was petulant. "You can turn back the clock. You can stay in
Ireland. You can marry that boy who wanted you to marry him before you
became a nun."

"God would not allow it," she answered. "I am sorry that I have become a burden to ye."

"You're not. It's me. It's what I see in my mind."

Her heart pounding, her fear of his touch increasing, she climbed fully
on the bed, laid herself down, and tugged on his arm. She was a bride and
she would act like one, no matter how much she dreaded the act of intimacy.
"Come. Lie beside me. Tell me what ye see in yer mind that troubles ye so."

Feeling childish, he lay on his back beside her, staring at the roof he had
built for her with such joy. "I see you with him. A man wants his wife . . ."
He shook his head.

"Pure? Unsullied? Virginal?" she retorted angrily, taking her hand away.

"Is it not enough I come to ye with me sins as cleansed as I could get them? I confessed to that priest, accomplished my penance with nearly unending prayers on the voyage here. And when ye expressed yer love to me, was I any different than I am now? Ye are being most unfair, Ready O'Neal!"

Ready was into his misery and couldn't stop himself from saying it all. "I married you under false pretenses. I cannot turn you over to that fiend." He sat up. "I can't stay here. I have to go."

She pulled him back, held him. Continuing to act as she imagined a bride would, she kissed him until at last he seemed to melt. She pulled off her gown and then, trembling, let him feel the length of her body. "Ready, I am yer wife." She waited but nothing happened. Then she asked brazenly, "Will ye not make ficky-ficky with me, boyo?"

"I can't."

Angry now, and feeling rejected, she climbed out of bed and stood with her hands on her hips. "Do ye want me to put the habit on? Is that it? Is that the fantasy ye have in yer twisted mind?"

He looked at her in the glow of her little candles, and what he saw in the flickering light and shadows was a girl, a young Irish girl, who was beautiful. "I would love you even if you wore nothing at all," he said.

Relieved, she laughed and spread her arms wide. "Well, yer in luck, Ready O'Neal!"

He stared at her for a long second, then, because he felt ridiculous, also laughed. "Come on then, me Irish lass. I have need of ye!"

She hopped on the bed and took him into her arms. Somehow, all her fear had been set aside. She felt, for the first time, like a bride and, better, was even glorying in the sensations it brought her. "Kathleen O'Neal, Irish lass at yer service, sor!" she cried and released herself from all care.

Kapura, a Ruka fella boy, placed on guard by Nango near the tree, heard the laughter coming from above and then the other noises that meant the marriage night was successful. Then he heard the school bell knocked off its table. It fell with a clang and rolled ringing across the floor. Kapura grinned and allowed himself a long pull of mangojack. "You fella boy Ready ring fella sister bell plenty too much," he whispered to himself, then moved to a tree farther away to give the happy couple a little privacy.

4 8

The story Kathleen told of the child she bore after being raped by the cruel Colonel Yoshu quickly became common knowledge. Everyone, especially the women, was sympathetic toward the former nun and thought she was very brave. The men thought she was brave, too, and understood now why the colonel wanted her back. Josh Thurlow once more tried to convince one and all to pack up and leave, but no one was amenable to it, including Rose. So Josh shut up about it and accepted the certain battle to come. If they were able to repel it, he rationalized, then perhaps he could convince one and all to run.

The marines, during this time, suffered. Colonel Burr gathered them at the boathouse, harangued them concerning their unauthorized departure from Tarawa, then yelled at them about their lack of discipline, their ragged utilities, and their women. "You have gone Turk!" he bellowed. "Drill, that's what you need, and that's what you're going to get!"

Burr lined up Tucker, Garcia, and even Sampson on his crutch and made them march with him calling cadence. "Hup-hup!" he bellowed. "Get in step there, Sampson. You think because you only got one foot, you ain't a marine? Once a marine, always a marine, son, don't matter how many body parts you might lose."

He marched them, even ran them, demanding that they sing cadence as they trotted along with Sampson held up between Tucker and Garcia. And so they did, with the villagers watching in astonishment as the marines struggled by, singing:

> *Ain't no use in going home.*
> *Jody's got your girl and gone.*

Ain't no use in feeling blue.
Jody's got your sister, too.
Ain't no use in lookin' back.
Jody's got your Cadillac . . .

"Sir, let's be honest," Tucker said to Burr during a short break. "None of us give a shit about Jody no more, nor Cadillacs. We got all we need right here."

"Don't say that!" Burr shouted. "You're in these latitudes courtesy of Uncle Sam, and it's your duty to miss back home and all its creature comforts, including Hershey bars, Coca-Cola, and American women, even if Jody, the rat bastard draft dodger, has stolen them all away."

Sampson was brazen in his reply. "Don't need no Cokes or Hersheys, sir, and I never met no American woman like the ones right here. You just wouldn't believe how sweet they are. Maybe you ought to get yourself one."

"Shut up!" Burr roared. "If I needed a woman, the Corps would've made her issue! Now, we're gonna run, boys, run like we're chasing Tojo himself. Now, up! Up, I say, and on your feet! Foot for you, Sampson! You're marines, and I'm not gonna let you forget it!"

So the sun rose, and the heat increased, and Burr and the marines marched and sweated and ran up and down the road and the beach. The villagers watched in awe while trying to imagine the purpose of such relentless exercise. The marines' women even went to Chief Kalapa to complain about Curbur, as the colonel was called. The chief in turn went to Josh, whom he found making a new batch of charcoal.

Josh inclined his head, listened to the cadence calls for a long second, then laughed. "Listen, Chief. It is good that the marines are being reminded who they are. We will need them to be marines if Colonel Yoshu comes, which could be any day. As for their women, sometimes I know something, though I don't know how I know it. If you let the colonel and his marines get through the day, and maybe tomorrow, I think things will settle down. This island takes hold of a man. I think it might even take hold of Montague Singleton Burr."

To the relief of the chief, Josh's speculation proved to be entirely correct. On the third night of his self-exile on Tahila, Burr retreated to his quarters, which had been Ready's house, now already known as Curbur's House. There he lay on a palm frond mat and stared up at the high-pitched roof. Although he didn't mean to, meant only to sleep, Burr began to contemplate his life. He rose in the dark and went outside and felt the wafting breeze against his face and sniffed the fragrance of the frangipani and the riotous scent of the gardenia. He heard the scrambling of lizards, the distant call of the Forridges *kukaboo* bird, and the sound of lovemaking in the various houses of the village. He thought about all that he'd done with his life, and why, and what it all meant, and then he was very sad. He was sad because of his ambition to receive a star on his collar, which he finally accepted was never going to be realized. He was also sad for the men whose careers he had destroyed through one stratagem or another in his quest for that star, and for the women he'd loved and lost for the same reason. By morning, he required conversation, a first for a man who liked to talk but seldom listened. He therefore visited Josh Thurlow, his ancient nemesis, who bade him to sit and have a cup of joe.

"Well, Montague, what's on tap for the Marine Corps today?" Josh asked as the man sat down in a driftwood chair and took the offered cup. "A fifty-mile hike with full packs? Or how about running up and down yon mountain a few times through the devil vine?"

Burr didn't answer directly. Instead, he took a moment to savor the delightful aroma of the wonderful coffee in his cup, rather than tossing it scalding down his throat as he did in ordinary times. "I think I have fallen ill, Josh," he said finally, then sipped delicately at the rim of the cup. "I seem to have heightened sensibilities. Last night, I considered my life. This morning, I feel as if every nerve in my body has been stripped bare. Do you think perhaps I have been drugged?"

Josh gave the question some honest thought. "There is something about this island that makes a man think. It's dangerous that way."

"Do you have a suggestion for what I should do?"

"That depends. What do you want to do?"

"I'm not sure. I think I might figure it out if I stayed here for a while."

"Then stay as long as you like. With luck, you'll have some days to relax, nap, and dream a little before the Japanese attack us and we're up to our necks in blood. Such an opportunity rarely comes to a marine, or any man."

Burr mulled Josh's words, then nodded. "I have misjudged you, Josh. You are perhaps not quite the shallow bastard I've always detested. If I've been wrong all these years, I would like to apologize."

Josh smiled, though it was a sad smile. "I'm sorry you thought I stole Naanni from you up there, along the Bering Sea."

"I always blamed you for her death," Burr answered.

"Maybe you were right. But I have a confession to make. Those fellows that killed her, they didn't live long to tell the tale."

Burr cocked his head. "You murdered them? I heard rumors . . ."

"I avenged my wife."

Burr drank his coffee, all of it, then poured himself another cup. "By God, I wish I could have helped you!" he swore. Then he said in a doleful tone, "Josh, I'm in disfavor, terrible disfavor with the Corps. They put me in charge of burying the dead on Tarawa, can you imagine? It's as shitty a job as there is, and surely not a proper job for a combat commander. It was that foul-up on Noa-Noa that started my downfall, a foul-up that had your fingerprints all over it."

"I didn't tell you to invade Noa-Noa, Montague."

"What did you think I'd do when I heard you were up there surrounded by Japs and cannibals? Let them cut out your liver and have it for lunch? Hell no. I got my Raiders together, shoved a boot up their patooties, and made one of the fastest operational landings ever in the history of the Corps. It was successful, too. It wasn't my fault there weren't any Japs on the island, nor much of anybody except you and that sad sack ambassador's son, Jack Kennedy. The word came down from Halsey I was too quick on the draw, had an itchy trigger finger, all them cowboy attributes he usually likes but apparently not in me. Next thing I know, just after we'd landed on New Guinea and started to move up, my Raiders were absorbed into division as a regiment and I was made into a damned staff officer."

"The world, and that especially includes the Marine Corps, ain't fair, Montague. You surely know that. The question is, what are you going to do about it?"

Burr pushed out his heels into the dirt and contemplated his brown boots. "I'm going to follow your advice and give it all a good think. This does indeed seem a good place to do it."

"It is that," Josh agreed, "but as I just alluded to, there's a problem, that mad Japanese colonel who wants to wipe us out and take back what he believes is his, namely Mrs. Ready O'Neal."

Burr nodded. "There may be some action, a chance for battle, our own little Alamo."

"Hold on, Davy Crockett. This ain't the Alamo. This is a village of innocents. What we really should do, and I keep trying to convince everybody of this, is load up the outriggers and head to the Gilberts."

"Yes, they have all told me your opinion, Josh," Burr answered, "and I see the logic of it, sure. But have you thought of this? You get that many boats out on the ocean, you're liable to get caught by that crazy Jap colonel. He'd wipe you out pretty easy then. No, I think it's better to sit tight, wait for Captain Wells to return. Then I'll go aboard his sub, get on down to Australia and convince the high and mighties to bomb Ruka down to bedrock. In the meantime, we'll take that bastard's measure if he tries to come ashore."

Josh was astonished. "Damned if you don't make sense for once, Montague."

"I've always made sense. You've just been too foolish to listen. Here's some more sense. It may be the Japs saw our submarine. If so, they likely ran back to Ruka. Maybe we've bought ourselves some time."

Josh smiled. "It's good to have a real military man to talk to. Have some more coffee, Montague. Wish I could sweeten it with Mount Gay."

"Thank you. Wish I'd brought some."

"Another thing we agree on," Josh marveled and toasted an enemy that just might be turning into a friend.

All the next morning, Tucker, Garcia, and Sampson waited as Burr had told them to wait with their rifles slung on their shoulders beside the schoolhouse while Mrs. O'Neal taught her class. When the colonel didn't show up, they went home for lunch and a little afternoon ficky-ficky with their women and then afterward dutifully returned to the school. They found Colonel Burr there, watching with interest the lesson that was being taught, that of the different types of flowers to be found in Ireland. Though the marines sat down on the bench behind him, he did not even acknowledge their presence.

"Mrs. O'Neal," he said after the lesson, while still ignoring the marines, who followed him to the front of the school, "I would very much like to teach a lesson on the flora and fauna of Kansas, my home state. Would that be all right? Good. Thank you. Tomorrow, yes. I will be prepared."

Burr finally turned to his marines. "Now, boys, I've talked to Bosun O'Neal and Captain Thurlow and reviewed the plans for defending this island. It's a good one. Go on home now, and do what you need to do for your women. All I expect is for you to man the machine guns at night and stay alert. Sampson, how's that stump? I'll see you get a Purple Heart. For that matter, all you boys, I'll get you some medals and your back pay, too."

"Are you sick, Colonel?" Tucker asked.

"Why do you ask?"

"I don't know. I thought you planned on working us some more."

"Do you need me to work you some more?"

Threatened with useless work, the marines instantly disappeared, an ability they had learned beginning at boot camp. That night, as Burr sat on the porch of his house, one of the widows who had first provided a bed for Sister Mary Kathleen brought him a dinner of chicken and rice, spiced with lemon, a local pepper, and ginger, along with a pot of mangojack. She sat beneath a waving palm near the porch and waited patiently until Curbur ate the meal and slugged back the drink. Then she came to sit beside him. After many minutes of silence, she suggested that perhaps he might like some company for the night. Burr perused her in the light provided by a nearby cooking fire and noted her fine, mature figure and her pleasant face and her compliant nature. He accepted the offer and woke the next morning feeling positively mellow. He wrapped a lava-lava around his waist and followed the widow's beckoning finger to the little pond. Along the way, he learned that her name was Nanura, which he shortened to Nan. On the path back, refreshed after his bath and eagerly looking forward to the big breakfast she had promised, he reflected on his present joy. "I've done it," he said aloud. "I've gone Turk, gone around the bend, gone native, pulled up stakes, lit out for the territories. Who'da thunk it of Colonel Montague Singleton Burr, the marine's marine?"

"Curbur," she said, daring to walk beside him while also trying out his name. "You belong Nan? Is good?"

"Is good," Burr replied with a satisfied smile, putting his arm around her and drawing her close as they walked. "It's all good."

And damned if it wasn't.

4 9

Josh woke with the roosters. Like most sailors, morning was his favorite time of the day. He took Rose in his arms and held her for a little while, marveling at how deep asleep she was, even though the roosters were vying with one another as to which could be louder and more obnoxious. Turu and Manda also slept through the raucous cock-a-doodle-doing. It made Josh softly chuckle to see them so securely asleep, without a single care. He knew it was because they trusted him to keep them safe. He loved his family, loved the island, loved the people and their village. He tried to think when he'd been as happy, and he guessed it was all the way back to Killakeet, maybe when he'd been a boy and his mother was alive. Though there were other times, such as when Dosie and he had held one another so close . . .

His thoughts unwillingly turned to her. How was he going to explain Rose to Dosie? For that matter, what about Penelope? Not for the first time, he also made the guilty wish that Naanni might still be alive. If she were, he believed, neither Dosie nor Penelope and now Rose would have ever happened. Yet how much he would have missed!

Josh tenderly pushed aside strands of hair from Rose's forehead, kissed her there, then eased her back beneath the blanket. Eager for the day, he tied on his lava-lava, plopped on his navy hat, and went outside and down the common road to the beach. There he found the sun having a grand old time pushing out of the sea. It was a huge flattened molten ball with vast streamers of golden light trailing from it as if blown by an invisible wind. The clouds on the horizon had turned into gold fluff, rimmed in silver. He applauded the sun and the clouds, literally clapped his hands. "Well done, old boys!" he said while the stars winked off one by one. Second by second, the great golden orb gathered strength, parting the clouds as Moses had once parted the sea.

Josh was distracted by voices. Down the beach came two of the marines, Sampson on his crutch and Tucker carrying an ammo box. Their duty at the eastern machine gun was done, and they were going home for breakfast and a deserved nap. Josh looked down the beach on the other side of the lagoon and saw Garcia and one of the fella boys also going off duty, trudging along the beach.

"Hidy, Captain Thurlow," Tucker said when he and Sampson got near. "Helluva sunrise, weren't it?"

"I'd give this one top marks, Tucker," Josh answered. "See anything last night?"

"Nope. Quiet as a whore in church, sir."

"Well, thank you for looking after us. Get yourself some breakfast."

"Breakfast and love, sir," Sampson said, stumping on. "What a great place this is!"

You'll get no argument from me, Josh thought, then called after the two. "How are you getting along with Colonel Burr?"

"Ain't seen much of him," Tucker called over his shoulder.

"My woman says that widow's wearing him out," Sampson added. "Been too long no ficky-ficky. Both of them."

Josh laughed heartily and turned for home. As expected, Rose was up, frying him some eggs on the piece of tin she favored for a griddle, along with some breadfruit fritters and, of course, the flavorful, aromatic coffee of Tahila, which apparently grew nowhere else, not even the other islands of the Far Reaches. *If coffee wasn't so cheap and anybody could brew it,* Josh thought, *I'd go home and open up a store and sell nothing but coffee.* He laughed at himself. The idea that you could have a business where you only sold coffee was ridiculous. Anyway, he was no businessman. He was a Coast Guardsman, or at least that's what he used to be. He ate his eggs, sprinkled this morning with a peppery spice that apparently also only grew on Tahila, and wondered what Frank Knox and the rest of the military establishment were doing at that moment.

"What are you thinking, husband?" Rose asked.

"I was wondering what is going on in the war."

"Do you miss the war?"

He considered his feelings, then said, "What I miss is the might of the United States Army, Navy, and Marine Corps. I wish they'd waltz into the

Far Reaches and solve our problem. But they won't, and we're on our own with a fight coming."

"You keep saying that, but nothing happens."

Josh had to confess that was true. Despite the evident scouting of the island by the Japanese, all had remained peaceful. "Maybe Curbur is right and the sub scared Colonel Yoshu away," he mused.

"That makes a great deal of sense," Rose agreed. "What else do you plan on doing with your day besides thinking about the war?"

"I think I'll carry the charcoal to Mr. Spurlock that he ordered. How about you?"

"Turu wants to go fishing this afternoon. I will go with him. I have decided I like to fish. You taught me well, husband."

"That's good," Josh said, though he'd actually not paid any attention to what she'd said. He was thinking instead about how happy Spurlock and his women would be to have his charcoal, and he liked the idea of climbing the mountain, where he would have a view all around the island and its coast. He would look for that Japanese barge again.

He lounged in his chair until he heard Kathleen ring the school bell, then escorted Manda and Turu down the common road and peeled off at the school. Kathleen waved to him. She still wore her long gown but lately had started cinching it at the waist, accentuating her fine figure. He watched her gather the children and begin her lessons. He admired the woman, no mistake, but he also believed she was selfish to put Tahila in danger. Then again, he reflected, she hadn't been on Burubu and Yoshu had destroyed it anyway. No, she was stuck here, just as he was, and the battle would have to be fought, sooner or later.

Josh returned to his house, dug out the boots Captain Wells had given him, and gathered some sacks for Spurlock's charcoal. Rose was puttering around with her gardening tools. He supposed she was off to garden for the day. He was well up the path to his charcoal kiln before it occurred to him that he hadn't told her good-bye.

5 0

Every day after school, Kathleen and Ready went sailing. "My husband is teaching me to sail," she made a point of telling any villager who might be curious about her sudden interest in boating. In reality, they were practicing for their sail to Ruka to capture her child. At night, in the treehouse, they plotted how they would do it, how they might be able to slip together through the streets of the township of Ruka and reach Colonel Yoshu's house, then somehow get past the guards to go inside, take the baby, and get back to the canoe. Kathleen eagerly approved all of Ready's wild ideas, knowing that it didn't matter. When they got within swimming distance of Ruka, she meant to slip from the canoe and go ashore, there to be captured and handed over to Yoshu. Her husband would have no choice but to turn back for Tahila.

For his part, Ready was pleased to take his wife sailing, for he loved the sea nearly as much as he loved her. He was happy to teach her how to raise and set the sail and how to pay attention to the wind and currents. But he had no intention whatsoever of taking her to Ruka. He had discussed everything with Mr. Bucknell and Chief Kalapa, and they had agreed that such a plan was impossible. So Ready stalled for time by proposing outlandish ways that they might capture her baby, such as creating diversions, perhaps even blowing up one of the barges. He thought it was remarkable how she thought every plan he proposed was a good one. It reflected her desperation, he supposed.

Kathleen was as unaware of her husband's deceit as he was of hers. What she did know was that he loved her, loved her with all his heart, because he showed it in so many ways. He showed it when he cooked her breakfast in the morning and cleaned up the treehouse and made the bed while she was at school; and in how he came to the school bringing her lunch, and how he helped her straighten the classroom after the lessons. He showed it when he held her hand and walked with her along the path to the treehouse. He showed it when he helped her cook supper and in how he never failed to compliment her cooking. He showed his love when he quietly read aloud for her enjoyment and amusement from a book borrowed from Mr. Bucknell's library. And he showed it when at night he held her. Oh, Ready O'Neal loved Kathleen, the fallen nun, and she believed it with certainty. And, before long, though she did not believe it would happen, she came to love him, too, at least as much as she could. It wasn't a passionate love, no, but a quiet joy at his presence, and a trust that he would always be there if she needed him to be.

Kathleen also showed Ready her esteem. She even said it aloud, at least once. "Ready O'Neal," she said one morning over a breakfast he had prepared of breadfruit fritters, fresh papaya, and coffee leavened with coconut milk and raw cane sugar, "yer a fine man, ye are. I'm glad yer my husband." This small compliment, as very small as it was, was enough to cause Ready to light up as if the sun itself had risen in his heart. This gave her nearly as much joy as apparently she had given him. She would miss him, she reflected, when she was back on Ruka. *If* she was going back. The truth was she was starting to change her mind about that. Ready had shown her love such as she never imagined existed. Perhaps there was another way; perhaps she might yet convince Captain Thurlow or maybe Colonel Burr to send after a mighty force to frighten Yoshu into surrender. Perhaps. There were so many possibilities. She felt hopeful, for the first time in such a long time.

Now they were at sea, he managing the sail, she sitting on the thwart of the canoe, with Laddy at her feet. The canoe was skimming along the clean, bright sea, and she was wondering what she might prepare for the evening meal. It was a serene, pristine moment.

Then the world changed completely and forever, as it so often does. Ready said, "Help me now, Kathleen. Help me quick turn about."

His sudden urgent appeal confused her, and at first she moved slowly. Then she saw fear in his eyes and turned to look where he was looking. Her hand went to her mouth at the sight of it, an ugly gray flat slab of a barge coming around the eastern headland. "Sweet Mary," she breathed and crossed herself, convinced that all she had dreaded, but wanted, was about to come to pass.

There was never a chance that they could outrun the barge, only that they might slip into water too shallow for it to follow. Ready had a pistol with him but kept it holstered. There were at least a dozen armed Japanese on the barge that he could see, not to mention a large-caliber machine gun on its bridge. Any shooting he did would invite instant annihilation.

"Ready," Kathleen said calmly, "Yoshu is on board. I'm certain of it. I think it's going to be all right."

"What are you talking about?" he demanded.

"I'll go with him." She unsheathed the K-bar they kept on board to clean fish, then stood and touched the point of its blade to her throat. She began to yell in Japanese at the barge.

"Kathleen, what are you doing? Sit down!" Ready scolded. "Put that knife away! And stop yelling. What are you saying?"

"I am threatening suicide if they harm ye. Yoshu may not believe me, but he will hesitate. Go into the water now, my sweet Ready. Swim to the village. Take Laddy with you."

Ready looked up at the sail, willing the wind to blow harder. Miraculously, it did. "I think we have a chance," he said and steered toward the western headland and the rocks.

"What are ye doing?" she demanded.

"He'll not have you!"

"Ready, spill the wind from the sail! I have to do this!"

But Ready kept the sail blooming in the stiff breeze. Kathleen grabbed a line and tried to cut it with the K-bar. Ready reached out and stayed her hand. "I said sit down! Obey me, wife!" Bullets sang past his head, but he kept his eye on the rocks ahead. "When we strike," he said, "we'll be knocked over. Brace yourself!"

Wild-eyed, she turned to face the onrushing boulders, saw the waves crashing on them, their beards of algae and sea grass whipping in the sea's spewing embrace. Then nothing made sense as the canoe tipped up on its bow, its mast and sail fell over, and the sea clutched her, tossing her into the turbulence. She somersaulted underwater and came up flailing at a big rock that stuck brazenly from the turbulent sea like a giant gray tooth. She grabbed it but the sea tore her off it, sucked her down, spat her out again until she found herself within a swirling eddy that gradually subsided. Her feet touched sand. "Ready!" she called, fearful that he had been smashed against the rocks.

"Right here, Mrs. O'Neal," Ready replied and swam across the white-flecked water into her arms.

She held onto him. "I was afraid I had lost ye."

"Takes more than a little white water to drown a Killakeet boy. Ah, here's Laddy, too."

She took the paddling dog under her arm, but then they heard the awful noise of machine-gun fire, mixed with the crack of rifles, though no bullets struck around them. Ready turned and saw the barge had disappeared.

"What's happening?" Kathleen asked as they scrambled up on the beach.

"They're attacking the village," Ready replied.

She began to pray.

"Kathleen," Ready said, "I think it's a time to fight, not to pray."

She crossed herself, then nodded. "Yes," she said. "Yes, we will fight."

Josh was on his way back to the village. It had been a good day. He had delivered the charcoal to the Spurlocks, then spent a few hours yarning with Carl and having a sumptuous lunch served by his wives, finishing with a drink or two of Spurlock's private whiskey stock. Josh had just crested the mountain when he heard the unmistakable chatter of a Japanese machine gun. Hoping the marines were just practicing, he ran to the clearing and up on the rocks for a view of the village. What he saw was the nightmare he'd been dreading for so long. A Japanese barge was entering the lagoon. He choked back his worry for his family and started running.

Ready and Kathleen dodged along a path skirting the sea. Both machine guns on the opposing sides of the lagoon were chattering away at the barge. The barge, shuddering from the impact of the bullets, had stopped. "It's snagged the cable!" Ready cheered.

They reached the machine gun being manned by Garcia and one of the Ruka fella boys. Here they had a clear view of the barge. Ready happily noted that at least a dozen Japanese soldiers had been shot down. The Japanese boatswain was desperately turning the wheel and pushing and pulling the throttle and gears, trying to break the barge loose from the hemp cable, which had apparently wrapped around the propeller.

Then a second barge came rushing into the lagoon and then slowed to idle behind the entangled one. Ready saw Kathleen suddenly dart down to the beach and throw herself into the water. She began to swim toward the barges. Ready, disbelieving at first what he was seeing, threw down the rifle and chased after her.

Josh had run all the way down the mountain to his house and looked inside but found no one there. He'd then sprinted to Rose's sister's house and found Manda. She looked up from her play with a smile. "Lots of noise," she said.

"Yes, dear, lots of noise," Josh answered. Then, to Rose's sister, "Where's Rose?"

"She went fishing," the sister said. "She said she told you."

Josh ran to the beach where he found Burr contemplating three dead Japanese who had slogged to shore, only to be shot down by the women's militia. "We took their measure, Josh," he said proudly.

"Have you seen Rose and Turu?" Josh cried, his voice wild.

Burr blinked in surprise at his demand. "Why, no. Why do you ask?"

Josh ran to the lagoon canoes and found his was gone. Nango was there. "I saw them, Jahtalo," he replied to Josh's desperate query. "They took the canoe. They were going fishing."

"But I didn't tell her good-bye," Josh croaked. "Nango, I didn't tell her good-bye!"

Ready pulled Kathleen ashore and threw her down, then got on top of her, holding her hands. She struggled briefly, then subsided. "What did you think you were doing?" he demanded.

"I was going to end this!" she cried.

"You were going to get yourself killed!" He looked across the lagoon. The first barge was still there, though empty of men. The second barge was steadily withdrawing with the men it had rescued.

Kathleen struggled to her feet and began to walk along the beach. She had seen Josh, and she needed to talk to him. Ready, still astonished at what she had done, followed.

Kathleen stopped Josh as he walked up from the canoes. He looked at her dully, noting somewhere in his mind that she was dripping wet. Ready, also wet, stood behind her, looking unhappy and not a little desperate. "Captain Thurlow, please, ye must listen," Kathleen said. "Take me to Ruka and hand me over. It is the only way to stop this. I tried to do it just now, but me fool of a husband stopped me."

Her demand had no meaning to Josh. Nothing had meaning except for the one thing, his family. "Have you seen Rose?" he asked her. "Or Turu?"

"No, I haven't. What's wrong?"

"She went fishing," Josh replied, his voice thick. "With Turu. Did you see which way the second barge came?"

Ready answered. "From around the eastern headland, I think. It must have been hiding in the cove behind it. What's wrong, Captain?"

Burr walked up to them. "I'm sure Rose and the boy are all right," he said. "Smart girl like her. Smart boy, too. Good boat handler. I'm certain of it!"

Josh wasn't certain. He wasn't certain at all. "I didn't tell her good-bye," he said hollowly, then ran toward the headland to climb it, to see.

He arrived there breathless, though he was scarcely aware of the climb. Perched on the point of the peninsula, he studied the cove below but, for the moment, saw nothing but a crystal sea, furrowed by small advancing waves that curved toward shore. Then he looked farther out, squinting, trying to pick up any object that might be dancing among the white horses of the turbulent sea. He saw nothing except the barge, which was heading eastward, receding into the gathering pallor of the late afternoon.

Kathleen, panting, came up behind him. "Do ye see them?" she asked with hope.

"No."

She stood beside him and caught her breath. "I'm sorry," she said. "I caused this. All of it."

"Yes," Josh replied bitterly. "You did."

"But I asked that ye hand me over to Yoshu."

Josh started to reply, then shook his head.

"Shall we pray for their safety?"

He looked hard at her. "It seems to me your prayers don't work."

She nodded. "'Tis true. They don't."

"It doesn't matter. I'll find them."

"How?"

Josh didn't answer. He knew anything he said would only come out filled with spite and anger. It would hurt her, and, though at that moment he didn't much care, he knew Rose wouldn't like it. He walked past Kathleen back to the village, not caring if she followed or not.

Night was falling and there was nothing he could do now to find his wife and son. But Josh would find them, and he knew where to look, though they weren't there, not yet. It would take a little while, but he intended to be there when they arrived.

5 1

Josh waited until sunrise. He did not sleep. There had been but one visitor in the evening, one of the lookouts. The fella boy had seen the second barge coming around the eastern end of the island. He had struck the alarm gong repeatedly to warn the village and also to warn Rose and Turu, whom he had seen in the cove. With great sorrow, he told Josh the alarm had not come in time. Though Rose and Turu were able to paddle out of the cove and into the open water, the barge had deliberately altered course and run over them. To his mounting horror and despair, Josh imagined the scene over and over, Rose and Turu desperately paddling while the big steel barge came down on them. The lookout had said there had been no shooting. It was a deliberate and callous act, no doubt meant to terrify the helpless occupants of the canoe for the amusement of the Japanese. The barge had struck the canoe broadside, spilling his wife and son into the water, then plowing across them with its giant, churning propeller. The lookout said he had spotted the broken bodies of Rose and Toru, bobbing loose-limbed in the wake of the barge, but then the attack had begun in the lagoon and he could no longer watch what happened to them.

Throughout the long night, Josh sat alone in his house. He longed for mangojack but resisted it. Though he did his best to keep his mind blank, the insidious thought kept creeping in that this had happened before. Naanni had been murdered, too, and her death had been because of something he had done. Now the deaths of Rose and Turu had been his fault as well. Why had he taught her how to fish? Why had he failed to listen when she'd told him she and Turu were off to fish? If he had listened, he might have stopped them from going without him to protect them. But he hadn't listened. He'd gone on his headstrong way.

The house was empty, silent to all but his own quiet movements as he made coffee, then hooked a gourd of water to his hip and gathered the other things he would need. Manda was with Rose's sister. She would be all right. He had sat with her for a while the previous evening and explained as best he could that something had happened to her mother and her brother but that he was going to find them and she was not to worry. It had made Manda sad, but children in those latitudes had an accepting manner about them, understanding that time rolled on, that there was no way of turning it back, that what happened simply happened, and there was no hope of changing it. *They are blessed that way,* Josh thought.

Josh passed Chief Kalapa, who stood in the doorway of his house. They did not speak. Nor did he speak to Mr. Bucknell as he passed the government house, though the old Britisher tipped his hat from his makeshift desk and his stacks of useless paperwork. Josh climbed the path up the great mountain, oblivious to the beauty of the blooming oleander and the waving elephant ears of the giant philodendron. He took no note of the myriad colorful birds in the high branches above, nor even heard their twittering songs, as he made his way to the Beach of the Dead Whales. For there, he thought, he would find his precious wife and beloved son, tossed up as jetsam by the odd current that carried all discarded things from the village.

In the late morning, he reached the ridge above the beach where once he had searched for ambergris and had instead received a lesson in humility and truth from Rose. He studied the cove far below, sorting through the bones and the other debris. His facial expression fixed in stone, his eyes claimed what he had come to find, though dreaded. For a moment, he thought that he might be overwhelmed by his grief, that he wouldn't be able to do what must be done. He searched for strength but there was little he could find. He felt hollow, depleted, and briefly wished that he might descend into insanity and not return. Better to wander through life with his eyes rolling and his mind empty than live with the self-loathing that pressed down on him like the taunting hand of a petulant giant.

A shadow passed over him, and he looked up to see what had made it. The sun blistered his eyes, but through it he saw what he somehow knew he would see. "Hello, Purdy," he said, putting down the shovel he carried and unslinging the rifle on his shoulder. "Come closer, my dear friend."

If indeed it was Purdy, the pelican complacently drifted in lazy circles, its great wings outstretched. "Why did you let this happen?" Josh demanded of it, then squeezed off his shot.

The rifle barked, the sound instantly absorbed by the great roar of the

sea smashing into the beach below, echoing up through the cove. The pelican, though surely struck, did not fall. Instead, it vanished, and then Josh
was aware that something else had joined him, something small but impossible to ignore. It was a megapode, a vulturelike bird that walked on big
webbed feet and could not fly, and Josh feared that he recognized it. "Is that
you, Dave?"

If it was Dave, the mascot bird of Josh's crew back on Melagi, it did not
signify it in any way. It climbed up on a small cairn of rocks and turned its
head, presenting Josh with one of its big black eyes, inviting him to look
inside.

"I will not look inside your eye," Josh told it. "I do not trust what
you've shown me, neither the past nor the future nor the present, for it is
seen through your own wicked light."

The megapode vanished. Josh felt abandoned, then realized with a start
it was the way he was supposed to feel, along with everyone on the earth.
"But why?" he asked heaven. Heaven did not deign to reply.

Josh followed the path until he reached the beach, and then he walked to
his wife and his son. They were lying as if asleep, their heads resting on the
wet sand, the sea washing gently at their feet. Nearby was the remnant of
their canoe. The scars on it showed clearly the marks of the barge's propeller
blades. Josh wept now and struck himself in the forehead with the flat of his
hand, for this was the way of these islands. He looked for a shell with a sharp
edge and used it to cut his forehead along his hairline, then felt the hot trickle
of blood flow down his face. Then he sat down beside them and put his arms
around his knees and drew them up and lowered his head, not to pray but to
seek the strength within himself to do what needed next to be done.

After a while, he raised his head, sensing he and his wife and his son were
no longer alone. It was *her*. He knew without looking, though it proved not
to be Ready O'Neal's wife, as he first thought, but Sister Mary Kathleen,
her white habit flowing like a flag of surrender in the wind, her pretty Irish
face framed by her wimple, corona, and veil. She knelt between Rose and
Turu, her knees in the wet sand, her lips atremble in prayer. She touched
them, then made the sign of the cross. Then, rising effortlessly, she began to
take off her clothing. First came the headdress, then the cowl, the cincture,
the scapular, and finally the habit. Underneath, she wore Marine Corps
utilities and Marine Corps boots, brought with her from Tarawa. She tore a
strip from her habit and tied it around her forehead. All the rest of her nun's
clothing she threw into the sea. "Let me tell you something of me family,"
she said. "Me old pap, to start."

"You told me once he was a farmer," he replied as if they were in a dream.

"Aye, he was," she acknowledged, "but he was also in the army that crawled through the Irish night, murdering the filthy occupiers. And a meaner, crueler man did not exist when he was at war."

She blinked into the salty air. "He would come home with his pistols stinking of burnt powder, and we kids would know he had been out killing the Black and Tans. Me mum, she would cry, but she never told him to quit, no. She believed in what he did, y'see, though it were a mortal sin according to the priest. All of the priests.

"There was the local constabulary," she went on. "Pap hated them the most, for these were his countrymen and they kept the British heel on our necks. He planned many a day for what he finally did to them. He and his fellows waited in the forest's edge near the chapel while the constab boys were at mass. When they came out, Pap alone stepped from the trees and confronted them, called them traitors, then shot one of them down. Then the others of his army stepped out and finished off the rest. When the priest came out of the chapel, Pap killed him, too, saying he had no right to give the Blessed Sacrament to such creatures as the constabs."

A windblown tear streamed across her rosy cheek. "The Black and Tans came for him a day later. Before our eyes, they shot him in the back of his head, then carried him off to be hung from the tree outside the chapel. When they cut him down, no priest would say a mass for him. We buried him, knowing he was bound for hell. Yet I have little doubt he preferred hell rather than the heaven of a God he had come to distrust."

She shook her head. "His blood, it runs through me veins."

"Yet you became a nun," Josh said.

"Yes, in the hope that God would provide me old man some comfort, even in hell. But then I came to love being a nun. There was no deceit in my heart when I wore the Church's cloth. It was my vocation, that which I believed was meant for me, that which made me happier than anything in life. Yet it was taken from me. God took it."

Josh looked out to sea, studying the distant line that marked the meeting of water and sky, then said, "Let me tell you something of my family. My father is the lighthouse keeper on Killakeet Island. He is a peaceful, gentle man, and he raised me to be the same as he. But, since it is a very small island, and everyone gossips, he could not hide the truth of my family. The Thurlows, from the beginning of the settlement on the Outer Banks, were wreckers who lived off the flotsam and jetsam of wrecked ships. Sometimes, they couldn't wait for the weather and the awful shoals to do their dirty work. The Thurlow family, all of them, men, women, and children, would go out into the dark and carry lanterns and walk back and forth on the beach. To a passing ship, it looked as if the lanterns were aboard boats safe in the stream. Unsuspecting captains would come near, only to strike Killakeet Shoals. Whether the sailors aboard drowned or not, few of them lived to see the new sun."

Josh continued: "The worst of the old wreckers was Josiah Thurlow, my great-grandfather. He was ruthless in his quest for treasure, even if it only meant a pair of ill-fitting shoes taken off a dead sailor. To stop the wreckers, especially the terrible Thurlows, the government built a great lighthouse on Killakeet and offered old Josiah the lightkeeper's job. He took it, though some say he never gave up his murderous ways." Josh paused and then said, "His blood runs through my veins."

"Did you try to be a good man like your father?"

Josh smiled. "No man could hope to be like my father. He's no saint, loves the girls too much for that, yet he is as good a man as there is. I do my best, that's all I will say."

All that could be heard was the keening of the gulls and the grumble of the sea. Finally, she asked, "Where shall they rest?"

He gestured toward the towering cliff. "Up there. Rose loved the view of this bay."

"I will say prayers over their graves, if you wish it."

"I do not wish it."

"Then may I say good-bye to them?"

"Yes."

"I should like the honor of carrying your son to his last resting place."

Josh studied her, then nodded his approval.

Josh tamped the dirt on Rose's grave with the back of the shovel, then leaned on its handle and was quiet until the lump in his throat subsided enough to allow him to speak. "Good-bye, Rose," he said. "You were a good wife. Good-bye, Turu. You were a good son, none better. I will miss you both forever." He tossed the shovel down and looked at Kathleen. "Why are you dressed that way?" he asked, as if noticing for the first time the combat utilities she wore and the rifle she carried.

"Because I have seen the light," she answered. "I finally understand that God loves war. I don't know why. Maybe without war, peace has no value. No matter. I am acceding to His wishes, which He has kept making plain, though I have for so long refused to listen." She looked across the sea, toward the pink and golden clouds that drifted so prettily and peacefully there. For just a moment, there was something of hesitation in her expression, a softening of her eyes; then she seemed to settle herself, to prepare. "For all the weeks after I escaped, I kept trying to get someone to chase the colonel away so I could have me little Monessa. But no one would do it. So I decided to go back to Yoshu, to give in to his demands, at least until I could find a way to escape with me child. It was why I married Ready, to use his love to get what I wanted. I am filled with deceit, Captain, and so very wicked."

"You shanghaied me, which was wicked, and perhaps so was your marriage to a man you didn't love. But what happened on Ruka, all that was forced on you by a cruel man."

"Thank ye, but ye are wrong. I sinned beyond measure on that island. And now, Captain, I will tell it to ye. My greatest sin."

So Kathleen told him her story, of her sin beyond sins, and when she was finished, Josh stood silent and shocked for a long time. Finally, he asked, "Who else knows this?"

"The marine priest. I told Mori and Rose early on about me baby, but the rest of it? Nay, Captain, only a priest could hear such a wicked thing. And now ye know."

"Why did you tell me?"

"Because I wanted you to know that I am dirt, and unworthy of yer concern. I am a grand sinner, Captain, but I can fight."

"Fight?" Josh shook his head. "When the submarine returns, Colonel Burr will go to Australia. He will request bombers to smash Ruka."

"Aye, and their bombs will murder the people there and me baby. Nay, Captain. I beg ye. Think what God has done. He has killed yer wife and yer son. He has allowed me to sink into depravity. He is telling us what He wants if we will but listen. Let us go to Ruka and kill the Japanese, or be killed. Maybe we'll win, and maybe I'll get me baby back. Or maybe we will die. I doubt that God cares. He only wishes us to fight. Finally, I understand this is His way."

Josh looked at the twin graves and something broke inside him, something that had never been real, something he realized he had invented to hide the awful truth of the kind of man he was. He steadied himself and allowed his dreams to fade until they disappeared altogether. "I don't know much about what God wants, Kathleen," he said, "but I do know this. Ever since I came to this island, I have tried to run away from Colonel Yoshu. I forgot the lesson Captain Falcon taught me so well on the ice. You do not run from evil. To hesitate allows it to grow. You go full throttle right at it, and when you get close enough, you reach inside its rotten breast and tear its heart out." He picked up his rifle. "It's time to go," he said roughly.

She shouldered her rifle. "Where are we going?"

Josh looked at her, then past her, to all that he had done, and all that he would have to do. "To war, Kathleen. We go to war."

5 2

In the darkness, the deep darkness of what seemed an endless night, Josh sat beside his daughter inside his sister-in-law's house. Manda's cousins were beside her, all asleep. Josh pulled the cotton quilt over Manda's bare shoulders, then leaned over and kissed her cheek. The evening before, after the other raiders had gone to rest prior to disembarkation, Josh had talked to Manda of many things, but mostly his reasons for going to Ruka. He'd explained that the bad men who had killed her mother and brother had to be punished.

Manda had looked up at him with her big luminous eyes, and the longing expression that reminded him so much of Rose, and had asked, in her innocence, "Will hurting these men let Mama and Turu come home?"

"No," he answered honestly. "Nothing can do that."

"Then I want you to stay," she said flatly.

Josh explained why he couldn't do that, as much as he wanted to. If he did, he told her, perhaps the bad men would come back and hurt other people in the village. "Evil cannot be allowed to win," he told her. "It must be destroyed by good men, else it grows."

Then, sensing that he could not convince her, he said simply, "I love you. I will always love you. I will always take care of you, too, even if I don't come back. You have to trust me on this."

Hearing these words, she did not cry, though Josh had supposed she might. He realized Manda was like most of the children on Tahila. She had a sure grip on reality and understood that things did not always go well in life. She also knew she was in the embrace of a loving village. Manda did not need him. It was he who needed her.

Still gazing at his daughter, Josh sat back. What had he become? Where was Josh Thurlow, the son of Keeper Jack of Killakeet? Where was that boy of the dunes and the sea, that gentle boy who'd risked getting a finger bitten off just to save an old mud turtle? How was it that this boy had become an efficient killer of men in the South Seas?

Josh didn't know, nor did he have time to think on it. *Not now,* he told himself. The time for such thoughts, or regrets, was past. The raid on Ruka was on. He would have to kill again.

Colonel Burr had organized the raid. There were to be thirty men and one woman in the party. Burr himself, of course, and his two marines would go, with Sampson remaining behind to help guard Tahila with the women's militia. Josh Thurlow, Ready O'Neal, and the eleven Ruka fella boys were also going, plus fourteen Tahila fella boys. The entire village was furious because of the attempted attack by the two Japanese barges and the deaths of Rose and Turu. It was necessary for Burr to turn away volunteers, including Chief Kalapa. The chief was too fat, but Burr told him he couldn't go because he was indispensable to Tahila, which would suffer mightily without his leadership. One woman in the party was allowed and that was Kathleen.

To prepare for the raid, Burr asked Nango to build a model of Ruka Township. He had done so from memory with contoured sand and shells and mangos for the structures in the town. Burr had carefully studied it; then he had instructed each of his squads on the route they were to take after landing in the harbor, and the Japanese positions that were to be destroyed. Rehearsals were accomplished. *"Toot sweet!"* Burr bellowed again and again to the fella boys when they became confused or tired. "Speed is required! All same run-run, you savvy?"

The Tahila fella boys savvied, and they savvied something else, too. It would be a desperate fight. That was when they threw down the rifles Burr had pressed on them and picked up their spears and machetes. This was the way they fought, the old way, closing on the enemy until his dying breath was in their face. Burr accepted it, made his adjustments, and kept training. For five days, they had rehearsed, and now midnight had come, and the raid was on. They would sail in the outriggers northwestward and then curve around to Ruka. This would take a day. At night they would rest, and land on the beach at Ruka Township an hour before dawn.

All was prepared. Nothing else left to do but go. Josh rose and, after kissing a sleeping Manda, walked through the dark to the lagoon, where the raiding party was gathering. Josh looked over the assembly. The marines were dressed in their Tarawa utilities with freshly honed K-bars strapped aboard their hips. Tucker carried a machine gun on his shoulder. Garcia was draped with bandoliers of ammunition. The marines' women wept silently beside them.

Nango and the Ruka fella boys held their Japanese rifles, and the Tahila volunteers gripped their spears and machetes. Behind them was the Tahila women's militia. Sampson, with a crutch under one arm and his hand on the holster of a forty-five pistol, stood in front of them. He nodded to Josh. If the raid failed, the Japanese would surely come again. Sampson and the women would somehow have to stop them. Behind the women warriors were the rest of the villagers, including Mr. Bucknell and Chief Kalapa, both registering deep sadness.

Pushing through the crowd came Carl Spurlock, a long-barreled pistol strapped to his belt, and beside him Gertie and Tilly. "The old girl wouldn't leave me alone about it, you see," Spurlock explained, nodding toward Gertie. "She's after some action."

Gertie, grinning, the whites of her eyes flashing in the torchlight, fondly patted a gleaming machete.

"Tilly will stay behind, to guard our house," Spurlock went on while the plump little woman wiped away her tears.

Burr nodded to Spurlock and Gertie. "You and Gertie are welcome, Mr. Spurlock. You'll be with the Ruka fella boys. Talk to Nango. He'll fill you in on the plan."

Kathleen bade all to bow their heads. "Go ahead, Captain," she said to Josh.

Josh said, "I'm no preacher, but my old skipper in the Bering Sea, Captain Falcon, prayed a special prayer before he went into battle. I don't know if it's a righteous prayer or not, but I never knew a man headed into combat who didn't like it said. Here it is, and bless me for a fool if God don't like it:

The Lord is my Captain. I shall not question Him!
His will takes me across the great waters.
He fills my sails and makes my heart strong.
He leads me to war in His Name's sake!

Yea, though I sail through the sea of death, I do not fear evil!
For He is with me! His powder and shot, they comfort me.
He makes me invincible before mine enemies.
His spirit is like rum; and my cup runneth over!

This much I know!
I fight for the right, the good, and the Holy.
I will therefore prevail and God's mercy will be mine.
For I sail in the gunboat of the Lord forever!

At Josh's "Amen!" the raiders lifted their heads. Burr walked up beside Josh. "Time to go," he said.

And go they did.

The raiding party surged forward and climbed into the outriggers while their women and the men left behind sang a low, ancient song, begging them to return safely from their long and dangerous journey. Paddles dug into the water as the boats flowed across the lagoon. The sails were raised, billowing and popping in the wind. The Tahila people continued to sing and then the outriggers disappeared, swallowed up inside a strange, cold mist.

Ready woke to stare at the interior roof of the treehouse. He blinked once, his eyes ahead of his mind, and began to sort through the odd dreams that had visited him as he slept. Somewhere nearby, there were voices raised in song. He sat up slowly, with both hands holding his head, which seemed thick and wooly. He pressed his eyes closed and tried to think more clearly. Then he felt beside him for Kathleen. She was not there.

A pale blue light flowed through the windows. Ready climbed from the bed, knocking a cup from the bedside table. It bounced on the bamboo floor and Ready stared at it, a dull memory returning. It was the cup Kathleen had given him. It was also the last thing he recalled. She had said it contained something the widows had prepared, something that would help him to sleep before the raid.

Ready walked quickly to the windows. The blue light was the rising sun, weakly permeating through a strange, dense fog that had rolled into the lagoon. He realized now what Kathleen had done.

He quickly pulled on his utilities, then his socks and boots, and picked up his rifle. Though his head was pounding, he ran down the spiral staircase and took the path to the beach. A few villagers watched him approach. Shockingly, the outriggers were gone.

Ready saw Chief Kalapa. "Why did no one wake me?" he demanded.

"Kathleen say you stay," Chief Kalapa quietly replied. "She say husband no die for her sin."

Ready's eyes landed on a canoe. It belonged to Chief Kalapa and it was very fast. "Chief, I need your canoe," he said urgently, and didn't wait for permission. He ran to it and pushed it into the lagoon and climbed aboard. He brought out the paddle and dipped its blade into the water and felt it bite.

"Canoe no belong big sea, Bosun!" Chief Kalapa called. "Too much rain, wind, canoe sink!"

Ready didn't care if his craft had been designed for the open water or not. He was a sailor. He would handle whatever came. With a dozen powerful strokes of the paddle, he ran the canoe through the passage between the coral reefs. Then he lifted the mast and raised the sail, which instantly ballooned in the vigorous wind that swept him and the fog along.

5 3

Throughout the night and much of the day, the anxious fella boys kept paddling, each flowing dip marked by their deep grunts, like a terrible war chant. Finally, fearing that they might exhaust themselves, Josh called a halt to the paddling and told the outrigger captains to make their men rest and let the wind do the work. Work it did, and the outriggers swept along, finally breaking out of the blue-gray mist and into the open air. The brilliant sun crept across the sky over the raiding party, while the sea remained empty of Japanese barges or any other vessel.

Toward dusk, Burr had his boat move so that he could climb across to Nango's outrigger, which held Josh and Kathleen. He had something he wanted to say. "I feel like Agamemnon, bound for Troy, Josh," he said. "Do you recall your Homer?"

"Educate me, Montague," Josh replied.

"*O excellency, O majesty, O Zeus,*" Burr quoted Agamemnon according to the old tale. "*Beyond the storm cloud, dwelling in high air, let not the sun go down upon this day into the western gloom, before I tumble Priam's blackened roof down, exploding fire through his portals! Let me rip with my bronze point the shirt that clings on Hector and slash his ribs! May throngs around him lie—his friends, head-down in dust, biting dry ground.*"

Josh smiled, though grimly. "As I recall, Zeus did not answer. It took ten years for Agamemnon to take Troy."

"We will do a mite better on Ruka," Burr swore.

"We'd better," Josh replied.

Kathleen listened but remained silent, for she had not the words that would tell anyone what she felt—and feared.

Then the sun, in a shower of fire, fell into the sea, and the little fleet pulled down its sails and waited, waited for the sun to return and the battle to begin.

During the night, the odd mist came again. A bit unnerved, the raiders floated along a gray, steamy wall. The fella boys, certain the fog had come from the gods, moaned and groaned at the sight of it. "Can we find Ruka, Pangoru?" Burr whispered to his outrigger captain, as they both peered into the great nothingness.

The big tattooed islander stopped his prayers to the old gods to answer the colonel's question. "Panua and Juki, they fight," he informed Burr, speaking of the two major goddesses of the Far Reaches. "Juki, she chase away Panua. She build dream wall. Say Panua no come these islands no more."

"Why are they fighting?" Burr asked.

"Juki say Panua too much jealous god," Pangoru answered, tapping his head. "But all gods too much crazy." He rapped the mast with his knuckles to ward off any listening god's revenge.

"How do you know all that?" Burr asked.

Incredulity showed on Pangoru's tattooed face. "Fella boys all time hear gods." He touched an ear. "Listen, Curbur. You hear."

Burr listened but didn't hear anything except the slosh of the sea around the outrigger. Then he noticed that a few of the fella boys had cut themselves along the hairline and blood was streaming down their faces. "Pangoru, tell these men to stop hurting themselves!" he cried.

Pangoru shrugged. "They say Panua, they sorry. They say Juki, they sorry. Gods stop fight so men they fight."

Burr sighed at the superstitions of all fighting men, then glanced at the sky. The stars twinkled back at him, but the moon was down. It was satisfyingly dark, perfect for a well-rehearsed raid. In two hours, he knew, the sun would boom from the sea and with it his hope for surprising the enemy. "We must go soon, if we're going," he said to the outrigger captain. "Whistle out now, Pangoru. Tell the others to raise their sails."

Pangoru nodded, then whistled across the darkness. The trilled replies were instantaneous. "All say, Ruka, we go!" Pangoru exclaimed. Very quickly, the little fleet was blown into the fog wall, the mist swirling around the boats like shadowy ghosts. The sails groaned as the wind became vigorous, adding to the sense that there were spirits all around. The fella boys started wailing, matching the groaning sails, and cast their prayers to Panua and Juki to leave them alone to fight the Japonee.

In Nango's outrigger, Kathleen prayed to her Irish child-saint. "Saint Monessa, let us find our way, we beg ye!" she said aloud, and her prayer was immediately seconded with a booming "Amen!" by Nango. Under her breath, she added, "Please give me the strength, dear Monessa, to do what I must do." She reflected then how different she was now that she had put her veil aside, how she saw humility and even inner serenity as her adversaries, perhaps even the reasons for her greatest sin. For had not her constant striving toward humility and a nun's natural subservient inclinations been the twin causes of her downfall? After enduring the greatest of humiliations, was it natural that she might accept the hand reached out to her, even though the bearer of that hand had abused her? She thought perhaps yes, though she was not certain, nor was she likely ever to be. That was part of her frustration, her pain, and her fear.

Kathleen forced herself to stop thinking along those lines. *I must not rationalize what I did!* she raged inwardly. Most of all, more than anything, she knew she could not allow herself to recall the sweetness of surrender. For it had been sweet and, in its own way, so terribly good. *I am damned beyond recovery,* she thought, then bowed her head. *Sweet Saint Monessa, save me. Stop me mind. Let me do what I must do!*

"Kathleen," Josh said, coming up beside her. "The fog is lifting."

Kathleen raised her eyes. It was as if someone were lifting a curtain on a stage. Clear air lay ahead, and somewhere out there, surely, the lights of Ruka Township.

The outriggers flitted along, and just before sunrise the town condensed in front of them. Exactly as they had rehearsed, the raiders swept into the big harbor without stopping, sailed past the pier where a bullet-riddled barge sagged into oily water and past a seawall of palm logs, and then landed hard on an open beach a hundred yards to the west. Just as the sun pushed itself completely from the sea, bathing the village in a harsh orange light, the raiders jumped from their outriggers and rushed into the town. Only one Japanese guard was found at the harbor, and he was asleep on the pier. At the sound of bare feet running down it, he rose only to be struck down by a machete. Silently, he died.

The raiders moved into the town built of plastered concrete and bamboo. They were prepared for violent combat, but nothing moved. Not even a dog barked. Burr was disappointed. He had planned his invasion carefully; they would seize one position, then move on to the next, until there was a crescendo of destruction. But there were no positions, only a slumbering, quaint little village built on two small hillocks. "Get out here, you damned lazy fools!" Burr finally yelled. He punched out a round from his pistol, then another. Japanese soldiers, most rubbing sleepy eyes, emerged tentatively from their houses only to be met by the machetes and spears and bullets of the fella boys.

"Never saw Japs like these," Burr said to Nango. He knelt beside one of the bodies. The man was dressed in a silk robe, and there were gold rings on his fingers. Two of those fingers were truncated. He had tattoos up and down both arms. "Little Al Capones, every one, I swear," Burr said, shaking his head. "Just ain't a proper war to be had with these fellas."

Within fifteen minutes of the landing, Burr knew the battle was essentially over. The Japanese had been caught completely by surprise and weren't much interested in fighting anyhow. All they wanted to do was run away. They were chased through the streets, not only by the raiders but by their house servants. When any Japanese was caught, he was knocked down, punched, kicked, and then killed in whatever horrible way the mob decided. None of it was pretty. Japanese heads rolled down the streets, kicked by laughing, chirping fella boys.

Burr watched it all with a bemused expression, then followed Nango and his friends to the house where they said their abusers stayed. Nango pushed open the door and charged inside, followed by the other Rukans. Burr watched from the entry as naked Japanese men rose to meet their former prisoners. Bellowing revenge, the fella boys knocked them down and slit open their stomachs. While the Japanese shrieked and clutched their spilled intestines, their misery was increased by the sudden sharp removal of their manhood. Blood flowed across the floor of the house like a river, drenching Burr's boots. He lurched back into the street, such mutilation too much for even a marine to bear, only to meet a Japanese soldier, perhaps the only one on the entire island who had decided to fight. The little man was in full dress uniform and clutched a rifle tipped with a long bayonet. Burr dodged his lunge, but his bayonet still got a piece of him. Gasping from the wound in his side, Burr jammed his pistol into the face of his attacker and pulled the trigger. Spattered with the man's blood and brains, the colonel sagged into the filthy street. "Nothing went as planned," he said to himself, but then the shrugged and added, most philosophically: "Thank you, General Sherman. You were absolutely correct. War is indeed hell, and not a little unpredictable."

Ready landed his canoe on the beach beside the outriggers. He had sailed directly for Ruka and waited offshore through the night. Shortly after sunrise, his wait was rewarded by the sound of a gunshot, then another. He sailed into the harbor, then spotted the beached fleet. Hearing screams, he ran into town but saw no fighting, only dead Japanese lying in the streets. A few Tahila fella boys emerged from one of the houses, their machetes and spears blooded. They ignored him and kept hacking at any Japanese they encountered. Then Ready came across Colonel Burr, sitting with his back against the plastered wall of a building and clutching his side. "Welcome to the battle, such as it is, Bosun," Burr said, in an ironic tone.

Ready knelt beside him, then gently pulled open his shirt to inspect his wound. It was not deep, but it had the potential for infection and Ready had not thought to bring his medical kit. "You're going to be fine, Colonel," Ready told the plucky little man, "but we'd best clean out that wound."

"Pour some alcohol on it," Burr said in a swaggering tone. "Surely a lot of sake around here. That will be the ticket."

Nango emerged from the doorway of the house. "Nango, come here," Ready said. "Take care of the colonel. Clean his wound. Use alcohol. Whatever you can find. Then bind it with clean cloth. You savvy?"

Nango nodded. "We kill too much Japonee," Nango proudly announced. His legs were drenched in blood that did not appear to be his own.

"Good, fine, Nango," Ready answered. "But now we fix Curbur, yes?"

"Nango savvy, stop along Curbur, makem OK," the outrigger captain replied and went back inside the house, soon returning with a white sheet, which he began to tear into strips, and a bottle of sake, which Burr snatched from his hands. The colonel took a long suck on the bottle, then poured it down his side, only wincing a little.

"Is good, Curbur?" Nango asked solicitously.

Burr smiled. "It's good, my boy. We won the battle, didn't we?"

"Colonel, where's Kathleen?" Ready asked.

"With Josh," he answered. "Gone to find Colonel Yoshu. If you hurry, you might still catch them."

Ready hurried.

5 4

Josh held his pistol and cautiously led the way down the empty streets. Tucker and Garcia, carrying their Japanese rifles, were just behind. Following was Kathleen with her M-1 Garand. Josh was taking them around the killing ground of the central town, through the empty streets of the native quarter, bound for what had once been Mr. Bucknell's house, now occupied by Colonel Yoshu. When he turned a corner, Josh saw he had indeed reached his destination, a gingerbread island-style house with a wide front porch.

Josh and the marines rushed up the steps and kicked in the door. Only silence and the ticking of an ancient grandfather clock greeted them inside. "Spread out, search the place, and be careful!" Josh ordered the marines. He started to tell Kathleen to be careful, too, but then he saw she was not with them. He went out on the porch. All he saw was an empty street.

As she ran past an alley, something caught Kathleen's eye. She stopped and backed up and saw that it was a girl, a very young girl. Remarkably, she was a white girl, and Kathleen could not imagine what she might be doing in Ruka Township. Her costume was also a little odd. She wore a golden robe and headpiece and looked, Kathleen thought, as if she were a little nun except she was underage and her habit much too gaudy. When Kathleen walked toward her, the little girl turned and ran away. Against all reason, Kathleen ran after her.

Kathleen caught only a wispy sight of the child's robe as she flitted around corners, but it was enough to keep track. Then Kathleen emerged in the town square, a grassy rectangle fronted by the chapel. The priests had built the chapel "of plaster and love," as Father Ballester had laughingly told her when she had marveled at its construction, majestic for such a tiny town on such a small island.

Then she saw Yoshu. He was on the steps of the chapel. He wore his dress uniform, braid and brass, a dandy even now. Calming herself, she called out to him, and he turned in her direction. When he saw it was she, he made a slight bow and put his hand to his heart.

"Where is our daughter?" she asked him in Japanese, though even in that language she had an Irish lilt that had often made him laugh. She was careful not to make a demand. Japanese never responded well to harsh words. She made her question a polite query.

"She is safe," he answered in the melodious soprano voice she recalled so well. "I have her here. Why are you wearing that uniform and carrying that rifle?"

"I have become a soldier."

His laughter was bubbly, like a woman's. "You are no more soldier than I."

"I want to see me daughter." This time it was a demand.

"She is inside the chapel," he answered. "Waiting for you. We've both been waiting for you for such a long time." Then he went up the steps and through the chapel's open doors.

Kathleen hurried across the square and followed him inside. Just as promised, Yoshu was there and so was Monessa. He had placed her on the altar of the chapel, where she lay naked, looking so small and vulnerable, atop a white silk cloth. The gossamer wisps that had been her hair when Kathleen had last seen her had grown out, full and thick and dark. Her little pink arms and legs were wiggling, and Kathleen could feel the fear and confusion of her beloved child. Yet Monessa did not cry. She was a good baby, so very good and innocent of all sin.

Now Yoshu raised a curved dagger over their baby, its wicked edge gleaming in the sunlight streaming through the chapel windows. "I wish I didn't have to kill her," he said dreamily, and Kathleen realized he had probably recently smoked his pipe. "But it seems I have no choice."

"Oh, Yoshu," she said conversationally, as if they were merely having an argument. "Ye have so many choices. I am here now. We will choose together."

He arched an eyebrow. "You abandoned us. Why would you care what happens to her or me now?"

"I care more than life," she said.

Tears began to leak down his face. He had always been so emotional around her. "I'm sorry," he said and raised the dagger higher as if for a killing swipe across Monessa's neck. But then she reached up to her father, squeezing her tiny hands open and closed, as if pleading to be picked up. He hesitated, holding the dagger quivering above her.

Though she was deathly afraid, Kathleen spoke to him in as soothing a voice as she could manage. "Our child needs ye, m'love." The candlewood floor of the chapel creaked beneath her boots as she took a cautious step forward, then another. "Just as I need ye. Come, now. We will be a family again."

Yoshu, who had been staring at the child, raised his tearful eyes to Kathleen. She had forgotten how striking his face was—thin, with high cheeks and full lips. He wasn't handsome so much as he was pretty. His eyes were deeply almond, and his lashes unnaturally long. She realized with a shudder that he could still enthrall her with a glance.

"Snow," he said, sniffing. "I've missed you so much."

Her finger crept to the trigger of the rifle. "Yoshu, I know ye are frightened," she said, taking another step, "but I will not let them hurt ye. Trust me."

"Why should I?" he whined in the little boy's voice he sometimes used around her. "You left me."

"I left because I made meself remember what ye did to the priests and me sister nuns."

"I explained that to you. I had to kill them. My men would have killed me if I hadn't shown strength. I made certain the sword was very sharp. They felt nothing. I love you, Snow."

"I am married now. To a fine man."

Yoshu's face registered disappointment, then resolution. He let the hand that held the dagger fall to his side. "It doesn't matter," he sniffed. "You were married before. To Christ, a god. Yet even a god for a husband was not enough to keep you and me from being lovers. We will be lovers again. I know you still love me. Confess it, Snow. To yourself as well as me."

She prepared herself. She wasn't that far away now, but she would have to shoot from the hip, and Yoshu was behind the altar with Monessa in the way.

He seemed not to care that she was drawing closer. He smiled, though his lips trembled. "Just like the snow, you were so light, so pure, and so easy to melt."

Kathleen's finger pressed against the trigger. She felt the resistance, knew if she only pressed a little harder . . .

"Do you recall the first *haiku* I wrote you?" he asked.

"Yes," she said and, against her will, faintly smiled at the memory. She had been so tired then, so dirty, so abandoned . . . *God, why hast thou forsaken me?* She had cried her plea to the ceiling of her filthy cell again and again. Then, later, when she had been raped a dozen times, and beaten until her body was blue, Yoshu had come to her, and it was as if he were a different man, a soft, warm, loving man who needed her to teach him what life was really about. Then he brought the pipe with the opium and told her how good it would make her feel. She had longed to feel good, if only for a little while, and it had worked its magic. For the first and only time in her life, the opium released her from her awful Irish inhibitions. She felt free, sexually and expressively, and morality was only a set of strictures to be overcome with ever more of the pipe whenever Yoshu would let her have it. And she had craved it so. The pipe had become her purpose in life, along with the man who filled it for her.

He seemed to sense the argument she was having with herself. "My first attempt at poetry," he said, his expression one of quiet pride. "A woman in white, gentle sweetness, your touch soft as snow." He tilted his chin. "You liked it, didn't you? I began to call you Snow after that."

"It touched me," she confessed. "I don't know why. After the things ye did to me. Maybe it was the pipe."

"No. The pipe only helped you to blossom into a woman." His smile broadened. "Then one day, one marvelous day, you wrote a poem for me."

"Strange man," she whispered, recalling how she had craved the pipe, and him. "Strange man. Filled with rage. Gentle when I smile."

"Ah," he breathed. "Yes-s-s-s."

"Ye said our love had changed ye forever. Ye said ye would work for peace. Then Nango told me what yer men had done to him, and the other fella boys. Yoshu, I discovered ye had sometimes joined in."

"I didn't want to do it!" Yoshu whined. "But I was afraid not to, afraid they would murder me for a weakling. And I am weak. You know that, Snow. But I felt so strong when I was with you."

"That was because I let the pipe make me weak. I broke the pipe after Nango told me what ye had done. I made meself well and whole again."

"No, you made yourself into the fiction you had constructed around your terrible church."

She stepped to the side, to get Monessa out of the line of fire. "Ye carved me symbol on the cross at Burubu," she said as if scolding a child. "Yoshu, I was disgusted."

His lips formed a pout. "It was the only way I had to talk to you. I did it so you would know how much I still loved you and wanted you to come home. Even though you abandoned me, I do love you so."

"That's why I know ye would not harm Monessa. She is the two of us made one, after all."

"I am very afraid," Yoshu suddenly said as she took another sideways step. "I am not ready to die. If you take another step, I will kill her." He raised the dagger again. "Snow, this I swear I will do. Put the rifle down."

Kathleen had no choice. She crouched and placed the rifle on the floor, then stood and spread her arms wide, showing him her empty hands. "Ye see? Ye have nothing to fear. We can be a family again. I love ye, dear strange man."

Yoshu lowered the dagger. "Then come to me," he said softly.

She walked to him, first touching Monessa with a trailing finger, hesitating for just a moment while the child cooed at her touch. Then she slipped inside Yoshu's familiar embrace. Sighing in submission, she kissed him, and her heart sang even as she made her calculations.

5 5

Ready finally reached Yoshu's house. His memory of the sand map of the township had served him well. Tucker and Garcia were lounging on the porch and grinned when they saw him. "Hiya, Bosun!" Tucker called. "How's the battle in town?"

"I think we've won it," Ready answered, relieved to see the two marines. "Where's my wife?"

Josh came out on the porch. "We came here to find Yoshu, but he isn't here, and I don't know where Kathleen is. She was behind us, but where she went, I don't know."

Ready paled. "I've got to find her, Captain!"

"And so we shall, Ready. I've been trying to figure out where to look."

"Maybe she went to church," Garcia suggested. "I mean, even if she ain't a nun anymore, she might still like to pray."

Josh snapped his fingers. "Out of the mouths of babes! The chapel!"

Ready didn't wait for Josh and the marines. He started running.

Though he still held the dagger, Yoshu lifted Kathleen's shirt during their embrace and explored her bare back with his free hand. She involuntarily shuddered, remembering how tender had been his caresses. She turned within his arms to face her baby. She laid her head back against his chest, sighing. "Kiss my neck, Yoshu. You know I always loved it."

This he did, and while he was distracted, she knew she had a chance. If she was very quick, she could pull away from him, pick Monessa up, and run with her from the chapel. But as she tensed to move, Yoshu pulled her shirt loose and she felt the dagger against her stomach. Why he had done this made no sense until he pressed its edge against her, then slid it hard across her skin. She felt something wet dripping down her legs. She clutched her stomach, then raised her bloody hands to her eyes. Horrified, she reached for Monessa, to pick her up, to hold her. She touched her, but Yoshu pulled her back by her hair.

"I'm sorry, Snow," he said, "but I knew you were going to try to leave me again. Of course, I couldn't allow that."

Kathleen was having difficulty standing, so Yoshu let go of her hair and gently lowered her to the floor. She stared up at him, still not quite believing what he had done. "Here we once made love after having our pipes," he said. "Do you remember? And here I have decided we will end it. First you will die, and then our child. After that, I will kill myself as the Bushido ritual requires."

For a very brief moment, Kathleen reflected that Yoshu had never been one much for rituals, Bushido or otherwise. Then a terrible, excruciating pain in her stomach tore her thoughts apart. She tried to scream, but it came out a sigh. "Such love we had," Yoshu crooned. "Such holy love. I wish only that we could have had one last pipe together."

Kathleen's eyes floated upward, and she saw a child sitting on the altar. It was the girl in the golden robe, and her skinny white legs were swinging back and forth. It was only then that Kathleen finally recognized her. "Saint Monessa," Kathleen said, though no words escaped her lips, "save my baby."

The child stopped swinging her legs and smiled.

Ready finally found the town square. His recollection of the sand map had not been perfect, and he had gotten lost. Finally, he'd run across Mr. Spurlock and Gertie, who was carrying a head under her arm. While his wife grinned and looked about for more prey, Spurlock gave Ready proper directions. Ready ran across the grass of the square and up the steps of the chapel and through its open doors. Inside was a disorienting patchwork of light and dark, the scalding sunlight flowing through the windows terribly bright, all else brooding and somber. Then he saw the altar, and something bloody lying on it. To his horror, he realized it was a baby.

"Kathleen?" Ready called and was answered by something rustling behind the altar. "Kathleen!"

Ready ran into one of the blinding rectangles of light thrown down by the windows. Then he came out of it and into darkness, so sudden it rendered him temporarily blind. He waited for his eyes to adjust, and then the suffused light allowed him finally to see her. At first, he thought she was lying on a scarlet silk cloth, but then he saw it wasn't cloth at all but shimmering blood. Then he saw a Japanese officer kneeling in one of the patches of sunlight on the other side of the chapel. A dagger lay beside him, and he was whining something in Japanese, something that sounded like begging for mercy.

Ready ignored the Japanese officer and knelt beside Kathleen. Her eyes were staring at the ceiling and blinking in a slow rhythm, as if they were counting seconds. He saw the terrible slash across her stomach. When he looked back at her face, he was startled to see that her eyes had focused and she was watching him. She slowly raised her trembling, bloody hands to him, except it wasn't for him. He knew what she wanted, the baby on the altar.

Ready felt as if his insides were turning to liquid. How could he hand her a dead child? But when he rose to look at the child, to decide, he saw she wasn't dead at all, just covered with blood. He realized it must have been Kathleen's blood. He lifted the child, her little hands clutching toward him, and handed her down to his wife.

Kathleen was happy, so happy. She held Monessa tenderly, though it took all her remaining strength. Saint Monessa stood now beside Ready, her tiny hand on his shoulder. "I should confess to him," Kathleen said to the little saint, though no real words passed her lips. "I should confess to my husband that I fell in love with Yoshu, against all reason. It is my greatest sin, the one that can never be forgiven."

"He knows," Saint Monessa replied in her little girl's voice. "He knows and forgives you."

"God forgives me?" Kathleen asked.

She inclined her little head, as if Kathleen had asked a very foolish question. "Your husband forgives you. God forgives you, too, but that is not as important."

Then, as Ready touched Kathleen's face, a touch she didn't feel, she saw Saint Monessa put out her hand. Kathleen felt humble and serene. She realized at that moment she had become the perfect nun. It was Sister Mary Kathleen who took the little saint's gentle hand and was lifted up.

Josh had been delayed by crowds of Rukans come out to celebrate. As he entered the chapel, he was cautious at first, as the sunlight through the windows was so dazzling he could scarcely see. But then, as he moved through the patches of light and darkness, he saw Ready and Kathleen and the baby behind the altar. And then he saw Colonel Yoshu. A bloody dagger lay beside him, but there was no blood on Yoshu. He looked up at Josh with his girlish eyes. His face was tortured, and tears streamed down it. "I surrender," he said in English. "I am prisoner."

Josh kicked the dagger away and took the colonel by his collar and pulled him to his feet. "Prisoner," Yoshu said again with pleading eyes.

"No prisoner," Josh said in his face so that Yoshu could see his outrage.

Yoshu whimpered as Josh dragged him out of the chapel and threw him down the steps into the square. There the Ruka fella boys, led by Nango, had gathered. Josh told them what Yoshu had done to Kathleen. Then he asked Nango to use what Japanese he knew to tell Yoshu what was about to happen. This was done, and then Josh turned away, closing his ears to Yoshu's screams.

Josh walked aimlessly through the streets of Ruka Township. He did not know what else to do or where to go. He had helped Ready get to his feet, then gently taken the baby from Kathleen's arms and handed her to the bosun. He had watched closely as Ready wrapped the little girl in the white silk cloth from the altar. "What will you do with her?" Josh asked.

"What do you think, Captain?" Ready had replied. "This is my child. I will raise her—and cherish her forever."

In the face of such goodness, Josh had turned away and made his way through the streets filled with celebrating Rukans. Before long, he came across Montague Burr. Burr, shirtless, his torso bound in strips of white cloth like a partial mummy, was sitting nonchalantly in a chair outside of what was evidently a bar, though it had been thoroughly ransacked. There was an empty whiskey bottle lying on the table before him and a half-empty one standing up. "Yoshu is dead," Josh told him. "So is Kathleen. Ready has her child. She is a pretty baby."

"I'll miss that little Irish girl," Burr said. "She had spunk." He pulled a chair back from the table. "Sit down, Josh. Have a drink. I think you could use one."

"Thanks, but no. I don't know what I need, but I'm sure it isn't a drink."

Burr shrugged. "So what are you going to do now?"

Josh gave the question some thought, then said, "The sea has always been an answer for me, no matter the question."

Burr knocked back his glass, then smacked his lips, island style. He poured himself another, then tossed the bottle over his shoulder, grinning when it shattered. "Will you go back to Tahila? You have a daughter there."

Josh nodded. "Yes. I will go back. After a short sail, I think."

Burr raised his glass. "Have fun, then, brother."

Josh walked away, and it wasn't too long before he found himself on the beach where the outriggers had landed. He noticed Chief Kalapa's fast little canoe among them and surmised it had carried Ready across the length and breadth of the Far Reaches.

Josh had always loved small boats, especially fast ones. He recalled he had risked his life to go after one a long time ago. It had been off Killakeet. He had been but a boy, minding his baby brother while their father was off the island. To Josh's joy, a pretty little red moth boat had gone drifting by. It had broken loose somewhere, and if Josh caught it, it would be his. Taking little Jacob with him, he'd sailed his father's spare dory after the moth boat but found instead a terrible storm. He had survived, but Jacob had been lost.

Josh pushed the canoe off the beach and hopped in. He used a paddle to maneuver it into deeper water and then set the sail. The breeze plumped the canvas, and very quickly the canoe was skimming across the water. An hour later, Josh thought to look over his shoulder. Ruka had disappeared. All he could see was the great circle where the ocean met the sky.

He sailed on while above him clouds gathered, fluffy and white at first, then darkening. He saw flashes of lightning on the horizon and then great blue-white streaks that hummed as they struck the water. He smelled the ozone-saturated air and it was clean and pure, washing the stink of death from his nostrils.

He longed for the cleansing rain to reach him, and reach him it did. He turned his face to it and let it flush away the dirt and grime of too many battles. The rainwater began to grow deep in the bottom of the canoe. He found half a coconut shell and bailed a little, though it was impossible to keep up with the sheets of rain. Finally, he tossed the shell away. He let the wind, howling now, blow him and the little canoe wherever it wished. Then the mast, not built to take the terrible energy of a vast storm on the open sea, cracked and fell. Huge waves pounded the canoe.

Josh let the angry water wash over him. Then he found himself no longer in the canoe but in the embrace of the sea. He lifted his head, thinking to perhaps find the remains of the canoe, to swim to it, to hang on. He rode the next swell up and up, then slid down into the valley between it and the next great wave. Josh swam on with his powerful stroke. He swam all night, but the boat eluded him, or perhaps it had sunk. When the sun again made its appearance, with all its usual gaudiness, Josh heard what sounded like thunder. It was waves crashing on a beach, he was certain of it! Exhausted but undaunted, the Killakeet keeper's son turned in the direction of what he hoped was an island, trusting the sea to help him on his way.

A HISTORICAL FOOTNOTE
AND A FEW REFERENCES

Although the Far Reaches are islands that exist only in my imagination, there were many such islands occupied by the Japanese during World War II that were bypassed by the United States forces on their march to Tokyo. The Japanese often removed their troops when they could, but sometimes they were left to fend for themselves against time and the elements, and also the resentful people they had brutally conquered. What happened to some of these abandoned Japanese troops is simply lost to history. I think it can be assumed more than a few of them met violent ends.

The battle of Tarawa as I recount it in this novel is accurate except, of course, for the participation of Josh Thurlow, Ready O'Neal, Colonel Montague Burr, the three marines Tucker, Sampson, and Garcia, and also Sister Mary Kathleen and her fella boys. Among the very real participants were Major Mike Ryan, Colonel David Shoup, Sergeant Bill Bordelon, Colonel "Red Mike" Edson, and Lieutenant Alexander "Sandy" Bonnyman.

The final American bill for Tarawa was 997 dead marines and 30 corpsmen, with 2,233 marines and 59 corpsmen grievously wounded and 88 marines missing. Another way of looking at it: Nearly 30 percent of the 12,000 Americans who participated in the landing were either killed or incapacitated by wounds. Ninety of their 125 landing craft were also sunk, wrecked, or battered into junk. The battle was three days of bloody mayhem. One wonders what the reaction of the United States public would be today after such a horrendous "victory." World War II in the Pacific, however, just kept grinding on after Tarawa with hardly a murmur of unhappiness on the home front.

The Japanese body count for the battle was 4,713 men dead. The *rikusentai* fought nearly to the last man. In 2004, the Japanese sent 600 troops to

Iraq, principally to support a variety of humanitarian projects, including water purification. Japanese citizens instantly began to fret over the safety of their soldiers, demanding that everything possible be done to keep them out of actual combat and to bring them home as soon as possible.

Obviously, there have been a few changes in the mindset of both Americans and Japanese since the 1940s.

Two excellent resources for the battle of Tarawa are the aptly titled *Utmost Savagery: The Three Days of Tarawa*, by Colonel Joseph H. Alexander, USMC, and *One Square Mile of Hell*, by John Wukovits. Another excellent book with many photographs and maps is *Tarawa 1943: The Turning of the Tide*, written by Derrick Wright and illustrated by Howard Gerrard. A most remarkable book I discovered told me the story of what happened on Betio immediately after the battle. It is titled *Tarawa: The Aftermath*, written by Donald K. Allen. It is an astonishing history of men living literally atop the shallow graves of thousands. An interesting recent memoir about life on Tarawa is *The Sex Lives of Cannibals: Adrift in the Equatorial Pacific*, by J. Maarten Troost. Despite its lurid title, Mr. Troost's amusing tale has nothing to do with cannibals or what they do in bed. It is, however, a good primer on how life has evolved in a most intriguing manner on those decaying little coral atolls.

Although the British government and church officials made an effort to evacuate missionaries off the Gilbert Islands (which included Tarawa) before the Japanese occupation in 1942, a number of them were captured, including approximately twenty Catholic nuns of various nationalities. Most of the male missionaries and priests were executed. The nuns were brutalized by the Japanese troops and then sent to the northern Gilberts. None were apparently on Betio when the island was invaded by the United States Marines.

Sister Mary Kathleen is fictitious, but many nuns of various Catholic orders have over the years dedicated themselves to service in the Pacific. These were and are remarkable women with an astonishing capacity for difficult and selfless work. They are rightly beloved by the citizens of Oceania's far-flung atolls and islands. To support these dedicated women, a contribution to Catholic Relief Services or directly to the various orders is always welcome.

To research Sister Mary Kathleen, it was necessary to delve into a variety of books written by and about Catholic nuns. Although fiction, *The Nun's Story*, by Kathryn Hulme, is still a powerful story and is based on a real woman's experiences during the same era as this novel. I found it invaluable because it told quite movingly how and why women became nuns just prior to and during World War II. Another novel that I enjoyed reading was *The Flesh and the Spirit* (a.k.a. *Heaven Knows, Mr. Allison*), by Charles Shaw. The movie's pretty good, too. An informative book on an Irish nun in the Pacific is *An Extraordinary Australian: Mary MacKillop,* by Paul Gardiner. I also found *The Habit: A History of the Clothing of Catholic Nuns,* by Elizabeth Kuhns, to be most enlightening.

I am particularly grateful to a Roman Catholic nun who wishes to be completely anonymous for her helpful correspondence during my writing of this novel. She provided me with much-needed research concerning the Catholic nuns in the Pacific during World War II as well as hand drawings to illustrate the various components of the habits they wore. I hasten to add that she was never aware of the plot of this novel or the imperfections of the fictitious Sister Mary Kathleen, who certainly does not represent her or most nuns. I hope she won't be too embarrassed by what I have written.

My research into native life on the islands of Pacific Oceania led me down some fascinating paths. Early on in my conceptualization of this novel, I decided that the people of the Far Reaches would be culturally closer to the Polynesian people of the nineteenth century, rather than the twentieth and certainly the twenty-first. With this in mind, *A Residence of Eleven Years in New Holland and the Caroline Islands,* by James F. O'Connell, first published in 1836, became pertinent, as did Mark Twain's *Following the Equator* and Robert Louis Stevenson's *In the South Seas.* To understand the navigational techniques and boat-building of the Pacific, *East Is a Big Bird,* by Thomas Gladwin, proved to be a wonderful resource. I only tweaked a bit the design of the oceangoing outriggers Gladwin writes about in his most excellent book.

Three books I used for insight into the minds of Japanese military personnel during World War II were *The Knights of Bushido,* by Lord Russell of Liverpool, *Senso: The Japanese Remember the Pacific War,* edited by Frank Gibney, and *Prisoners of the Japanese,* by Gavan Daws. *Japanese Pacific Island Defenses, 1941–45,* by Gordon L. Rottman, illustrated by Ian Palmer, was an excellent manual to help me understand Japanese field fortifications.

I also used portions of many other books, manuals, and personal recollections to get into the minds of the men and women of that era and place. If there are errors in this novel concerning technical details of the American and Japanese war machines, I regret them. But if I have captured the emotional souls of the people involved, while providing a little entertainment and history for my readers, I will have accomplished my goals. As for Josh Thurlow, if I have anything to say about it, he will sail again across adventurous seas.